Don't You DARE

CE RICCI

Don't You Dare
Copyright © 2022 by CF Ricci
Publsihed by Deserted Press

All rights reserved.
No part of this book may be reproduced in any form or by any electronic or mechanical means, including information storage and retrieval systems, without written permission from the author, except for the use of brief quotations in a book review.

This is a work of fiction. Names, characters, businesses, places, events, locales, and incidents are either the products of the author's imagination or used in a fictitious manner. Any resemblance to actual persons, living or dead, or actual events is purely coincidental.

The author acknowledges the trademark status and trademark owners of various brands, products, and/or restaurants referenced in this work of fiction. The publication/use of these trademarks is not authorized, associated with, or sponsored by the trademark owners.

Editing: Zainab with Heart Full of Reads Editing Services
Proofreading: Amanda Mili with Amandanomaly

Cover Design: Sarah Sentz with Enchanting Romance Designs

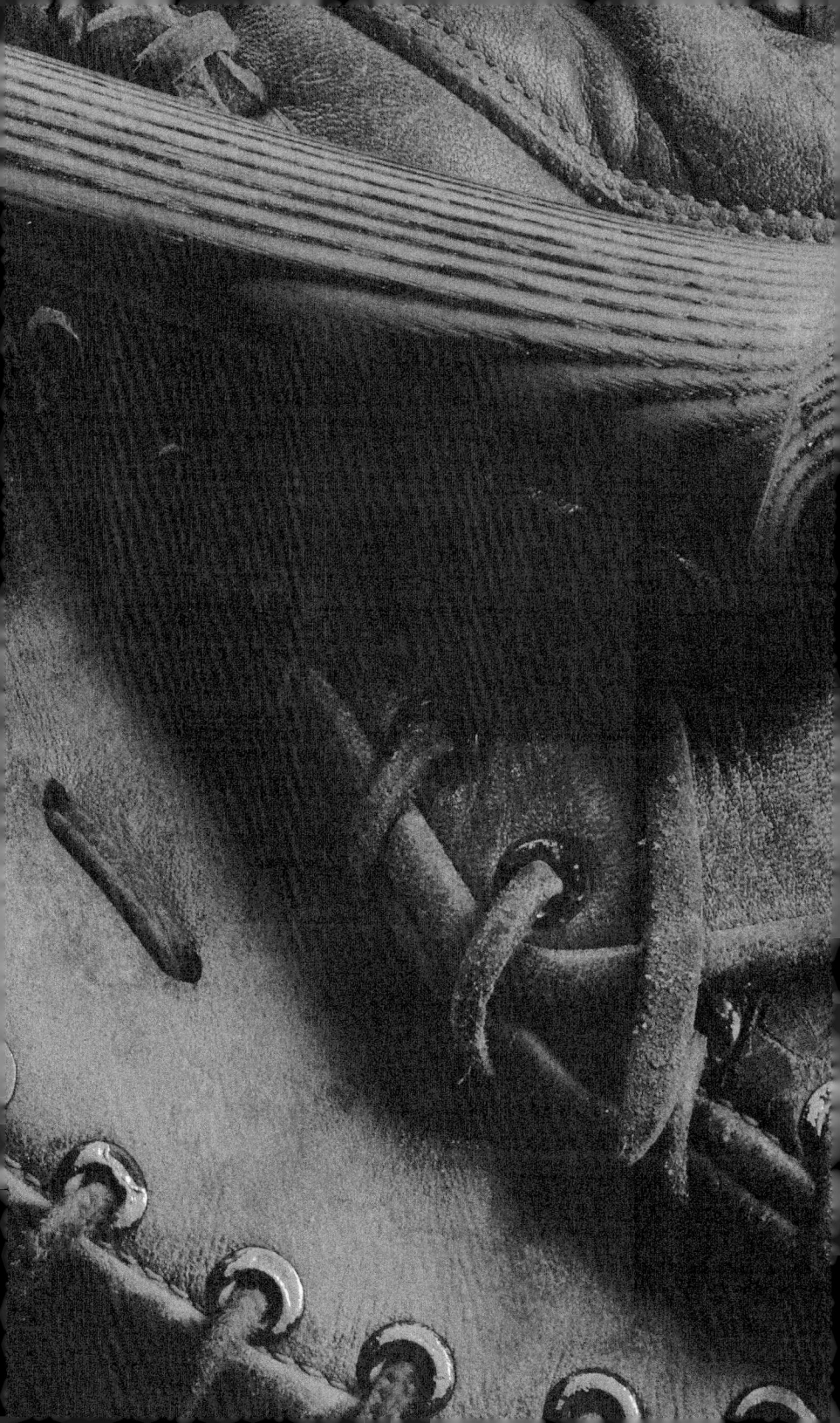

2

To the lifelong friends that are more like family.
To the few who've stuck by my side through it all.
This one's for you.

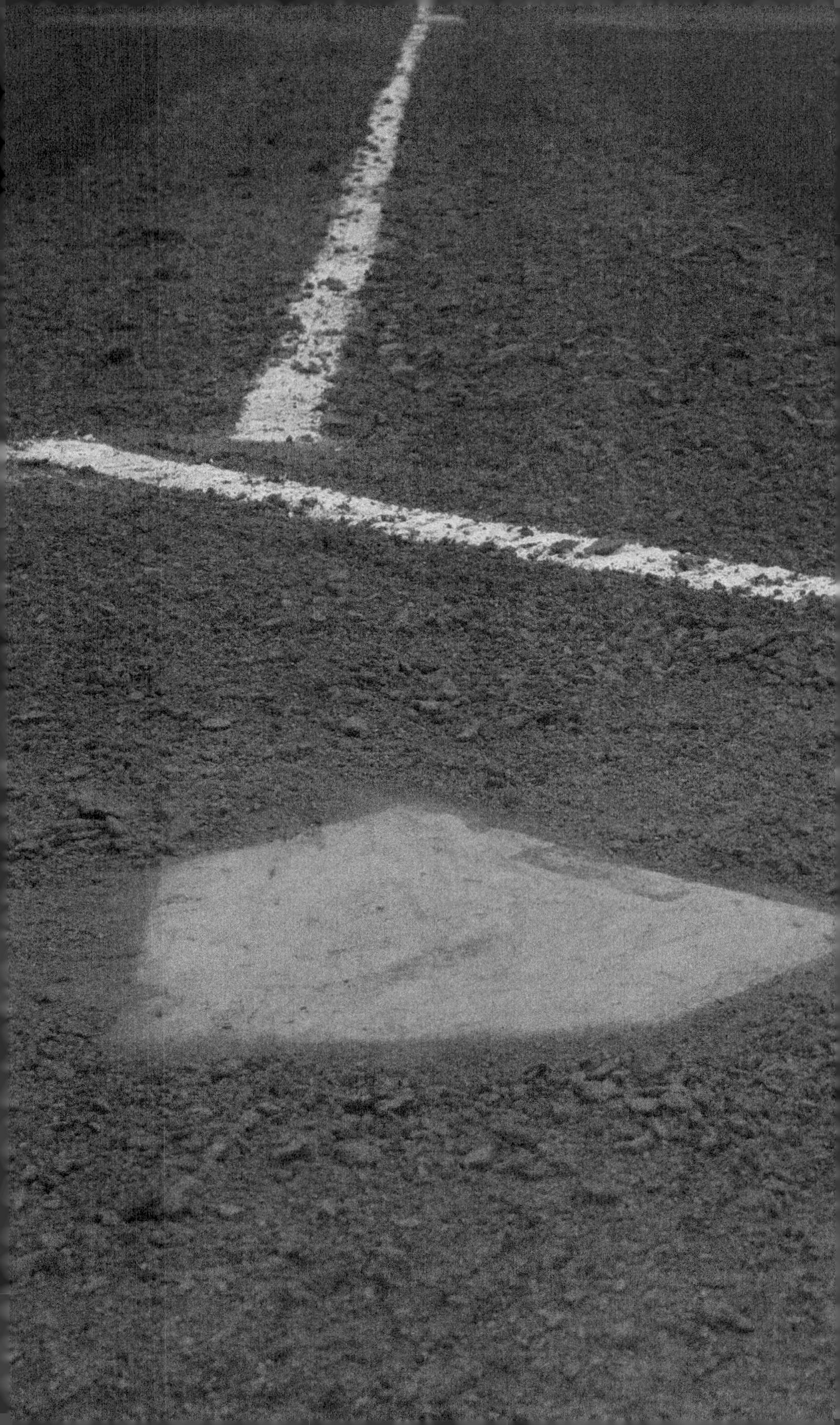

True love exists in moments
stumbled upon by accident…

— *Atticus*

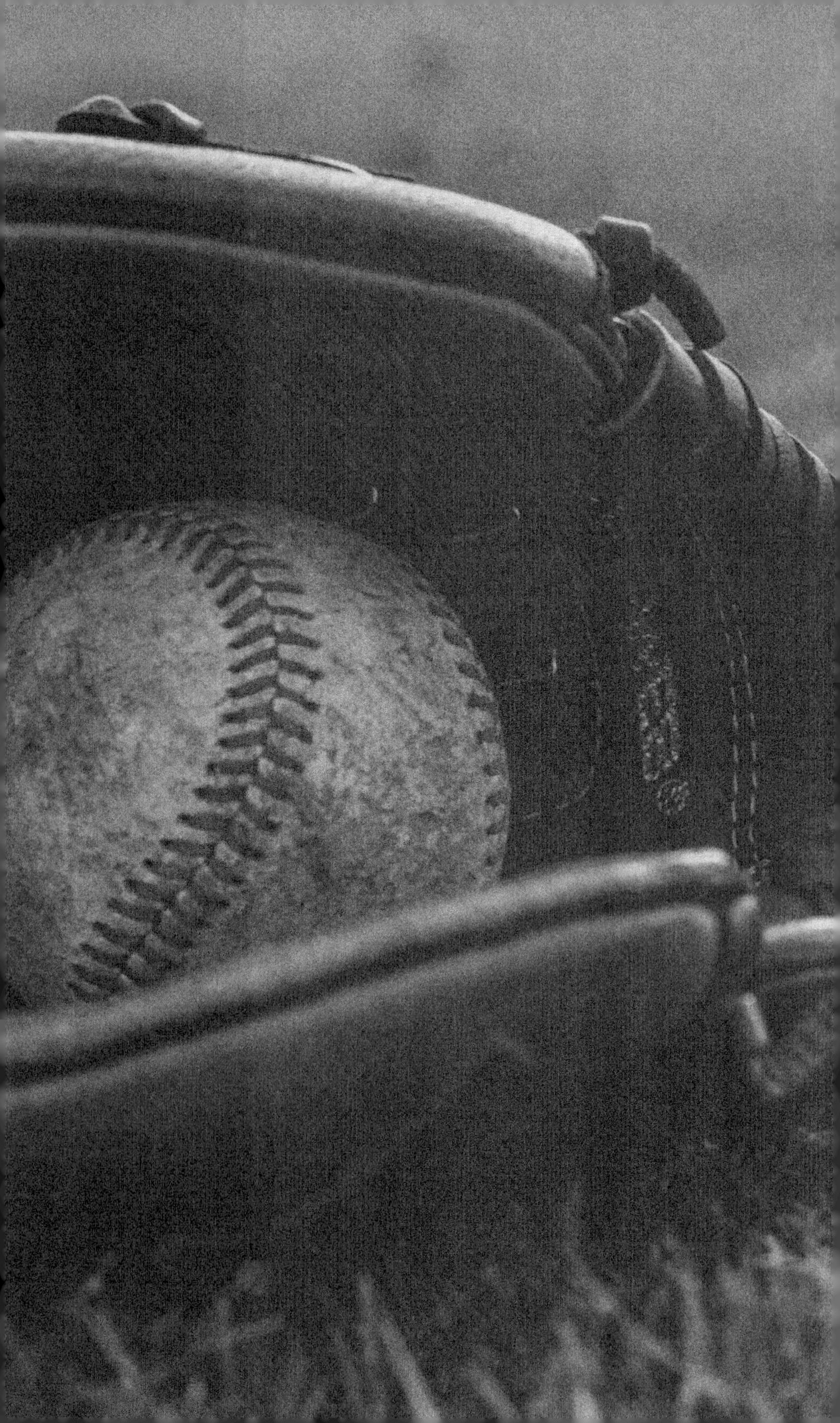

THEME SONG:
Once In A Lifetime — All Time Low

PLAYLIST:
3AM — You Me At Six
the 1 — blackbear
Alone — I Prevail
The Hills — The Weeknd
Favorite Place — All Time Low feat. The Band CAMINO
My Thoughts On You — The Band CAMINO
Fireworks — You Me At Six
All Over You — The Spill Canvas
Reckless — You Me At Six
You Broke Me First — Conor Maynard
Don't Miss Me? — Marianas Trench
Lost in You — Three Days Grace
Like I Do — Rain City Drive
Voicenotes — You Me At Six
Better Now — Post Malone
Good Things Fall Apart — ILLENIUM, Jon Bellion, Travis Barker
Bones — MOD SUN
You & Me — LUNDON
Everything We Need — A Day To Remember
Leave a Light On — Tom Walker
Bleed For Me — Escape the Fate
Don't Forget About Me — Emphatic
In Your Arms — ILLENIUM, X Ambassadors
If You're Gone — Matchbox Twenty
Come Back Home — Calum Scott
Pens and Needles — Hawthorne Heights
mother tongue — Bring Me The Horizon
Daphne Blue — The Band CAMINO
Pieces of You — nothing,nowhere.
My Home — Thousand Foot Krutch
Collide — Howie Day

Find the playlist on Spotify

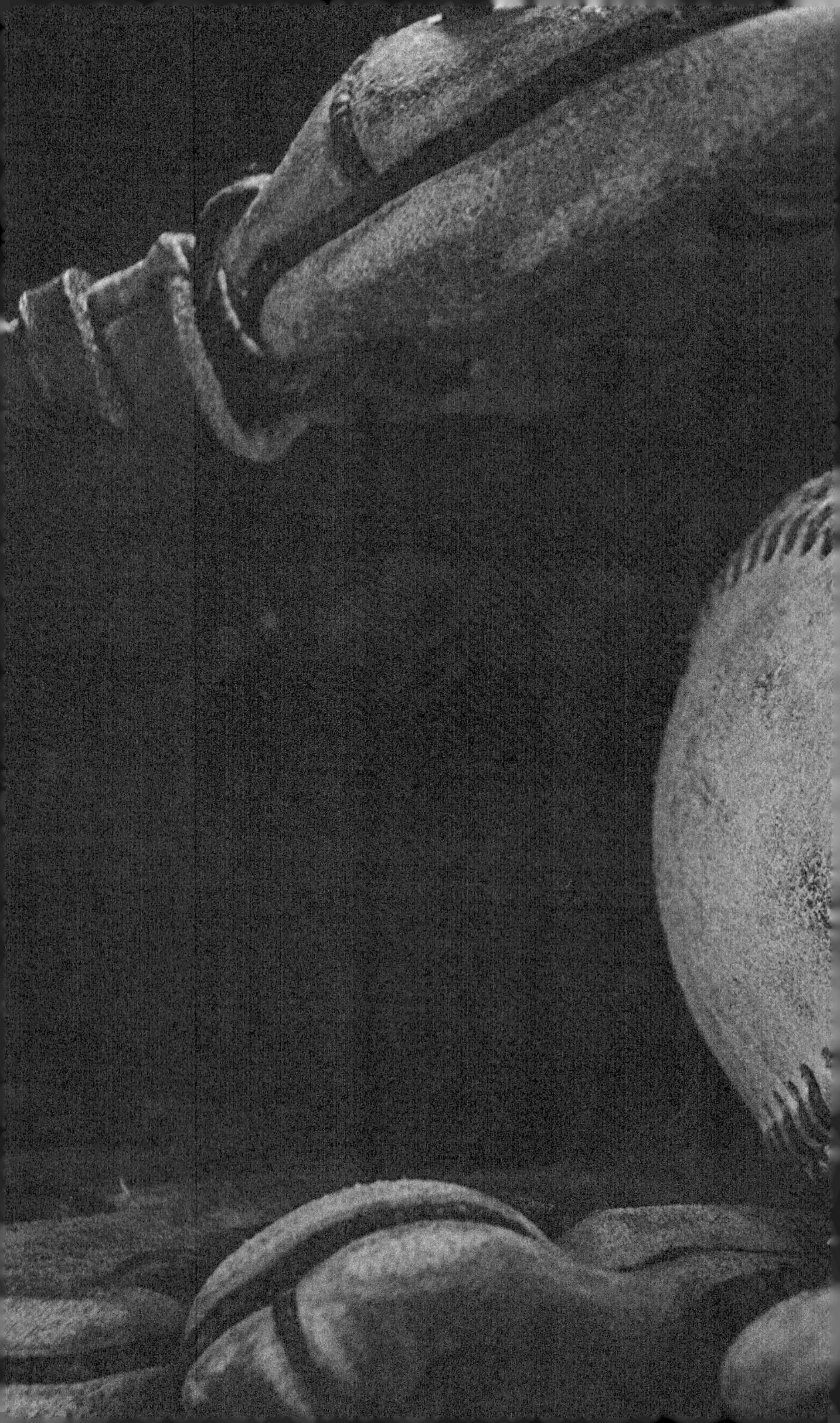

PROLOGUE

Keene

Almost Two Years Ago

"Don't you dare?"

I sigh and glance at Aspen next to me, raising a brow as if to ask, *is there even a second option here?*

The answer is no. Not unless I wanna be kicked out of the game. Something that's never happened to me in the history of this altered version of Truth or Dare…where there's no truth option.

"Do your worst," I tell Ashton, the girl in charge of my fate.

Her smirk turns deadly. "I dare you to kiss Aspen."

Well, I should've seen this coming a mile away, because Ashton loves to do anything she can to get under Aspen's skin.

I glance between the two of them, wondering how I keep getting stuck in the middle of their feud, before my eyes settle on her. "There's no use trying to measure cocks against Pen," I tell her, Aspen's nickname rolling off my lips. "He's gonna win every time."

Her smirk remains painted on. "Well, you'd know all about that, wouldn't you?"

I roll my eyes. "Funny, Ash."

"I suck his dick better than you too," Pen cuts in, and *goddamnit,* I can't help laughing. He's got some balls to say that shit with a straight face, considering he *is straight* and has never touched my cock in his life.

He raises his eyebrows and glances over at me, confirming my acceptance of the dare, to which I pucker my lips like a fish and start making kissing noises while I lean in toward him.

I think that's enough of an answer.

He lets out a soft laugh, the tiny dimple below the left corner of his mouth making a rare public appearance. "Nah, man. Not gonna happen if you're doing that shit. I have no problem with letting you drop out of the game early."

I narrow my eyes on him. "You wouldn't fucking dare."

I actually *know* he wouldn't. We're the kind of best friends who would do anything for each other. Even kiss each other for a stupid dare.

"We don't have all night," Ashton singsongs from her seat across the sectional from us. "So, let's get a move on."

Sometimes I wonder how I dated this girl. This is one of those moments.

I meet Pen's eyes again, muttering, "Ten seconds."

He nods. "Stick your tongue in my mouth and I'll bite it off."

Chuckling, I decide to play into his earlier comment to ease the weird tension simmering between us. "That's not what you said when I put my dic—"

I don't get to finish, though, because his lips are already pressed against mine.

The first brush of contact is electric, coiling my intestines in knots. I'm surprised by how soft his lips are and how gently they move against mine. I wouldn't think Aspen capable of being able to kiss like this. Sweet and sensual. Tender.

He's handling me like I'm made of glass, capable of shattering in his hands, and right now, I think it's very possible I could.

It's the strangest feeling in the world.

It makes my heart leap into my throat and does something weird to my stomach. Makes it flip and somersault, but not with nerves or anxiousness. With something else entirely.

And it spurs me into action.

My hand reaches up, cupping the side of his jaw to tilt his head right where I want it. A tiny part of me has the urge to deepen the kiss, maybe slip my tongue out just to fuck with him, but I rein myself in enough to keep it a simple press of our lips.

But then, something happens.

His tongue brushes against my bottom lip, and my entire body lights up like an inferno. My pulse kicks up into overdrive, and that electric feeling from earlier intensifies. And as my cock twitches behind my zipper, starting to thicken, I realize what it is.

Lust. Desire.

For...*Aspen*.

It hits me like a brick wall, simultaneously scaring the shit out of me and sending a thrill rushing through me that's nearly impossible to keep control over. My mind races to a thousand different places, seeing vivid scenarios playing out behind my closed lids.

Hot, naked skin brushing up against mine. Hard, smooth muscle beneath my palms.

Raven black hair anchored between my fingers.

Fantasies run rampant in my thoughts, and I don't know how to stop them. I don't know if I even want to, because nothing's ever felt like this.

All I know is, I want more of it. More of whatever addictive magic Pen's lips possess.

I don't even notice when the ten seconds are up until Aspen's mouth leaves mine, and I try not to think about the small pang of sadness flashing through me at the loss of contact. Because it doesn't make any sense for me to feel it. His cobalt eyes are cloudy and his breathing shallow when he meets my gaze, giving me a look I can't place.

Fear washes through me, and I'm terrified it's because he can read every filthy thought I just had running around in my brain written on my face, clear as day.

And more than that, I internally plead to whatever higher being that exists for me to not be hard enough for anyone to notice. Especially Pen.

I might never see most of these people again after tonight, but I have to *live* with Pen in a few months, once we head off to college. I don't think I'd be able to look him straight in the face if he knew the type of visceral reaction I'm having from just kissing him.

He pants against my lips, still close enough that I could close the gap between us and take more. Thrust my tongue into his mouth and let it tangle with his the way I wanted to before he cut us off at the knees.

Someone—Cameron, I think—clears her throat, though, and it snaps my common sense back into place.

"Uh, is anyone else now pregnant because of that?" she asks with an awkward laugh.

I glance up in time to catch a couple other girls nodding. Even Ashton's eyes are wide, lips parted in shock.

"Oh, fuck off," Pen mutters, releasing me entirely as he clears his throat too. "It's not like it meant anything. Just fulfilling another stupid dare."

"Yeah." I swallow. "Just a stupid dare."

But the way my heart's hammering against my ribs, far harder than it should be, tells me it was so much more than that.

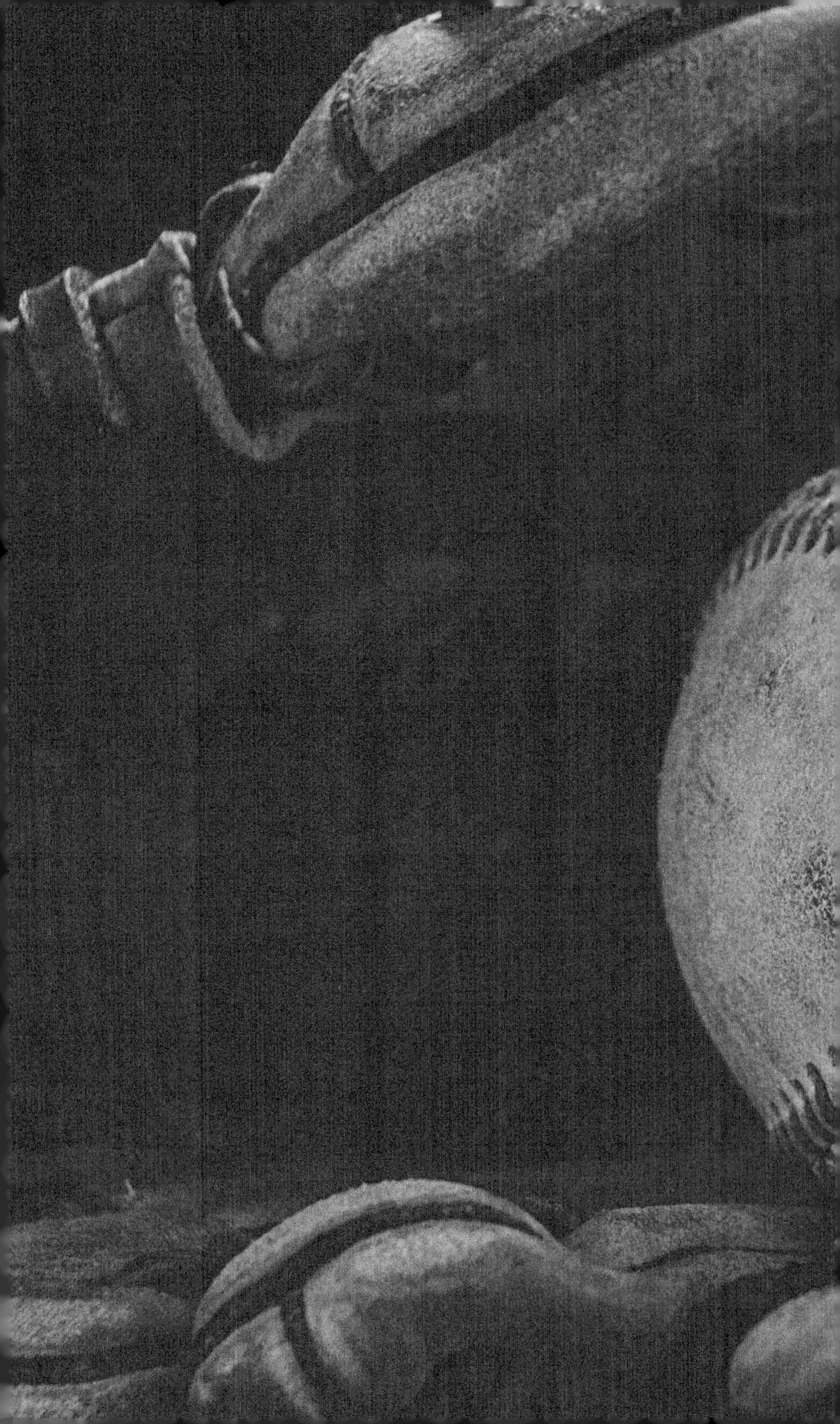

ONE

Keene

Present Day - January

Never—not in my entire damn life—did I think I'd grow up to be an alarm clock.

Plenty of things were on the list over the years of my adolescence. When I was a young kid, they were the fun ones and nothing out of the norm: Astronaut. Firefighter. President of the United States, on the days I was feeling particularly ambitious. Sometimes, I could see myself jamming out on stage as a rock star, despite not having a musical bone in my body. All the dreams of a kid with nothing but my imagination holding me back.

When I grew older and a little wiser, discovering my true talents along the way, things became a bit more clear. I thought maybe I'd be a professional athlete. Part of me still thinks I could be. Spending my days playing the game I love. Traveling around the country with a team. Being part of the one percent of the population that was able to truly hone my skill and craft enough to make it to the big leagues.

All in all, from start to finish, none of those are anything atypical for a regular, run-of-the-mill guy.

But last I checked, being the annoying, awful thing to wake a person up in the morning wasn't on that list.

Yet here I am, slamming my fist into Aspen's door to wake his sorry ass up. Irony that's not lost on me, considering he's usually awake at five in the morning to run and is normally the one to make sure *I'm* awake in time to make it to early morning lifting or PT sessions.

Not this morning, though. At least, if his running shoes by our door and AirPods on the coffee table—or the noises coming through his wall until late last night—are anything to go off of.

A good ninety-eight percent of the time, those are the only mornings the asswipe never manages to get up on time. When he's been busy *entertaining* whatever girl he's decided to bring back to our dorm room. Thankfully, they've been few and far between over the last three semesters we've been roommates here at Foltyn.

He seems to be starting this term with a bang, though. Pun absolutely intended.

"Wake up, Pen! We have to get going!" I shout, still pounding my fist into the wood.

And I'm gonna be late too, because you're *my damn ride.*

I glance down at my watch to find I have exactly thirty minutes to get to the field. I prefer to be early, even if it's only weights this morning. And seeing as both the team's facility and the field are on the other side of campus from our dorm, walking is out of the question. My only option is the car.

And the owner of said car is fast a-fucking-sleep.

A low rumble of irritation slips from my throat as I slap against the door again.

"For fuck's sake, Pen. Get up! You're gonna make *me* late!"

It takes a few seconds, but I finally hear stirring behind the wood and let out a breath of relief. Leave it to a threat to *my* well-being to get him going. I can say what I want about my best friend, but at the end of the day and for all intents and purposes, he's a brother to me. Cares about me on a level not many other people do. Only my mother and sister can compare.

No more than a minute later, the door is yanked open by…not Aspen.

Nope.

I'm met face-to-face with Bristol, dressed only in one of Aspen's ratty t-shirts.

I sigh as I take in the girl he's been seeing for the past year or so. If you can call it that, considering I don't think they've actually gone out on a single date. Fuck buddies would be more accurate to describe their relationship. And again, from the sounds they were making last night and the sated smile currently on her lips, she's definitely okay with it.

Her blue eyes roam my face as she combs her fingers through her long, dark hair.

"Hi, Keene. He'll be out in a few."

I plaster a fake smile on my face. "Didn't realize you were his secretary now too."

She isn't taken aback by my slightly insulting comment or tone. Instead, she just smiles and crosses her arms before leaning against the door frame.

"Someone's feisty this morning," she quips. Deep maroon nails tap against her tanned skin as she studies my face. "If you need to get laid, baby, all you have to do is ask to join."

My stomach swirls at the offer, but I snort and shake my head. The annoyance is still there, but I can't help being amused by her quick wit.

Honestly, I like Bristol. Not in that way, but as much as I possibly can like the girl my best friend is screwing regularly. On any other given day, I'd chat with her while waiting for Aspen to literally get his shit together so we can get out of here. Make the small talk that isn't all that awkward anymore, since we've gotten to know each other a bit.

But today isn't a normal day, and the first regular season practice always has me on edge.

Something Aspen knows all too well, so why he pulled this crap with me this morning is…

Just cool it. He'll be out in a few. It's fine.

"I'll keep it in mind," I tell her, instead focusing my attention on flipping my snapback backward on my head to give me something to do other than lose my shit on Aspen.

She shrugs at my dismissal of her offer, slipping past me to head to our kitchenette to make herself some coffee. Which only serves as a signal that I won't be leaving anytime soon.

Goddamnit. I should just take the car and go.

Just as I'm entering his room to suggest it, I collide with a hard, bare chest. On instinct, I reach out to steady myself by putting a hand on his shoulder, and while his skin should just be warm beneath my palm, it sizzles uncomfortably.

Clearing my throat, I release him quickly and glance at his face. His sapphire eyes are wide and alert—almost in a state of panic—and the long midnight strands of hair on the top of his head, a disheveled mess.

"You look like you had fun last night," I say dryly, taking in his sex hair. My eyes move down his body of their own accord to find he's half-dressed in jeans and socks. Three-quarters, if the shirt in his hand that he's clearly about to toss on counts at all. "Sounded like it too."

He glances over my shoulder, presumably to where Bristol is, and shrugs. *I will not commit murder this morning. He is the only way I'm making it to practice on time.*

"Ready in less than five," he tells me as he tosses the shirt over his head. "Just wanna brush my teeth."

I grind my molars and nod, though he's already slipped past me, out of his room, and into our shared bathroom connected to the little communal living area we have.

Turning, I find Bristol leaning against the counter next to the coffee maker, sipping a steaming cup. I cringe absently at the smell. Neither of us particularly cares for the stuff, but when Pen has to pull all-nighters for his studio classes each semester, he caves for any form of caffeine. Even that nasty stuff.

"Early day for you, isn't it?" she asks over the rim. "I don't think I've ever seen you up before ten."

True, she hasn't.

Spring semester of last year, Aspen was usually the one doing the walk of shame from *her* dorm, so she's never been around when the season starts. I'd like to think it was a respect thing for me, that he kept the location of their hooking-up elsewhere, but I'd probably give most of the credit for that to his low-key issues with intimacy.

His space is his own, and he's not really one to share it with just anyone. Which is why it's slightly surprising that she's been sleeping over the past few times they've hooked up.

"First day of regular season practice," I say, my smile forced.

At least she has some form of social cues, not bothering to try to make any other conversation with me after that.

Just like he promised, Pen's by the door with keys in hand the second he's done brushing his teeth. He doesn't look at me, clearly aware of my irritation with him this morning. Instead, he looks at Bristol while she continues to drink her coffee, watching us with the utmost curiosity.

"Let yourself out, and I'll meet up with you later," he tells her as he slips into his Vans. Only then does he look up at me. I can see the silent apology in his eyes as he slides into the worn leather jacket he favors this time of year, and it's enough to melt my icy mood into a puddle. "Ready?"

"Have been," I tell him matter-of-factly before clearing my throat. My irritation is completely gone now, but that doesn't mean I won't still give him shit. "For the last fifteen minutes."

He just licks his lips and smirks, seeing right through me. "Well, why didn't you just say so?"

My eyes roll and I shove him out the door, smiling to myself as he stumbles for a second before calling a goodbye to Bristol over his shoulder.

Less than a minute later, we're sliding onto the bench seat of his '67 Impala and making our way to the team's practice facility.

"You could've just let me take the car," I tell him, flipping through the radio until I land on a station playing The Weeknd. The bass thumps through the speakers, settling my pulse into a steady rhythm with the beat.

Aspen being who he is, though, glares at the radio like it's offended him. The only reason he allows anything in the Top 40 countdown to play in his car is because it's what I like. And he's probably letting it slide because *he's* the reason I'm cutting it close for practice.

His brows raise as he glances over at me, and he barks out a laugh. "You're kidding, right? No one drives my baby."

Cue an eye roll. "Okay, *Dean*," I say, my tone laced with sarcasm.

Truth be told, I've never watched a damn episode of *Supernatural*, but I'm pretty sure everyone knows how Dean Winchester feels about anyone besides him driving his Impala. I actually think the obsession Braden Kohl—Aspen's father—had with the show is the reason he bought the exact same car and restored it.

I remember, clear as day, when he hauled the junker to Aspen's house across the street when we were younger. And I also remember the coronary Aspen's mom had when she saw it sitting in the driveway.

The damn thing didn't even run, but Braden changed that with six months of hard work. By the time it was all fixed up, it was his prized possession.

And anything his dad loved, Pen loved too. Maybe that's why I found it a little poetic when the Impala became Pen's once we were old enough to drive. Now, it's all he has left of him. That, and the old leather jacket he's wearing.

"It's not like you don't let me drive it sometimes," I point out. "When we go home. Or to the beach. Or on our annual road trip."

He nods thoughtfully. "True. But I'm in the car with you. Able to take over at any time."

I snort. "You act like I haven't driven more than a day in my life."

"If the shoe fits..." He trails off, the smirk that pops the dimple below the left corner of his mouth crossing his face.

"Oh, fuck you."

"Not my fault you've *barely* driven since you got your license."

"Not my fault you got yours a month and a half before I did, so I didn't really need it at all."

He just grins, seeing the truth in my words.

It's not obvious from looking at him with the leather, shaggy hair, and general *fuck off* vibe he radiates, but Pen's one uptight motherfucker. Always the one in charge. While driving us around wherever we wanna go might be included in that, it's pretty much true in any and all aspects of our friendship.

Don't get me wrong; I have my own thoughts and opinions, and I'll voice them with a blowhorn if needed, but being the more laidback one makes it a lot easier to just be along for the ride.

Hell, the only time I ever feel the need to control things is in relation to a baseball diamond, but that comes naturally with the position I've played for three-quarters of my life. Probably because catchers are the most important position on the damn field, bar none. But besides then? Basically never.

But that's our dynamic—complete opposites—and has been for as long as I can remember.

Ever since our dads died in a car accident right before we turned eight.

Before then, Pen used to be a lot more carefree. But after that night, he shut down and shut out everyone in his life. Besides his mom, the only person he let in was me. Even to this day, not many people get to see what he has beneath the surface. Picking and choosing a select few who've earned a glimpse inside.

Control is his suit of armor. Reclusiveness, his shield. Both of which I'm more than happy to lend him; whatever he needs to protect himself. He's never needed them with me, anyway.

Moments later, he rolls to a stop outside the training center and throws the car in park. "Do you need me to pick you up too, Your Highness?"

"You think this is a chariot?"

He glares. "Never mind. You can walk. Last I checked, it's supposed to start raining right when you're done lifting."

Ah, Oregon. Always raining.

I smirk as I get out, slinging my bag over my shoulder and calling through the open door. "Thanks for the ride, Mom. Meet you here after practice."

The words "fucking asshole" are just loud enough for me to hear before the door slams shut and I turn to walk away.

TWO

Aspen

That little shithead.

My eyes bore into Keene's back as he walks away from me and into the university's practice facility.

He's always known how to push my buttons better than anyone else. Probably because I gave him the damn nuclear codes years ago. Hard not to when we've known each other since birth.

I'm still staring long after he's passed through the doors leading to the team's weight room, indoor cages, and all that shit. Not for any reason in particular, other than I'd prefer to wait long enough that Bristol isn't at the dorm when I get back.

It sounds shitty, I know. But her habit of staying over has become more than a little cumbersome as of late, and not just because she hogs a lot of room for such a small human.

The girl's a great time; that's not the issue. We get along easily enough, and the sex since we started this friends-with-benefits arrangement our freshman year has been top-notch. And most importantly, we're on the same page about keeping things casual between us. Keene doesn't quite understand it—the monogamist he is—but at least he keeps it to himself.

He might like the whole cute, cuddly thing that you get from relationships, but it's not my jam. I prefer the zero-attachment style of hookup. The kind where we fuck, she leaves, and I get to crash alone. In fact, sharing a bed with someone is probably in the top five of my least favorite things on Earth.

I just don't like the intimacy of it all. The closeness that comes with waking up next to someone after screwing the daylights out of them for a good forty-five minutes the night before.

Plus, the amount of awkwardness—and subsequently, guilt—I feel whenever she stays over weighs on me. Awkward, because I never know how to say something like, *okay, you can leave now,* without sounding like a complete tool. And guilty for not only wanting her to leave, but also because I know Keene has to hear everything through the paper-thin wall we share. Brist isn't exactly discrete in bed.

A loud honk behind me sends my pulse into hyperdrive, and a quick glance in the mirror reveals a car trying to pull into the spot I'm blocking with my Impala.

Dad's Impala.

But the car is a Mercedes G-Class, and in the driver's seat is none other than Avery Reynolds. Also known as one of the starting pitchers for the Wildcats and the biggest douchebag I've ever had the displeasure of meeting.

How Keene deals with him on a day-to-day basis, especially working so close with him as a catcher, is beyond me. And don't even get me started on the way he talks down to Keene, even in the middle of the game. I have a hard enough time not cussing him out every time he calls Keene out to the mound for one of their little huddles, knowing damn well he's giving Keene a hard time when it's *his* pitches that aren't hitting the target Keene sets.

I'd deck him the first chance I got if he started popping off at me. Then again, this is why I don't play team sports and keep to running instead. My preference lies with things that don't require me to talk to other people, unless it's jumping into a squad while I'm gaming.

But I digress.

Avery honks again before urging me to move forward and out of his way by revving the engine.

Like I said, douchebag.

Oh, and look. Getting out of the passenger side is his right-hand asshole, Reese. Also known as the best first baseman in the conference, as if it's any sort of accomplishment.

I'm kind of sick of all these guys thinking they're hot shit just because they're playing college ball. It's not like they're over in Nashville playing for Vanderbilt. Baseball at Vandy might as well be compared to playing football for Alabama; where the best of the best want to be.

Where Keene could've gone, if I was less of a selfish dick. Or a fucking coward, too chicken shit to uproot out of my comfort zone permanently.

Keene's mom even tried to talk him out of staying, to truly follow his heart when choosing where he wanted to land. That he and I would still be best friends, even if we were no longer attached at the hip like we've been our entire lives. All very valid points.

But like he could sense the fear radiating from me while we all sat around the Waters' dinner table at one of our weekly dinners, he said the Wildcats made the most sense for him.

I try to ease the guilt I feel for that by telling myself Keene made the choice to stay here, though deep down, I know that the only reason he did so was for me. And if I would've given Vandy a chance—because, yeah, I applied and got in—he'd be working with some of the best coaches to garner his shot at the MLB.

And we wouldn't have to deal with jack knobs like Avery if we were at Vandy.

Knowing what I do now, that would've been my selling point to drop everything and head to Music City. Hindsight, and all that.

Speaking of the devil, Avery's now outside my driver's side window, rapping on the glass with his knuckles and one pissed-off expression.

I sigh and roll the window down halfway. Enough for him to talk, but not enough for him to do something stupid, like get close enough for me to sock him in the mouth if he makes some com—

"If you're planning to wait all day for your boyfriend, I'd suggest moving this hunk of junk into an actual parking spot. You're making us late for practice."

The boyfriend comments from Avery are new, just starting near the end of last semester, but it's gotten old real quick. Just another way for him to be a piece of shit and bully people who aren't intimidated by him or all the money his daddy threw at school as a "donation" for a new stadium.

A generous one, and the only reason Avery's even on the team in the first place.

My brow arches and I look around at the practically empty lot we're in. "Ah, yes. How could I forget the world revolves around you? Heaven forbid you be inconvenienced."

The sarcasm in my tone is potent, completely obvious to even this Neanderthal, and it shows when his glare turns into a sneer.

"It's not hard to move the car, Kohl. So, do it."

I give him a thoughtful look and nod. "You're right. It's not hard at all. So why don't you get back in yours, put it in drive, and go around me."

His stunned expression is priceless as I pull out my pack of Marlboros, stick one between my lips, and light it.

I picked up the habit last year when I was outside my architecture studio late one night with another classmate, taking a break from working on my midterm project. He offered me one, and though I'd never had the urge to smoke, I did it. And just like that, I was hooked. Not to the cancer stick itself, but the feeling that came when I inhaled.

I felt lighter. Calmer. Less stressed. More in control.

Keene hates it. Even told me he'd throw the pack away anytime he caught it lying around, and I don't blame him for it. I wouldn't want to watch him suck all the toxic shit into his body either. But I don't make a habit to smoke often—only when I really need to cool my shit—and next to never when he's around.

Avery's lip curls up in clear disgust when I flick ash out the window in his direction.

Good. Let him think what he wants of me. I don't give two shits about his opinion, or Reese's, or any of the other douche canoes on Keene's team.

I exhale slowly, letting the smoke blow out at him. "Didn't you say you were gonna be late?"

His jaw ticks, and he waves his hand angrily to fan the smoke away. "Why're you such a dick?"

I snort. "Coming from you? Please."

"Just move the fucking car."

I raise a brow. "How about…no?"

The vein in his temple becomes more visible, and the part of me that hates this guy as much as I do is begging him to deck me. I'd take the shiner if he broke his damn hand in the process. I can tell he's getting close to that point too. The way his face reddens says it all.

But instead of dragging me from the car and beating my ass, his fist slams down on the roof. My vision goes black. Or maybe it's red, from all the blood of his I'm about to spill if he doesn't back up in the next two seconds.

"Do that again. I fucking dare you."

"Or what? What's your punk ass gonna do about it? I'd rock your shit, Kohl."

Again, I could give two shits if he kicked my ass. No doubt, with one or two of his cronies holding my arms back, because he's not the type to fight fair. But the funny thing about having nothing to prove is you also have nothing to lose.

He has both.

"Then do it."

He blinks at me. "What?"

I shrug. "Hit me. Fight me. I don't care."

The shock on his face makes me chuckle, but not nearly as much as watching him stammer and grapple for some sort of rebuttal. I give him a second, though, because no one ever accused this meathead of being smart.

Finally, after a minute, he settles on something. "Yeah, but then go home to have Waters nurse you back to health. Hell, I bet I'd be doing you a favor." He pauses, then adds, "And I can't risk an injury to my hand."

The smirk that slides on my face is one of victory, and man, it tastes sweet. Only getting better when his glare takes on a mixture of anger and resentment for embarrassing him.

How dare I call him out like that?

"Your hand. Right," I say, nodding. "Well, if that's all, I've gotta get going. You mind?"

Oh, does his face turn into a damn tomato when I say that, but he turns and heads back to his car without another word. He's getting what he wanted, after all. He just got his ego knocked down a few pegs beforehand. And his sense of entitlement checked.

Assholes like him need that every once in a while.

Of course, he's not the only asshole here, so I roll my window down completely to lean out and call back to him, "Oh, hey, Reynolds!"

He's got his hand on the door to his Mercedes when he looks back up at me.

"Next time you touch my car, I'll hit you with it."

Then I flip him the bird and punch the gas, speeding away with winter air and cigarette smoke filling my lungs.

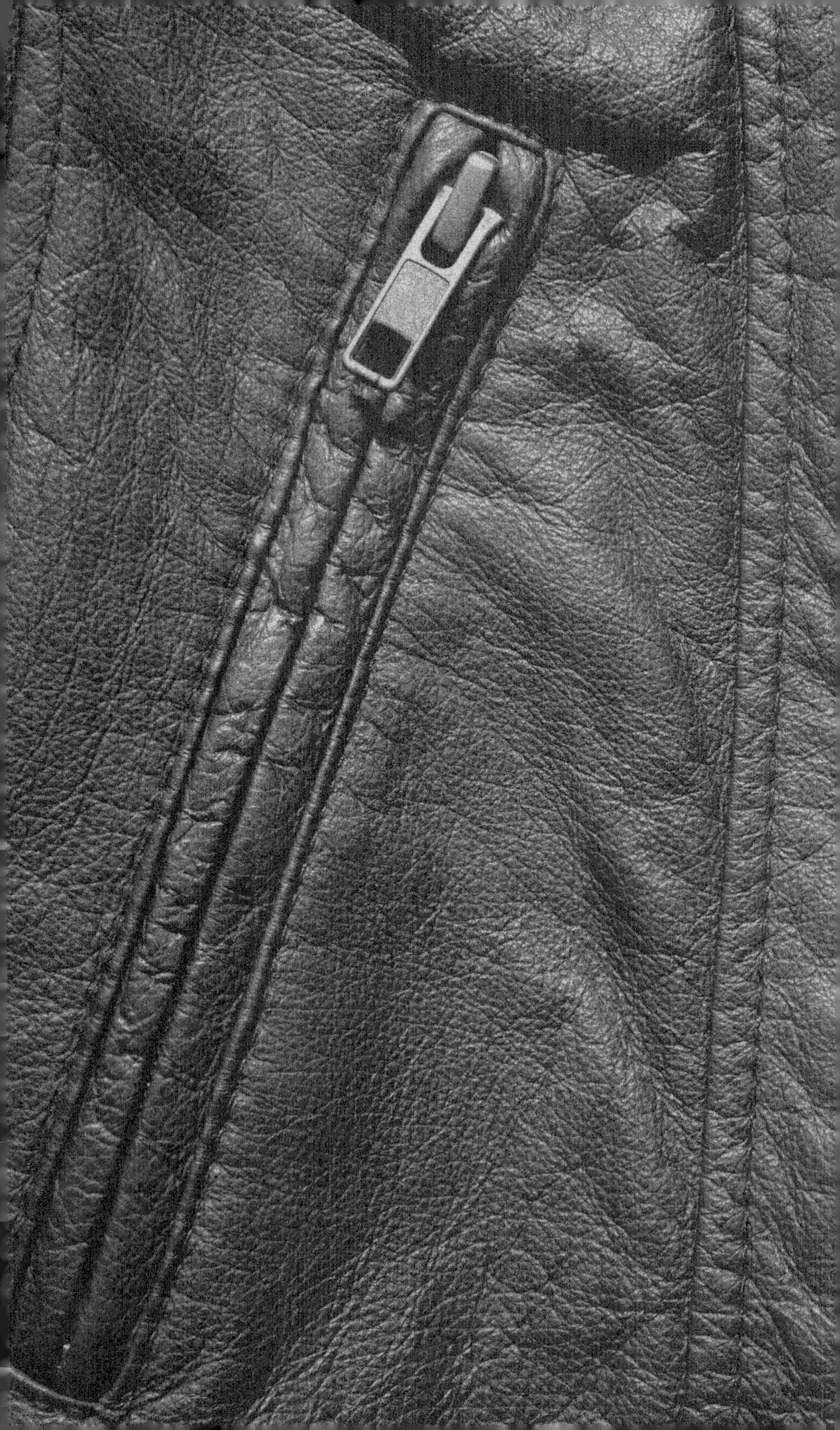

THREE

Aspen

With school back in session after winter break, a lot of my time is about to be consumed by my studio class alone, not to mention my other lecture classes.

I was clearly mistaken for thinking it was smart to take eighteen credit hours this semester. Call it the overachiever in me. Or that I'd rather graduate as quickly as I can, so I can get a job and pay off the insane amount of debt I'm wracking up in loans.

All that school work leaves little time to play, and that also means Keene and I barely see each other. Spring semesters are the worst, since that's when baseball season really starts kicking into gear. But since things don't really get heavy for another week or two for the both of us, I use the time to hang with him instead.

Well, if *hanging out* is me playing *God of War* on the couch in our dorm suite's tiny living room while he's occupied with icing his knees and messing around on his phone.

I'd offered to do something else, maybe go for a run or even hit the gym with him, but he's been pretty beat from getting back into preseason training and practices this week. He's not out of shape by any means, but when he goes back to squatting behind a plate in full gear after months of not doing it, I'm sure it takes a toll.

And he seems content with this, so I'll take it.

"So what're you thinking for plans this summer?" I ask, tapping away on my PlayStation controller a little harder than might be necessary. I'm having a bitch of a time defeating this boss, and it's starting to piss me off.

"In terms of…" Keene says, trailing off.

I roll my eyes, not bothering to look away from the TV. He knows exactly what I mean.

Each summer since we turned sixteen, Keene and I have taken a road trip together. In high school, it was usually just up to Washington or down into Cali, but the summer we graduated, we went all the way to Nashville. Don't ask me why, seeing as we both hate country music, but it's somewhere we'd always wanted to go.

And maybe I wanted a chance to see the city we could've been living in for college instead of staying on the West Coast. See if there was any regret on Keene's face while we explored the city.

Thankfully, I didn't find any.

Though we take turns choosing where to go each year, I always let Keene have some input. Even when it's my turn to decide, like this year, he should know by now that I'll always give him a say. I'm not nearly as much of a control freak as he makes me out to be, and it's meant to be fun for the both of us.

Even if he puts on his shit music in my car.

His silence makes it clear he wants me to spell it out for him, so with a quick glance at him on the other side of the couch, I say, "Why're you playing dumb? The trip, of course."

I feel him shift on the couch before asking, "Isn't that like six months from now? Little early to be thinking about that, isn't it?"

"Um, no?"

Okay, so maybe he's a little right about the control freak bit.

But the chuckle that floats out of him is somewhere between true laughter and his mocking laugh, giving him away. It's the one he makes before he says something like—

"You and your goddamn plans."

Yep. That.

"Fuck off, Kee. Someone has to be the responsible one," I grind, speeding up my fingers on the controller.

His go-with-the-flow style of life isn't usually a bother to me. It's just who he is, and he's been that way since…well, forever. I swear, the only real "plan" Keene has had in his life is to play baseball for as long as he could. It's more of an ambitious goal, and though I'm biased, I think he has the talent to make it happen.

But even then, I don't know if he even has a backup for if something happens and he *doesn't* go pro. Like if an injury takes him out of the game for good. Living life and thinking it'll all just work itself out is insane to me, and no matter how hard I try to get it through his thick skull that plans are a good thing, he doesn't get the hint.

"Just like you were the responsible one on Monday when I was almost late to practice?" he points out, and even though I'm not looking at him, I know his brows are raised at me. "It's your year to pick, anyway. You just let me know where, and I'll be there. Just remember, we only turn twenty-one once."

I'm not at all surprised by this response. But like I said, that's just Keene. Flying by the seat of his pants. Though, I'll admit, his carefree attitude might actually be one of my favorite qualities of his. Sometimes.

Other times, it just pisses me the fuck off.

Hell, I remember plenty of times when we were kids, or even teenagers, where he'd forget his swim trunks for a weekend beach trip because he didn't pack until ten minutes before we left. Or he'd have to stay up until four in the morning to finish papers in high school because he's the world's best procrastinator…and also hated English with a passion. At least the latter has gotten better with age and discipline—and because he has to stay on top of his grades to play baseball. Yet he almost always forgets *something* whenever he leaves for an away series, even if he's learned to pack the night before, thanks to yours truly.

Most of the time it's socks, so I've learned to pack an extra pair in his duffle, just in case.

Biting my lip in concentration as I go in for another attack in the game, I offer, "Vegas?"

He's silent for a moment, but I glance up briefly to see him wrinkling his nose. "I feel like we'd need money to go there. A lot more than we have, at least."

Touché.

"Hmm. Maybe when we're like twenty-five and you're making millions in the majors, we can revisit it."

He snorts, eyes still locked on his screen. "Planning to make yourself my sugar baby, Pen?"

"If you're making millions, I think you can spare a couple grand for us to play some poker."

Right then, the boss I was fighting on the screen kills me with a sword to the chest.

"Fuck," I mumble, and I drop my controller onto the coffee table with a clatter of annoyance before looking at him again. "New York?"

He glances up over his phone, brows raised. "Might as well drive to Alaska at that rate. It'd be closer."

"You don't need to exaggerate."

He takes that as a challenge, the dick. But two minutes and a Google search reveals that Juneau, Alaska, is four hours closer to here than New York City.

Go figure.

"Alaska could have some killer hikes."

"But at least they have baseball in New York," I counter.

At the end of the day, I could win this non-argument with that point alone. The only thing Keene really cares about are the activities we do on our trips. Usually, it consists of hiking and sightseeing, but visiting every MLB stadium is on his bucket list, so knocking one or two off every time seems to be a common theme.

Take the year we went to Nashville, for example. We stopped in St. Louis and Kansas City on the way back, per Keene's request, to catch a game at each one. Or the year we did our trip to Cali, we got to all but one of the stadiums there, and that's only because the Giants were out of town the days we were near San Francisco.

If I've counted right, I think he's up to twelve now. Or is it thirteen?

Regardless, he's got plenty to go. And an East Coast road trip could knock a bunch off the list if we planned it at the right time.

"We'd need at least a month," he says in rebuttal. "And while I know we're both adults, our mothers would throw a bitchfit if we were gone for that long."

He's got a point.

"Fine." I sigh, running my hands through my hair. "I guess we've got a bit of time to think of something else."

"If by *a bit,* you mean months?"

"Oh, bite me."

His brows raise, eyes still fixated on his phone. "You'd probably like that too much, kinky fucker."

I'm half tempted to smack his phone clear out of his hand for that one, but I refrain. Barely. I'm not one to be needy for his undivided attention, but the level of distraction he has tonight is a bit…weird.

"What're you doing on that thing, anyway? If it's porn, it must not be very good if you're still out here."

He doesn't even laugh at the joke, giving me a clipped response. "Just texting."

Vague isn't really his style, but letting him get off that easy isn't mine, so I dig further. "And what's her name?"

Keene looks up from the screen and blinks. Then blinks again before saying with a perfectly straight face. "I have no idea what you're talking about."

I give him a knowing smirk. "If you say so."

"If there was anything to report, you'd know about it."

Normally I'd believe that, but the way he rolls his lip with his teeth after he says it gives him away.

Keene's not one for hooking up often, and as a monogamist, it makes sense. So if he's wanting to keep this to himself, I'll let him. For the time being. But I'll get it out of him eventually. Probably when the seat next to me at his home games is taken. Or when she starts staying over. Hell, part of me hopes the latter starts happening here soon. Then I wouldn't feel so bad about the racket Bristol causes.

He locks his phone and taps it against his knee. "By the way, the party the Chi O's throw for the baseball team at the beginning of each season is next weekend."

"Nice subject change," I note before actually registering *what* he said. Then I let out a low groan, hating any time a sorority party is brought up.

"I guess you mentioning this to me is your way of saying that we're going." And now I'm tempted to smack his face for the smirk he gives me. "Is that your way of saying you're not gonna go?"

Damn him.

I hate parties, at least the kind thrown in high school and even college. They're just an excuse for a bunch of stupid, horny people to get shit-faced and do things they'll regret the next day. It never fails that some kind of drama happens too, whether it be a very public break-up or a fight between two drunken fools.

It's just not my scene. At all.

But for Keene, I'll go. He knows that too, which makes it all the more irritating.

I'm not one to worry about something as trivial as *fitting in* with the jock or Greek crowds, and I don't go actively seeking out chances to be around those people either. They're just not *my people*.

Then again, no one really is besides Keene. Maybe a couple other people I've met last semester in my studio. They could be friends, if I put in a little more effort, but my inability to trust anyone sort of inhibits turning acquaintances into anything more than that.

Having a bunch of friends isn't all that important to me, anyway. When it comes to close relationships, I'd rather have quality over quantity.

It's not to say that I *can't* have a good time at parties. I did in high school, though I was a lot more comfortable letting loose around people

I've known my entire life. Hell, Keene and I used to run the beer pong tables whenever we'd get a group of people together, though flip cup has always been more my speed. And it was a great time.

But college is just different.

Eventually, I always end up having a good time, though. It just takes a bit for that to happen.

Letting out another groan, I cave. Like I always fucking do. "Fine. I'll go."

He grins. "You can never say no."

Truer words have never been spoken.

"What can I say? I'm whipped, and you don't even put out."

He lets out a bark of laughter, rubbing at the back of his neck. "Best friend perks, I guess."

"Maybe for you," I grumble. "I don't see any perks for me, though."

"Free beer?"

I cringe. "That tastes like piss."

A nod, then he says, "The joy of my company?"

"Someone's stroking their ego a little too much lately."

He laughs again. "Okay, okay. Point made. Wouldn't be the same if you didn't go, though."

That makes me smile.

No matter how many friends he has or how popular he gets as the years pass, I'm still his number one. Just like he's mine. We might've been basically family since we were born, but we still choose each other.

Always have, always will.

And damn if that doesn't make me feel like a million bucks.

FOUR

Keene

The second we make it through the door of the Chi Omega chapter house, my senses are assaulted with pounding music and the smell of body odor and spilled beer.

Ah, college parties.

I'll admit; I'm not a big partier or drinker, seeing as I'm not twenty-one yet and I have an athletic scholarship I need to keep, but this is one of the few parties I always make sure I attend. After all, the girls at the Chi O house put this on *for us* as a way to kick off the season, so it'd be rude if we didn't show up.

I don't waste a minute once we're inside, grabbing Pen by the sleeve of his jacket and dragging his ass to the backyard before he can disappear off to some dark corner and sulk the way he normally does.

Okay, so sulking might be the wrong term, but it's close enough to be accurate. The last party he came to—which was almost three months ago, I might add—he barely talked to anyone. Myself included. And there's no way I'm letting him go through all of college without having at least one good party experience.

And it's happening tonight. Even if he's still planning to be the DD.

"Man-handle me much?" he bitches, trying to yank his arm free from my hold.

"I'm not letting you leave this party until you admit to having fun," I tell him as we weave our way through the back door.

The back patio is lit up with hanging lights under one of those pergola things, multiple kegs off to one side and three beer pong tables front and center. I forego the main attraction for a moment, grabbing us both a beer.

"Oh, really? I can't leave?" His tone is skeptical at best, but when I glance over and catch him eyeing the beer pong table, I can tell the idea of having fun might be piquing his interest.

"Yep," I say, handing him a cup of frothy liquid. "Now let's show these fuckers how to run a damn table, yeah?"

He looks at the cup in his hands, then back at the table.

"Ah, fuck it."

Tapping the rim of his cup to mine, we make our way over to call the next game. It takes a lot longer for us to get in, but we shoot the shit with a few of my teammates while we wait.

My phone's been dinging with message notifications from that stupid app since we walked through the damn door, and finally, I silence it and quickly slip it back into my pocket right before we're called for our first game.

Our opponents are two guys from the football team—they always crash our preseason party just like we crash theirs—and I'm pretty sure one is the new quarterback...which might be a bad omen for us. After all, his job on the field is to throw balls *accurately*.

And when I shoot, going a little long, I'm pretty positive we're gonna have the floor wiped with us.

Aspen lets out a low laugh as he lines up his shot, and I cross my arms. "Like you're gonna be any better."

He arches a brow and shoots, hitting the rim of one cup before the ball bounces in the one next to it. "You were saying?" he taunts as one of the guys on the other team pulls two cups.

I gape at him. "How are you still good at this?"

He shrugs, watching the other two take their turn. "Physics."

I scoff. Leave it to Aspen to bring math into this. Wait, science? It's one of the two, but hell if I know which physics technically falls into. I'm a business major, and that shit's way over my head.

"Well. Okay, then," I say with a grin.

With Aspen's magical secret weapon, running the table isn't hard for us to accomplish. We're a team that feeds off each other, picking up our game where the other is weak. His game is stronger at the beginning and can't seem to finish—something I'm sure to give him hell for later—but that's where I pick up the slack.

And hell if we don't knock out team after team that comes up to call the next game.

Our fifth game wraps up—where we defeat Avery and Reese in a blow out, by the way—and I'm somewhere in that wonderful place between buzzed and drunk. The fuzzy state where life is a little bit off-kilter, and if I keep going at this pace, there's a good chance I'll end up sleeping on our bathroom floor tonight, since I'm downing the majority of the drinks for both of us.

There's no way we're giving up our spot at the table until we lose, though. Which doesn't look like it's happening anytime soon, since Aspen and I both sink our first shots against two Chi O sisters, earning us balls back. Then Pen makes the second shot too.

I burst into laughter and wrap my arm around his shoulders, dragging him into a clumsy hug. "You're on fire."

He turns his face toward me, a small smirk tilting his lips. "Dude, that was only two. On fire is three. How drunk are you?"

Pretty drunk, apparently. And with him this close, his mouth only inches from mine...the feeling of intoxication only gets worse.

"Can you two just get a fucking room?" Avery calls from the table two over. "Oh, wait. That's right. You already have one together."

Reese and a couple other people around chuckle and laugh at the comment, and normally, I would too. There's no point in doing anything but that when it comes to guys like Avery. Fighting them or talking back only riles them up more.

Except I feel hot all over and so transparent, I might as well be a piece of glass.

"The amount of toxic masculinity you radiate is truly disturbing," Pen retorts, rolling his eyes before shrugging out of my hold and looking at me. "This is getting a little too easy. I think we need to up the stakes or we're gonna end up passed out here at the end of the night."

Checking out the table, I see we only have three cups left to their eight.

Shit, he has a point.

"He's right," Tori—one of the girls we're playing against—agrees. "And Keene, I'm sorry, but you're a sloppy drunk. There's no way in hell I'm taking care of you."

I clutch my chest in mock offense. "*Tori.* And I thought we were friends."

She and her partner, Kensie, both laugh as they take their turn to shoot. "Friends are honest with each other, honey. I'm sure your bestie there agrees with me."

I turn and look at Pen, who catches the ball Tori just shot when it bounces off the table. When he realizes I'm waiting on an answer, he just smirks and mimes zipping his lips closed.

"Fucking assholes, all of you," I mutter with a shake of my head. Which was a bad idea, because it just makes me dizzy.

"Why don't we up the stakes by adding in that game you guys used to play?" Kensie suggests, shooting and missing her toss turn too.

"Don't You Dare?" Pen asks, cocking his head. "How do you know about that?"

He stole the words right outta my damn mouth, but then it dawns on me, and I can't believe I didn't recognize her sooner when she's been to countless parties where DYD was played, even if she didn't go to our school.

"Oh, shit! Kensie *Dalton?* Who used to date Frankie Sanders?"

"Took you long enough to put it together, Waters." She smirks, tapping her finger to her lips. "So let's change the rules a bit. Sort of combining the two games. For every shot you make, a dare is tacked on. If you don't do it, the cup stays on the table. Both of you pass on the same dare, then you forfeit the game."

Seems fair enough, so we both nod in agreement and start back in on the game.

It takes a few tries for Aspen to hit another shot, for which he's dared to strip to his underwear and play the rest of the game like that.

I'm already pretty useless in my inebriated state, and his almost-naked form shivering beside me makes it even harder to focus on shooting. To no surprise, I miss the next three rounds. Add in that the girls somehow start heating up and get balls back on a round, and we're at two cups to four.

We've also garnered quite the crowd ever since the new dare rule was implemented. Mostly girls staring at Pen half naked, not that I can really blame them.

"Fuck," he mutters when I miss again, glancing at me. "Some closer you are."

"I'm a *catcher*. I *catch* balls."

He snorts and shakes his head, and Landon—our team's *actual closer*—chips in with, "If you wanted to call a celebrity shot, you just had to ask."

I flip him the bird just as Aspen takes another shot toward the cups, this one spinning in one before popping into the other. Normally, that would be game over, but when the girls call for Pen to drink a cup of eight different beers and liquors mixed together, he goes pale.

Well, paler than his already pasty ass is.

"Absolutely not. I'm driving," he says, eyeing the cup. "And even if I wasn't, there's no fucking way."

It ends up being a compromise that they pull one cup, leaving us up one to four. Which quickly dwindles down to one to two after another couple rounds. These girls are making the comeback of the century—okay, of the party—and the crowd around us grows more.

Aspen misses again when Tori decides to play dirty by leaning over and pulling her top down to show more cleavage. The ball goes long, hitting her right in the chest, and both girls start laughing.

"I don't know why you're laughing," Pen says in a tone more flirtatious than normal. "I hit my target."

It earns a wink from Tori before she leans down to do the same thing to me.

I have to say, it's definitely distracting. Her rack's a thing of beauty. So I don't know how I manage to land the last shot with them staring me in the face, but I do.

It spins around the cup, and Tori tries to blow it out unsuccessfully.

The crowd cheers, the game over if the girls miss their rebuttal shots. Which, of course, they do.

And just like that, all that's left is one final dare.

I raise my brow at them, silently asking them to do their worst. But I must be asking for a death wish when I do, since Tori smiles deviously when she leans in to Kensie and whispers something in her ear. They both take turns giggling and nodding, taking their sweet-ass time debating before they turn back to me.

I'm hit with the weirdest sense of déjà vu when Kensie smiles, the picture of innocence when she says, "Well, Waters. Don't you dare?"

The feeling gets stronger, spiking my heart rate.

"Just get on with it, baby girl. We've got another game to win after this."

That gets a laugh outta some people watching.

She bites her lip for a second, a clear sign of indecision. But then she says, "I dare you to make out with Aspen."

Just like that, I'm hit with a bucket of cold water. In fact, I've gone from drunk to stone-cold sober as her words register in my brain.

Oh, fuck, no.

I know for a fact she wasn't there the one and only other time Pen and I kissed, since it was after she and Frankie had broken up. There's no way she's aware of an eerily similar dare being tossed on my plate previously, or they would've decided on something else.

Why go with a dare we've already done? It wouldn't make sense.

But here we are, and—

"Fucking done," Pen mutters, turning to me and grabbing the back of my neck.

An aching want fills my veins at the same time panic seizes me. Because this time, it wouldn't just be a dare. It didn't even end up being *just a dare* last time, and it certainly wouldn't be just kissing between two straight best friends.

That's the only excuse for why I react the way I do as his mouth closes in on mine.

I hold my hands up and shove Pen. On his *bare* chest, because he's still stripped down from one of the previous dares, and apparently, I do it hard enough to send him flying into the table next to ours. He hits it with full force, and when it flips on its side, cups, cans, and bottles scatter, crashing to the ground with him.

Gasps echo out into the night, but then the entire party goes dead silent. The music pounding from inside the house fades into nothing as ringing starts in my ears. It's possible time even comes to a standstill as I stare down at Pen on the ground. Practically naked. Dripping wet with water and alcohol.

Seething mad.

"What the *fuck,* Keene?" he hisses, wrenching his body up from the ground and shaking his limbs out. A couple girls gripe when they get misted, while some start murmuring and snickering at the scene I've just caused.

Of course, public humiliation wouldn't be complete without Avery being the first person to make a jackass comment.

"Aw, would you look at that? Kohl just got rejected by his boyfriend in front of everyone."

Fortunately, the comment only earns a few awkward laughs as Pen grabs his clothes from the ground beside the table.

Unfortunately, Pen looks more than just rejected, which is clearly written in his eyes. He also looks ready to commit murder. And though I'm usually the one who'd help bury the body…I'm pretty sure *I'm* the body this time.

I blink back at him, my thoughts a jumbled mess and emotions running haywire.

Why did I do that? Why did I fucking do that?

I don't have the chance to open my mouth, let alone say something, before Aspen grips my arm like a vice and drags me out the back gate and into the alley.

"Pen, I—"

"Shut the fuck up, Keene," he snaps.

I shut up. Zip my mouth closed, as hard as it is for me, and let him steer me away from the party to where the Impala is parked down the street.

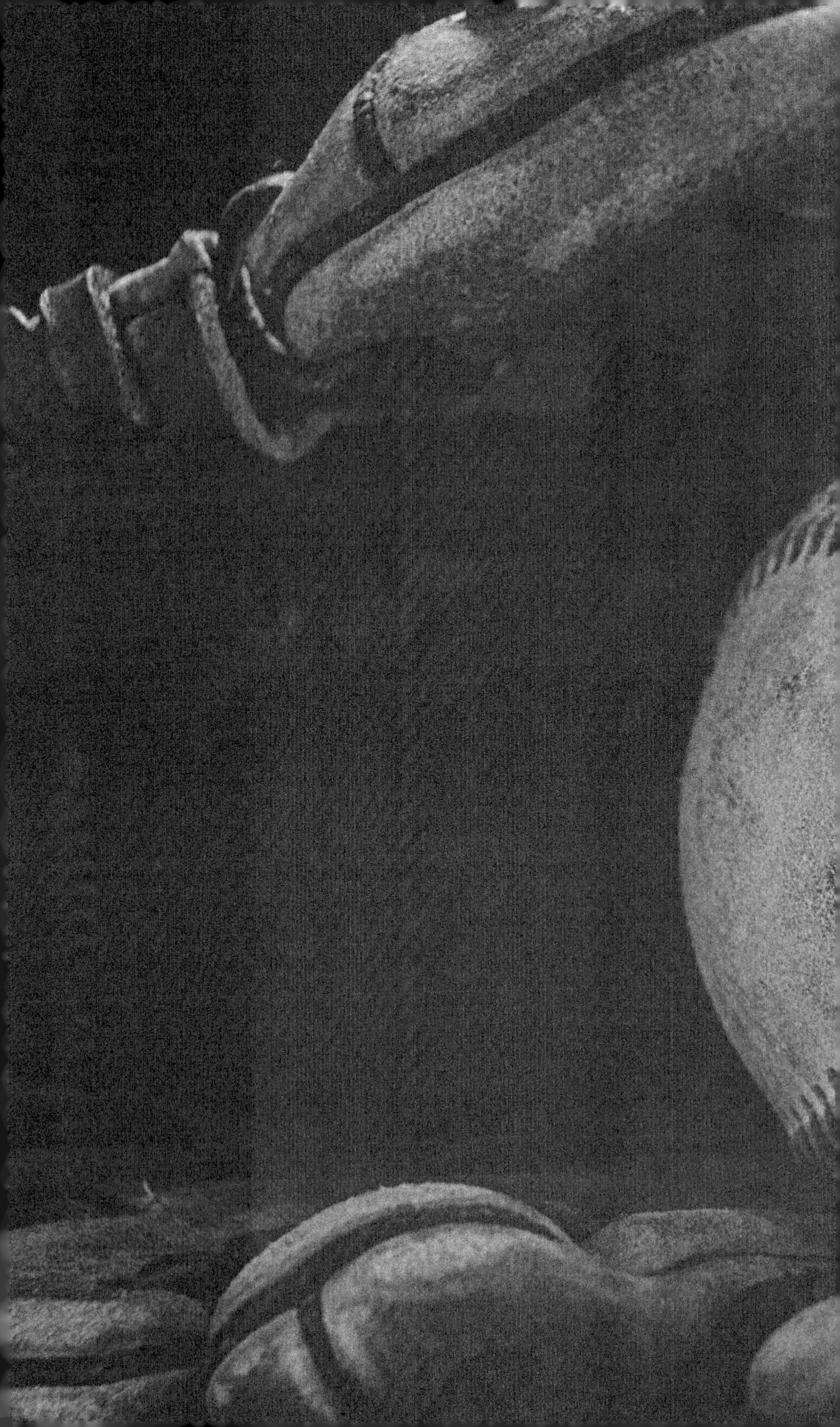

FIVE

Keene

I don't need to be his best friend—or sober—to tell Pen's pissed.

Hell, it was obvious the second he grabbed me at the party. Even more when we got to the Impala and he shoved his limbs through his clothes so violently, I thought he might rip them apart at the seams.

To most people, his emotions are hard to read. He's good at keeping them hidden, always has been. But goddamn, when he's pissed, the entire world is sure to know it. It's written all over his face as the door to our dorm slams closed behind him.

I'm clumsily sliding out of my jacket, maybe not as sober as I thought I was twenty minutes ago, but still perfectly aware of Pen's irritation when he kicks off his shoes by the door and tosses his keys on the TV stand. His fury is stifling, filling the air with a toxic fog that's sure to kill us both if we don't air out what's going on.

I just…don't know what that is.

Or maybe the problem is that I do, I'm just too much of a chicken shit to deal with the unresolved repercussions of kissing Aspen almost *two fucking years ago.*

Being that it woke something up inside me. Something unexpected and life-changing.

Something I've been keeping from him ever since.

I track his movements as he starts straightening up the dorm room. It's one of his tells that he's really pissed or stressed out—cleaning. He says it's better to use his anger to be productive rather than destructive, and I have to admit, it makes sense.

But right now, I don't want him to *clean*. I want…

Fuck. I don't know what I want. To know what he's thinking would be a good place to start. Or maybe I should start with an apo—

"What the hell was that?" he asks out of nowhere as he arranges a few pairs of our shoes in a neat row by the door.

I open my mouth to say it. To tell him everything.

That, even though he's the only guy I've kissed, ever since that night, I can't stop thinking about wanting to just grab him by the shirt and haul his mouth to mine again. That I'm not entirely sure how I feel about it, either, besides being completely scared shitless that he can somehow read my mind and know what I'm thinking whenever he looks at me.

But what my brain decides to let my lips utter is, "What was what?"

"Don't fucking play coy with me, Kee," he snaps, rising back to full height. "What was that shit back at the party?"

Tell him. Tell him right fucking now. End the misery.

I clear my throat. Rub the back of my neck. And lie.

"It wasn't anything."

He shakes his head and steps closer, pointing an index finger at me. "I don't believe that for a second, Keene. I know you too well. If it was nothing, then why wouldn't you kiss me?"

This is about to be the most ridiculous argument ever between two guys who are supposedly straight.

My lips curl into something like a sneer. "Because I need a reason to not kiss someone? I should just walk around letting anyone do it?"

"I'm not anyone; I'm your best friend. Who does whatever *you* want, by the way. Whenever you pull me into your shit and ask me to do things with you that I hate, I still go. I try. Because that's what we do for each other."

"Aspen, the saint. Always putting everyone before himself, right?" I snap right back.

I know it's the wrong thing to say almost immediately. In fact, I'm about ready to yeet myself out this fifth-floor window for being such a dick. But if I'm gonna dig a damn grave by continuing to lie to him, I might as well bury myself in it too.

"My point is that if I can do something like put myself in a situation where I'm stripped down to my underwear at a party with a bunch of people I don't know and we're about to win a fucking game, why would you bitch out on something as simple as a kiss?" His fingers snake through his hair in frustration, and I watch as he fingers the pack of cigarettes in the front pocket of his black jeans. "Seriously, Keene. It's not like we haven't done it before."

"But like you said," I grit through my teeth. "It was just a game."

He scoffs, rolling his eyes at the same time my phone goes off in my pocket. I'd turned it off silent in the elevator so I wouldn't oversleep and miss practice tomorrow afternoon, completely forgetting about the message notifications I was avoiding most of the night.

It pings two more times, and Aspen's eyes fly to where it's housed in my pocket.

"Are you seeing someone? Is that the issue?"

Aw, hell.

"No," is all I say, checking the screen before I drop it on the coffee table. "I'm not seeing anyone. I'm too busy for that shit right now, and don't you think if I was, you'd know because I'd be around *even less* than I already am?"

"Maybe, but you've been talking to *someone* a lot recently and—"

"Jesus Christ, Pen. Just drop it."

His nostrils flare, and he steps closer. And I can tell. That this is just the beginning. He's locked in on this now, like a hound on the scent, and there's no way he's giving up that easily. We're not the type to keep shit from each other, after all. Not the small stupid shit, and definitely not something as life-altering as this, no matter the catalyst of it all.

"I don't even know what *it* is, so how can I drop it? Would you just talk to me about it?"

"There's nothing to talk about!"

"Bullshit, Kee. I call fucking bullshit," he snarls, his arm cutting through the air. "You can't lie to me, remember? I know when you do."

Except I have been. For over a year, and you're only just now catching on.

And hell if that doesn't make me feel a stupid amount of guilt.

I might as well be going insane, the war battling inside me to either tell him or keep this to myself is literally tearing my insides apart. Nausea racks me, sweat starts gathering at my hairline, and I do my best not to lose the contents of my stomach as I sit down on the couch.

He clears his throat. Clasps his hands behind his head. Paces in front of the TV before stopping directly across from me, anguish etched in his eyes. "Do you…not trust me with it? Is that what's going on?"

"No," I say again, my head falling to my hands.

"To which one?"

Oh, my God.

"Jesus Christ, Pen!" I shout, the thin shred of sanity I had left snapping in an instant. I drop my hands and glare at him, the words tumbling from my mouth without my permission, "I didn't want to kiss you because I didn't want it to mess me up all over again, okay?"

His brows furrow and he blinks, taking a step away from me. Like my tone was enough to physically move him. Or maybe it was the words themselves to garner the reaction.

My stomach rolls again when he whispers, "What are you talking about?"

How the hell am I supposed to do this? Admit that, ever since that stupid dare...I've looked at him a little differently. In a way that's more aching want than friendship, because the sound and taste and feel of him from the night we kissed have all been seared into my brain with a white-hot brand ever since. Swirling around there rent-free when I should've done the smart thing, locking them away in a safe at the back of my mind and losing the combination forever.

But instead, I kept thinking about it. Letting it fester in my mind like a disease, infecting every viable part of my brain until it's become impossible to ignore. And only continues to confuse me.

"What are you talking about, Keene?" he asks again. Slowly, like he's unsure if he wants to know the answer. But then he adds in, "Mess you up, how?"

Of course, my phone takes that opportunity to go off again, and his eyes move to it on the table between us.

I watch as the gears turn in his head. Thinking. Calculating. Debating. Then he takes action.

There's only a moment of hesitation on my part, but it's enough. And even if I have a bit of extra muscle mass on him, the asshole is faster than me. He snags my phone from the coffee table and steps back out of my reach, making me barrel over the table to grab it from him and shove it back in my jeans.

But the damage is already done.

He saw the screen and the notifications waiting there for me. I'm sure there's plenty of them.

Why did I leave it out for him to see, like a damn idiot?

His hand is still held out, though my phone's safely in my pocket now. The expression on his face is blank, devoid of all emotion as he blinks. Then blinks again before he looks up at me.

I think I'm gonna be sick. Really, truly puke as he stares at me in wonder. Because I see the questions in his eyes. Can feel them filling the room in wave after suffocating wave, worse than his anger was earlier.

Still, it doesn't prepare me for the first one that leaves his lips.

The same lips responsible for this whole fucking mess.

"What are you doing on Toppr?"

I remain silent, willing myself to keep from opening my big fat mouth about why I'm on the gay version of Tinder. Urging myself to do everything possible from screwing shit up. Because this is my mess, and I refuse to drag him into it more than he's already been involved.

He's always been my crutch, my helping hand or whatever, but this is something I need him to stay far away from. It'll only make things more difficult in the end.

Pen steps closer to me, closing the few feet between us, and I take a step back on instinct. Hurt and anger flash in his eyes when I do, but he doesn't make another move toward me.

"Keene. Why do you have that app?"

There's a sharpness in his tone, and I can't really blame him for it. If the situation were reversed, I'd be getting pretty irritated with my lack of answers too. But it's enough to have me breaking my vow of silence, practically biting his head off with my response.

"Why do you think? Why does anyone have a hookup app?" I pause, then supply, "To hookup."

"Yeah, but…" He trails off with another shake of his head. Like his mouth and brain can't compute what he saw and put it into words. But the question continues in his eyes when he stares into mine.

Why that one?

And so, for the first time, I say the words I've been grappling with for over a year. The ones that have shaken me to my very core to even think.

"I think…I'm bi, Pen."

His expression shifts, and though the proof was right in front of him, stunned doesn't begin to cover it. "What?"

I let out a sharp laugh and step away from him, suddenly needing a lot more space. And maybe some air.

Maybe yeeting myself out the window isn't such a bad idea after all.

"I might be into dudes," I say, the words feeling strange on my tongue. But hey, they're the truth, or at least as close to the truth as I have right now. "Figured that one out, thanks to kissing you last time, so I wasn't about to go on another self-discovering mission without completely finishing the first."

The silence between us stretches on for an eternity.

"You…" He sighs. "Kee."

His tone, the softness in it…guts me. I can't tell if it's pity or something else, but right now, I don't wanna know. I sure as fuck don't wanna do this while I'm still half drunk. So like the coward I am, I avoid it. I run. I bolt. I flee the scene of the crime in favor of the safety of my room and lock the door behind me.

Good thing too, because he's there moments later, rattling the handle a couple times.

"Keene," he murmurs from the other side of the door. His forehead connects with the wood, a soft thud echoing through my room. "Please, let me in."

The irony, the double meaning of his words, isn't lost on me. And though I know I should listen, get up, and unlock the door…I don't. I can't.

Not now. Not tonight.

It might've been hurtful, shutting him out like this when he clearly doesn't want that. Hell, what I said before probably was too. But at least it was honest, which is more than what I've been doing ever since the night at that damn party.

Kissing him, it flipped my life upside down. Opened up a whole new curiosity I never knew I had. One I still haven't figured out, and I've been struggling on my own to understand what it means.

And it's something I'm scared shitless to try and navigate, whether it be with or without his help.

SIX

Keene

Most of the weekend passes without any sighting of Pen. The only time I managed to catch a glimpse of him before Sunday night was when I happened to get home from practice early Saturday afternoon before he retreated back to his room.

Now, if this were later in the semester, I wouldn't be concerned. During Hell Week—what we call the week of finals—I can go days without seeing him. He's either locked in his room studying or over in his studio at the Arts building across campus, finishing up whatever design project he's been working on the entire semester.

But I know that's not it.

He's only giving me what he thinks I want. Space and time. Which I do…but I don't at the same time, and it's almost as confusing as this whole situation to begin with.

Maybe because by giving myself space, I have no way of knowing what he's thinking or feeling. Sure, I've made exactly no effort to find out, since I'm still reeling from the entire situation, but the not knowing is still suffocating, nonetheless.

Fuck, I can't really say I blame him for holing up, either. Not after the way I slammed the door in his face.

And let's not forget, *I* was the one keeping a massive secret, only to drop it like an atomic bomb at what might be the worst possible moment. We've been best friends for two decades. Literally our entire lives…and that was how I decided to bring up my *maybe* attraction toward men.

Which is still only a *maybe,* because even with taking the step to download Toppr, I'm still clueless.

Chatting with the guys on the app was supposed to be a way for me to sort of play it safe. I kept my profile image anonymous, only using an abs shot, and you don't have to make anything public but your user name. Keep my identity under wraps—especially since there are *a lot* of guys at this school on Toppr—until I figured out if I'm even into it. Then maybe even explore it if the stars aligned and the opportunity presented itself. See if any interest is sparked.

Only one guy really has as of late, which is a number far smaller than I would have figured.

He goes by the username *balls4lyfe,* and I'll admit, I got a kick out of that play on words after I commented on it, only to find out he actually plays a sport *with balls.*

I think that's part of the reason it's been so easy to talk to him, since he's in a situation sort of like mine. Another college athlete who wants to get his shit figured out privately without the gossip mill running amuck. It's been hard, though, wondering if he's my teammate. Or if maybe he's a guy on the football or basketball team. Shit, maybe even soccer. I'm not really ruling anyone out at this point.

Or…maybe he's lying and he's not an athlete at all. It's that last little theory which keeps me from revealing I'm also an athlete.

From his body, though? I'd say he's probably being honest.

And I'll admit, I have the urge to see more than what he's shown me. I think I'd even be cool with getting nice and sweaty with him, because I definitely like what I see…but it's still just off. Something I can't quite put my finger on, but our interactions all feel weird to me. The flirting is too forced, maybe? And he's kind of…clingy. He's always wanting to talk. Blowing up my phone like crazy, especially when I was at the party. Of course, at one point when I gave into temptation and checked the DMs when I was pissing, I realized why.

He was there. Or, at least, I'm almost positive he was. His status said *within .1 mile,* so I'm sure it wasn't a coincidence. But the slight panic I felt in my stomach that he might recognize me—even when I knew he couldn't because my face and name aren't public on Toppr—tells me I'm not ready for whatever we have to be anything more than virtual conversation.

I feel really shitty for keeping it all from Pen, though I had my reasons. Plenty of them, in fact, and all still feel valid and justifiable.

Would he look at me differently? Will he be mad that I didn't tell him sooner? Is it going to change the friendship we've had for years if I really do like guys too?

Basically, I've been afraid to rock the boat because I didn't want to fuck something great up in the process. Yet the boat's still been rocked. And the fears and worries and doubts are more prevalent than ever, no matter how hard I try to shove them and him to the back of my mind.

Which is why, as I lie across my bed and stare up at the ceiling on Sunday night, I take the first step. I might be a coward to do it through a text, but it's still a white flag. I just hope he sees it that way.

Me: Hey.

I hear the ping of the notification through the wall as I stare at the screen, waiting for it to show as read. When it does and he starts typing back, my heart crawls in my throat.

Pen: You ready to talk about it?

And just like that, I'm hit with another massive wave of guilt. I shouldn't feel guilty, though. Not for trying to understand who I really am and certainly for not being ready to talk about it. That's the biggest thing I've tried to tell myself for over a damn year now, and what countless blogs and Reddit feeds I've skimmed through have said too.

Being your most authentic self is the only way to ensure your happiness.

I never really thought of it that way, but it makes sense. I can't see anyone being truly happy if they're hiding who they are. Especially such a massive part, like their sexuality.

Even Pen, who hides the deeper pieces of himself from the entire world. It has to chip away at him, having his guard up all the time. Never letting people in. The only time I ever see him at his happiest is when he's around me or his mom, the people who know what lies beneath the armor.

But I guess he's not the only one doing it these days…and I think it's finally time I let him in too.

Me: Yeah…I'm sorry. Dropping that on you how I did was fucked. It wasn't fair, and I don't want you to be pissed at me for it.

Pen: I'm good. Well, now I am. But are you?

Me: I feel a little better now that you know.

Pen: Can I ask why you kept it from me?

Me: I didn't want to say anything until I knew for sure, ya know?

Pen: Makes sense. And now you do?

Me: Not even close.

I hear his deep chuckle through the wall, and I picture that damn dimple popping out below his mouth as he smiles at his phone. It does something stupid to my stomach. That mixture of butterflies and straight up desire.

Pen: Have you tried any gay porn?

Yes, and while I found some of it really hot…

Me: It's too unrealistic at this point.

Pen: And hooking up isn't helping?

Me: I haven't exactly used the app to hook up.

Pen: Might be a good thing. If you can't even kiss me, how can you hook up with someone you don't even know?

Yep, and this is why he's the smart one. Level-headed and always thinking big picture instead of me, who lives more in the moment.

Me: Maybe I'm just not ready yet.

Pen: Maybe not. You will be eventually.

I know he's right. I've known that for a while as I've tried to navigate this on my own. But having someone to validate it makes it a little easier, for whatever reason.

Me: Thanks.

Pen: Always got your back.

Me: So it's not weird?

Pen: That kissing me made you realize you were MAYBE into dudes? Not at all. It's kind of a compliment, if you think about it.

A warm feeling fills my stomach, and I have no idea why I was so freaked out about telling him about this sexual awakening. Granted, he doesn't know about me still wanting to maul him on the regular or about my attraction to him specifically. But this is a start, and I already feel like the weight of the world's been lifted off my shoulders.

Another text pops up, making me laugh.

Pen: You think I'm hot.

Me: I can hear your ego inflating from here.

Pen: It was good to hear you laugh, though. And don't worry, I think you're hot too.

Me: *insert Ryan Reynolds rolling his eyes gif*

Pen: He's definitely hot. No man can deny that. I'd say you have good taste.

Me: Why do I think you're gonna want to help me match people on Toppr now?

Pen: Uh, that's what best friends are for.

I have to laugh, knowing his friendship is so much more than just helping me pick out hot dudes from an app, though the fact that he'd even be willing to says a lot about who he is. And again, I wonder why the hell I was so afraid of opening up to him about this.

He's the person I can count on to get me through the hard shit. The brutal moments, like the deaths of our fathers. Or even just the smaller shit, like having no energy to go get food after a long day, so he does it for me.

When school or baseball or life feels fucking impossible, he's the one who makes it better.

Pen: Have you thought about trying sexting with a guy on the app to start? Sending dick pics and trying to get off to them? Maybe that would help you start to picture it happening IRL.

Pen: Is this weird for me to be asking that? It feels weird.

Yeah, it might be weird if we weren't us.

But what's also weird is the idea rolling around in my head. Or maybe it's not weird as much as it is insane. And it probably crosses more lines than any best friends should, which is why I should keep this crazy idea to myself. It's better—safer—that way.

Yet my stupid fingers, guided by my even stupider brain, still types out the message before I can back out of it.

Me: Don't you dare?

Pen: I have a feeling I'm about to regret my inability to say no to that question.

I smirk, despite my anxiety ramping up. It's true that he's never been one to pass up a dare, though I don't point out that he technically did say no when he passed on that dare to drink that nasty alcohol mixture at the party.

Rolling my tongue over my bottom lip, I lean back against the wall and…I hit send.

Me: I dare you to send me a dick pic.

I watch as the three little dots at the bottom of my screen pop up, type for a few seconds, then disappear. A minute passes, then the dots come again…only to disappear once more.

Fuck.

This was a really bad idea. Colossal mistake. I'm probably making things more awkward between us…and if he refuses, I swear I'll probably jump off the damn roof rather than look my best friend in the eye after asking him to show me his cock.

Especially when we both are more than aware *why* I'm asking.

I'm about to send him another text, telling him to forget it or that I was joking when one from him pops through.

Pen: …hard, I'm assuming?

I chuckle, the panic that was rising in my chest subsiding ever so slightly.

Me: Isn't that the point of a dick pic?

His response is immediate.

Pen: Good point. And I want you to know I'm smart enough to see what you're doing here.

My heart plummets, but the dots keep moving.

Pen: If you need a picture of my hard dick to figure out if you're into guys, that's fine. I'm happy to be your sexual guinea pig. But this is leverage. You could do anything you want with it, like send it to everyone on your contact list. Or post it on Reddit.

A snort escapes me because he's not entirely wrong, though I don't think I'd ever do something like that to him on purpose. I'd never intentionally try to hurt or embarrass him. To *that* degree at least. But at least he's being a good sport about all this shit.

Another text pops up before I can respond.

Pen: My proposition: I show you mine if you show me yours.

My eyebrows shoot to my hairline as I type out a response.

Me: Blackmailing me? I never asked to be part of a dare.

I can practically see the grin on his face as I read his next text.

Pen: We can rectify that. Don't you dare?

I laugh, knowing full well I'd go through with it just because he asked. It's just how this works between us, the banter and egging each other on to the point of idiocy. Because...that's what this is. What most of our dares have always been.

Me: Okay, fine. Any additional terms?

Pen: I dare you to send me a NEW dick pic.

My brows furrow.

Me: As in one no one has ever seen?

Pen: As in one you take right now.

My heart starts pounding in my chest as I reread his text about thirty times, doing my best to process the request.

He wants a dick pic no one has seen. He wants me to get hard...right now...and send him a picture.

And now I'm circling back to my point from earlier about this being insane. Literal fucking insanity.

So...naturally, I text him back with a revision to my own dare.

Me: Same to you, then. Even the stakes.

Pen: Done. Five minutes.

I shake my head, not really believing where this is going right now. In all the years we've been friends, seeing each other's penises has never entered the equation. Well, scratch that. I'm sure I've seen it, considering our mothers bathed us together as kids, but it's not like I *remember* what it looks like. And well...I'm sure it's a lot bigger now.

Guess I'm about to find out just how big it is.

And I'm astounded to realize the anticipation of him sending me the image is more than enough to make my cock thicken beneath the mesh of my athletic shorts. Obscenely quickly, I might add.

Not one to waste time, I quickly slip my shorts down to my knees and wrap a fist around my length. Barely two strokes have made me rock solid since I was nearly there before I even touched it, and I don't think it takes more than ten for me to be ready to explode.

But not before I line up a shot for Pen, snap it, and send it off before I think better of it.

My eyes sink closed then, reality and my biggest fantasy mixing for the first time as I picture Pen in the room beside me, lying across his bed just like I am, fucking his fist.

Does he cradle his balls? Knead them in his palm while he jacks his length? Does he like fast, short strokes, or long and torturously slow ones?

My brain imagines it all, every possible scenario, and it only gets me hotter.

A groan of frustration slips from me, and I release my cock to roll to my side. Searching my bedside table, I find a bottle of lube and coat my shaft with it. Taking a few more long, steady strokes, I feel like I could blow at any second.

Then my phone pings with a text, and I peel my eyes open to look at the screen to find a two-word reply to the pic I sent that nearly makes me choke on my own damn spit.

Pen: Stroke it.

I type back one-handed, the other doing exactly what he said.

Me: I already am.

Pen: Prove it.

Proof? But how, unless...

I shake my head and laugh, letting the idea marinate for a second. Thinking about how weird this is and how many lines we're crossing by sending dick pics alone. But for me to send him a *video* of me jacking off has to cross so many more. Ones I probably don't even know exist.

It's not like I let it stop me, though.

Nah, I hop, skip, and take a grand fucking leap over every one of those lines as I take my cock in my hand again, adjusting the camera so my full length is visible. It glistens from the lube, and it aches for release already.

I'm so hard for him. Only for him, and this incessant want I have for him is making me crazy. Irrational. That can be the only reason I hit record as I let my fist slide up and down the length, rolling it over the head on the upstroke.

"This what you want, Pen?" I whisper, my voice graveled as I continue to work my cock for him and the camera. "You want to see my hand wrapped around my cock? See how hard I get just thinking about the pic you're about to send me?"

I swallow harshly as I stop the video after about ten strokes and hit send, not bothering to care that the lust in my voice as I spoke was far too obvious, or that the words I spoke were ones I should never speak to him.

My only hope is by some miracle, things between us aren't weird the next time I see him. Though I doubt I'll be able to look him in the eye for a few days after this.

Only a minute passes before he texts back again.

Pen: You sound like you need to get off. Might as well make use of it.

I smirk, already way ahead of him this time.

Me: What's that saying about great minds?

Pen: Glad to see we're both thinking with our heads.

A bolt of lust zaps through me when I read the text, seeing the double meaning behind his words. And I grip myself harder. Tighter. The ache in my balls only intensifies.

My eyes roll back in my head as I start fucking my fist more furiously, those two words—*stroke it*—replaying in my mind on a loop. I hear it in his voice, complete with a lilt of unmistakable desire. See his lips forming the words before they collide with mine in a brutal kiss that has my toes curling. His tongue tastes like mint and smoke in my mind, as he takes over for me, jacking my cock until I'm panting and writhing for him. Begging. Pleading into his mouth for him to let me come.

The fantasy is so intense, it has my back arching off the bed slightly as my hand keeps shuttling over my shaft.

I hear my phone ping as I start getting close and I debate just checking it after. I'm so fucking close, and entranced by the scene behind my eyelids, breaking away from it now is sure to only leave me with blue balls. But I'm hopeful the sight of his cock is what's waiting for me behind the dark screen, so I grab for it anyway.

There's no photo waiting.

It's a voice message.

Damn it.

Annoyance hits me for a split second as I go to press play, adjusting the volume and setting it beside my head. And the second it starts playing, I forget all about the non-existent photo.

This is so much better than any picture.

"I can hear you through the wall, you know that?" Pen's voice spills from the speaker, floating over my skin in his smooth cadence. "Every pant and sigh while you're getting off to thoughts of me, I can hear. And that's what you're doing, right? Jacking yourself while picturing me?"

Oh, my God.

My cock throbs in my palm, pre-cum dripping and leaking all over my stomach and hand as I stroke faster to the sound of his voice.

"What filthy things are we doing together in that head of yours? Am I sucking you? Swirling my tongue around your cock? Teasing you before taking you deep? Or are you the one with a cock down your throat while I fuck your face until you can't breathe?"

He's trying to kill me. And he might just succeed.

I've never been one for dirty talk before, but holy shit, do I ever want more of it from him. I want every dirty, wicked word he has to say right now.

I pound on the wall adjoining our rooms, and if I wasn't so close or half the chicken I am, I'd go in there. Fuck the consequences, I'd walk in there and slam my mouth to his and rut myself against him until I came all over him.

Fuck the picture too; I'd settle for getting my mouth on him instead. Let him do whatever the hell he wants to me as long as I learn the taste of his cum and the sounds he makes when he loses control.

Like he knew what I needed, he's there moments later. Right on the other side of the wall. Speaking low and seductive through the drywall barrier, just loud enough for me to hear.

"Fuck your fist, Kee. Fast and hard. Let me hear how much you want me." His voice is raspier than normal, and far less composed. "Get there for me, baby."

He almost sounds as needy as I feel, and that sends me straight over the edge, falling off a cliff into the sweet, sweet oblivion.

With a low moan, the sound rumbling from deep within my chest, I'm overcome by my release. Cum shoots from my dick in thick ropes, coating my abs and hand with the sticky liquid. I feel like I've been hit by a freight train of pleasure as I try to slow my heart before it pounds its way out of my chest.

My entire body feels high on endorphins and adrenaline, floating on a hazy cloud of ecstasy as I listen for him on the other side of the wall. But it's silent, save for the sound of my own heavy breathing as I try to come down from my orgasm.

Then I hear a soft thud from beside me, something hitting the wall on the other side, before his voice comes through again.

"That's it," he breathes. "Fucking perfect, Kee."

My eyes sink closed, a small, sated smile resting on my lips.

I'm so blissed out on a high from my orgasm—one brought on by the strangest exchange of nudes I've ever experienced—I might pass out without cleaning up first.

In fact, that's exactly what happens.

Which is why it's not until the next morning, when I wake up covered in dry cum and lube, that I realize something.

He never actually sent a pic back.

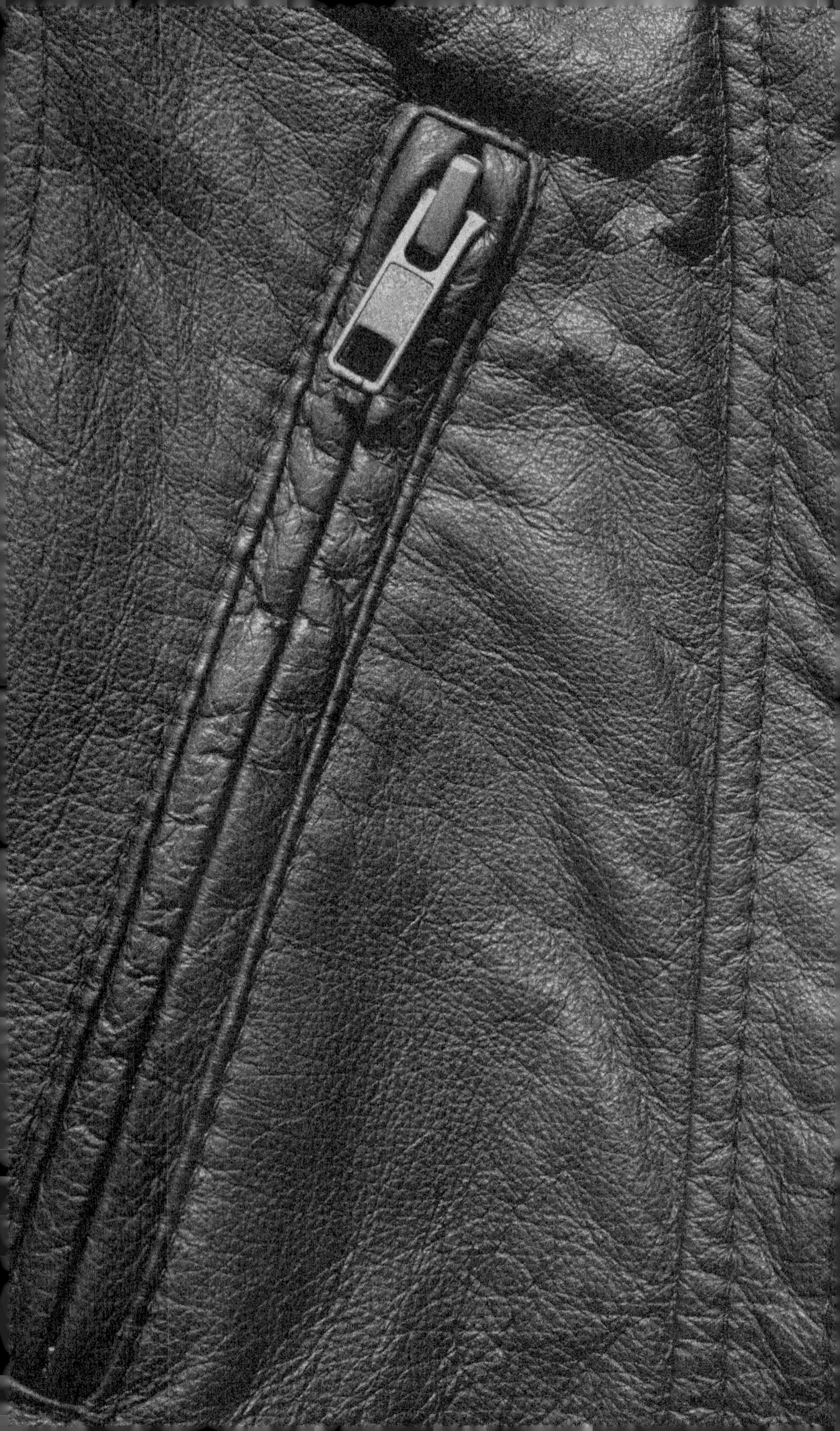

SEVEN

Aspen

I am a piece of shit.

If the dictionary were a picture book, it'd be my mug staring back at anyone who looked up the term. Hell, I'd be surprised if Urban Dictionary didn't already update it to include me in the definition.

The feeling of self-loathing inside me isn't quenched with any attempts I make to sleep, either. Futile attempts, I might add, because I've been staring at the ceiling for hours now, and there's been no sign of being pulled under into blissful unconsciousness.

And all that lack of sleep…it gives me way too much time to do something I really shouldn't do right now.

Think.

And more importantly, *over*think.

I truly don't know how we ended up where we did last night, only that it confused the shit out of me. Not because of Keene's admission of his sexual identity being muddled from that kiss two years ago—but hell if that isn't another piece to this weird, Tetris-style puzzle.

No, my confusion stems from how in the ever-loving fuck sending one, single dick pic turned into a masturbation video, filthy voice notes, and me listening to him through the wall while he fucked his fist.

My alarm beeps softly, signaling it's five and time for my run, and I do my best to shake the thoughts away. Rolling off my mattress, I search for clothes in the darkness, careful to be quiet enough to not wake Keene. Not that it should be an issue, considering he sleeps like the dead ninety percent of the time.

But every once in a while as I drag clothes onto my body, my attention gets snagged on the wall between our rooms, and my mind latches on to last night all over again.

Shit.

I rush through lacing my shoes, grab my AirPods, and I'm out the door in hopes that some cool winter air will help me sort through this. The pound of rubber on asphalt is my own form of therapy most days, since there's nothing a long run, when everyone else is still asleep, can't fix.

But it doesn't take more than five minutes of jogging down the paths of the dorms to realize it's not working. Instead of clearing my head, my thoughts become more jumbled than they were before. I'm a mess, actually. So much that I almost run straight into the road without stopping once I hit the edge of campus.

At least traffic is almost non-existent at this time of day.

As I turn down the block toward the Arts building where my studio is, I debate locking myself up in there for the next few days, maybe get a head start on this semester's project and simultaneously escape any awkward encounters with Keene that are sure to happen after what went down last night.

I mean, how can it not be awkward as shit between us now?

Honestly, why I even put myself in this kind of situation with him, knowing he was already confused about his sexuality, is clearly beyond my comprehension. I should've said no the second I realized where the dare was going, but only hindsight is twenty-twenty.

There must be something about him that makes my brain go all stupid, letting me agree with the bad ideas he cooks up in his head.

The reality of where those bad ideas took us plagued my mind all night, slamming into me in wave after wave of shame and guilt. I know I shouldn't feel those things. I shouldn't be ashamed of helping him get off, even if it was to thoughts of me. And I really did mean what I said to him; if me sending him a picture of my cock would help him get his shit figured out, I'd do it.

I just never intended for shit to get so out of hand.

But when I could hear him, right there on the other side of the wall, my body took over. Took notice. No matter how hard I tried to push it out of my mind, it wanted release.

It wanted…him.

My eyes slam closed momentarily, and I try to push the thoughts back again. But my stupid brain won't let me.

All this shit between us has managed to do is stir up memories I'd completely forgotten about. Like the night when we kissed at the end of high school. A kiss that I haven't thought about in almost two fucking *years,* which now seems to be dancing in my brain like it's the star of the show.

It didn't freak me out that he's a guy and we kissed back then. Just like it wouldn't have if we'd kissed again at the party the other night.

After all, I'm a firm believer in love being love, and I've never batted an eye seeing couples in the LGBTQ community out in public, loud and proud of finding a partner to love. Actually, I find it pretty awesome, especially when it's a testament of just how far we've come as a society. To accept people for being true to who they are and who they love.

I've just never pictured *myself* as a member of that community.

In my measly almost-twenty-one years on Earth, I've only ever kissed girls. And fucked girls. And dated them, though that one's a lot less common overall. But at least it was consistent with the way I've approached things like attraction and sex.

Up until that graduation party, I'd never even *thought* about trying anything different. Not because of some screwed up sense of what is "right" or "normal," but because there's never been that urge to try something other than what I've always known. Certainly not with my best friend.

Then again, just because I've never thought about it doesn't mean I'm against it.

At the end of the day, a kiss is just a kiss, and I know it doesn't automatically make me gay or bi. That's not the way sexuality works. There's a lot more to it than that. Yet, I can't help but wonder if this *more* part is the way my mind can't stop thinking about it. If that's the reason why I have the want or desire to do it again.

Maybe even take things further, like we did last night.

The thought alone makes me halt in my tracks, and I skid to a stop outside one of the local coffee shops on the edge of campus.

What the hell is happening?

Turning back toward campus, I pass by the baseball and football stadiums as it starts to drizzle, the elements matching my shitty mood and even shittier state of mind.

I don't know why I'm so fixated on this. After all, I've never been one to overthink something as trivial as sex. It's always been fun and enjoyable to me, but I've never put a whole lot of stock into it the way Keene has. The way it forms deeper attachments to the person you're banging, which ends up turning into some sort of romantic relationship.

Yeah, I understand the sentiment just fine, and maybe even why someone would want that kind of partnership with another person. It's just never been appealing to me before, never been a part of the life I've pictured for myself. Which is one of the millions of reasons why what happened with him last night should never happen again. The last thing I need to happen is for him to want something I can't give him.

Unfortunately for me, my mind and my dick are on two very opposing teams when it comes to this. Meaning, as much as the idea of messing around with Keene freaks me out because of all the issues it could cause, it also turns me on. A fucking lot.

"Goddamnit," I growl under my breath, shaking my head to clear the thoughts away. I turn up the sound of You Me At Six in my headphones, hoping to get lost in the beat or lyrics enough to let my mind have a break from the circles it's been spinning in for hours now.

It only works for a little while before the thoughts return, revolving around the filthy sounds Keene made last night. For me. Because of me.

Soon, pants and moans echo through my memory loud enough to drown out the music pounding in my ears.

And they're not just his. They're mine too.

The ones I bit back as I jacked myself until I came with his name on my lips.

〈〈

My mind is a vault for the rest of the day after my run when it comes to Keene.

Okay, so that might be seriously stretching the truth, but I do manage a full twenty-four hours where I don't let a single stray thought of what happened between us come crashing through the eighty-foot wall of willpower I've created in my mind.

It's easy enough the first day, since Mondays are his busy days this semester. Even Tuesday, I manage to avoid him, save for one run-in at the bathroom door in the morning. Of course, the second I see him again without his shirt on, all those memories come rushing back in high definition, making my body crave another round.

Maybe this time, in person—thoughts I later reprimanded myself for having.

The war between the head on my shoulders and the one in my pants is starting to wear on me. The one with an actual brain wins out ninety-eight percent of the time, thank God, but that measly two percent is still dangerous.

Dangerous enough to have me replaying that stupid video he sent me again Tuesday night, just to see if my body reacts the same way it did the first time.

Spoiler alert: It does. Of course it fucking does. And it causes me to smoke half my pack of Marlboros from the roof of our dorm building afterward just to cool my shit.

Which is why, by Wednesday, I've come up with a brilliant plan. Or maybe it's a really stupid one, but I'm letting my brain convince what's left of my sanity that this is a good idea. A way to get my dick back on straight, so to speak.

I'll admit; asking Bristol out on a date—one where I wine and dine her before taking her back to her place before screwing the daylights out of her—might be a cheap, shitty way for me to get my crap together again and stop thinking about Keene, but it's the only thing I can think of that just might work.

Of course, getting Bristol to actually take me seriously about the whole date thing was another issue altogether. Especially from the thousand—not exaggerating on this—"hahas" in the text she sent me when I asked if I could take her to dinner.

Still, after about twenty minutes of back and forth, I got her to agree. It might be wrong, but I'm choosing to take that as a step in the right direction.

Though, by Friday night, I'm standing in front of my closet filled with regret for ever coming up with this cockamamie idea in the first place. To the point where I'm tempted to text her and cancel to hang out with Keene instead…until I remember we're still sort of tip-toeing around each other like two teenage girls in a petty-ass fight.

And I also recall finding him smiling at his phone earlier today when I got home from my architecture studio, no doubt texting one of those guys from Toppr.

Just the memory of that smirk has me seeing red as I grab my only pair of jeans that aren't black or shredded or both, and slide them on before snagging a button down off a hanger. A black one, because this is me we're talking about, and I'm still gonna look halfway like myself on this sham of a date.

I'm almost finished with the buttons when my door is flung open, revealing Keene strolling, looking stupidly good in his signature snapback, a pair of sweats sitting low on his hips…and no fucking shirt.

Of course he isn't wearing a shirt, because God hates me.

"Hey, I just wanted to see if you had a—" His words cut off when he notices my appearance. "The hell? Did you lose a bet I don't know about?"

I scowl, fastening the last button before raking my fingers through my already styled hair for the hundredth time. "Bite me, asshat."

His brow arches, a devious grin forming. "If that's all you wanted, you could've just asked for it. No need to get all dressed up only for me to have to strip you back down."

I feel the tips of my ears heat, and I continue messing with my hair some more in the mirror while trying to tell my dick not to get any funny ideas about what he just said.

The whole point of this shit was for me to want *Bristol*. Not Keene.

"I have a date," I find myself muttering. When I can't find another hair out of place on my head, I glance over my shoulder, meeting his gaze through the mirror.

"A date," he repeats dryly. "You?"

I scowl again. "You act like I've never gone on one before."

"You haven't since we were in high school and you were expected to take a girl out before getting her into bed," he points out.

"Tell me what you really think there, Kee," I snap, turning around to face him. "Though I don't remember asking for your opinion on my social life."

"Forgive me for being a little shocked about you suddenly *wanting* one."

My molars grind, irritation settling deep in my bones as I glare at my best friend. "Fuck off, Waters. You're the one always saying I need to get out more. This is me doing that."

His jaw ticks. "And just who are you getting out more *with?*"

"Does it matter?"

He shrugs. "Call me curious, seeing as I have a hard enough time getting it to happen, and I'm supposed to be your best friend. Though it doesn't really feel like it the past few days with the way you've been avoiding me." He crosses his arms. "So, please. I'd love to know who outranks me these days."

The low blow hits its mark, guilt surging through me like a tidal wave.

"Bristol," I say softly, not meeting his eyes. But I don't need to see him to hear his scoff.

"Guess you've finally decided she's worth more than just a lay, yeah?"

"It's never been like that," I say, but it comes out way too defensive to be anything close to the truth.

He snorts. "Who are you trying to convince here, Pen? Me or yourself?"

Not bothering to stick around for an answer we both know already, he turns and leaves for the living room.

Fuck if it doesn't piss me right off that he'd call me out like that. Judging me for how I handle my relationships and hookups when I've never once said a bad thing to him about his own.

Fuck that, and fuck him too.

I'm still stewing about it when it's time to leave twenty minutes later, and I don't even bother looking in his direction to where he's seated on the couch when I leave my room. Instead, I just pass in front of the TV where he's watching an episode of *New Girl* and slip into my leather jacket and black Vans.

Keys in hand, I'm about to head out when he calls after me.

"Hey, Pen. Don't you dare?"

Though I know I shouldn't, especially with how things turned out last time he asked me that question, I turn around and arch a brow.

But I'm not prepared for the shit about to come out of his mouth.

A deadly smirk sits on his lips when he says, "I dare you to think of me when you fuck her tonight."

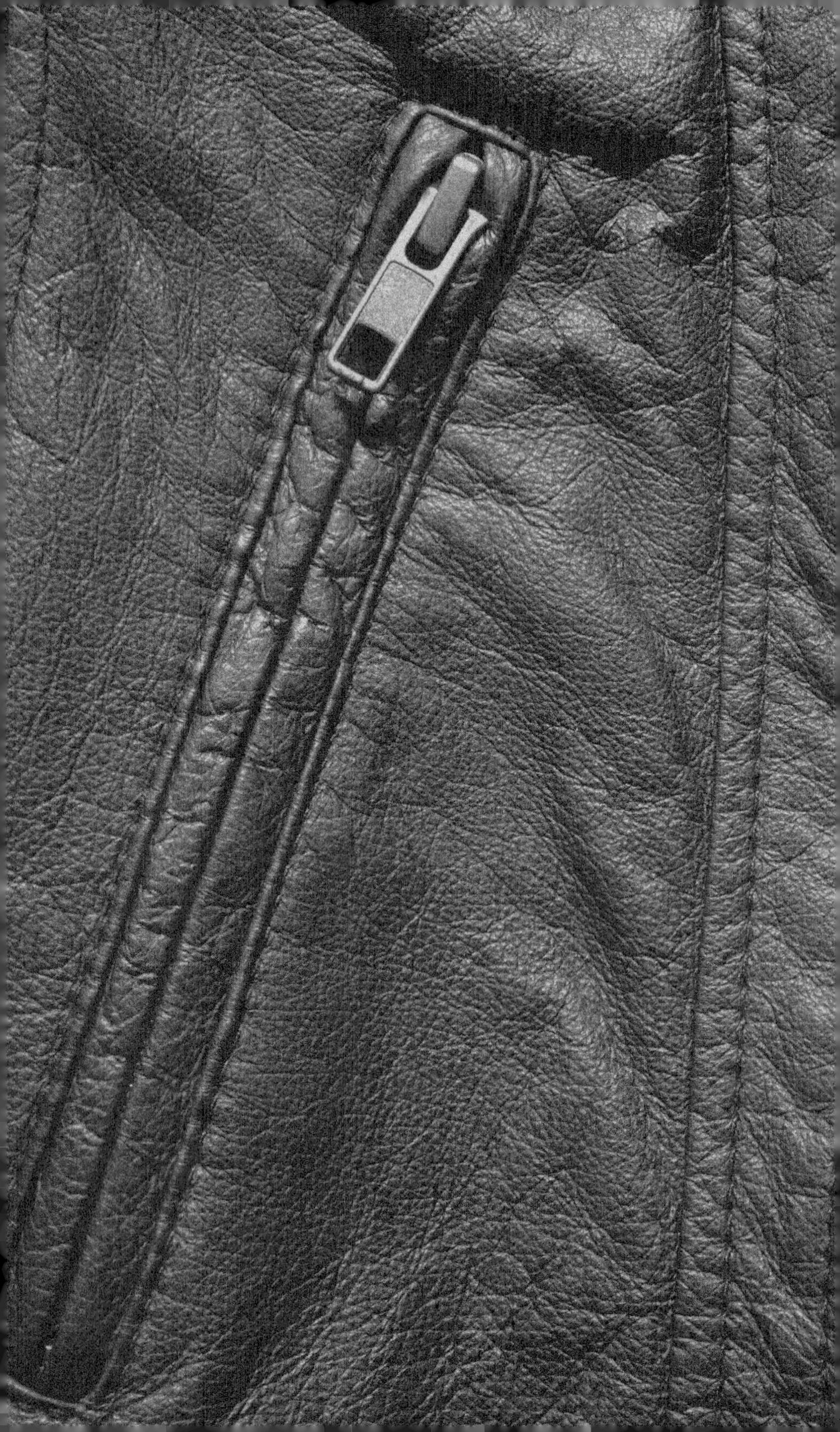

EIGHT

Aspen

Sitting at the table in the Italian restaurant I said I'd meet Bristol at tonight for our date, I rub my palms over my jeans and try to push my anxiety down. More than anything, I wish I could be excited about it, but all I feel is a pit of dread in my stomach.

I should've known this was a bad idea the second it crossed through my brain.

Hell, I did know it was a bad idea. But here I am, still doing it anyway, out of sheer pettiness and spite toward Keene.

Maybe some other being has taken control of my brain and all motor functions. Aliens, probably. Or maybe it's a brain tumor. People do stupid, out of character things when they have those, right?

I shake my head, trying to focus on anything other than my spiking heart rate while I wait for my first date in years. Which, of course, sends my mind to think about the only other thing I don't want to be thinking about: Keene Waters, and the irritating way he's been getting under my skin ever since last weekend.

I think part of the issue stems from knowing someone for two decades. They know every little thing that makes you tick. How to coax whatever emotion they want out of you at the drop of a hat, and they make it look damn easy when they do.

After this long, Keene's apparently become really fucking good at pissing me off whenever he wants.

The soft classical music playing from hidden speakers throughout the restaurant does nothing to help my nerves or frustration, either. It sets a tone, along with the dim lighting, which gives off a more romantic and intimate vibe than I'd like on a first real date.

I run my fingers over the table cloth—yeah, a fucking table cloth—and sigh to myself.

I should've just canceled.

But hell if I was gonna sit there all night with Keene while we don't talk to each other and let the weirdness happening between us just stew and simmer uncomfortably.

"Stop thinking about him," I mutter to myself as I fiddle with a fork on the table. "That's what he wants you to be doing right now."

He also wants to drive me to the brink of insanity, apparently. Talking to myself is a clear indication I'm already halfway there.

Keene knew exactly what he was doing by saying that shit to me before I left the dorm.

He was doing his best to get in my head. And sure as shit, those words have only kept my mind circling around the bastard since the minute I left. No more than five goddamn minutes pass without him in my brain.

It only enhances the frustration I'm feeling, knowing he's getting exactly what he wanted, even if he isn't here to see it for himself. Yet another sign that fucking with my head might be his new favorite pastime. Last I checked, that's what he has baseball for, but apparently he's moved on to much more *entertaining* options.

"Hey," a soft voice says from behind me. The pressure of a hand on my back has me turning in my seat to find Bristol standing behind me.

"Hey," I say as I take her in. She looks absolutely stunning, dressed in a knee-length black dress with a cutout between her breasts that's just toeing the line of sensual and completely inappropriate. But it's also enough to let me know that if I wanna get laid tonight, I absolutely will.

I dare you to think of me when you fuck her tonight, echoes in my head, and I let out a low growl as I rise from my seat.

"You look amazing," I tell her truthfully as I kiss her cheek and pull out the chair across from me.

Her eyes rake over my body before a sinfully seductive smirk appears on her blood-red painted lips. "You don't clean up bad yourself, Kohl."

I smile tentatively, trying to ease some of the tension in my stomach as I take my seat across from her again. Thankfully, she launches right into making fun of my request to take her on a date, and honestly, I'll take a bit of roasting over the uncomfortable weight on my chest.

But that tiny bit of comfort is gone quickly when we start stumbling through some pretty awkward small-talk after we order and wait for our food. Most of it surrounds her ballet—which I don't know jack shit about—or my classes—which she doesn't care about either.

Needless to say, this date's taking a fan-fucking-tastic turn after only ten minutes.

That's probably the main reason my mind starts to wander off where it damn well shouldn't. Like to Keene, and wondering what he's doing right now while I'm not there.

The paranoid, slightly manic part of my brain is ridiculously fixated on the idea of him talking to another guy on his stupid hook-up app. But I'm sure that's what he's still doing right now. Maybe even sexting him, if the confidence he gained from what happened with me is anything to go by.

It shouldn't matter if he is. I shouldn't even care, because if Keene's happy, that's all that matters.

Yet all I feel is this overwhelming sense of…jealousy.

It's not just from someone else taking his attention, either. I've learned to share him a long time ago in that regard, especially because he's always been the more outgoing one of us.

I just don't want to share *that* piece of him. The piece that started questioning his sexuality *because of me*. And in the fucked-up logic of my mind, because it's me that he figured it out with, it should also be me he does all that other shit with.

Jesus Christ, I sound neurotic to my own self.

But it's how I feel, and if I've learned a damn thing in life, it's that my feelings are valid, no matter how misplaced they might be.

Our food arrives moments later, and I take the opportunity to dig into the lasagna sitting in front of me…which happens to be Keene's favorite Italian dish. I didn't even realize I ordered it until now.

What are you doing to me, Kee? Why can't I get you outta my head?

Bristol lets out a low moan when she bites into her carbonara, and the sound brings me back to another moan that's been stuck in the back of my mind ever since I heard it.

My cock twitches in my pants as I zero in on the memory. Rewinding and replaying it, as I envision the video of Keene stroking his cock for me in view of the camera. Then my mind takes it a step further, pairing it with how soft I know his lips feel pressed to mine, or how the slight stubble of his jaw feels cupped in my palm from when we kissed all that time ago.

A moment that might've been shoved to the recesses of my mind, but is back with vivid clarity now.

"Aspen," Bristol says, snapping her fingers in front of my face. It's enough to startle me and pull me from my daze.

"Shit," I mutter under my breath. "I'm sorry, Bristol. I didn't mean to space—"

"You're not really into this, are you?"

My teeth sink in my lower lip and I let out a disgruntled sigh.

"It's not you, I swear. And I'm not normally this much of a headcase. I'm just…" I trail off, scrubbing my palms over my face. "I'm just a mess right now."

She smiles, warm and kind, and reaches over to pat my hand resting on the table. "We're all a bit of a mess sometimes. But I think this might be more than that."

Leave it to Brist to pick up on the shit vibes I wasn't even aware I was giving out.

A low groan slips out of my throat, and I shake my head. "I'm so fucking sorry."

Her shrug and carefree smile let me know she isn't mad before her words have the chance. "Believe me, Aspen. I was more shocked than anyone when you asked me to dinner tonight. That's why I was giving you hell about it, because I honestly thought you were kidding."

What?

"Why would you think that?"

"You're…" She trails off, measuring her words. "You're not a relationship guy, really. You could be if you tried, but you're too detached for it."

It's not like she's telling me something I don't already know. I've *made* myself this way. Isolated sex from emotions, making it so no one would dare try to get close enough to hurt me.

I guess I just didn't realize other people saw right through it.

"I hope that doesn't offend you," she continues, picking at the food on her plate and avoiding my eyes. "You're a lot of fun to be around, but it's all surface level, ya know? I don't think you let anyone but Keene see past that, which makes it impossible for anything deeper between us." She pauses and meets my gaze. "And thinking about it, even after a year, I probably know Keene better than I know *you*."

Mention of Keene lights a bit of a fire inside me. Mostly because I'm trying *not* to think of him, but somehow, he's fucking everywhere.

"Keene's an open book," I tell her. "Of course you'd be able to get to know him better than me. He's basically a golden retriever in human form."

"Maybe, but I'm not sleeping with Keene," she counters. "Don't get me wrong, the sex with you is some of the best I've ever had, but in no way would I want to taint that by attempting to turn this into something more than just a physical relationship. That's not what I'm looking to get into in college anyway."

Wait a minute.

Is she saying—

"Oh, God." I look at her for a second, taking in her expression. "This wasn't me trying to…" I trail off and laugh some more. "Shit, Brist. I'm not trying to make you my girlfriend or anything by asking you on a date."

She frowns and sits back in her chair. "Then why did you?"

Well, isn't that the question of the fucking hour.

"I just…" Searching for the words isn't easy, but finally I settle on, "I'm trying to figure myself out. Who I am and what I want. And part of me thought that taking you out on an actual date, not just to my bed, might help with that."

She blows out a long breath and nods. "Well, that makes a lot more sense. I get it, and I'm all for it. But I don't think we should be seeing each other anymore."

I go to object, but she holds up a hand.

"If you're serious about trying to figure yourself out, I don't want to make it harder by letting you get comfortable again in what we had."

I nod a couple times, a small amount of unexpected sadness hitting me.

"I can't say I'm surprised to hear you say that. No matter how much I don't want to hear it, because I do like you, Brist."

"I like you too. And I truly am sorry." Her hand lands on mine from across the table, and she gives it a squeeze. "I think it's better for you to put the focus on yourself. But just know, I'm happy to help however I can. I'm sure you've got Keene to help you too."

That sends my mood nosediving further.

He'd be a lot of help, if only he weren't the entire fucking reason for this little crisis I'm having in the first place. Then shit could just go back to normal, and I'd be getting laid tonight without worrying he'd pop into my head when I'm about to come.

Jesus, I need a drink.

"Yeah, thanks," I say, scratching the back of my neck awkwardly. "I'm sure it'll be fine."

From the look in her eyes, the slight amount of sympathy there, I'm not really sure she believes me. Hell, I don't think I believe me.

Still, she nods and murmurs, "You'll find yourself, Aspen. That's what college is for, right?"

I nod back. "Yeah. It's just…hard."

Her lips twitch into a smirk. "That's what she said."

I bark out a laugh, immediately more at ease, and squeeze her hand. "But can we circle back to that let down, Brist? 'I like you enough to fuck you, just not enough to date you.' You're as savage as ever," I tease.

Her blue eyes roll and she smiles. "I must've learned from the best, Mr. Love 'Em and Leave 'Em."

And now it's my turn to roll my eyes. "That's an exaggeration, and you know it."

She lets out a scoff. "Well, in that case, you're still buying dinner. Dessert too."

I chuckle again and shake my head. "Okay, I think I can do that."

NINE

Keene

I'm three beers and what must be close to eighty games of *Call of Duty* deep in my sad, little pity party when my phone starts buzzing on the coffee table. My immediate thought is to ignore it, not being in the mood to talk to anyone until Aspen is back from his *date*. With fucking *Bristol*.

But seeing as ignoring people, even when I should, isn't my strong suit—case in point, the interaction I had with Pen earlier—I grab it and check the screen.

My brows furrow when the name of my left fielder is glaring back at me.

Kaleb: Dude. Come get your boy from Stagger. There's no way he's driving home after the way he's been pounding back drinks.

I frown and text out a response.

Me: What're you talking about?

Less than a minute later, an image pops up from him instead of another text.

I don't know what I was expecting to see in the photo Kaleb sent me, but it sure as hell isn't what I'm staring at on the screen. Because there's Pen sitting at the bar in Stagger, a line of empty shot glasses set out in front of him.

My stomach rolls as I start counting them, and when I reach six, I stop altogether and text Kaleb back instead.

Me: Whatever you do, don't let him leave. Be there soon.

All I get back is the thumbs up emoji, and I quickly pull up the Uber app to order a ride. Not even thirty minutes later, I'm flashing my fake ID to the bouncer and walking through the front door.

My eyes automatically dart to the back of the bar where Pen was in the photo, but my stomach sinks when I find the spot completely empty.

Fucking hell.

The bar's packed because it's a weekend, and it's almost impossible to tell anyone apart in the swarm of bodies covering the dance floor between the door and the bar. Finding Pen in this mess will take forever. What was he wearing when he went out on his date again?

My eyes scan the crowd in search of his leather jacket I know he was wearing when he left, but a hand on my arm drags my attention to my side.

Kaleb.

"Hey!" he shouts over the music, pulling on my arm. I follow him over to a table on the side wall, and that's when I notice a couple other guys from the team I'm pretty good friends with, like Castle and Reyes.

There's also some I'm not all that fond of, including Reese and—unfortunately—Avery.

Of course, Avery happens to be sitting right next to Pen too. Something I'm sure isn't a coincidence from the pissed off look on Pen's face.

Well, fuck a duck. This can't be good.

Pen's temper is short when it comes to Avery on a good day, so I can only imagine what's been happening since they've been sitting at the table together while Pen's more than likely sloshed out of his mind. I'd honestly be surprised if punches weren't already thrown, or at least attempted.

How did he end up over here anyway?

As if reading my thoughts, Kaleb yells in my ear, "I grabbed him about ten minutes ago when he paid and started for the door. Didn't want him to leave before you got here."

Letting out a long sigh, I give him a nod of gratitude. "Good looking out, man. I appreciate you texting me."

"No problem." He claps me on the shoulder as we stop in front of the table before taking his seat.

The second Avery's eyes land on me, he gives a delighted jeer and shoves Pen's shoulder. "Look who's here to be your knight in shining armor."

I ignore him, instead letting my eyes rake over Pen's slightly disheveled appearance. His hair that was perfectly styled before is now a mess from him clearly raking his fingers through it, and the top button on his dress shirt is undone.

"Date go that well?" I can't help but ask. And because I'm petty, I don't bother to hide my sarcasm.

He glares at me with sapphire eyes. "Perfectly."

It's barely enough to even be considered a conversation, but the tension between us would be obvious to the blind, and it fills Avery with an obscene amount of joy.

"Aw, are the love birds fighting? Someone stepping out and looking for a new butt-buddy?" He leans back in his chair as he gives Aspen another shove before wrapping his arm around the back, behind Pen's shoulders. "You really should be more considerate of my teammate, Kohl. Can't have him crying over you when we get to the playoffs."

Is this dickhead serious?

Between the shit with Pen earlier, having to pick him up drunk, and Avery acting like a tool, my patience has long since left the building. So I can't be held at fault for the slightly violent way I push Avery's arm off Aspen's chair.

"Touch him again, and I'll fucking deck you, Reynolds," I say, painting on a fake smile before turning my attention back to Pen. "It's time to go."

As expected, Avery makes another comment, but I'm too busy watching Pen's bloodshot eyes roll so hard, I wanna smack him upside the damn head just to see if they get stuck like that.

Thankfully, he follows without argument, sliding out of his seat and allowing me to practically drag his drunk ass out the bar.

Once in front of the Impala, I hold my hand out. "Keys."

Even though he's plastered, he must be able to sense my irritation, because he hands them over silently and moves to climb in the passenger seat.

Moments later, I'm pulling out on the road for the ten-minute drive back to our dorm, my favorite rap station on the radio to keep me from losing my cool on him for trying to drive home like this. It's the only sound in the car besides the hum of the engine until Pen decides to break our stalemate.

"Turn that shit off in my baby," he mutters from the passenger seat.

I send up a prayer to whatever God exists that I don't murder my best friend tonight before I roll my eyes and turn up the sound of Post Malone. Ignoring him might be childish, but he's just looking to pick a fight with me, and hell if I'll let him.

Plus, he lost his right to have an opinion on my music selection when he decided to be a dumbass by getting shit-faced with no way home.

He grumbles some more before letting out a disgruntled sigh and starts digging in his jacket pocket. I know what he's doing the moment he starts to roll down the window, but the second his cigarettes are pulled free from his jacket, I slap them out of his hand.

"Not when I'm in the car," I snap, knowing full well he's aware of my distaste for the nasty habit he picked up last year.

His lip curls into something of a sneer before he looks away to stare out the window until we park. Which, thanks to the hour of night, there's shit for parking and we end up having a good half-mile walk back to the dorm.

A fucking blast to do when Aspen can barely walk straight.

Of course, getting the asshole home when he's plastered is no easy feat *ever,* so I'm not surprised tonight isn't any different. He's stubborn and more than irritable as I drag him through the door of our dorm, letting the lock fall in place behind us.

"C'mon," I say, grabbing his arm and moving him in the direction of his room. "Let's get you in bed."

Instead of following suit, and once again, showing his stubborn side, he rips his arm from my grip and glares at me for a solid ten seconds. No words, just glares.

Whoa.

My blood boils when he brushes past me like I'm not even there, and that's all it takes for me to let my control over my temper snap completely.

"What the hell is your issue?" I snap, crossing my arms. The way he stumbles across the living room of our suite is slightly endearing and makes me want to laugh, but my frustration with his crap attitude wins out in the end.

"Nothing. I just don't wanna go to bed," he says, grabbing the remote to the TV. Then he plops onto the couch and starts surfing through Netflix aimlessly. He's going so fast, I don't even think it's possible for him to read the movie titles. Then again, I doubt he has any intention of actually watching whatever he puts on. He's just doing it to be a dick.

I'm exhausted, and I really don't have it in me to fight with him right now. Or go digging for answers as to why he's in one of his moods—though I'm almost positive it has to do with his date. But neither of those things would be worth my time when he's drunk, so I let it slide.

"Fine." I sigh, moving over to slump down on the opposite end of the couch.

"You can go to bed. I don't need a babysitter."

Yeah, you really proved that tonight.

"I'm fine right here. Just pick something."

It takes him thirty minutes to decide on some documentary I have no interest in watching. So I lean my head against the backrest of the couch and let my eyes sink closed as the droning coming from the TV starts to lull me to sleep.

I'm not sure how much time passes, only that I'm startled awake by a foot kicking me in the thigh. My eyes shoot open to find Aspen sprawled over the couch, his feet now on my lap.

"What the—"

"You were snoring," he mutters, giving me a quick glance before turning his attention back to the TV. A look over to the clock on the microwave lets me know it's only been about an hour since we got home, and well past the time I'd like to go to sleep, so I let my eyes fall shut once again.

"Thank you," he says a few minutes later, his voice gruff and low.

I'm assuming it's for making sure he didn't do anything stupid tonight and got home safe, so I just say, "You'd do the same for me."

"No, that's not…" He trails off, and it has me leaning up to look at him. When I do, I see mixed amounts of apprehension and tension on his face. Like he's almost nervous to be here with me, and it's putting him on edge.

Okay, what the fuck?

"Then what is it, Pen? I'm not a mind reader."

He doesn't say anything, just stares at me in the dim flickering light casting off the television. His eyes float between mine, studying me like it's the first time he's ever looked at me. It's not, obviously, since we've known each other for years. But I absolutely believe this is the first time he's looked at me and actually managed to see me.

Maybe even see me the way I've seen him for months now. Hell, longer than that.

It causes my chest to tighten, and I don't know how to feel about that.

"Kee," he whispers, still searching my face.

I lick my lips, not missing the way he instantly tracks the movement.

My blood heats, and I swear, I better not be seeing things. So I do it again to be sure, and yep, his eyes follow again.

Shit.

Is it because he's drunk? Is that the only reason he's looking at me like he wants to shove his tongue down my throat? Or is it possible he's been feeling this tension between us too?

Goddamnit. I hate this. Not knowing. The questions that always ran through my mind whenever our eyes would meet this past week. Looks I swear were a little more than platonic.

But fuck it. He's shit-faced, and I've had a few beers myself. If anything, I can blame this on the alcohol tomorrow.

Decision made and before I can think twice—or more importantly, bitch out—I shift and allow my body to crowd his. I lean over him, one hand planted firmly on the arm of the couch, the other resting beside his waist. The movement has my knee sliding between his legs and as I lower my body closer to his, my pulse races.

"What're you doing?" he breathes out the question, barely loud enough for me to hear. If I wasn't hovering inches away from him, my chest brushing his, I probably would have missed it entirely. I'm not too focused on his words right now though. Not when I can practically taste the liquor lingering on his lips from here.

"I don't really know."

Truthfully, I don't know what I'm doing. I don't know why I'm even bothering to take the chance, only that everything inside me is telling me I need to. If only to know for sure.

As much as I hate to admit it, the way it felt to kiss him back at the end of high school has been permanently ingrained in my brain. I haven't been consumed by it or anything like that. Intentionally, at least. But ever since DYD came up at that party and then the video…it's there again, fluttering in the background like white noise I can't seem to get rid of.

I just wanna figure out why this is happening. Because while I'm definitely attracted to the guy I've been chatting with on Toppr, I sure as fuck don't get this feeling when we talk.

So, is it only Pen?

The words that slip out of my mouth next, without my permission, make me think it might be.

"You're the only guy I've ever kissed," I tell him, fingers of my free hand dancing over his jaw. They coast along the sharp angles, tracking to the spot below the left side of his mouth where the dimple I'm obsessed with pops when he smiles. Currently, it's nowhere to be seen. If it was, I don't think I could stop myself from licking or biting at it, consequences be damned.

I work to swallow, ignoring the way my stomach ignites as his stubble scrapes against the pads of my fingers, or how the thought of my lips on any part of his body has my blood heating beneath my skin.

Touching him like this, even though it's nothing overly sexual, has every inch of me on fire. Or maybe it's the way it feels to have his hard, lithe body pressed against mine that has me all worked up.

But this is Pen. My best friend. And while I'm confused as hell, I don't want to scare him off. So I do my best to keep my thoughts tame and *away* from how good he feels.

That's before I catch that same look in his eyes. A hint of lust and interest mixing with the fear, sending any thought of keeping things tame right out the goddamn window.

I hear the slight intake of breath as I move my fingers over, tracing his lips. They part slightly and I feel his hot breath coasting over my skin. Every sensible part of myself, every ounce of my self-preservation, is screaming at me to stop this. Stop what I'm doing. Get up and go to my room and forget this night ever happened.

But I can't.

I have to do this. I have to prove it was just a fluke. It was the connection we share from years of friendship, nothing more.

I have to know if he's the exception to the rule.

"Fuck, Pen. All of me wants to kiss you again." His eyes widen slightly as I say it, but again, I just see lust and confusion in them.

He swallows, and it takes all my willpower to not lean in and lick his Adam's apple. But my self-control isn't strong enough from keeping my stupid lips from spilling more thoughts that'd be better kept to myself.

"I'm done holding back. Not when refusing to give in only makes it worse."

"Give in," he repeats in a whisper, almost in reverence. Or maybe anticipation. As if he likes the idea as much as I do.

I nod. Swallow. Tamp down the nerves.

And lean in.

"Please, don't deck me for this later."

Before he has the chance to protest, my mouth descends on his until they mold together. Tentative at first, but quickly growing more confident in what's happening. His lips are soft against mine, softer than I remember them as I tilt his chin up toward me. A soft groan manages to slip past our fused mouths, but I'm not sure who it came from. I think it was him, but honestly, I don't even care.

One of Aspen's hands grabs at the front of my shirt, the other coming up to the back of my neck. The blunt tips of his fingers scrape against my skull as he kisses me back, slowly and seductively.

It feels so damn good.

My heart hammers in my chest, pounding a mile a minute, as my brain attempts to play catch up with what's happening. Namely, that I'm kissing Aspen again for the first time in what feels like a lifetime. Only this time, it's a real kiss. And he's *letting* me.

Not because of a dare, but because…fuck. Because he wants to?

Goddamnit.

Whatever it is—whatever has taken over all rational thought from either of us—it's emboldened me enough to keep going. Asking for more. See how far he's willing to let me take this.

My tongue slides against the seam of his lips, seeking permission as much as it's coaxing. He surprises me yet again when his lips part barely a second later, granting me the access I'm craving.

The taste of whiskey on his tongue is instant as it brushes along mine, and this time, it's definitely him who lets out a low rumble from deep within his chest. A sound I wanna hear again and again. I'd give my last breath to never forget the feel of it against my mouth. It sends a bolt of lust straight to my balls, and when his tongue starts tangling with mine inside his mouth, the need within me builds astronomically.

And that's what it is. Need.

It's a yearning I've never felt before. One that consumes me to my core and only builds the longer we're like this.

My hips move of their own accord, sinking down against his as I fuck his mouth with my tongue. The fingers that were gripping my shirt have now slid beneath it, and holy—

He thrusts up into me, and I'm floored to feel that he's just as hard as I am. Long and rock solid, and when our dicks brush against each other beneath the confines of our clothes, I moan into his mouth.

"Fuck," he mutters against my lips, his breaths coming out in ragged pants.

Part of me worries he's about to break this off and push me away. Honestly, I wouldn't blame him if he did, especially with how things just went from zero to sixty in no time at all.

But then he keeps kissing me. Like a man starved. Greedy for more.

I must be too, and soon enough we're clawing at each other, nothing more than desperation and unbridled lust driving us.

A tiny part of me wonders if he even knows it's me. Or if he thinks I'm Bristol. Maybe some other girl he picked up at Stagger.

Those thoughts are quickly put to rest when his hand cups my jaw and he breaks away to nip at the skin there. "Goddamnit, Kee. What're we doing?" he mutters against my jaw before taking my mouth with his again. This time, it's him who thrusts his tongue in my mouth, making it impossible to think.

"I don't know," I breathe into his lips, shaking my head as I grind down against him. The groan it elicits from both of us is intoxicating. "Just don't stop."

Truthfully, stopping isn't an option at this point. Every single thought is now circulating around Pen and his lips and the blissful torture that is his body against mine.

Both his hands fly to my hips, digging in at my waist as he pulls me down against him. Each and every bump and grind of his cock is enough to send me over the edge, but I can already feel this is going too far, too fast.

But even though I know I need to break this off soon—mostly because I have no clue how drunk he is still—at least something came out of this moment. Well, besides the single greatest kiss of my life.

That fact in itself confirms what I've been wondering these passing months.

I'm not as straight as I thought I was. Especially when it comes to Aspen Kohl.

He might be like a brother to me, but this goes way beyond that. Past friendship, and right into desire.

Because I want this. I want him.

I've never been more sure of anything.

I just have no idea what it means for our friendship.

TEN

Aspen

Keene's mouth on mine is the equivalent of a taser to my balls. A straight up electrical jolt that sends my senses into overdrive. To the point where I'm so keyed up, the only thing I can think about is stripping out of our clothes and doing…fuck.

I don't even know what I wanna do to him. Anything and everything. I wouldn't know where to start.

The thought alone has me completely terrified.

He's my best friend, the only person in this world I chose to be like family to me. It's so much to risk, knowing if this goes too far, we might never come back from the lines we've crossed.

Then there's the fact that this is also uncharted territory.

The only cock I've been acquainted with is my own in my twenty years on Earth, and for the life of me, I never imagined that changing. Almost all of me *still* doesn't because…I've been straight my entire life. It's what I am.

Right?

Then again, I'm definitely not in this current moment, with my tongue in Keene's mouth and my cock hard and aching as our hips roll together in a desperate chase of release. Right now, the only thing I'm sure of is I don't want this to end, no matter what it's doing to my sanity.

Namely, making me lose it all together.

Nicotine might be my vice of choice, but that's all changing with his lips on mine. Barely a goddamn taste of him has me reeling, ready to trade my soul for more.

I'm not sure which of us moves first to shed shirts, only they're ripped from our bodies and soon tossed over the back of the couch. Maybe it was me, because my confidence is high and inhibitions low, thanks to the copious amount of alcohol I've ingested tonight.

Both my hands at his hips shift, slipping down to the outside of his ass. It's firm in my palms, more than any woman's, and I can't help but give it a squeeze. The taut muscles work beneath my touch each time he rolls his hips against mine, and it's got my cock weeping behind my zipper.

Or maybe that's because we're dry humping and making out like two sex-starved teenagers. It's gotta be one of the best moments of my life. Go figure that one out.

"Goddamnit," he whispers, when my fingers move to slip beneath the waistband of his sweats. The smooth skin of his ass glides against my palms, and it somehow feels right. As if touching him like this is how it's supposed to be. And that's enough to have me grabbing on to him to help pace each and every grind of his body.

"You feel..." I trail off, my brain short-circuiting when his teeth lightly sink into my jaw. He feels amazing. Hard body and strong muscles and smooth skin rocking against me. It feels perfect.

Like home.

He's always felt like home to me, but not like this.

"You too," he mumbles. Sharp teeth bite at my lips before he devours me some more. My hold on his ass becomes firmer, and I lock him tight against me. As close as humanly possible.

"Can you come like this?" I hear myself utter, and hold the phone— *Can you come like this?*

Goddamn. When I go gay, I bat for the fucking fences. Normally, that's Keene's job. Both in reference to baseball, but also acting without thinking. Because I'm the rational one. The one who knows and understands that all actions have consequences, and *these* actions can have consequences of the life-altering variety.

Doesn't seem to matter though, because all rational thought left the building the moment his lips met mine. All I can focus on is the way he feels against me and how much more I want than just this.

His forehead rolls against mine, signaling a nod of confirmation before his teeth grab my bottom lip and tug. My hips buck up into his in response.

Oh, shit. This is bad. Really, really fucking bad.

Yet, never in my life, has bad ever felt so good.

Good enough to where I have no qualms about what we're doing. I've never wanted anything more in my entire life.

"Why does this feel so good?" he murmurs against my mouth before trailing his lips over to my ear. "Why do I want more?"

Fucking hell. It's like he's crawled inside my mind and can read every thought and desire bouncing around in my brain. Then again, it's always been that way with us.

Instead of answering—mostly because I sure don't have answers for him right now—I let my hands slide further inside his shorts, my fingers teasing his crease as I give his ass another firm squeeze. This time, a moan rips from his throat that's so erotic, it should be criminal.

His head falls into the crook of my neck and he rasps, "Fuck, Pen. Give me more."

My teeth sink into my bottom lip and I try not to think about what more entails, or I'm bound to get carried away to places we aren't ready for.

"You want my fingers sinking inside you? That it, Kee?" I pant as I thrust up again. He groans, and the sound does something to me, and I grind out, "God, you're gonna kill me."

The heat of his breathy laugh on my skin sends goosebumps breaking out over my skin, despite the fire burning through my veins. He nips at the skin of my throat, then sucks it into his mouth in a way that's sure to leave a mark for all to see tomorrow. Claiming me as his.

Do I care? Maybe if I was stone-cold sober and in my right mind, sure.

Right now, it only makes me hotter for him. For the sinful and slightly forbidden way we're going at each other like animals in heat.

"I want your fingers inside me. Your cock rubbing against mine until I come," he murmurs against my throat before he takes my mouth again. His tongue slips between my lips to keep me from answering. Not that I'd want to when his tongue rolls against mine in time with his hips.

Oh, my fucking God.

My dick is aching behind my zipper, my balls throbbing with the need to release. I don't think there's ever been a time in my life where I've been as turned on as I am with him, here and now.

Jesus Christ, I need to get a grip on myself before I come in my pants like a goddamn preteen the first time his dick is touched. But from the way Keene keeps grinding against me, making no move to get the rest of our clothes out of the way, that's exactly the point.

Wrenching my mouth from his, I gasp and pant for air while he dry fucks me into oblivion. I'm about to explode at any second.

"I'm right there, Pen."

The rasp in his voice, rough like gravel, combined with the sheer need in the words is enough to have my balls seizing up. One, two, three more rolls of his hips over mine have my eyes slamming closed as I lose myself in pleasure.

Keene slips his hand into his sweats, pulling them down just enough to release his cock. He continues to rock into me, his balls rubbing against my sensitive dick as he strokes himself. All my senses are working overtime, every touch and sound more than enough to get me right where he wants me.

But it's the sight of his hand wrapped around his cock that undoes me entirely.

Cum jets out of me, filling my underwear in a way that, if this wasn't Keene, I'd be really embarrassed about. Part of me still is, but the filthy smirk that crosses his face when he must feel the warm liquid seeping through our clothes quickly turns embarrassment right back into lust.

"Goddamn," he marvels, still smirking as he works himself over. "Wrecked is a good look on you. Wrecked just for me."

He's not wrong, though I doubt I looked nearly as wrecked as I feel inside.

It only takes him a couple more quick jacks of his cock while he stares down at me before his release shoots from him too, coating my stomach in thick ropes. This time, it's my turn to smile at the sight of him losing control for me. He's quick to kiss it right off my lips as he collapses against me when the last of his cum is milked from his body.

He rests both forearms on either side of my head, just above my shoulders. We're chest to chest now, and both his hands move to wrap around the top of my head. Fingers snake into the longer strands of my hair, and his mouth continues to thoroughly ravish me.

I'm literally wrapped up in him. Cocooned by his body. And that feeling I had earlier of being at home? It's all-consuming now.

And all of me knows just how dangerous it is, because it's something that'd be all too easy to get used to.

We continue to kiss, every inch of our bodies pressing into each other. His cum has the firm ridges of his abs sliding against mine, and I can feel myself getting hard all over again.

How am I ready for a second round already?

We don't make a move to take it further, though. In fact, all grinding and movement has stopped entirely, except the way our lips and tongues glide together. And soon, the sated feeling takes over both of us and the kissing stops too, leaving us panting. Consuming each other's air as we try to calm the rapid pace of our breathing.

"I might be fucking stupid for admitting this," he mutters against my mouth, placing one last peck on my swollen lips. "But I really hope you're sober enough to remember this tomorrow."

My heart is still hammering in my chest at double time, and I manage to rasp out a soft, "Why?"

His lips and teeth leave a searing path on my skin as he kisses and nips his way to my ear. "Because we've barely stopped, and I already wanna do that all over again. And again. And again."

God, if that wasn't already completely obvious from the way he keeps on touching and licking and kissing me. Like he can't stand the thought of stopping. Of breaking the spell.

I can't either, though I know we have to eventually.

A groan slips from me before I'm turning my head to lick a path up his throat to his ear. Partly because I love the taste of the salt on his skin, but also to keep myself from saying those two words dying to slip from my mouth in response.

Me too.

Or worse, the words that sure as hell have no business coming out of my mouth until I'm comfortable...well, *coming out*. If not to the world, at least to myself.

I want you.

But he deserves more than just my lust. More than a heated kiss or a half-drunken dry-fuck fest. And there's a massive piece of me that wants to give him everything he could ever want or ask for.

It's like Bristol said, I'm not the type to date. Fuck buddies are the only thing I know, the only way sex doesn't become a messy complication that impacts my life on a daily basis.

And Keene could never be that. A fuck buddy. A friend with benefits.

It would be the quickest way of screwing up the relationship we already have, and ruining us is the last thing in the world I'd ever want. So instead of responding, instead of saying anything that this situation would call for, I go the route I always do.

Deflection.

"You gotta get up."

His body goes rigid over mine, and I immediately know it was the wrong thing to say. Too late to change it or take it back now though, so I double down by patting his ass as a signal to move.

"Right," he whispers, lifting off me. Instantly, I miss the warmth of his bare skin on mine and the cocoon his body had mine in.

A tense cloud falls over us, thickening the air to uncomfortable levels as he looks down at me, looking as destroyed as I feel. He fixes himself up, tucking his half-hard dick back in his sweats, but I can still see the wet patch on the gray material from my cum seeping through my jeans.

I didn't mean to make it a rejection of any kind by asking him to get off me. I just needed space. No contact of his body against me until I know what to do or say or think.

Keene chooses to clear his throat and speak instead, giving me an out I don't deserve.

"I'm gonna clean up." His tone is as detached as he can manage, but his eyes give away his hurt. Even in this dim lighting from the television.

Part of me wonders if that was an offer for me to join him, because I'm definitely the messier of the two of us right now. But fear and doubt have me rooted in place and my mouth zipped shut. In the end, I just clear my throat and nod in response, no longer trusting any part of myself to know the right way to handle this.

My eyes stay locked on the ceiling as I listen to him run the faucet and rummage around in the bathroom. Self-loathing and regret begin churning inside me, not for what happened, but for the way I just reacted to it being over. I push it down best I can, but it doesn't do much good.

In fact, it only grows when, five minutes later, he exits our shared bathroom and slips into his own room without a word or a glance in my direction.

Shit.

Rising from the couch, I take my turn to get cleaned up in the bathroom. Since both of our cum is covering a good portion of my lower torso, a quick shower is the only sensible option for getting cleaned up.

My mind races as I rinse my body and then dry off. It doesn't stop, even when I toss on a new pair of boxers and slide into my bed. Or when I lie there, staring at the ceiling once more, and begging for sleep to take me out of my own head, if only for a few hours.

But how can it?

His taste still lingers on my tongue. Branded there in a way I won't soon forget.

And the kicker of it?

Everything inside me wishes *this* would've been our first kiss.

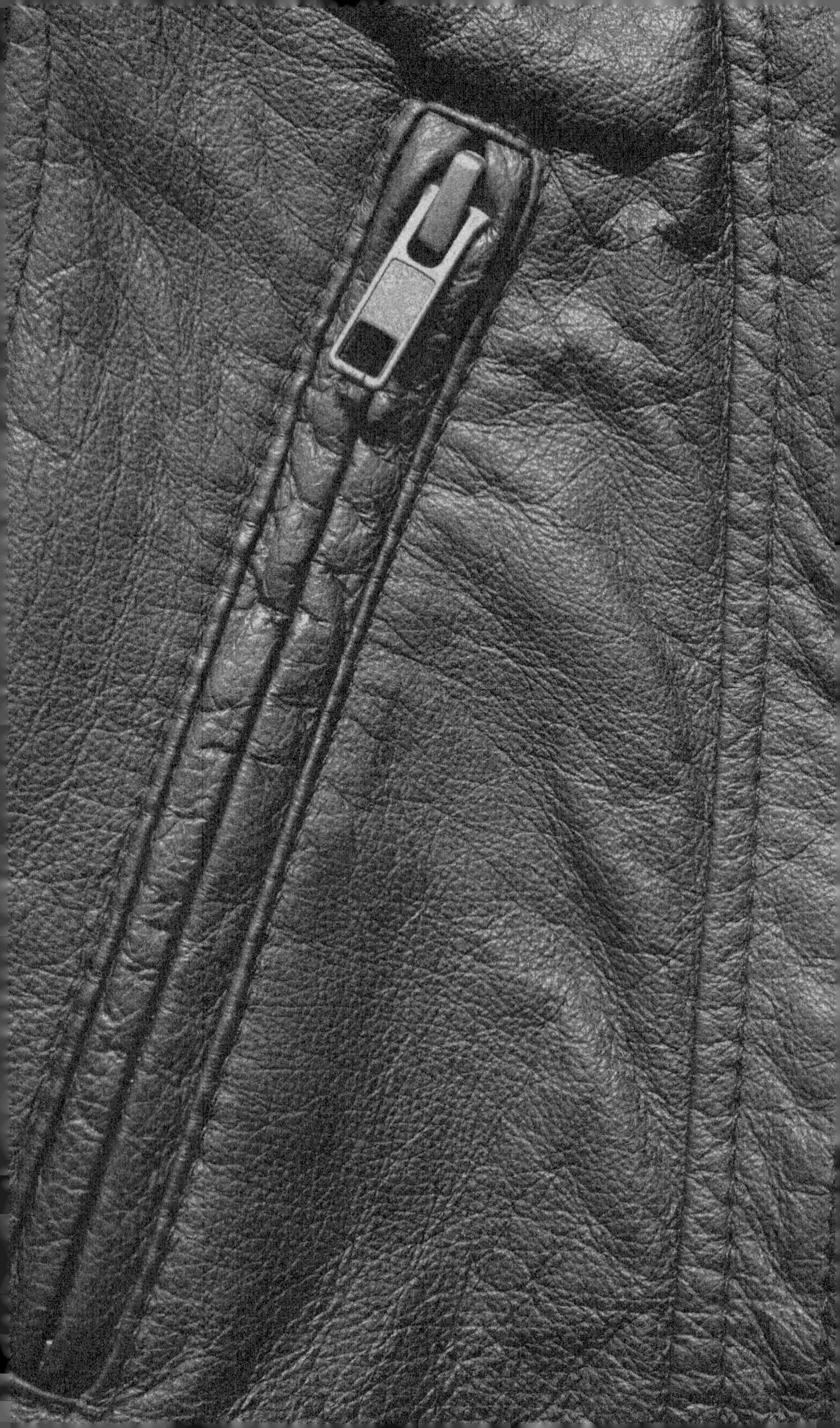

ELEVEN

Aspen

Keene ignores me for the two days following the night he picked me up from the bar and brought me home. Also known as the night we made out like two lust-drunken idiots and came all over each other.

Well, he came on me, and I came in my pants. To-ma-to, to-mah-to, at this point.

Though, I'm not entirely sure if *ignore* is the right word. Being distant might be the better term. Whatever it is, he's made himself very scarce around the dorm. Staying out to study at the library until he knows I'm in bed or spending time at the team's practice facility for extra batting practice. The latter is how I know something is definitely wrong. Keene hates taking BP off the machine and avoids it at all costs during the regular season.

Guess he's choosing the lesser of two evils in this instance.

But when it comes to the third day and I still haven't seen more than a passing glance of him, I've had about enough.

I know I screwed up a bit, pulling a classic Aspen and shutting down immediately post-hookup. I also know I haven't done shit to broach the subject about what happened the other night because I really don't know how. But I also know I can't keep living like this: two ships passing in the night like the other doesn't exist.

If anything, I understand—now more than ever—why he kept the questioning of his sexuality under wraps. Because after what happened when we were texting and then the other night on the couch…

Hell.

I think I'm questioning *mine*.

The door to our dorm clicks open, revealing Keene with his bag slung over his shoulder. He pauses when his eyes lift to find me on the couch working on my architectural studio project—which is toeing the lines of Frank Gehry level in abstraction—and his brows lift in the way they do when he's taken off guard.

"Oh. You're still up," he says after kicking off his slides. Long fingers grip the bag slung over his shoulder far tighter than they should be, and I can tell he's looking for an out. Hilarious, considering Keene's always the one to make us *talk about our feelings* when we get into a fight.

The only exception to that has been the past few weeks.

But pair his clear desire for avoidance with the way he still won't look at me, and I know this is necessary. No matter how uncomfortable it'll be. And I know it'll be awkward. Especially if we aren't on the same page as to where we go from here.

"Yeah," I say slowly. "I think we need to talk."

He nods a couple times before finally meeting my gaze. An impassive look is plastered on his face, completely unreadable. My stomach rolls at the sight of it. Part of me thinks he might even tell me *no* or to fuck off.

I don't think I'd blame him if he did. Rejection stings from anyone, but I'm sure having it come from one of the people you care about most hurts like a bitch.

But in true Keene fashion, he just lets a confident smirk cross his face. One he and I both know is faker than Dolly Parton's tits.

"Okay, so talk."

Then he walks right past me and into his room, clearly meaning for me to come with.

Well, shit. I wasn't expecting him to make me go first. Spew my guts out without knowing what he's thinking or feeling beforehand. Then again, this is Keene. If I can't be open and honest with him about this, I can't do it with anyone.

Moving my laptop to the side, I follow behind him, anxiousness and dread settling low in my stomach. I have no idea where to start, and I think that's the biggest issue. I don't hate what happened between us, but I also don't know what any of it means. I don't know if I *want* it to mean something, other than a stupid, drunken moment where we got carried away more than we should've.

Well, at least for me, it was partially due to intoxication. Though, as far as I know, Keene was sober when he came all over my stomach in what might be the hottest sight I've ever seen.

Passing through the doorway, I find Keene's back to me as he tucks his duffle in the corner of the room. Plopping down in his desk chair, I take a deep breath and open my mouth to start out with what sure is gonna be a ridiculous amount of word vomit—the first few being *I'm sorry*. But then he strips out of his cut-off and tosses it with the rest of his dirty clothes, his shorts and socks quick to follow. Soon enough, he's left in only a pair of black compression shorts.

And I'm left completely tongue-tied.

There are plenty of times I've seen Keene in this state. Being around each other in only underwear has been a pretty regular occurrence since we moved in here freshman year. Probably well before then too. We also can't forget the hundreds of times I've seen him in swim trunks, which is basically the same damn thing.

But never before has the sight caused my brain to short-circuit like this.

Miles of tanned skin over perfectly sculpted muscles greet me, and I'm both shocked and horrified to find myself greedy for more. For him to drop the briefs entirely, so I can get another look at his—

Jesus Christ, stop it.

My eyes snap away, shame coursing through me for ogling his body… because for fuck's sake, why is this happening? I most certainly haven't wanted to get an eyeful of another dude's naked dick before. Hard, flaccid, or anything in between.

When I flick my attention back to him, my eyes are immediately glued to his package again, so apparently that's not the case anymore.

Why the way I look at him has suddenly changed, I don't know. But now, I see the way his obliques carve his lower torso with that sinful V girls lose their shit for. The defined indentations of each of his abs, eight in total. And then there's the sculpted curves of his shoulders that meet the sharp lines of his collarbone.

The urge to run my lips over the hard lines is unreal. Unfathomable, even.

And it's so far off course from what I'm used to feeling, that I have no idea what to do with it.

How did we end up here?

He's completely oblivious to my eye-fucking session—or at least pretending to be. And my internal existential crisis, which is far more important. Thank God, though, because I'm not looking to make the conversation we're about to have even more awkward.

He must get tired of my silence, though, because his attention finally lands on me when he drops onto his bed across from me.

"Normally when you wanna talk to someone, you have to speak words, Pen." His eyes give nothing away. Not an inkling into how he's actually feeling.

Okay, so that's how we're playing this. Good to know.

My eyes narrow on him, and I cock my head to the side. "You might be cool with pretending like nothing's going on after the other night, but I'm not."

His shoulders go rigid. Imperceptibly so, and I almost don't catch it. But it's the way his eyes widen that give him away. And it's then I realize what's really going on here.

I really hope you're sober enough to remember this tomorrow.

As if I could forget anytime soon. I think the groan he let out as he came all over me is permanently seared into my brain. A sexy, forbidden soundtrack playing on repeat ever since I first heard it.

"I remember," I murmur, confirming what he's thinking as I glance away. "I remember all of it, Kee."

He lets out a sharp exhale, relief crossing his face momentarily. It's quickly replaced by a look of irritation, his eyes narrowing on me.

"If you remember, why'd you wait three days to say something?"

"How was I supposed to when you were avoiding me at all costs?" I counter, a slight bite to my tone.

He blinks a couple times, shaking his head. "I guess that makes sense, but you can't blame me for wondering when you're hardly the one to talk about shit unless I force it out of you."

I frown. "So then, why didn't you force this conversation the morning after?"

His lips roll in, forming a thin line, and he sighs. "I guess I didn't want to freak you out if you didn't remember. Or worse, have you think I was like...taking advantage of you or something. I don't know."

A pang of guilt rushes through me, and I roll the desk chair until I'm sitting right in front of him. "I'd never think that, Kee. That's something you should know."

"I should..." he starts, shaking his head, "but things have been so weird lately. Ever since that Chi O party where we played DYD, I've felt this..."

"Tension?" I supply. A little too quickly, because his head snaps up and it feels like he's staring right through me.

"So you've been feeling it too?"

Hard not to when that video has been on a loop in my mind since the first time I saw it. Or that the sound of your moans has been cemented in my brain and I can't stop thinking about how they'd feel around my cock.

Oh, and then there's the other night when you got pissed at me for taking Bristol on a date and dared me to think about you while I fucked her...which led to the hot-as-shit make-out session where we came all over each other.

I don't say any of this, though. After all, I don't feel like adding more fuel to this awkward fire we've already got burning between us. Honestly, I'd rather go back to pretending all that shit didn't happen in the first place, but we're way past that now.

So instead, I just nod. That's the safest bet here.

He nods too, eyes sinking closed. "Okay, so it wasn't just me. That's good to know." The words are muttered softly, almost to himself, and another wave of guilt hits me.

Just because I wasn't able to express what's going on in my head about all the shit escalating between us—let alone talk about it with him—doesn't mean it was in his head. Or one-sided.

That's the last thing I wanted him to think.

But again, the coward in me won't dare voice this.

As unfair as it might be to him, it'd be even worse if I were to say one thing and then end up taking it back later. I'd rather know for certain before taking that kind of leap. With anything, really, not just him. But because it's him…it's almost more important to be sure.

Keene lets out a long sigh, breaking me from my thoughts, and starts shifting his weight back on the bed until he's leaning against the wall and his feet are dangling off the edge near my knees.

Which would be fine if the movement didn't make me realize…he's still in his damn compression shorts, and *only* the compression shorts.

Damn.

Clearing my throat, I glance away from him, but that only makes him burst out into laughter.

"For fuck's sake, Pen. You act like you haven't seen me half-naked before. Or completely, seeing as we used to take baths together as kids."

I feel my cheeks heat, and I snap, "Yeah, well, baths as toddlers when we don't know about dicks and sex is completely different than making out and dry-humping each other to the point of climax."

The feeling of embarrassment immediately increases the second I realize the shit that just spewed from my mouth, and I clamp my lips closed on instinct.

Shit, shit, shit.

Keene just continues to stare at me, lips parted slightly in something like shock. After knowing him for years, I can tell he's doing his best to read between the lines. Seeing what I'm not saying. I'm kind of terrified of what he might find…because I don't even know what's hiding there myself.

Eventually, he clears his throat, eyes darting around his room before they settle on his hands. "Can you just tell me what you're thinking? Because I can't figure it out anymore."

Those words aren't anything close to what I thought he was about to say. And honestly, what kind of question is that? How am I supposed to answer it?

I've never come harder in my goddamn life than I did the other night, and that scares the crap out of me because he's not only a guy, but he's *Keene*. My best friend in the entire world made me come in my fucking pants.

And I can't stop thinking about doing it again. Another *huge* problem.

I have no interest in messing around with any attraction toward men. Honestly, I've never really experienced it past seeing a dude and thinking, "yeah, he's good-looking," or something like that. A regular acknowledgment of male beauty, not some sexual desire to get them naked and lick their entire body. I don't even know if that's what I'm feeling now with Keene. I just know kissing him and touching him makes me feel things.

Unexpected things, like stupidly turned on.

But Keene isn't good at the hook-up culture, and even if I like doing sex stuff with him, it wouldn't change the whole *I don't do relationships* bit.

I sigh, resting my face in my palms. "I don't want to want you. Not like that."

"And you think I do?"

Lifting my head to meet his gaze, I'm surprised to find a pained, worried look on his face.

"You think it hasn't been fucking torture to keep this shit to myself? *From you* for this long? I've been living in hell ever since that kiss, and it's only gotten worse over the past few weeks. So do you really think it's been easy to want you, but know I can't have you?"

No. If what I've been feeling—the confusion and overwhelming lust every time I look at him—is any indication of what he's been going through, I don't think it's been easy at all.

He shakes his head, sitting up and combing his fingers through his hair before continuing. "Look. I've been wishing I could just get over whatever happened that night for a long time, Pen. But I can't. I've tried."

My head hangs. "I just wish you would've told me. So you didn't have to go through it alone."

He shrugs off-handedly. "I mean, I didn't even know at the time if it was something I needed to *go through,* you know? Like I said, I tried to ignore it, get over it, whatever. But I can't, and it's made me realize this is something I just have to figure out for myself. I can't not know."

"Then you should." I pause, my stomach rolling with worry. "But Kee, you have to be able to trust the person you're gonna be exploring this with. I…" A knot works its way into my throat, and I swallow it down. "I don't want someone to just take advantage of you. Something like this is a big deal."

"Coming from the king of no-strings hookups."

I smirk, because yeah, the irony isn't lost on me.

"Well, the only person I would trust is you." He lets out an awkward laugh. "But I can't ask you to be the guinea pig in this either. Sending me a dick pic is one thing. I can even rationalize what happened on the couch as us getting carried away with something that felt good in the moment, even if it wasn't smart for us to get caught up in. But sex is something else entirely."

My brows furrow, and while I understand what he's saying, I find myself disagreeing. Because *I am* the king of no-strings hookups, and the fact of the matter is, I don't think I'd mind Keene figuring this out with me.

I don't want him doing it with someone else.

We could have each other in the ways our bodies are clearly craving. As long as we made some guidelines and were open with each other, there's no reason for us *not* to.

The only thing stopping us is…me not offering it up.

"But you can."

His forehead creases. "I can what?"

"Ask me." When a look of doubt crosses his face, I roll the chair closer to him until my knees brush against the mattress. "I'm serious, Kee. You know I'd do anything for you, and if this is what you need, then sign me up."

"No fucking way."

You stubborn shit.

"Well, I'm not gonna take the chance on you finding some asshole on Toppr who doesn't care about you at all and only ends up making it bad for you because he's a dickhead."

The point I'm making is completely valid, but from the way his features flicker with a mixture of apprehension and uncertainty, he's not feeling the same way.

As much as I don't like being the catalyst to this whole sexual discovery in the first place—only for him to keep it from me for as long as he has—I want to help him with this. Any way I can. So if I was the reason it started, I'm gonna make damn sure I'm the way he figures it out too.

It takes balls to put yourself on the line for another person. He's probably the only person in the world I'd be willing to do something like this for, just like I know he'd do the same for me.

Maybe that's why I find myself uttering the question that keeps getting us into this mess.

"Don't you dare?"

His eyes heat dangerously. "Pen."

I shake my head. "Yes or no, that's all I need."

His jaw ticks, and I don't think I've ever seen him look more pained in my life. Torn between what he thinks is right and what I can tell he really wants. And make no mistake, he wants this. He's just too afraid to take it. I'm almost positive he's gonna say no when his eyes sink closed and his head slumps back against the wall.

Until he nods. The slightest movement, but it's there nonetheless.

And fuck if I'm gonna let him start overthinking and take it back, so I blurt the dare out before he has the chance.

"I dare you to suck my dick."

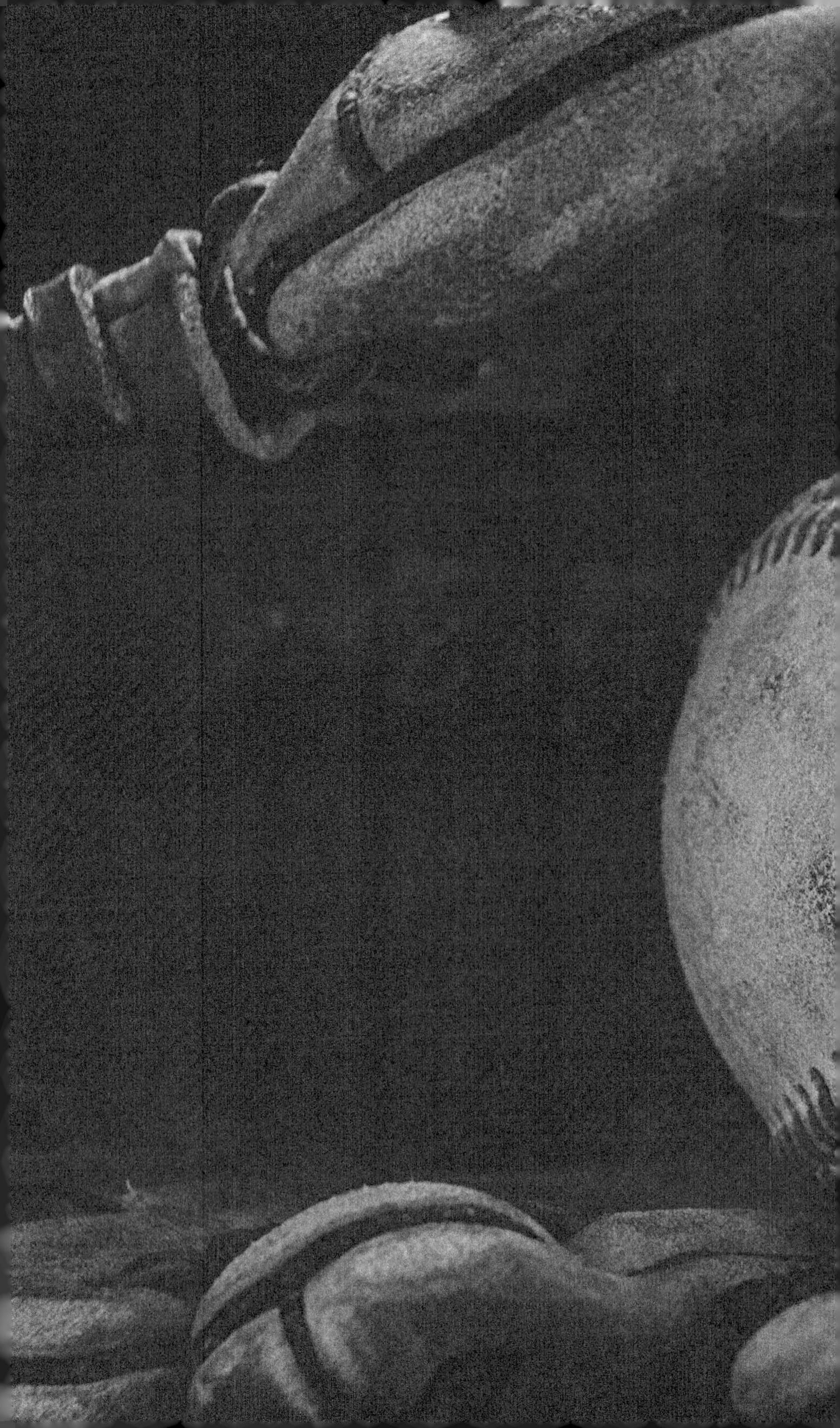

TWELVE

Keene

My eyes snap open.

"*What?*" I ask in complete disbelief.

"You heard me."

No. No, I don't think I did. I think I'm in a dream and my brain is working up some wild shit to keep it interesting. Or maybe I've been thrust into an alternate reality. Either way, there's no fucking way Aspen just dared me to blow him.

Yet from the look on his face as he's staring at me, waiting—albeit, impatiently—for me to respond, tells me this is really happening.

"You're serious," I say slowly. "Like, deadass serious?"

He nods. "You wanna know if you like dick for real, so what better way than to start with a blowie?"

Maybe, but…Jesus.

Everything inside me tells me to bolt, yet the way my dick decides to thicken in my compression shorts gives me away. He's quick to notice and nods toward my crotch.

"It's clear just from the tent you're pitching you want it, Kee. So don't pull a me by starting to overthink this."

Okay, now this is literal insanity. Have we pulled some *Freaky Friday* shit, switching bodies, and I haven't noticed until now? Aspen doesn't do shit without thinking—that's my MO, not this worrying bullshit. The worrying is all *him*.

But God, can he really blame me for overthinking? This is a recipe for disaster if I've ever heard one. Sex between friends is *always* a bad idea.

Yet I don't object when he starts making his points, working out yet another one of his plans for us to tackle this together.

"We'll make some rules to follow, mess around a bit, and when you feel comfortable with *knowing*, we'll end it. It doesn't have to be more than that, Kee. It doesn't have to be complicated."

I nod in agreement, but an unsettled feeling still sits in my stomach. "How aren't you completely freaked about this?"

He sighs, running his hands through his hair. "I was before. I mean, maybe I still am. I was definitely confused by how turned on I got with the whole…sexting thing."

I narrow my eyes on him. "Is that why you took Bristol out on a date?"

The tips of his ears pink slightly. "The thing about overthinking is that sometimes it's easy to convince yourself something is a good idea, even when it isn't."

In a way, I can see it. Understand what he was trying to accomplish. Hell, I've tried a ton of shit over the last year and a half to get my dick to walk on the straight and narrow.

None of it worked, obviously, and that's why we're here.

"But if the other night taught me anything, it's that it felt really good to be touched by you, even if it did freak me out a bit. So...I'm not gonna be one to get hung up on it."

"Which goes entirely against the way you're programmed," I note, dryly. He shrugs. "It's sex, Kee. And if sex with you feels as good as it does with any other partner I've had, then..." He trails off and shrugs again. "Then that's all I really need to know about it."

I wish I could be as cavalier as he is about sex and hookups, but I've never been able to separate my emotions when it comes to intimacy. I can count the number of one-night stands I've had on one finger, and it only happened because I was in desperate need to get out of my head about this whole attraction-to-men thing by making sure I still got it up for women too.

"So...you mentioned rules?"

"We only do what we're both comfortable with should be the big one," he says, leaning back in the chair. "And we're not fucking around with other people while this is going on."

My ears perk up at the exclusivity clause, and I'm glad he's all for it. I don't know why I thought he wouldn't be to begin with. Pen might have a major detachment when it comes to sex, but it's not like he goes around screwing anything that moves.

And that's also why it doesn't surprise me when he brings up his next point.

"Our friendship is the most important thing. Maintaining it at all costs. We have to be honest with each other when it comes to what we like, how we're feeling, everything. Especially on the big things, like anal." The red on his ears deepens and his cheeks turn pink, but this time, I can't tell if it's embarrassment or something else. Maybe even lust. "Who would top, if it ever came to that, being the main thing."

My blood might as well be boiling in my veins. "I can tell you one thing: the way I've pictured this going puts you on top ninety percent of the time."

"So you've pictured it."

Yes.

I lick my lips. "Maybe."

Any question I had about it being lust or embarrassment is immediately answered by the heat in his gaze at my answer. And though it makes me feel so much better, knowing this turns him on as much as it does me…I'm still worried.

I can't shake the feeling, which is why I shine the light on the elephant in the room.

"You know this could fuck up everything, right?"

"I know." His smile is soft and reassuring. "Believe me, I know it could. But I also know I'm not gonna let you figure it out with anyone else but me. Call it possessiveness or jealousy, I don't care. But it's not happening with anyone else, so you might as well get on your knees right now before I walk out the door and make you come begging for it."

While that's meant to be a threat, my cock definitely takes it as more of a promise. In fact, ever since anal was brought up, I've been rock hard and ready to get this show on the road.

But I'm nervous. Really nervous, actually. Which is something I'm not used to feeling when it comes to sex or being around Aspen. I can't help it though, when I want this to be good. I want him to like this, the same way he liked what happened on the couch the other night.

He's the one person I've always been able to be vulnerable with about anything—and if we aren't letting these hookups change the way our friendship's been for the past twenty years—then I shouldn't have any issue letting him know my insecurities.

"You'll tell me what you like? Or if I'm bad at it?" I murmur while sliding off the mattress and to my knees between his thighs.

The desire in his gaze is still scalding, but his eyes soften around the edges as he looks down at me. "You're always stupidly good at everything you do. I doubt this will be any different, Kee."

His reassurance sends a surge of confidence through me. One I didn't realize I needed to feel twenty times more at ease with where this is going.

Somehow, Pen always knows exactly what I need to hear, no matter the situation.

"Then take your shirt off," I find myself whispering as my hands come to rest on his thighs. They're warm beneath my touch, practically searing through the fabric of his sweats.

Arching one brow slightly, he does as I ask. My eyes latch on the smooth expanse of his abs as the cotton lifts away from his skin.

Pen's always been fit, despite not being an athlete like me. His daily runs and our hiking trips take care of keeping him lean, along with the few days he goes to the gym to keep his muscles toned and sculpted. And his pale skin makes him look like a marble statue of some sinfully beautiful god. With the dark hair, bad-boy aura, and wicked gleam in his eyes, I wouldn't say anyone but Hades.

And I'm more than happy to let him drag me to Hell.

Gripping the waistband of his sweats, I start to pull them and his boxers down. His hips lift, allowing me to slide them past his ass easily. The second his cock springs free of the fabric, my heart jackhammers against my ribs hard enough to crack them.

"Shit," I whisper.

It's long and thick, a deep blue vein running up the bottom that I can't wait to run my tongue over. An angry, red tip stares back at me, a drop of pre-cum seeping from the slit already.

Part of me is so glad I didn't get the picture from him the night we were sexting, because seeing it for the first time in person is so much better. When I say it might be an actual work of art, I'm not kidding. And even thinking it tells me, while I might not know if I like all dicks, I most definitely like his.

"If you keep looking at it like that, I'm gonna come before you even get your mouth on me."

My eyes snap to his face, and the unmistakable lust written in his expression eases any tension left in my stomach.

Smirking, I wrap my fist around his shaft and angle the tip toward me. "Someone a little quick on the trigger, Pen?"

I swipe the flat of my tongue across the tip before he can answer, lapping at the bit of pre-cum. It's a burst of salty flavor on my tastebuds, heady and not what I was expecting. Even more unexpected…I don't hate it. At all.

A sharp inhale causes me to look up, and when I do, I swear *I* could come just from looking at him. His eyes are two balls of blue fire, burning with an intensity that sears right into my soul.

"Not a fucking chance," he mutters. "Now, suck."

My balls seize at his command and the rasp in his voice. I've never let myself think something like his voice is sexy before, but his tone is so seductive, I'd do whatever he'd ask of me just to hear him keep talking.

I stroke him a few times, getting used to the weight in my palm before taking the tip in my mouth. Giving it a gentle suck, I flick my tongue across the head and am granted with more pre-cum leaking on my tongue.

I'm already addicted to the flavor of his lust.

His hands latch onto the chair's arms, something like desperation written on his face when he looks down at me. Up until this point, right now, I've questioned it. If this is really just something he's doing for me as a favor and as a friend. Or if, maybe, this is something that feels as right to him as it does to me.

But with the desire in his eyes and the way he's straining to hold himself back, I know.

He wants this as much as I do.

The second the realization hits, it's like I'm able to stop thinking and just breathe. Feel and touch him the way my body tells me to, without question or worry. And my God, it might be the greatest feeling in the world. To be free like this.

I pull him deeper into my mouth, taking care to run my tongue down and around his shaft as I go. A low moan slips from him and his fingers release the chair to grip my shoulder, digging into my traps with a surprising amount of force.

"Shit," he whispers, licking his lips as he watches me bob over his length a couple times. "Your lips look so fucking perfect stretched around my cock."

Jesus Christ, that mouth might be the end of me.

Every filthy word that he's ever spoken to me has gone straight to my balls, and these are no different. They make me ache for him with a need so severe, I don't know if I'll survive it.

His head rolls against the backrest as I continue to suck and lap at his dick, getting lost in the pleasure I'm bringing him. But God, I want his eyes on me. I need to see the look in them and on his face when I make him come harder than he has in his life.

I want to suck his dick so well, nothing and no one else can compare.

My fingertips dig into his hips as I breathe through my nose, allowing him to slide in deeper. The first time he hits the back of my throat, my immediate response is to pull away and gasp for air. But I'm anything but a quitter. Instead I open more to him, letting his length slip into deep-throating territory.

I gag when he gives his hips a tiny thrust up, tears pricking at my eyes when I glance up at him to see him watching me again, completely entranced in the way I move over him. It sends a shiver of desire down my spine.

I keep fighting through every bob and thrust, lavishing his cock like it's the last thing I'll ever do as I try my best not to come from the sounds he's making. Which I manage, but it's damn hard—no pun intended.

The pace I'm keeping is comfortable, alternating between short, fast strokes where I use my hand to help get him closer and taking him as deep as I dare down my throat. My cock is aching between my legs, the pressure of my compression shorts containing it nearly unbearable. To the point where I think I could get off just from getting *him* off. Which is new to me.

"Shit, shit, shit." The hiss comes out strangled as his fingers move into my hair. "Fuck, Kee. I'm not gonna last much longer."

I smile like a Cheshire cat around his shaft as I continue to lick and suck him like he's the best thing I've ever tasted. His length slides in and out of my mouth more and more as I take him down my throat again. My nose brushes against the trimmed hair at the base of his cock, the scent of him musky and manly and overwhelmingly intoxicating.

His grip on my head tightens as he gives a few tentative thrusts up again. I'm prepared for them this time, doing my best to relax and let him use me to get him to where he needs—

"I'm gonna—"

He doesn't get the chance to finish his sentence before he literally explodes. Spurts of hot cum hit the back of my throat in an instant, and though I wasn't expecting it, I swallow down everything he's feeding me, ready to beg for more. It's messier than I thought it'd be, drops of cum escaping my lips as he continues to thrust. I keep lapping it up though, the taste unfamiliar but not unwelcome on my tongue as I milk him for all he has. All my senses are overwhelmed by him. The taste of his cum, the smell of his skin. Watching as he loses control before my eyes, groaning and panting like a marathon runner until the painful grip he has on my head relaxes.

I lick him clean before popping off his softening cock to catch my breath, pressing one final kiss to the tip. When I raise my eyes to find him watching me, I'm not prepared for the sexy, sated look on his face.

Blissed out doesn't even begin to cover it.

"That was so hot," he breathes, swiping his thumb over my lip. Cum collects on the digit, and I wrap my lips around it on instinct, sucking it free of his release.

I'm surprised by the way he reacts, nostrils flaring and gaze smoldering, while he watches. I swear, I even see his dick twitch a little outta the corner of my eye.

"You're gonna fucking kill me, Waters," he mutters.

I smirk around his thumb, giving it a quick nip before releasing it. "Mmm, but what a way to go, Kohl."

I rise back up to sit on the edge of the bed, still harder than a rock and in dire need of release. And I truly mean *dire*. Like if I don't bust a nut in the next five minutes, they might fall off altogether. But I can't bring myself to move from this spot, wanting nothing more than to just stare at him like this, knowing I was the one who put him in this state.

"What a way," he agrees as his teeth sink into that plush bottom lip. A lip I'd actually give said nuts to bite into right now.

Before I can do anything about my wayward thoughts—particularly, act on them—he shoves me back onto the mattress, crawling up until his body is plastered over mine. Any semblance of him being tired is gone as he licks his way up the side of my throat.

The cool air from where the heat of his tongue passed sends a shiver racing down my spine.

"I'm still all sweaty from the gym." I laugh, my hands landing on his chest to shove him off me. "What do you want?"

He sinks his teeth into the side of my neck before soothing the bite with his tongue.

"You. On your back. I wanna taste my cum on your lips while you fuck my fist."

THIRTEEN

Aspen

February

Any and all worries about Keene and I hooking up wrecking our friendship are completely gone after a week.

Sure, the first couple days after the first hook-up were still a little awkward, but not because of him sucking my dick until I came literal buckets. It wasn't even because we were busy tip-toeing around each other, nervous to say something.

It was more one of those things where…do I kiss him goodbye before I leave? Or do I just go on about my day the way I always have and not worry about it?

Under any other circumstance—like with Bristol, for example—I'd just dip out for class or my run with a goodbye and have absolutely no concern about it. After all, it was just a hook-up, and we both knew the score.

But this is Keene. My best friend. And with this being a sexual exploration of sorts, the last thing I want him to think is that I'm just using him. Or vice versa. Even though…that's kind of exactly what we're doing.

He's using me to learn about his attraction to guys, and I'm using him to…well, shit.

To get off, I guess? I hadn't really thought about what I'd gain from this situation, besides the peace of mind that some jack knob from Toppr isn't gonna mess this up for Kee. Honestly, that's more than enough for me.

And yeah, I guess getting sex out of the deal is pretty great too.

Once we got over the whole idea that we needed to act any one certain way, the awkwardness in the air went away entirely. It also helped when we both agreed that keeping this thing between us on the down low would be the best option, only acting like we're hooking up when we're in the safety of our dorm room. It wasn't a hard sell for either of us, especially with fuckheads like Avery already running his mouth and calling us boyfriends and shit.

The last thing Keene needs is someone else messing with his head when it's already all sorts of confused. And I doubt I'd have it in me to keep from punching Avery if he did anything to make Keene feel bad about his attraction to me. Or any other guy that comes along after me.

And from the way Keene couldn't get enough of my dick…I'm almost positive there will be one after me. Something I don't know how to feel about quite yet, though I'm choosing to chalk it up to thinking no one on the planet is good enough for him.

For now, it's just me. Even if we've been too busy to do much on the friendship *or* hook-up front.

Since the world's most epic blowjob, we've only gotten horizontal one other time. Though I don't really call Keene high-jacking my shower, only to wrap his fist around our cocks and take us to heaven with his hand, as *horizontal* anyway.

Tonight, though, we're both in the same damn place, and we're choosing to take advantage of it. Well, *I* am. Keene, on the other hand, has decided to be a good student and study, rather than game with me or watch a movie.

But beggars can't be choosers.

"What do you wanna do for food?" I ask Keene from where I'm lying across my bed.

He's sitting at my desk, working through his reading for one of his business classes this semester, meanwhile I'm screwing around with my new camera lens I got for Christmas. It was a joint gift from Mom and the Waters'—something that was completely unexpected, considering how much it cost. Especially when it's only for a hobby.

How Keene managed to zip his damn mouth closed about this one is a shock, but he did. Though, at the time, I didn't know if I wanted to kiss him or punch him for keeping the secret from me.

Now, as I sit here snapping random candid photos of him while he tries to work, I'm firmly leaning toward the former. But kissing his lips ends up wanting to kiss him everywhere *else*, and I'm trying to *not* jump him at every spare moment we're together.

If I did, he wouldn't be getting jack shit done in the studying department.

He glances up at me briefly and picks up his phone. "I dunno. I'm kinda feeling pizza, if you are."

Pizza's always a good option. I mean, really, who doesn't like pizza?

"Okay," I say, grabbing my phone and pulling up the delivery app. "Your usual?"

When he doesn't respond because he's still typing on his phone, I pull a sock off my foot and toss it at his head. It hits the target perfectly, and I smirk, thinking I could be a baseball player too. Granted, I'm only a couple feet away, but still.

His head snaps back up from the screen, and he glares at me. "What?"

"You want your usual?" I ask again. "For pizza?"

"Oh. Yeah, that's good."

I finish up placing the order, but I'm hyper aware of him busy with his phone now instead of studying. He could be doing a number of things on there. Innocent things, like looking up his stats from last season or some shit. But my mind wonders if he's still texting one of those guys on Toppr, even after we started hooking up.

The feeling doesn't settle well with me, but I'm not gonna bring it up. It's not like Keene and I are dating. I'm not his boyfriend, he's not mine, and we don't really owe each other anything at this point when it comes to romance.

We're just…messing around.

One of my stipulations for us to do it was we're exclusive *sexually*. As far as I can tell, talking to someone isn't breaking that rule.

So why does the mere thought of him still talking to someone else make me see red? Or maybe it's…green, because when he smiles at his phone, a ridiculous surge of jealousy washes through me.

I don't act on it, even though it just about kills me.

Instead, I grab my camera again and aim it at him, snapping more pictures. This time, close-ups of his face. I study his features through the lens, the sharp line of his jaw, the bow of his lips. The subtle bump on the bridge of his nose where the freckles dotted there are getting darker. When I tell him this, it causes a blush to creep over his skin.

"Why're you blushing?"

"I'm not."

The way his cheeks get redder begs to differ. "Really?"

"Really, really."

My brows furrow as I continue to watch him through the viewport, taking in the slight frown at the corner of his lips. "I don't believe you."

He lets out a long sigh before turning to face me. "Pen. You're distracting me."

Deflection. Nice.

I drop the camera down enough to meet his gaze. "You're the one who decided to come in here to study. You only have yourself to blame."

His teeth sink into his bottom lip, and my cock does that little twitching thing it's been doing around him lately. Guess that's what happens when I know what it feels like to have those teeth scraping against it.

"I just felt like I haven't seen you a lot recently. Figured this would be the only way to change that since I've got an away game this weekend and we're not gonna be back until late on Sunday."

It's true. We've both been really busy with class and him with practices on top of it. And now that the season is kicking into full swing, he's gonna be spending a lot more time everywhere but here with me.

Him wanting to make time for me during his busy schedule actually makes me really happy. And more importantly, that it's just *friend* time. Not hooking up or anything of the sort.

I already love the time we've spent together when we're both naked, but the last thing I want is to lose our friendship in the sex.

"I was just giving you shit, Kee." I look down and fiddle with the mode dial on the top of my camera. "I'm always happy to have you around."

Way to be a fucking sap.

"Good," he says, a small smirk on his face when I glance back up. "Now, stop taking pictures of me while I'm working."

Rolling my eyes, I set the camera on the bed beside me. "You love it, you attention whore. Don't act like you don't."

He lets out a bark of laughter and goes back to what he was doing.

"It's like you don't know me at all, Pen. I just deal because you like taking pictures of me, and I like making you happy."

My stomach swirls at his declaration. "Really?"

He nods, not looking at me when he responds. "I mean, it's not like I really mind. But I dunno…every once in a while I wish I was the one taking *yours* for a change."

I snort out a laugh, leaning back against the wall. "You lost me."

"I'm serious."

Rolling my head back and forth against the wall, I think about it.

I don't hate having my picture taken. I'm not one of those people who covers the camera whenever it's shoved in my face for family events or whatever occasion it might be. Hell, I even snap selfies with Keene often to send in the group chat we have with our moms and Keene's sister, Alexis.

But at the same time…

"I belong behind the lens," I tell him, which is the truth. "That's where the artists go, you know? And pretty boys like you belong in front of it, Waters."

This time, he's the one to roll his eyes. "Okay, Picasso."

I blink at him. "You know he was a painter, not a photographer." When he doesn't answer, I add, "…right?"

His gaze meets mine again. "Please don't insult my intelligence. Of course I know that. I paid attention in third grade art class, thank you very much."

"Okay, okay."

I'm not about to correct him by saying we didn't learn that shit until middle school. I've learned to pick my battles with this one.

Keene refocuses on his work for a while, and the asshole I am, I grab my camera again to keep snapping photos of him once in a while. I try to be discreet, of course, but it's kinda hard to disguise the sound of the shutter clicking, so there's no way he's unaware of what I'm doing.

Especially when he flips me the bird in the middle of a series of shots. *Busted.*

"You really don't know how to listen, do you?" He says it with a smile though, so at least he's not actually mad. His head cocks slightly, and he narrows his eyes on me. "One of these days, I'm getting payback."

I snort, dropping the camera to the bed again. "Oh, yeah? And how would you have me pose?"

His lips curl up at the corner. "Naked, obviously."

Set myself up for that one.

My eyes roll. "Not at all what I meant, but good to know you wanna perv out on me."

"Is it really perving when we both know you'd like it?"

Nope. It's not. And apparently, I'm as transparent as cellophane if that's his first response.

Clearing my throat, I reroute the topic ever so slightly. "You know, models have to trust their photographer implicitly if they're shooting nudes."

He arches a brow. "Are you saying you don't trust me, Kohl?"

I trust you enough to get naked with you when I've never messed around with another dude.

"Oh, fuck off. You know I trust you. Way more than anyone else."

The arch in his brow increases. "Enough to take pictures of you naked?"

My fingers dance on the comforter before messing with the dial again. "As long as you never show them to anyone, I don't see why we can't… maybe discuss it…one day."

He bursts out laughing. "That was the most roundabout *no* I've ever heard."

I look up then. "If it's that important to you, I'd do it."

His expression sobers. "Same goes to you." Then those sinful lips twitch into another smile. "Just make sure it's after a workout if we're doing nudes, 'cause I wanna look good. Even if you're the only one to see them."

"That's so cheating," I say with a chuckle.

"Coming from the biggest catfish I know? Please."

My brows shoot up. "Come again?" He gives me a filthy smirk, and I realize my poor choice of words before correcting. "I mean, how am I a catfish?"

"Look at what you look like," he says, motioning to me.

I look down at myself, finding my regular black jeans and a black hoodie, completely missing his point. "Okay?"

"Your looks don't match your personality at all."

Has he lost his damn mind?

I frown. "Last time I checked, I wasn't a ray of fucking sunshine, Kee. Black matches my personality perfectly."

"Maybe, but you've got the whole bad-boy persona when you're also a massive nerd."

Now he's really lost me. "I'm a nerd because I like photography?"

I grab my camera again, snapping more pictures of him to prove a point. And, no surprise here, he flips me off in every single one.

"And videogames. And anime. And you're going to school to build buildings." He smirks, yanking my other sock off my foot before tossing it at my face as I click the shutter. "Nerd."

Lifting my eye from the viewport, I scowl. "You really wanna start calling out stereotypes, macho-jock face? Because two can play that game."

His hands raise in mock surrender. "I'm just speaking the truth. You're the biggest nerd I know, and if any of those girls got to know you one iota, they'd realize you're just an e-boy genius disguised as a degenerate."

My mouth opens to toss a rebuttal back at him, but my mind gets caught on what he said, and—

Hold the goddamn phone.

"What did you just say, Waters?"

He grins. "You heard me."

"I don't think I did over the shutter," I say, clicking the button and holding it while I glare at him. "Maybe you should say it again."

"Take your finger off the button."

"Still can't hear you," I tell him, shaking my head, my face the picture of innocence.

I see the words *challenge accepted* written in his eyes as he vaults from the chair to the bed, tackling my ass backward as soon as he hits the mattress.

We're both laughing as we roll around, wrestling for a hold of the camera. My finger is still pressing down on the shutter button as I try to keep it from his reach, so God only knows what my SD card will be full of after this. Definitely a good time to sort through.

I flip him over, and he flips me right back. Elbows and knees are flying everywhere, and it takes me right back to when we were kids and would wrestle for the TV remote or the last PopTart for breakfast.

Only, my cock never used to take notice of the way his body presses against me when we were younger, and he's definitely never had this look on his face as he straddles me and pins my hands above my head with a vice-like grip on my wrists.

It's a look that says he wants to devour me whole. Leave no inch of me untouched.

Right now, I sure as hell wouldn't stop it from happening.

In fact, my dick keeps thickening against his thigh, wanting to get in on some of the action. Just like the ridge of his erection presses into my stomach as he leans over me and gently removes the camera from my trapped hands.

His eyes never leave mine as he slowly sets it on the bed beside us.

Adrenaline courses through my veins, along with enough lust to put a brothel out of business. And I don't know what to do with it.

"Stop looking at me like that," I whisper, licking my lips.

"Like what?"

"Like you want to eat me alive."

His lips twitch slightly before he leans and brushes them over my throat. "Maybe I do."

I turn my head away in indignation…which only gives him better access to my throat. And fuck if he doesn't take advantage of it, nipping and licking at the skin there.

"You're not getting lucky after calling me an e-boy."

His fingers slide between mine, clasping tightly as his lips skim over my jaw. "Don't get mad, Pen. You're like my own, personal, sexy-as-sin e-boy."

"Call me that again and I'll—"

I don't get to finish that thought because Keene decides to crush his mouth to mine, spearing my lips apart with his tongue to put my own to much better use than arguing.

And yeah, I guess I was wrong about sex stuff overshadowing our friendship. Friendship is a lot more fun when kissing's involved.

FOURTEEN

Keene

As much as I enjoy playing ball, sometimes I really hate the travel schedule. It's not like I didn't understand what I was getting into when I signed with Foltyn College. Just like I know if I end up going pro, it'll only get worse. I'll be on the road half the season, sometimes two weeks straight without sleeping in my own bed.

It's never been much of a thought or issue before now, though.

Then again, I've never really had much of a reason to *want* to be in my own bed. Or someone else's bed back home, either. But now that things between me and Pen are escalating—in all the best ways—I'd rather have the comfort of his nearness and regular sexy time over weekend travel for baseball.

To even think that is literally…insane. That seems to be my mantra when it comes to this whole situation, but I honestly can't come up with a better way to describe it. Pure insanity.

And sure, I don't like being away from Aspen for more than a day or two at a time, but I've always just attributed that to our slightly unhealthy level of codependency. Of always being near each other since I was born, which is the fault of no one but our parents.

It's never been anything more than that.

Yet I can already tell that the discomfort in my chest while I'm away from him this time is completely different. It's not the normal *damn, I wish he was here* feeling I used to get whenever I'd leave. It's an ache of longing, and it's deeply unsettling. Especially considering I shouldn't miss him already. *Truly* miss him.

I haven't even left Portland, for fuck's sake. I shouldn't even be thinking about him at all, let alone pining for the moment I'm back in our dorm room with him.

And as I sit and wait for the rest of my team to board the plane, I'm annoyed to find myself checking my phone constantly for a text from him. Or maybe a Snapchat. Something to let me know I'm on his mind the way he seems to be on mine.

Seriously, what is that shit?

Finally, I just give into the urge to hear from him and shoot him a text first…only to type out close to ten different things before settling on the most obvious opening.

Me: Hi.

Jesus Christ, I've turned into a thirteen-year-old girl, I think as I stare at the message, waiting for it to show up as read.

It takes a couple minutes, but soon enough it does, and the three little dots reveal him typing a response.

Pen: Hi yourself. Everything good?

I realize my error when I read the message. Of course he'd think something's wrong. I never send him texts randomly like this. We rarely text at all, usually going for the easier option to FaceTime if we're not in class. There's not really another option for us right now, though, otherwise I definitely would've just done that instead.

Apparently sucking his dick has turned me into a stage-five clinger.

I stare at the screen and wonder how to respond without being completely obvious about what I'm wanting from him. Which…I don't even think I know what that is.

His attention, I guess?

Ugh.

As I think about how to answer him and keep the conversation going, a dangerous yet alluring idea starts to take root in the back of my brain. It's stupid, seeing as I'm on a plane full of my coaches and teammates, and he's probably walking to his boring-as-hell architectural history class right now.

But…

Fuck it. I type out the response, baiting the line for him to latch on to.

Me: Yep. Waiting on the plane. Bored out of my mind.

Pen: Listen to your crap music. Do some homework. Read a book. You know how to do that last one, right?

It takes a lot for me to ignore his barb for my hatred of reading, but I'm sorry I'm not one of those unicorn people like him who see a movie in my head as I read. All I see are words on a page, and they never fail to put me to sleep.

Fucking sue me.

Me: Or we could play a game.

I smirk, typing out another text and sending it before I can think better of it.

Me: Don't you dare?

The dots appear and disappear for a few minutes, and I chuckle to myself as I wait for his response to pop up on the screen. Finally, he settles on a single word.

Pen: Always.

And just like that, I know I've got him. Hook, line, and sinker.

Me: I dare you to finally fulfill your end of the bargain. You know, the one you conveniently forgot because you were too busy talking filthy through the wall?

It's a risky move, asking him to do this when I know he's in public. But I love getting under his skin, and I have no doubt in my mind that this will get him good and fired up. Which is why I'm surprised at his reply.

Pen: Fine. I'll be back to the dorm in an hour.

Me: Nope. Right now. Five minutes, like last time.

Pen: I'm about to walk into a lecture.

Me: Your point?

Pen: Are you insane? Do you want me to be arrested for public indecency?

Ah, there we go. There's the reaction I was waiting for.

Glancing around to make sure none of my teammates are paying me any attention, I chuckle softly and reply.

Me: It doesn't have to be bare.

Pen: Still a fucking problem when there are 200 people sitting around me. And it's not like listening to Hendrickson talking about the Baroque period gets me all hot and bothered.

Me: Sit in the back row, AirPods in, and watch my video. I know you still have it.

His lack of denial about the video makes me preen in my seat when I read his response.

Pen: You've actually lost your mind.

Me: Are you about to bitch out of a dare? For the first time in the

history of DYD?

I can practically see the steam blowing out of Aspen's ears. I know he's gotta be pissed since he already said yes to the dare. But pushing his buttons—and his limits—is one of my favorite things to do. And this is one time I actually have zero faith he'll go through with a dare.

Aspen might have the sexy bad-boy persona down to a T, but I know him better than anyone. There's no way he'll give in to sending me a dick pic in the middle of class.

Pen: I don't negotiate with terrorists.
Me: Do it and I'll send another video. Tonight. After the game.

Fuck, just thinking about sending him something else has my cock twitching behind my zipper.

Pen: If I do this, I want more than a video.
Me: Now we're talking. Whatever you want, it's yours.
Pen: Promises, promises, baby.

The term of endearment at the end of his last text sends my stomach into backflips, which ends up being more confusing than this attraction I have for him. But I ignore it, watching as the dots appear and disappear some more before they're gone entirely.

Shit.

After a couple minutes, they're still not back, and worry starts to niggle in the back of my mind. I didn't think taunting him would make him go dark on me. I thought he'd just tell me to fuck off or something.

Letting out a deep breath, I glance around the plane again. Most of the guys have boarded, we're just waiting on a few stragglers before we can get ready for takeoff.

When five minutes have come and gone with still no response from Aspen, I'm about ready to turn my phone into airplane mode and worry for the entire flight that I did something to mess this up already. Crossed some sort of boundary line we haven't really defined yet.

Then my phone vibrates in my palm, and when I look down, I'm speechless. Actually, I think I might be imagining things, because…there's an image waiting for me.

There's no way he did it. Not in the middle of class.

My heart hammers as my fingers open the message.

No way in fucking he—

"Shit," I mutter under my breath, sliding down a little in my seat, so anyone behind me can't see if they looked over the backrest. At least Avery is sitting a few rows in front of me, and I don't have to worry about him being the one to see it.

The shot is aimed at Pen's crotch, I'd recognize those black jeans that hug his ass so perfectly anywhere. It's slightly showing the row of seats in front of him too, further proof he's actually in the lecture hall while sending this. His leather jacket is tossed on the seat beside him, a pack of Marlboro's sticking out of the inner pocket. Even his backpack makes an appearance next to his knee.

But what catches my attention is nothing other than the beautiful, hard outline of his cock beneath his jeans. Jeans he absolutely needs to buy more of because holy mother of God, I think I can even make out the ridge of the tip as I stare at the outline.

Pen: Just thinking about you in that video gets me so fucking hard.

My dick twitches again, thickening behind my dress slacks. Knowing he got hard just thinking about me? I can't even describe the way it makes me feel.

Powerful, for one. A feeling I'm not used to having when it comes to Aspen Kohl.

Me: God, now I'm gonna be thinking about your dick the entire flight to Phoenix.

Pen: No one's fault but yours. Just know you're taking care of this the minute you walk in that door Sunday night.

Is that supposed to be a threat? All it sounds like is an invitation I'm more than happy to accept.

Me: Believe me, I can't fucking wait.

Pen: Me either, baby.

That zing happens again when I read the last word, but it's short lived when the pilot calls over the intercom that we're getting ready for takeoff.

Me: Hate to cut this short, but we're about to take off. Call you after the game.

After waiting a couple seconds to at least see him read the message, I switch my phone into airplane mode and settle into my seat.

I didn't really think my dare through all that well, because that picture only ensures I'm horny as shit the entire flight to Phoenix. Which is almost unbearable as it is for someone who hates to fly *without* adding something between a half-chub and full-fledged boner to the mix. Especially in a suit.

It only gets worse when I switch my phone out of airplane mode as I wait for the pilot to let us deplane, only for two more images to pop up in our text thread.

My jaw drops—actually fucking drops open—and I'm left completely speechless.

Because there, on my screen, is a pic of Pen in his bed, positioned to show the cut lines of his abs and torso…and his hard cock in hand. There's a bead of pre-cum glistening on the tip, blue veins popping out of the sides from beneath his fingers.

Holy shit.

I might not have been on the receiving end of a dick pic before, but I sure as hell have taken and sent them. But I don't think I've ever seen a better one in my life.

Then again, Pen has an eye for taking pictures. I'm not surprised he found the perfect lighting and angle to create the holy grail of cock photography.

The second image is nearly identical, but this time, the skin beneath his palm looks slick with lube, and there's a pool of cum resting on his abs. It makes my mouth water, and I'm hit with the urge to lick that salty liquid from his skin before tasting the rest of him.

If only I wasn't in fucking Phoenix for the next forty-eight hours.

After saving both images to a locked folder in my phone, I scroll down and read the text he sent after.

Pen: Couldn't stop thinking about that damn video and had to put myself outta my misery. Still as sexy as it was the first time. Too bad my hand doesn't feel nearly as good as your mouth.

Goddamnit.

Quickly, I pull up the keyboard and type out my response before everyone starts getting up and moving.

Me: I've never needed to rub one out as bad as I do right now. Thanks for that.

The issue is, there's no way I'll be able to. We're going straight to the field from the airport, and hell if I'm gonna jack off in the locker room with my entire team around. I might like to live on the edge, but I'm not stupid.

My phone dings with another text from him.

Pen: Ask and you shall receive. You only have yourself to blame.
Me: I asked for a pic, not torture.
Pen: Semantics ;)

FIFTEEN

Aspen

I lean back against the wall, tapping against my knee with my phone as I debate on how to spend my Friday night.

In my dorm suite.

Which I have all to myself.

For the whole-ass weekend.

Alone.

Fuck, I sound like a pussy right now. And *feel* like a goddamn puppy sitting by the door, waiting for my owner to come home after being gone all day at work.

Pathetic, if you ask me. And that's coming from someone who *likes* dogs.

It's not that I haven't lived through Keene being gone during baseball season. This is completely standard in comparison to last season. It's just strange to not have heard from him by this late in the night. I know the game is over; I watched the damn thing on the local channel that broadcasts all Foltyn athletics.

Normally, if it's close enough, I just go watch instead. Support my best friend the way he's always supported me in whatever I decided to set my mind to. And if I can't go watch, like tonight, he'll call me and bitch about his mistakes after the game instead of focusing on what he did well.

It happens like clockwork, a constant cycle with Keene the second his back hits the mattress of his hotel room. Ready to lay out all the ways he saw himself as inadequate during the game.

He's always been like that, the perfectionist he is when it comes to the game. It usually takes me reminding him of the things he did well before he calms down enough to realize that *hey, maybe I'm not a trash baseball player like I think I am when I'm not on my game every single day.*

I learned so much about baseball to do this for him over the years, even when the sport held little to no interest to me. But I did it anyway, because he's my best damn friend.

It was worth it in the end, just to get him to stop stressing out about his abilities on the field. Hell, I didn't even dare make jokes about *performance anxiety* to him, knowing it would only earn a death glare and an ass chewing. While we were in high school especially. Shit got pretty rocky when scouts were coming around and recruiting for colleges our junior and senior years.

But...it wouldn't be Keene if he wasn't too hard on himself.

Tonight is different though. They flew to Arizona this morning for the four-game series over the weekend, and I haven't heard anything from him yet. Fucking *radio silence*. Which wouldn't freak me out under normal circumstances.

But with the shit we've been doing together lately, it's got me feeling a little on edge. Itchy. Like at any second, our friendship is going to completely implode because we've touched each other's dicks and know what the other sounds like when we come.

Not things best friends typically do with each other.

I gnaw on my bottom lip, spinning my phone atop my knee and debating calling him to check in. There's no harm in that, right? We do this all the time. Regularly. The only thing that's different is *I'd* be the one calling him instead of the other way around.

God, I need a cigarette to chill out.

Checking the time, I see he most definitely should have been back to the room by now. It's been almost two hours since the end of the game and lights out are usually by eleven for the team while they're on the road.

Why hasn't he said anything?

They lost tonight, though from my end it seems like he played really well. Again, not a baseball expert, but I know enough by now to know when he plays like trash. And *again*, not one of those times. Yet I know he's going to be in his own head unless he talks it out.

Jesus Christ, stop overthinking this. It's Keene, *for fuck's sake.*

Scrolling to his contact, I tamp down the sudden bout of anxiety that hits me and tap the FaceTime icon.

It rings three times, each passing one causing an increase of adrenaline to pump through my veins at an unprecedented rate. It's stupid to be nervous about calling Keene, but I am. So much that I'm about to end the call when he picks up, but then I'm greeted with an extremely unexpected sight.

Keene.

In the *shower*.

He actually answered the damn phone completely naked and propped it up in the shower while cleaning himself.

Now...at this point, I've seen his cock. I'm well acquainted with that particular part of his body by now. And if that isn't a damn kicker in itself, I'm surprised to find myself *disappointed* when I notice it's out of view, the camera cutting off just below his belly button.

I'm quick to cut that line of thinking before I can do something stupid like ask him to *show me* his dick, instead choosing another opening.

"Why're you answering the phone on FaceTime when you're in the *shower?*" I ask, trying to keep my eyes on his face while the water pours down over his head and chest. It doesn't work, though. The stream sends trails of water cascading over his pecs and rippling down his abs enticingly before running out of view, and my eyes greedily follow.

My own cock twitches at the thought of tracing their path with my tongue.

What the fuck is happening to me?

"Why're you FaceTiming me while I'm *in* the shower?" he replies, smirking slightly as he runs his fingers through his hair before his hand reaches out and grabs a bottle of shampoo.

"I didn't *know* you were in the shower, Kee. Don't you shower at the field anyway? Why are you taking another?"

"I always take a second one after getting back. Ritual thing."

Damn superstitious baseball players and their rituals.

He glances up at the camera, a shit-eating grin crossing his face as he pours some in his palm. "You miss me already, yeah?"

I roll my eyes, already much more at ease. "Sure, shithead. We can go with that. Not like I haven't been waiting for you to call and bitch until my ears fall off about how shitty you played tonight."

His grin widens as he lathers the shampoo in his hair. "I played great. I don't know what you're talking about."

My brows rise as I settle into my pillows and prop my phone on my knee. "Who are you and what have you done with Keene Waters?"

A soft chuckle floats through the phone as he tips his head back, closing his eyes and letting the water rinse his hair. My mouth goes dry watching the suds slide down his toned torso, coating his tanned skin with bubbles. Even through the tiny phone screen, I feel like I'm there with him. Seeing it in real time.

I glance away, clearing my throat, and try to keep my mind *off* his sinful-as-hell body.

"I actually feel great about how the game went. Which is weird, knowing me. Especially with it being a loss."

Swallowing roughly, I let out a wry laugh. "If I didn't know any better, I'd think you're high."

"High on life, man. Kaleb grabbed some beers and we hung out in his room for a while. Bullshitted and whatnot. Which is why I hadn't called yet. I just got in."

My skin prickles at the idea of him spending time with one of his teammates alone in a hotel room. Where somehow, Kaleb was able to keep Keene out of his head when that's what he relies on me for.

What were they doing in there that allowed Keene to let off enough steam that...?

Images, ones I never want to see or think, flash through my mind. Kaleb and Keene *together*. The pinpricks along my skin only grow into a sense of revulsion when I realize...it's *jealousy* I'm feeling. Again. Which is *ridiculous* because Keene is my best friend and Kaleb is straighter than an arrow. At lesat, I think.

I shake my head to dislodge my train of thought, bringing my attention back to my screen. Keene is silent on his end, not paying me any attention as he washes his body with soap. More and more suds cover every inch of him, and I feel my dick getting thicker behind my shorts at the sight.

It's confusing—the way my body reacts to his. Even through a *phone screen*. This doesn't happen to me with any other guys—fuck, it doesn't happen often with *girls*—so why is it so different with him?

What is it about Keene Waters that's different from the rest of the world?

I don't know, but I sure wanna figure it out. So naturally, I do the only logical thing that comes to my idiotic twenty-year-old mind.

"Don't you dare?"

He makes a choking sound as his head snaps to the phone, his hand wiping away the water pouring down his face. "You serious? While I'm in the shower? Reyes could come back to the room at any minute?"

I nod and smirk, rolling my tongue across my teeth.

He scoffs and shakes his head. "Asshole. Fine. What do you want from me?"

Weighing my options is the smart move, though it's something I should've done before I even brought the game up in the first place.

The dares...they're just a cover. A way for us to have fun while we explore this with each other. Adding a little bit of friendly competition between us.

Exhibit A being the dare he tossed out at me today, which was really awkward when I had to tamp down a boner before one of my two hundred classmates saw it.

Which is why I'm going for some payback.

"I dare you...to prep yourself for me. Right now."

His eyes lock on mine in challenge, his nostrils flaring. I swear I can see the water turning to steam as it hits his skin beneath the spray of the shower.

"You want me to touch myself while you watch, Pen?"

His tone is playful. Taunting with a touch of defiance. It always is when we get like this, in the middle of a dare.

My smile is wicked. "Damn right I do. I wanna watch as your fingers stretch yourself for me. Making yourself feel so good, Kee." I lick my lips, feeling his lust through the phone screen. "I wanna see you come apart while you imagine my cock sinking deep inside you."

His throat works to swallow, and I can see his mind spinning.

We haven't broached this subject past the day we agreed to start messing around. The *anal*. But logically...that's the next step. And as insane as it might sound, I want it. To be buried deep inside him. I wanna be the first person to give this to him, while he tries to sort this shit in his head.

And yeah...my dick really likes the idea of fucking my best friend.

Keene's breathing slows and he steps closer to the camera so I'm only able to see his collarbone and above. I'm transfixed on the way the water falls over the freckles on his shoulders in vividly high definition this close.

His voice comes out like gravel. "You want that?"

Mine is just as rough. "Do you?"

I watch as his head dips down, seemingly looking at the floor before brown orbs grab hold of mine once again. Instead of answering me, he reaches over again and brings a bottle of conditioner I know smells like citrus into view.

Then he steps backward, away from the camera.

Once. Twice.

And then I see it.

His cock. Standing at full mast, begging to be touched as he pours the liquid into his palm.

"Yeah, Pen," he finally says, his voice low, almost blending with the sound of the water. He grabs his cock, sliding his fist up and down the length, coating and lathering it. "I think it's pretty clear I *do* want that."

I'm transfixed by his cock, the way he strokes it. Rolls over the head on every third upstroke. Fuck, even when he's prepping his *dick*, his slight obsessive compulsive tendencies have a way of coming out.

I don't know why my noticing makes this even...hotter. But I'm scorching.

"That's mine," I tell him, my dick aching for me to take pity on it and join him in this little display. But I hold out. I have to or I'll come within ten seconds of watching him. "What makes you think you can touch it like that?"

The desire in his expression wavers for a moment and he smiles from ear-to-ear. "Yours, huh? Never took you for the possessive one. You jealous of my hand?"

Yes. I want it to be my mouth.

But I'm not about to give him the satisfaction of admitting I want him coming on my chest or down my throat rather than in a shower over a thousand miles away.

God, I'm well and truly fucked here.

"I'm not just talking about your cock, Kee," I growl out the words. "I'm going to lick every inch of your body before fucking you so hard, you have no choice but to remember what I'm about to tell you. No *option* but to hear me when I say this." I lick my lips and lower my voice, my eyes locked on the hand still wrapped around his cock. "You. Are. Mine. You belong to me and me alone."

I hear a soft intake of breath before Keene visibly *shudders* at my words. It makes me feel on top of the goddamn world, seeing my effect on him mirrors his on me.

"Fuck, Pen." A groan escapes him as his hand moves faster over his shaft. "Why're you not here right now? Why am I in Arizona instead of in your bed?"

"Because you're the best goddamn catcher Foltyn has had in years. And because if I was there right now..." I trail off, swallowing. "I don't think I could stop myself from railing you into the goddamn tile wall of that shower."

"I want that," he pants, his head lulling back against the wall with his eyes closed. "I want that."

My cock is throbbing and I reach down and squeeze it, doing my best to tamp down the ache, but it's not working. At this rate, watching him alone will have me blowing in my pants like a preteen.

Again.

"You're not ready for me yet," I tell him. "You have to prep. Go get some lube. Use your fingers. Work yourself open, right now. So I can make it good for you."

He swallows, still stroking his cock. His head sinks back against the tile wall, getting lost in the pleasure he's bringing himself. "Keep talking to me, Pen. I'm so close."

"*Keene*," I growl out his name, forcing his eyes to snap back open. He's not coming. Not until his fingers are in his ass and my name is on his fucking lips. "Put your fingers in your ass."

He shakes his head. "No lube."

I lick my lips and squeeze my shaft, refusing to pull myself free. I need my full attention on him. "Use something else. The conditioner."

Keene releases himself instantly, grabbing for the bottle of conditioner. He squirts a small amount on his fingers before rubbing it around.

"In your ass, Kee. I don't have all night." My voice comes out strained. I'm barely keeping myself together as I watch his dick sway when he props one leg up against the wall of the shower stall best he can to get a good angle.

I don't miss his wince as his index finger presses into him either.

"God, it burns."

Shit.

"I know, but it'll get better. I promise. Just breathe."

I don't know this. Not at-fucking-all. I could be cluelessly feeding him lies and it gets a lot worse. But I do know one finger won't be worse than my cock if he isn't prepared for it.

A deep breath leaves him as he starts working his finger inside him, but his leg keeps slipping down the wall, halting him from getting to where he needs to be. Where *I* want him.

"Turn and press your knee into the corner."

He obeys, giving me the most glorious angle to see both his cock and his ass swallowing his finger whole. The new positioning works for him better. He's able to get in deeper and he even starts stroking his cock again after leaning against the wall to his side for better balance.

He's a literal wet dream. Hard and muscled and all man, fucking his fist and his ass at the same time. Giving me my own private show.

My God, I might burst at the seams. Nothing I've ever done has been this erotic.

A soft moan escapes him and his hand starts moving faster again. But I'm greedy. I need more from him.

"Add another finger. Work yourself open for me."

"You're killing me here," he grumbles, his head slanting against the tile. He listens though, and I watch as a second finger starts to ease inside with the first.

"That's it, Kee," I praise him, my voice dripping with heat and arousal, a vice grip around my shaft. I don't even catch the term of endearment slipping past my lips right away. "You're gonna be such a tight fit around my cock, baby. Snug and warm and fucking perfect."

His throat bobs as he swallows. "Fuck, fuck, fuck," he chants, pumping himself harder. Faster. Fucking *frantic*. I can tell the moment he hits the right spot inside his ass—the promised land that is the prostate—because a string of expletives leaves his mouth and cum shoots out of him, coating the wall he's facing.

And my entire body is on fire.

No, I've ignited into an inferno of desire, disintegrating into finely ground ashes as he strokes himself through his climax. Two fingers lodged in his ass. A fist around his cock.

My name leaving his mouth in an impassioned growl, thick with lust.

It's the greatest thing I've ever witnessed. I'm not sure I'll ever be able to wipe this memory from my brain, even if I wanted to.

Keene is a shuddering mess as he pulls his fingers free and starts cleaning up best he can. I can tell he's exhausted from the heat of the shower, the orgasm, and I'm sure from the game he played earlier as well.

But he's smiling like an idiot, so that must be a good sign.

Once he's cleaned himself off as well as the shower, he turns off the water, grabs the phone, and slides down the tiled wall.

"God, that was amazing. I've never come like that before." He runs his fingers through his wet hair, his biceps flexing at the movement.

The sight of them makes me perfectly aware of how hard I still am.

Still, I smile in accomplishment. "Looks like you were right. You have bottom written all over you."

He snorts. "Until you try it and want to take it away from me, the jackass you are."

My throat seizes at his words, my skin crawling slightly at the idea of a role reversal. But I don't comment back sarcastically like I normally would, just hit him with facts.

"You need to keep doing that if you want a dick to fit. I don't want to hurt you."

His eyes roll. "I know that. It's not like I'm gonna try to ride your dick tomorrow or something."

I try to push that image from my mind, because *holy shit,* it might be the hottest thing I could imagine. Keene on top of me, my cock sliding in and out of his ass.

"I want you to be able to take a third finger by the time you're home on Sunday," I growl out. I try not to think about him spending his downtime finger-fucking his own ass over the weekend because the pain my dick is in might actually cause it to combust. "Do you hear me? I want three of my fingers milking your prostate on Sunday night when you get home."

He smiles at me through the phone, still sated and happy as a clam, and lets out a sarcastic, "Yes, *sir*."

My dick officially has a *pulse* at this point. "Call me that again. See what happens next time I have you alone."

Keene just grins wider. "Goodnight, Pen. I'll call you tomorrow."

I swallow, desperate to keep him on the line so I can get off too, yet knowing he needs to rest for tomorrow. "Of course. Night, Kee."

The call disconnects and a massive weight hits my chest, more cumbersome than an anvil being dropped from the Empire State Building. Yet instead of focusing on it, I push it aside for the time being. I have to take care of the insane boner tenting my shorts first before I allow myself to analyze what just happened.

Pulling my cock free, I feel hotter and thicker and heavier than ever. It's almost painful.

Scratch that, it *is* painful and I need some relief. I don't even bother with lube, just spit a few times into my palm before taking care of the ache.

And as I picture my best friend fingering his own ass, I come harder than I ever have in my life.

SIXTEEN

Keene

Our flight lands back in Oregon later than I would like on Sunday evening. I'm down-right exhausted from playing the double header today and my body is literally *aching* from squatting behind the plate all day.

Even though my body is used to this, trained for it year-round, I always feel like an extra on the set of *The Walking Dead* when we play so many games in a row, but especially with going into extra innings last night. I didn't even have time to call Pen after the game before I was knocked out from fourteen innings; just a quick good night text to tell him I'd talk to him today.

That was before one of the games went long today too, making it thirty-five innings total in less than twenty-four hours. Needless to say I didn't have time to do anything but eat and sleep and play ball since Pen and I...*FaceTimed* in the shower on Friday night.

God, even if I haven't had the time or energy to do as he asked and prep myself for him apart from Friday, that phone call has been replaying through my mind at every moment when my head hasn't been focused on the game.

Never in my life would I have thought I'd be fingering my own ass in the shower while on FaceTime with another dude, let alone with Pen. But hell if that wasn't the hottest thing I've ever experienced in my life. I loved every second of it. Not a goddamn thing about the act felt weird or foreign or wrong.

Listening to the deep growl in his voice, obeying his demands, it was *natural*. Instinctual, even. Like my body and my mind just *knew* that if I did what he said, there was no chance in hell I wouldn't enjoy myself.

I wasn't kidding when I told him I've never come harder in my life.

And I want that again. And again and again and a-fucking-gain.

With his fist wrapped around my length, his fingers deep inside me. His tongue even, because I'd be willing to try anything once.

And his cock? Most definitely.

I want his dick inside me like I've never wanted anything more. I want to know what it feels like to be fucked by my best friend. While that might sound and be problematic, I still want it. There's no other person in this world I'd trust with something like this. Only him.

Which makes me insanely grateful he offered himself up for this.

My jeans tighten slightly as I try to stop my train of thought. I'm not exactly looking to be sporting a boner walking through campus. Even if it's deserted at this time of night.

I'd be lying if I said I wasn't glad to be back and able to see him, though.

I barely had time to eat and sleep, let alone talk to him much while I was gone. That's standard for a lot of road trip weekends, but usually at least once a day, I have some downtime. So I don't know if this time it feels different because I really was *constantly* going or because our relationship is...shifting.

Either way, I'm not about to overanalyze it.

But I will say, when I opened my phone to see a *see you soon* text from Pen, one that had a fucking smiley face emoji after it, my stomach did a little flip. Because Pen doesn't smile all that often, and definitely not in texts with emojis.

And I don't know; it made me feel good. Even in a state of being asleep as I walk on my Jell-O legs into our dorm, I still feel my stomach trying to learn gymnastics. Butterflies or whatever.

I slide my key card into the slot of the door and enter our suite as quietly as possible, surprised to find a lamp left on in the living area. It's almost one in the morning and I know Pen has to be asleep since he wakes up early—at five in the morning—to run before class on Mondays. And usually every other day of the week.

The guy is legit crazy to wake up that early by choice. I purposely don't have class until after noon on Mondays in the spring semester because of this exact situation, and honestly, even in the fall term, I'd prefer not to learn before ten. What can I say? I'm not an early bird and I have no desire to catch any worms.

Still, there's no way he's awake right now. Which means he left it on for me.

I try not to focus too much on how that realization sends my stomach into more somersaults and fucking backflips.

Slipping quickly into my room and closing the door, I discard my bag and strip down, welcoming the sight of my bed. Even if it's not the best bed in the damn world, it's at least mine. Not in a hotel room thousands of miles from here. From normalcy.

From Pen.

For as long as I can remember, we wouldn't spend more than a few nights, a week at most, away from each other. Sure, we lived in our own homes, but our bedroom windows faced each other from across the street for our entire lives. It was just the way things were between us. Even shared a bed on occasions, and there was never a time when it became *a thing*. Even at sixteen, we'd sleep in the same damn bed, no issues to be found.

I mean, it's not like we *snuggled* or anything. Hell, most of the time he'd flail to the point where a pillow ended up lodged between us, anyway.

But now...

I shake my head, trying to shake off the thoughts I'm having. It doesn't seem to work, though. Instead I find myself tiptoeing out of my room, under the impression I'm going to grab some water from the small kitchenette we have in our suite. Which I do. But as soon as it's gone, I find myself at his door.

It's slightly cracked, the way it always is. He hates sleeping with his door closed completely, though that's one thing I've never asked why. Just like he always has a thunderstorm podcast playing while he sleeps. Things I don't question anymore, they're just *Pen things*.

Peering into his room like this sets me on edge and I feel creepy as hell. But God, all I want is to curl up next to his warm body right now. Let his presence soothe the ache in my muscles and in my chest from being away from him the past few nights.

Damn, I sound like a needy bitch right now.

Still, it doesn't stop me from crossing the room and peeling back the covers from his bed, sliding into place beside him.

He's facing the wall, not stirring at all as my weight shifts the mattress. It's not 'till I turn on my side and wrap my arm around his waist beneath the sheets that he literally bolts upright in the bed.

"It's just me," I whisper, grabbing his hand.

"Kee?" My nickname comes out filled with sleep and gravel. It's sexy as hell, even more so than the dominating voice he used with me while I showered the other night.

Goosebumps rise on my skin at the thoughts reappearing, though I'm not about to act on anything. I'm too exhausted to even think about blowjobs or hand jobs or even making out. My body might dissolve into a puddle of goo if I have to do anything other than sleep for the next ten hours.

"Yeah, it's me. Go back to sleep."

He lets out a soft groan before stretching and sliding back down into place beside me. A warm, muscular arm reaches around me and pulls me against him, and I almost stop breathing when he nudges his head into the crook of my neck.

"You turn off the light I left on for you?" He speaks the question into my shoulder as I slip one arm under him, the other over him. His hot breath on my skin has me on full alert.

My words come out mangled. "I did. Thanks."

He pulls me tighter against him, our bare chests pressing together as our legs tangle. Holding me closer than he ever has dared before as a kiss is pressed to the side of my head.

And I can't breathe. We've never been this close. He isn't affectionate. *Ever*. But right now, it feels like...fuck, I don't want to think about how it feels.

Then he rests his forehead against mine, and I can't stop myself from snaking my hand up to the back of his head to hold him there. Never fucking let him go. Not until I ingrain every second of this moment in my mind.

"I'm so tired," I grumble after a few quiet beats, rubbing my nose against his. "But my mind is still wired from the games."

Just the game. Not about how whatever is happening right now might send me to my grave from asphyxiation or a heart attack.

A low rumble comes from deep within his chest and throat. "Do you want to talk it out?"

I glance up at the ceiling where his fancy-ass alarm clock projects the time, telling me it's almost one-thirty in the morning. Less than four hours from when Aspen wakes up.

I feel guilty as hell for waking him up in the first place. No way will I make it longer.

I shake my head, my forehead brushing against his. Fingertips trace along my spine, then up to my shoulders where he starts drawing random lines and shapes with the heat of his skin.

It's an act I'm becoming dangerously attached to, even if it's the first time I've ever felt it.

But it's soothing and loving. Exactly what I need to calm my mind, even if it causes my heart to pound in return.

"I'm fine."

"You sure? I watched both games. I swear, I don't mind."

I smile. Of course he did. He always watches my games. And I'd almost believe him about staying up to talk through them with me if it weren't for him turning away to yawn before nuzzling against me again.

"Yeah, I'm sure you don't." I laugh softly, running my hand through the closely cut sides of his hair, up into the long strands he keeps on top. It's so silky and smooth and smells like his shampoo as I rustle it. I could play with it all day and never get bored of it slipping between my fingers.

"Mmm. Feels good," he murmurs, his lips brushing mine as he speaks the words. It emboldens me to take them for a few seconds in a gentle kiss. It makes him smile against my mouth. "That does too."

I can't help but grin back. "Go back to sleep."

"Mmm," he mutters again before pressing a kiss to my lips once more.

The pads of his fingers continue to dance over my skin for another five minutes or so before coming to rest. His breathing evens out, but just when I think he's back asleep and surely not going to remember a goddamn thing from this encounter, he lets out a soft whisper.

"Hey, Kee?"

"Yeah?"

"I missed you."

My stupid heart squeezes. "I missed you too, Pen."

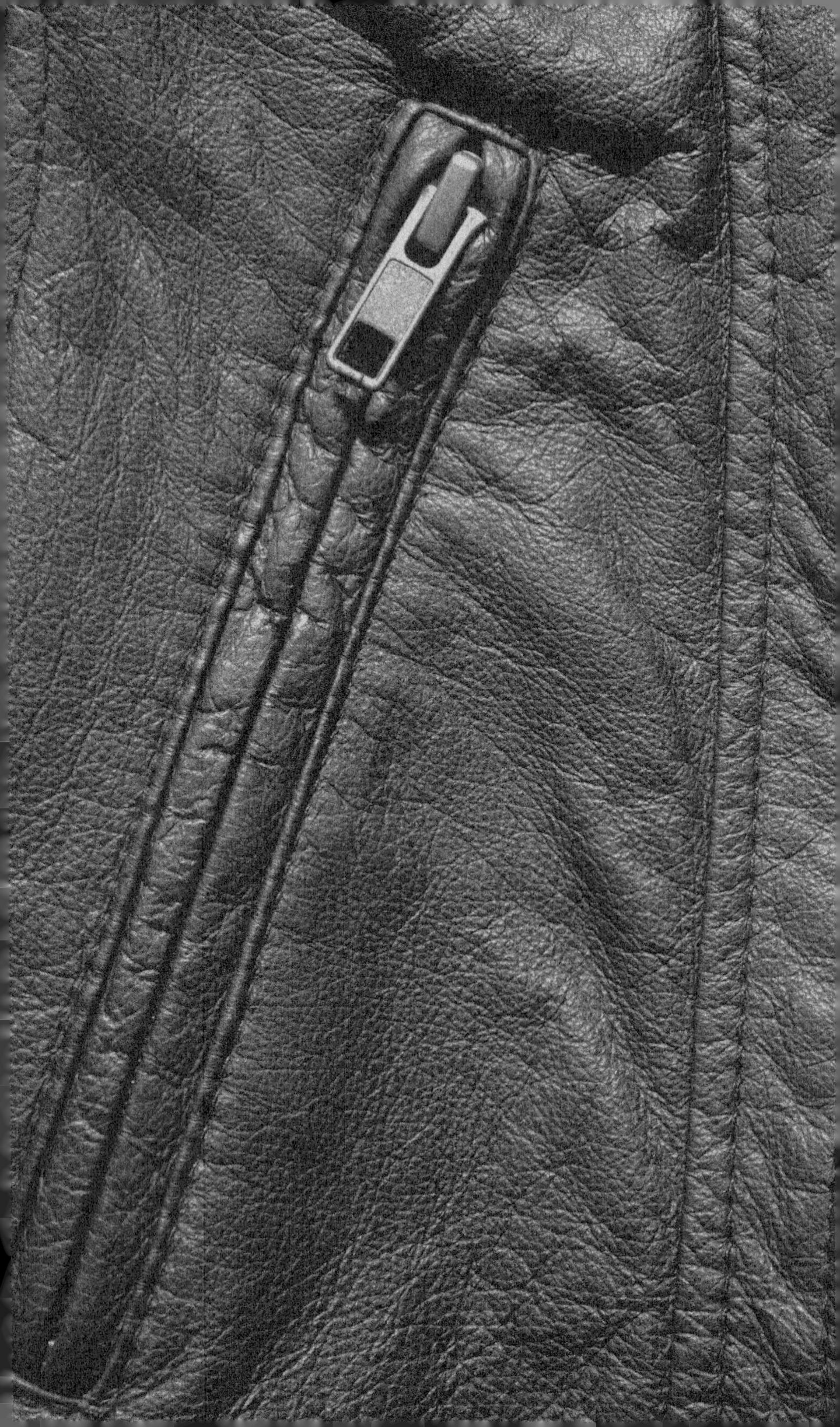

SEVENTEEN

Aspen

The Friday following Keene's Arizona trip rolls around quickly, and since the Wildcats are home this weekend, it means more nights of him here with me instead of some stupid hotel room in another state. Which, as much as it shouldn't matter to me, I'm grateful for.

Ever since the morning I woke up after he returned from Arizona to find him in my bed, half of my body sticky with sweat since he's a literal space heater, I've come to crave more contact with him. And as much as I despise sharing a bed with anyone—and Keene takes up more room than any girl I've ever had sleep over—I can't help but love waking with our limbs tangled together.

It's just…different with him.

I'm different with him.

He hasn't tried to crawl in my bed since, but I'm to the point where I don't think I'd stop him if he tried. In fact, I think I'm more disappointed he *hasn't* snuck in here in the few days since. Besides, I'd love nothing more than to wake him up with a blowjob in the middle of the night, one of these days. Which I haven't gotten to do yet, since he keeps denying me the chance.

I could be a little more vocal about it, or maybe even forceful and take what I want…but when this whole thing started, it was about Keene and *his* sexual exploration. It was never meant to be about me and what I want to do to him. I guess I can't really complain either, because *damn* is his mouth talented, but I haven't done much more than fuck him with my fist, and it makes me wonder if there's a reason *why* he doesn't want my mouth on him.

The only thing I can think of is that he thinks I don't want to give back to him.

It definitely seems that way, no matter how ludicrous the theory is. I love sex, and Keene knows that. Add in that I definitely love what Keene and I are doing together, so why wouldn't I want to make him feel as good as he makes me feel?

But I can't lie; I'm craving him. To know how he tastes and feels sliding over my tongue. And the last thing I want is my partner in the bedroom to feel like I'm not giving them the same amount of attention they give me.

I'm a tit-for-tat kind of guy.

Which is how I end up basically sprinting to his room after cutting out of my studio early today, ready to start making some demands of him. Namely, to let me suck his dick until he begs me to stop.

Except when I burst through the door of his room to find him lying across his bed—sans shirt, as fucking always—he shoots a glare at me and snaps his laptop closed before pulling it closer to his stomach. I halt in the doorway, taking in the slight scowl on his face.

Whoa. What the hell?

"What're you doing?" I ask slowly, taking in the blush creeping from his cheeks down his neck—a telltale sign of his embarrassment.

"Nothing," he says a little too quickly. "Just some homework."

I give him a knowing look, my brows arching as I cross over to him. "Really? Then why do you look like you were about to rub one out to some porn?"

One of the benefits of knowing Keene as well as I do is that I'm able to read him way too easily. He doesn't even have a chance to hide the guilt on his face before a smile breaks across my face.

"Oh my God, you totally were." When he doesn't respond, the blush now starting to spread to the top of his pecs, I let out a laugh. "If you wanted to get off, you could've just waited for me to get home."

In fact, now that I'm here…

He frowns, his hands tightening on the laptop. "Maybe I wanted a solo session, okay?"

The corners of my lips curl up at the lie, which I know it absolutely is, because who the fuck would prefer to masturbate over someone else's hand or mouth?

"If you say so," I say with a shrug before plopping down on the bed and crawling up beside him. His frown deepens as he watches me settle in, my back against the wall and thigh pressed against his. "What?"

"Don't you have something to do?"

I shake my head. "Nope. So what're we watching?"

He lets out a long-winded sigh, his eyes sinking closed as he taps his fingers on the laptop. If I didn't know any better, I'd think he's counting to ten, so he doesn't murder me or something.

"If you're actually planning to be a dickhead by staying in here, you can't judge me. I was just…retrying something you'd suggested."

What?

I'm completely lost on what he's talking about…until he lifts the laptop open, and my eyes take in the screen before me.

And the thumbnail of *two men* making out naked on a couch is the one pulled up.

Oh, shit.

"Gay porn," I say softly, trying to keep the surprise out of my voice. I must not manage it very well, though, because Keene aims another glare at me.

"I said, no judgment."

"I'm not judging," I say quickly. "Just…observing."

"Great observation, Pen." He rolls his eyes. "So now that you know it's gonna be two dudes fucking, will you go?"

I honestly wasn't prepared to watch gay porn with him. Hell, I wasn't really prepared to watch any porn with him for more than five minutes before jumping him. But my curiosity on how *I'll* react to this is planting me firmly in the *hell no, I'm staying* category.

Instead of answering though, I smirk and ask, "Don't you dare?"

His nostrils flare, the pink on his cheeks returning when he realizes where I'm going with this. "I hate you so much."

"No, you don't. Now answer."

The tick of his jaw makes me think he'll actually say no and tell me to get the fuck out so he can have some privacy. So when he whispers *fine*, my stomach does a little flutter of happiness. And maybe a little bit of nervousness too.

"I dare you to let me stay and watch with you."

I think I hear him mutter something along the lines of *Jesus, take the wheel* before he looks at me, his entire face as red as a tomato now.

"If you start doing anything stupid, I'm kicking you out." I go to reply, but the second I open my mouth, he glares and says, "I'm dead serious, Pen."

All I do is nod in acceptance of his terms, then he clicks into full screen and hits play before setting the laptop off to his side where we both can see it.

I'm not really sure what I was expecting of gay porn, but it sure wasn't to start off with one dude on his knees while he straight up deep throats another dude's cock within the first five seconds. And though I know it's porn and it's actors who are literally paid to fuck, these guys make it look easy to take an eight or nine incher to the hilt.

It's impressive.

"Damn," I whisper, my eyes wide as I flick my attention to Keene briefly before moving back to the screen.

It took Keene a few tries to really get the hang of taking me as deep as this guy on the screen is—and while I'm a good size, I'm not nearly as thick—but he made it look pretty easy too.

Which makes me wonder if…is it even that hard to deep-throat a dick?

From all the girls I've been with, they made it out to be a challenge. Then again, none of them were nearly as enthusiastic about my cock as Keene is.

I watch as the scene shifts, the guy who was sucking now bent over the arm of a couch as the other one fingers the hell outta his ass. Like, he's really pounding into him, and I swear, something like that should hurt like a motherfucker. Yet from the pants and moans coming through the laptop speakers, the dude getting finger-fucked is loving every second of it.

Keene shifts beside me, one hand coming to rest on his lap as he discreetly tries to adjust himself without me noticing. I notice, though. Because Keene's reaction to this is far more interesting than the acts playing out on the screen.

Even when the top slides inside his partner and starts fucking him hard and relentlessly, I'm still more entranced by Keene. Literally, these two guys on the screen are going at each other like they're starved animals and it does nothing for me. I'm not hard or turned on in the slightest. Which should be confusing as hell for me, considering how hot I get just looking at Keene without a damn shirt on.

Who—speaking of—is now pitching a rather impressive tent beneath his sweats while his attention stays fixated on the screen.

He's liking it, apparently.

But it's *that* sight—of Keene's arousal, rather than the porn—that finally gets my cock perking up behind my shorts.

Huh, how 'bout that?

The memory of him in the shower the other night as he came apart by his hands and my words floods my mind as I stare at him. That was basically live action porn, so why did that get me geared up and ready to go, but this isn't?

It makes no sense to me, no matter how I try to rationalize it, so I'm done trying to figure it out. I'm just gonna go with it instead of overthinking things like I always do.

This is sex. Sex with Keene turns me on. That's all that matters.

Keene clears his throat, the hand resting across his stomach adjusting his hard-on again briefly. I swear I even catch him giving the tip a little squeeze, a clear indication of trying to calm himself down while I'm still in the room.

But I have *zero* intentions of letting him take care of that by himself.

"This getting you hot?"

He glances down at his obvious erection before his gaze—practically searing with heat—lands on me. "Not at all."

My lips twitch into a smile, and I catch his attention moving to my dimple. "Damn shame."

"It really is," he says, a sharp laugh coming from him before his attention moves back to the screen. "Guess I better keep watching."

He can keep watching all he wants, but I'm over this shit. Nothing's turning me on more than he is right now, seeing his want and desire before me plain as day. Which is how I find myself leaning over him until my lips press against the column of his throat, just below his ear.

His breath hitches before his hand lands on my thigh, latching on tightly as he arches his neck to give me better access. My cock is aching now behind the zipper of my jeans as I continue to explore him with my mouth, tasting him as I lick and kiss a path down his neck until I reach his collarbone. It protrudes slightly, forming a smooth ridge beneath his skin that I map with my tongue.

"Fuck," he groans, his grip on my thigh tightening. "What're you doing?"

"Exploring," I murmur into his skin. "Just keep watching."

Before he can disagree, I slide further down his body, stripping him of all clothing along my way. His cock slaps against his stomach, hard and waiting for me, but I plan to take my time with him. Add in a little torture to the pleasure I'm about to give him.

My tongue slides down his abs before paying special attention to the smattering of freckles near his belly button, looking eerily similar to the constellation of Orion's Belt. At least, that's what I've always seen them as, since for as long as I can remember, I've been obsessed with Keene's freckles. That might be weird, but as someone who has absolutely none, I'm mesmerized with his and how they darken and seem to spread when his skin takes a deeper, golden tan in the summer.

When we were kids, I used to joke about connecting all the dots across his back and shoulders. Even pulled out a Sharpie one time when we were in elementary school to give it a whirl, but didn't get to even press the ink to his skin before his mom put a stop to the shenanigans.

"Pen," he rasps, a mixture of want and need in his voice as a hand slides into my hair.

Slowly, I lift my gaze to meet his eyes. I'm not prepared for the sheer amount of lust darkening his to damn near black. He's not even paying attention to the screen anymore, his attention completely locked on me.

"Yeah?"

He swallows hard and his eyes slam shut again, almost pained. And when they reopen, I understand that he really is in pain. Maybe not physically, but emotionally.

He's at war with himself. Caught in a battle between whatever is rampaging through his head and the want his body is feeling. It's more than evident in his voice when he lets out a ragged sigh and murmurs, "You don't have to."

And it hurts. Damn, it fucking hurts to hear how much he wants this, but he can't bring himself to ask for it. Demand it, even.

My tongue lashes against his tip, the bead of pre-cum hitting my tongue with a salty tang. He hisses out a curse, the hand in my hair tightening painfully, but nowhere near as much as the ache in my chest or throat when I see that look in his eyes, barely discernible in the dim light.

"I want to," I mutter, the hand still wrapped around his shaft stroking him slowly. Tentative and unsure.

If he asks me to stop, I will. I'll get up and go for a run to clear my head. Do my best to forget the sting of rejection from the one person on this Earth I'm not equipped to handle it from.

He licks his lips, searching my face. "Are you sure? I don't want you to think—"

"I want to, Kee," I say again, more firmly this time. "Let me make you feel as good as you make me feel every time the roles are reversed."

The uncertainty etched into his features doesn't lessen as he nods once, loosening his grip on my hair.

"Tell me if I'm bad at this," I murmur, still holding his stare. "Show me what you need. I want it to be good for you."

He cracks a small smile, then. "I doubt I'll even last long with a view like this."

I smirk and lower my head more, taking the entire tip of his cock in my mouth while still holding his gaze. Hollowing my cheeks, I give him a firm suck and watch his eyes roll back into his head.

"Oh, fuck. Do that again and this will be over before you know it."

Being the asshole I am, I do it two more times, drawing out the sexiest groan from deep within his chest. The sound, mixed with the soft sounds of sex coming from his laptop, has my own dick throbbing painfully and my balls seizing up with anticipation. But it also gives me more confidence to take him deeper in my mouth, seeing just how much I can handle.

Letting instinct take over, I bob up and down on his length while I cup his balls in my palm, tugging on them gently. He rocks into my hand, seeking more of what he likes, and it makes me smile around his dick.

Going down on Keene is *nothing* like going down on any girl I've ever been with. And not just for the obvious reason of *he has a dick and not a pussy*. It's just…all around different.

The musky taste of his skin and the saltiness of the pre-cum on his tip. How hard and smooth his shaft feels slipping in and out of my mouth. And the way he responds to my touch; it's like nothing I've ever experienced before.

He's rough with me, keeping his fingers anchored tightly in my hair as I work him over. Unashamed in the way he pants and groans when I cup his balls in my hand or take him deep enough to gag. And hearing, seeing, *feeling* him so turned on only makes me hotter for him.

I try to take him deeper, the way that guy in the video was doing, inhaling through my nose to let him slide to the back of my throat. But the second I do, I start to gag even more.

Jesus Christ, please don't let me vomit on his dick mid-blowie.

Keene inhales sharply as my throat constricts around his length, loosening his grip on my hair to gently pull my mouth off him. My hand takes over where my mouth was, jacking him in long, measured strokes as I raise my gaze to his. Brown eyes full of trust and desire stare down at me, and I can see the flush painted across his cheeks even in the dim light.

He huffs out a breath before sliding his hand down to my cheek. His thumb brushes over my bottom lip, which I'm sure is swollen to hell from blowing him, and the sweetness in his touch has my stomach doing backflips.

"What's wrong? I—"

A grin forms on his face, and he shakes his head. "Not a damn thing could be wrong right now, Pen. Not one goddamn thing." His tongue wets his lower lip, my eyes greedily tracking its entire path.

My brows furrow. "Then why'd you stop me?"

"Because, as much as I love the thought of you deep throating me, you don't have to take the whole thing to get me off. Just do what you're comfortable with." He traces his thumb over my lip again before pulling it away. "I promise, everything you're doing feels fucking amazing."

Do what I'm comfortable with.

Sounds simple enough, so I push back at the slight niggle of insecurity and go back to my task of making Keene come apart for me in the best way. And it only takes a few minutes to get him completely primed and ready to explode all over again.

"Mmm, more tongue," he coaxes, his hips rising in shallow thrusts to meet me. "Along the bottom."

Doing as he asks, I glide my tongue along the underside of his shaft, paying special attention to the sensitive spot just below the head. Then for good measure, I lightly scrape my teeth along the same path as I pull him back so just the head is in my mouth.

"Fuck, yes. Just like that, Pen."

Pride surges through me, emboldening me to take things a step further. To something else we just watched happen on his laptop.

One hand slides down between Keene's thighs, bypassing his balls altogether in search of his taint. My thumb runs along the sensitive patch of skin, and his cock twitches between my lips at the contact.

"If your goal is to kill me, you're almost there," he pants, rolling his hips a little quicker.

His shaft thickens against my tongue as I continue to bob and suck, teasing the head as I continue to play with his taint. And when my middle finger reaches back further, brushing over the tight rim of his ass at the same time I suck hard on the head of his cock, he lets out the most tortured sound I've ever heard. Something between a gasp and a moan that could surely wake the dead.

My finger continues circling the ring of muscle in a taunt, my mind all too aware of this line neither of us has crossed yet. Well, *together* at least, because my cock is still aching from the way I watched him finger his ass for me through the phone last weekend.

I wonder if—

Popping off Keene, I pull back and roll toward his nightstand. I fumble blindly in the drawer for the bottle of lube he keeps there as my eyes stay locked on Keene, taking the sight of him in and filing it deep in my memory bank. I quickly strip myself down while he takes over stroking himself, studying me. I remove every article of clothing from my body, my skin heating where his eyes eat me alive, before I take the lube in hand and coat my index and middle finger with the cool liquid.

"Are you gonna…" He trails off, and lets out a rough exhale. "I don't know if I'm ready—"

"I'm not fucking you, Kee," I assure him, moving back between his legs. My fingers move down, sliding over his taint and circling his rim slowly. A soft chuckle escapes me, because holy shit do I ever want to drive my cock inside him right here and now. But—

"Honestly, I don't think I'm ready for that yet either. We need to work our way there. Together."

He runs his tongue over his bottom lip. "But on the phone last weekend. You said—"

"I know what I said," I cut him off. "But that was just to get you hot and hard and coming for me. I wanted to see you fall apart while I watched, wishing I was there to make it happen myself. My fingers"—I press the pad of my thumb against his ass, and he gasps—"the ones inside you. My hand"—I take his cock in my free hand and stroke—"the one wrapped around you."

"Jesus Christ," he breathes, his hips rising off the mattress as he seeks more of the friction my palm is giving him. "Don't you dare stop."

I smirk at his unintentional use of our game and keep stroking him while moving to start working a finger inside him. He swallows hard, moving and fucking himself further on the digit, until my knuckles brush against his ass cheeks.

It's a damn sight to see, Keene splayed out below me and at my mercy.

"You should see yourself right now," I murmur, squeezing his tip on the upstroke. "Watching you do this for me on video is nothing compared to being the one actually touching you."

"Having it be you is a thousand times better," he rasps in agreement.

Sliding my way back down his body, I bite and nip at his abs before my tongue dips into his belly button and continues the path back to his cock. He lets out another shuttering gasp, his ass clenching around my finger.

"Did you work yourself up to three like I asked?" I murmur against his hip, thrusting a second finger inside him. The groan it elicits has my cock aching even more to be inside him.

"I thought you said you weren't fucking me?"

"I'm not." *Today, anyway.* A grin creeps over my face at the thought of stretching him with my dick one day soon. "I just want to know how much more you can take before you come down my throat."

Because make no mistake about it, I'm not bitching out. Keene's swallowed every damn time he's blown me, so there's not a damn chance I'll be doing anything different right now.

Taking his cock in my mouth again, I swirl my tongue around the tip before playing with the slit.

My fingers curl up on the out stroke, searching for his prostate. It takes a few passes, and I know the second I find it because he lets out a chain of expletives a sailor would gape at.

"Ohholymotherfuckingshitgod," he babbles when I swipe over it again.

His cock twitches against my tongue, and I can tell he's close. Right there on the edge, exactly where I want him to be.

My hips grind into the mattress, desperation clawing at me while he continues to push himself onto my hand. Every drive up has him thrusting into my mouth before sinking back on my fingers, and I let myself get lost in it. In the way he takes what he needs from me, unashamed and unrelenting.

It might be the sexiest thing I've ever seen.

"Pen. I...I—"

The grip he has on my hair tightens, his cock throbbing in my mouth as I register what he's trying to tell me. He's there, about to come, and I'm dying for it.

But nothing could prepare me for the way my body would react from the first burst of cum hitting my tongue, because the second I taste his release, my own hits me like a fucking freight train.

I moan around his cock, rutting myself faster against the mattress as I milk both our cocks dry before easing into the state of post-orgasmic bliss. Keene doesn't let me linger there for long, though, before he's grabbing my arm and tugging it up.

"Get up here," he demands. "Want my mouth on you."

I shake my head, pressing a kiss to his V. "No need."

"Pen, I'm serious," he says, pulling at my arm again.

"So am I," I murmur, nuzzling against his softening cock. "I'm all good."

"So you're just gonna—" He cuts himself off, his fingers raking through the hair on the top of my head before pulling them enough to make me look at him. His eyes narrow in on my face. "Did you come in your shorts again?"

Well, I'm technically naked, but...

I groan, yanking my head free from his hold to rest my forehead against his taut stomach. "Any chance we can pretend this never happened?"

He lets out a deep belly laugh before dragging me up his body. The second his mouth lands on mine, any sense of embarrassment is gone. All I can focus on is his tongue rolling against mine and the way his palm cups the side of my face.

"Is that a yes?" I mutter, slightly breathless when he finally releases me.

Another chuckle warms my lips. "Not a chance in hell."

EIGHTEEN

Aspen

"I figured it out," I say the next week when we're both lying across my bed.

Glancing up to where Keene's sprawled across the mattress beside me, I find myself smiling because of his presence alone. And it has absolutely nothing to do with the fact that he's shirtless with his textbook laid out in front of him, attempting to study for his history class.

We've taken up studying together a lot more recently, seeing as that's pretty much the only time we can be together with his season in full swing now. And yeah, we do study…in between the hand jobs, blowjobs, and occasional prostate massages, at least. But he made it clear that we're not messing around tonight until he's ready for this test, and like the good best friend and sex partner I am, I've listened.

I even put a pillow wall between the two of us, as if that's enough to keep me from ripping what's left of his clothes off and devouring him like a man starved.

With this sex-ban in place for the evening, I'm also meant to be working on my studio project. It's a productive way to distract myself from the delectable specimen sitting beside me—though it's nearly impossible these days. So my lack of focus has me creating a list on my phone of all the places we're going to visit on our annual road trip this summer, rather than drafting floor plans on my laptop.

"I don't know how you're figuring much of anything out when you're not actually working," he points out. His gaze flicks up to mine, brown eyes piercing me with irritation. "You're a really shitty homework partner, and that's coming from the most easily distracted person around."

I smirk and flick at the brim of the hat resting backward on his head. "My project lasts an entire semester. Your test is tomorrow. I think I can slack off for one night."

He adjusts his hat back into place and glares some more, though this one is not nearly as effective. "Yeah, but how can I stay on task when you're sitting there having a grand time doing whatever it is you're doing. Not working, clearly. It just makes me want to be doing anything else but this," he complains, motioning to his textbook.

I can't help but laugh. Maybe our moms weren't far off with this codependency thing after all.

"Well, then how about a teeny, little brain break?" I ask.

I don't wait for an answer, pushing through the barrier of pillows and flopping down on my stomach. My skin heats as I settle in beside him, noting every point of connection between our bodies before holding my phone out to him.

"What do you think about doing another National Park road trip?"

"Which ones?" he asks, taking the device from me and unlocking it with my passcode.

The summer after Junior year, we did all the parks in California over a two-week period. It's actually where I truly found my love for hiking—not at all something I thought I'd enjoy as much as I do.

Anything outdoorsy, hiking included, has always been Keene's thing more than mine. I've always been an inside person, preferring to spend most of my time gaming unless I'm messing around with my camera. But when Keene suggested I take my camera with us on the trails to take some landscape shots, the whole game changed.

I'd never messed around with landscapes before, being more of an urban photographer since we grew up in the city. Capturing candid photos of people on the bus or shots of some of my favorite buildings in the city were my main subjects.

To say I fell in love with nature on that trip would be the understatement of the century, and I have Keene to thank for it.

"Well," I say, reaching over and tapping on the image folder I've been compiling over the past couple hours, "I was thinking we could hit all the ones in Utah. Maybe even—"

"Utah in the middle of summer?" He barks out a laugh. "We're gonna die from heatstroke if we do that."

I roll my eyes. "Always with the theatrics. Are you sure you're not a drama major? It'd be a far better fit."

The shove he gives me with his foot is almost enough to push me off the bed, even from this awkward angle. I always seem to underestimate the strength in his legs, despite knowing he literally does squats on a daily basis by being a catcher. Which…could definitely be useful down the line if I ever want him to ride my dick.

The thought makes said dick twitch against the mattress.

"Shut your cakehole, Pen," he says playfully. "Before I make you."

Oh, I'd love to see him try. And if shutting me up means my lips around his cock?

Well, I'm fucking sold.

"We'll put a pin in that," I say slowly. My eyes heat as I crawl back over to him, telling myself to cool it before I end up breaking the one rule he set tonight by jumping his bones.

"But back to more important topics, you've bitched about every option I've given you since the beginning of the term. Quit being so damn picky and then maybe I'd stop calling you dramatic." I grab the phone from his hand, opening my Maps app to show him the route I planned out. "Just hear me out. We could hit all five National Parks in Utah, and if we really wanted, the four in Colorado too. Maybe stop at a couple other hotspots on the way there and back to make a big trip of it. A full month, maybe a bit longer?"

If I had my way, we'd be gone the whole summer. Check out all the parks not just in Utah and Colorado, but even New Mexico and Arizona too. A four corners trip. Spend both of our birthdays out on the road, getting hot and sweaty from the sun during the day, only to shower and do it all over again at night while we devour each other's bodies.

Sounds pretty damn perfect to me.

He asks a couple questions, mostly about dates and costs, uncertainty etched into his features as he continues to flick through the pictures. I answer them honestly, having already worked out most of the details before I mentioned it to begin with.

And who said making plans was a bad thing?

I don't tell him about the ones I've made for his birthday, though—staying in one of those swanky-ass glamping tents for a few nights outside Moab. They're the ones that are air-conditioned and have a freaking bathroom inside, not at all the kind of camping we're used to doing, or the shit motels we've stayed at in the past.

It's expensive as shit, but I know it'll be worth it to see his eyes light up when we get there. Not to mention, Moab has those side-by-side and ATV rentals for us to go explore some canyons on the days we aren't hiking Arches or Canyonlands. Something that's been on the list of things we've both wanted to do on one of our trips.

Overall, I think it's the best way to turn twenty-one besides going to the bars and getting shitfaced. Especially since our fake IDs have allowed that since we started college. And it's so…*Keene*. Everything he'd love, all packed into a couple days of non-stop fun.

His teeth roll over his bottom lip for a few seconds as he looks at the screen before flipping back to the folder of all the places we could hike or sights we could see.

Raising his gaze, it collides with mine, and he asks, "Could we stay in Denver a couple days and catch a Rockies game?"

And that's the moment I know I've got him.

My lips twitch at the corners. "Whatever you want."

"Then…okay. Let's do it."

Hell yes.

"Utah and Colorado, here we come." I grin at him.

His eyes latch on to my mouth as he smiles, two rows of perfect teeth framed by the most kissable lips I've ever seen. And the way my heart thuds harder in my chest at the sight is the main reason I close the space between us entirely, rolling him to his back before taking his mouth.

I knock the hat from his head by sinking my fingers into his hair as his arms wrap around my waist. Warm palms slide under my shirt to find skin, and I shudder against him. We've been doing this for weeks now, and I don't think I'll be getting used to what his touch does to me anytime soon.

"I told you no sex until after I've studied," he says against my lips.

"I don't want sex," I murmur, the truth in those words hitting me harder than anticipated.

"Then what're you doing?" His whisper is gruff and grated when he breaks away from me to meet my gaze. The confusion written in them increases the ache in my chest.

"Just kissing you."

"But...why?"

Because you're mine.

I've said that to him before, in the heat of the moment. But saying it now, it feels so much more...real? So instead of answering, I kiss him again. Needier, this time.

But something doesn't sit right with me, and I can't push the thought away now. Not even his lips are enough for me to let go.

Why the hell am I not trying to get this to lead to sex? That's all this is supposed to be between us. Fun and fucking. That's what we agreed to. That's the rule *I* put in place for us to follow, trying to make sure we didn't cross any invisible lines so our friendship survived.

So it makes no sense for me to be the one to break them, especially as the one who thinks things through before acting. Who knows all actions have consequences, and the fallout of this could be downright catastrophic. A ticking time bomb lodged right next to my heart.

An emotional Chernobyl, leaving only devastation in its wake.

Knowing this, realizing it at this moment, it still isn't enough to stop me, though. So I take his mouth harder, tugging the bottom lip between my teeth until he gasps from the bite of pain. Giving him the tiniest amount that I'm feeling.

His hands grip the front of my shirt, curling it in his fists to pull me closer.

Closer than he should ever dare.

Closer than I should let him, out of self-preservation and fear alone.

But how can I be afraid when everything about him screams things like safety and security and *home?*

My tongue pillages his mouth, coaxing and wanting and taking everything he has to give me. Greedy and aching for it as I burn up in the slow, searing agony that is the war between my head and heart.

When I'm forced to break away for air, I still can't find a molecule of oxygen when I let my eyes wander to his face. His lips, red and swollen from my kiss and the slightest hit of stubble burn, steal my breath.

He reaches up, fingers curling around the back of my neck and brings my forehead down to rest against his. I breathe him in, all citrus and musk and Keene, letting the scent overwhelm me until I'm cocooned in it like a security blanket.

In the safety that is Keene.

At least, I thought so until his breath, hot against my lips, destroys it all with three words.

Not *those* words, but ones that answer thoughts I never spoke aloud.

Ones with the power to detonate that fucking bomb sitting inside my chest.

"You're mine too."

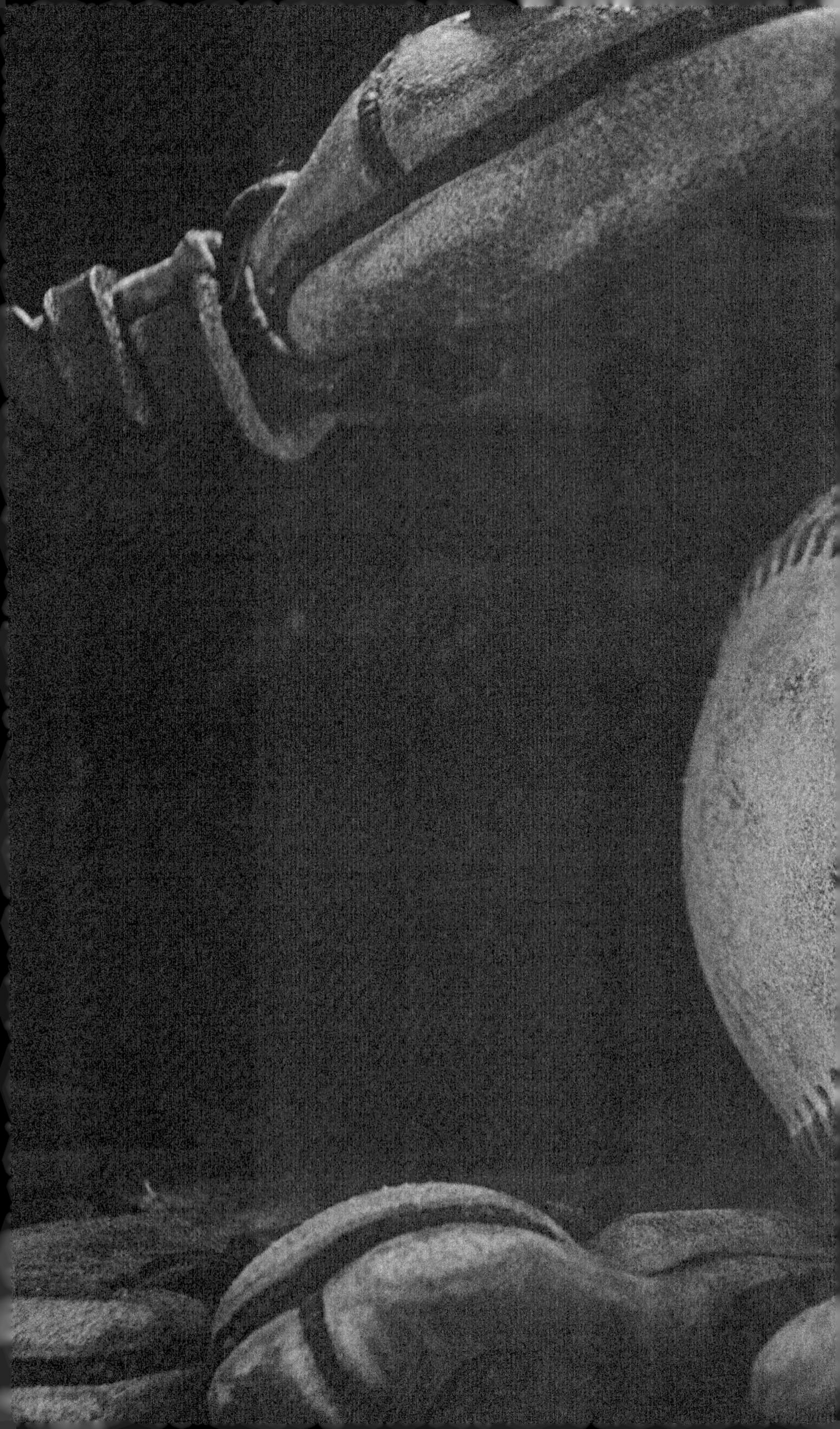

NINETEEN

Keene

March

I have the dumbest smile on my face as I sit on the bus to our away game against Washington, and it's all because Pen and I are having a conversation consisting of only GIFs. It's stupid and not in any way a real conversation, but here I am, grinning at my phone like an idiot anyway.

It's been a few weeks since my last away series, and I was really starting to enjoy all the time on our home field and being able to sleep in my own damn bed.

Or Pen's bed, that one time. Which is where I want to be *every* night, but I know he likes his space. I don't want to infringe on that, best friend or not. Even if the dorm room is the only place I can act the way I want with him, it doesn't mean he always wants me fawning on him or whatever.

Not that I exactly fawn on him…I don't think.

Hell if I know.

Lately, I've been questioning every interaction I've been having with him. The way it makes me feel. The weird, lingering ache in my chest when

I can't bring myself to ask for what I want. For what I crave down to a cellular level.

It's like the night he went down on me for the first time. I couldn't ask it of him because…I don't want to force any kind of sexual exploration on him. Sure, he offered because he didn't want me doing it with anyone else—Pen's protective nature coming out in full swing. Yet, the last thing I need is for him to feel bad for me or do something like sucking cock out of some screwed-up sense of obligation to our friendship.

Lots of hetero guys are friends with guys in the LGBT community. Doesn't mean they have to experiment together because of it.

"Waters!" Coach barks from beside me in his deep, booming voice that scares me enough to drop my phone to my lap when I jump slightly.

"Yeah, Coach?"

"Rooming assignment," he says before looking at his clipboard. "You're with Castle."

"Sounds good," I tell him.

He nods before proceeding further down the aisle, and I let out a sigh of relief. A quick glance up reveals Castle, our second baseman, sitting a few rows in front of me. And while he's a cool kid—albeit, very shy—I can't help the pang in my chest that it's him I'll be sharing a room with tonight instead of the person I want it to be.

I wish, more than anything, Pen could come up for the games against Washington this weekend. After all, the drive isn't too far, but his studio is starting to get more demanding, so he chose to stay behind.

I can still daydream about it, though. If he'd managed to stay at the same hotel as us, I could sneak into his room without Castle knowing and fall asleep with him pressed against me after we defile each other's bodies.

My ass clenches just thinking about it. About his fingers inside me, the warm, velvety heaven of his mouth milking me for all I'm worth. A feeling that hasn't gotten old, even weeks after experiencing it for the first time.

It's almost scary how quickly I've become addicted to getting naked with him. Touching and tasting him, sure, but also the filthy things he whispers to me while my mouth's wrapped around his cock or his fingers are screwed up my ass.

Even more, it's downright freaky how fast I've embraced things like sucking dick and having fingers there in the first place.

By now, it's safe enough to say I'm attracted to Aspen. Absolutely, one hundred percent, no doubt in my mind, not that there ever has been since the damn kiss that started this whole thing. But one thing I've discovered through our hookups is I'm definitely attracted to guys in general. Not *just* Pen.

Now, the thing I'm running into is, the more I feed my attraction to Pen specifically, the less I want anyone else. Take the porn experiment, for example. Once he started getting turned on, it didn't even matter that the porn was there. I didn't even notice the two guys going at each other like two wild beasts after Pen started kissing my throat.

At this point, I don't see anything or anyone besides him.

That happens to be one of the many reasons why I've decided to delete my Toppr profile. At least, for the time being.

With my focus being almost entirely on Pen lately, I'm not feeling it anymore. It doesn't help that I can't help but compare all the conversations I'm having with whoever I match with to the way Pen and I talk to each other. How easy and natural it is, regardless if we're in a friends-only zone or lying naked together and covered in cum. I'm not nearly as comfortable with anyone else.

Not to mention, it just feels wrong to be talking to other guys—or girls, for that matter—while screwing around with him. Almost like it's some form of betrayal. Sure, we agreed on not hooking up with other people while we're doing this, and just texting guys like balls4lyfe on Toppr doesn't really cross into that realm.

Still, it doesn't stop me from feeling any less…itchy.

Which is why I'm currently telling balls4lyfe that I'm not really looking or interested in anything right now. That I've sort of started seeing someone—not a lie—and that I need to focus on that more.

The message is long and far more detailed than it needs to be, considering I don't really owe him anything. After all, I've been keeping him at arm's length a lot more since things with Pen have picked up, not wanting to be the kind of person to lead him on, unintentionally or not.

After reading it over once, I hit send just as the little red dot beside his name turns green, signaling he's now online and updating his location.

Within .1 miles.

I do a double take, rereading the distance before my stomach rolls. Realization hits me like a Mack truck, panic surging through my veins.

Quickly as I can, I delete my account altogether before uninstalling the app from my phone and tucking the damn thing away in my bag. I don't know if he had time to read the message or if it will even show up anymore after deleting my account, but it doesn't matter.

It's better for him to think I flat out ghosted him than to know the truth.

That I'm his fucking teammate.

{{

The high from our wins over the past two days—and the fuckhot phone sex Pen and I had afterward—has long since faded by Sunday morning. I was hoping to ride that wave into today's game, but I guess fate had other plans. We've been a complete and utter shitshow since the beginning of this game against Washington. It's like we're a completely different team than we were the last two days on the field, and while I wish I could say I have no part in the clusterfuck, I'm just as guilty as some of the other guys.

It started out great, going through the first inning with a shutout, thanks to some stellar fielding by Castle, and our shortstop, Reyes. The issue is, Avery's on the mound today, and he's been off ever since he stepped foot on the damn field. Even back in the bullpen before the game started, I could tell something was off with him.

By the middle of the third inning, we're down 4-1, and it's not looking to get any better when the heaviest hitters in our line-up are either struck-out or send dribblers to Washington's infield for easy outs.

By the sixth, I'm ready to demand that Coach pull Avery. Why he hasn't already is beyond my comprehension. He shakes off every other pitch I call, which serves to do nothing but piss me off and hand over hit after hit to Washington until they lead us 8-1. Thank God Reyes is on his game tonight—the only one on the whole team, it seems—because it's his diving catch on a line drive up the middle that gets us out of the inning before more damage can be done.

At least Coach has enough brains to finally pull Avery before we head out in the seventh. Hopefully our relief pitchers can keep the scoring for Washington to a minimum for the rest of the game.

Of course, I'm entirely wrong, and by the top of the ninth, we're looking at a nine-run deficit.

"We're not out of this yet," Coach barks as we head back into the dugout for our final chance at bat. "So get your heads out of your asses and start playing ball like you know how!"

We're completely out of it, actually, but leave it to Coach to give the most bullshit pep talk of the year.

Avery's still not happy about getting yanked, even innings later, because he's slamming around the dugout like the petulant child he is. Apparently, throwing a temper tantrum is something that helps him deal with the way he played today.

Whatever works for him, I guess.

I slide out of my catcher's gear in favor of my bat and helmet, heading out to the on-deck circle to wait for my turn at the plate.

Hanson—Washington's starter—was on fire today, giving up only one run, and we haven't got many hits off him either. The ones we do end up just getting stranded because we can't piece together enough of an offense to push them around the damn bases.

The bad news for us is that his replacement, Jacobs, is just as good.

Just as I'm thinking it, the crack of a bat sounds out as Reyes connects with the ball in a line drive right back where it came from. Elation spikes through me until Jacobs is quick enough to snatch it out of the air a second later.

Damnit.

I step into the batter's box and take my signs from Coach where he's positioned down the third base line. He's telling me to hold off and make the count work for me, not unlike any other time I'm at the plate.

I do just as he says, making Jacobs work for it, no matter how hard I wanna swing at any zingers he throws my way. Especially the fastball that barely clips the inside of the strike zone.

Everyone in our conference knows I have a weakness of inside fastballs. It's a surefire way to get me to swing, even if they're some of the harder pitches to hit. A lot of pitchers and catchers rely on them to get a batter down in the count early on. Hell, I've been known to call for them often when I'm the one behind the plate. But when I've got a bat in my hands? Those pitches are my bread and fucking butter.

I'm up in the count with two balls and one strike when I pull my front foot from the batter's box and look down at Coach. He finally gives me the go-ahead to swing if it's something I like.

Perfect.

My eye stays locked on the ball in Jacobs's hand with precision focus the moment I step back into the box. I watch as he nods to his catcher, taking his sign before hiding the ball in his glove.

I wait for the pitch, the best kind of adrenaline coursing through my veins. The anticipation. The high. It surges through me and makes me feel more alive than I do anywhere else.

When the ball leaves Jacobs's hand, I can already tell it's exactly what I'm hoping for. An inside fastball, just waiting for me to smack it out to the outfield.

But something's wrong.

I realize too late that the ball hurling toward me is a little *too* inside for me to do anything with it at all besides hope to get out of the way.

There's not enough time, though, and the ball collides with my ribs. The wind is knocked out of me instantly, and I drop my bat to the ground and curl into myself on instinct. My knees hit the dirt, my entire side vibrating with bone-searing pain as I gasp for air that won't fill my lungs. It feels like all the oxygen in the atmosphere has suddenly been completely used up.

Coach is at my side moments later, urging me to breathe deeply with a gentle palm on my back. I heave for air a couple times before I manage to finally catch my breath, coughing and sputtering once I finally have a steady flow of oxygen again.

Clapping sounds from around the stadium as I rise back to my full height. Really fucking slowly, because I feel like a kid with asthma trying to run a marathon. The umpire signals for me to take my base, and I make my way down the baseline to first.

In hindsight, trying to get out of the way was probably the worse thing I could've done. Taking a ball to the shoulder or forearm is a cakewalk in comparison to the ribs. It sure as hell wouldn't have been enough to take me to the ground.

"All good?" my first base coach asks when I make it there. "Need a runner?"

Fuck, no, I don't need a runner. My side might be hurting like a bitch, making it difficult to take a deep breath, but there's no way in hell I'm stepping off the field right now. Not when my team needs me.

I'm one of the faster guys on the team, and I need to score in order to have any chance of starting a rally. Getting from here to home plate within the next two outs is the only thing I give a crap about. Not my goddamn ribs, even if they did just take a ninety mile per hour fastball to them five minutes ago.

But none of that matters, as it turns out. Getting a runner, my speed around the bases, all of it ends up being irrelevant when two batters and outs later, I'm still left standing on first.

The entire team is dejected as we shake hands with Washington and head to the locker room for an ass-chewing from Coach. Which, of course, only makes the vibe in the air twenty times worse afterward.

By the time I hit the showers, I'm in immense pain. It lances up my side every time I try to lift my arm or twist my body in a mixture of searing and stabbing, and drying off my skin afterward might as well be the equivalent of sliding a dagger between my ribs.

Back in the changing area, I towel off my hair as best I can before slipping into clean boxer briefs. I move slowly to grab my dress pants next, but as soon as my arm extends, a rough hand lands on my shoulder. I don't have time to react before I'm spun around and pushed back against the wooden cubby. My eyes slam shut as pain ricochets through my side and chest, and when they slide open again, I find my attacker is none other than Avery.

Wonderful.

"Get the fuck off, Avery," I growl. The arm on my good side lifts to give him a shove, but he's just as big as me, if not bigger. One arm against his entire body weight doesn't do jack shit to move him more than an inch, especially when I can barely put any strength behind it.

"You'd like that, wouldn't you," he snarls, pressing into me harder. His forearm digs into my chest and it feels like my ribs are splintering under the pressure. Even worse when his other palm slams against the already-forming bruise on my side from where I was hit by that pitch.

The pain—damn near debilitating—comes rushing back instantly, and I hiss through clenched teeth as it makes my vision go blurred. To the point where I think I might pass out if it doesn't stop. I can't even speak, let alone shout at him to get off me again, or better yet, to leave me alone. The way he's pressing against my injury makes even breathing seem impossible.

"This loss is on you, Waters." The bite in his tone is icy and ruthless as he pushes against me harder. "If you hadn't fucked with my mind by calling all those bullshit pitches, half of those runs could've been prevented."

Yes, because one person on a field with eight other guys has the lone responsibility for winning or losing.

If I had enough air in my lungs to tell Avery that, I would. Or point out the clear flaws in his math skills. The problem is, I literally can't form words, let alone summon the brain power to speak them.

Something he takes advantage of, letting venom drip from his words.

"At least you have your little fuckboy to go home to." The pressure on my ribs increases. "I'm sure he'll make everything all better with a nice, sloppy blowjob."

I grit my teeth and push back against him, but to no avail. In fact, all it does is make his sneer turn into something of a smile, clearly entertained by getting a reaction out of me.

"Aw, is he a sensitive subject? You two get in a fight about which one gets to top when you get home?" He lets out a menacing laugh. "I bet you're the one who gets fucked. All that squatting behind the plate would help you ride your boyfriend's cock better."

Embarrassment and fury surge through me at his insinuation, heating my cheeks. My stomach is seizing from the pain and his wicked onslaught of insults, but I tamp down the vomit threatening to make an appearance. I'm not letting this homophobic asshole see me lose my lunch while he's got me pinned like this.

"Would you cut it with the stupid boyfriend shit?" I snap, finally finding my words before making another futile attempt to shove him off me. "I'm sick of you running your mouth when it comes to Pen."

"And I'm sick of your queer ass walking around here like you're God's gift to baseball."

Either he's delusional or he's lost his damn mind, because that sounds more like something *he does*. Not me.

Something everyone on this team realizes.

And look at that, a quick glance around the locker room reveals quite a few of them gathered around to watch the showdown between us. What's more infuriating is that none of them are making any attempts to stop this.

"Reynolds!" Coach barks loudly from behind where Kaleb's standing. He shoves his way through the team quickly and lands what must be a bruising grip on Avery's shoulder, if his wince is anything to go by. "Unless you've suddenly become the team trainer, I suggest you get your hands *off* Waters."

Avery's nostrils flare, and from the tick of his jaw, he's barely preventing himself from flying off the handle at Coach. Yet, somehow, he does, shoving off and away from me to his cubby after a muttered, *Yes, Coach.*

I gulp down oxygen greedily now that I'm free of his wrath, slumping down to sit at the bench as I wait for the agonizing pain in my ribs to subside. When it still doesn't after a minute, I look up at Coach helplessly.

"Go see the trainer about that side before we get out of here," he murmurs just to me before turning to the rest of the guys. Some are still milling about, watching the outcome of this with interest. "The rest of you, get your shit together and get on the bus so we can get home!"

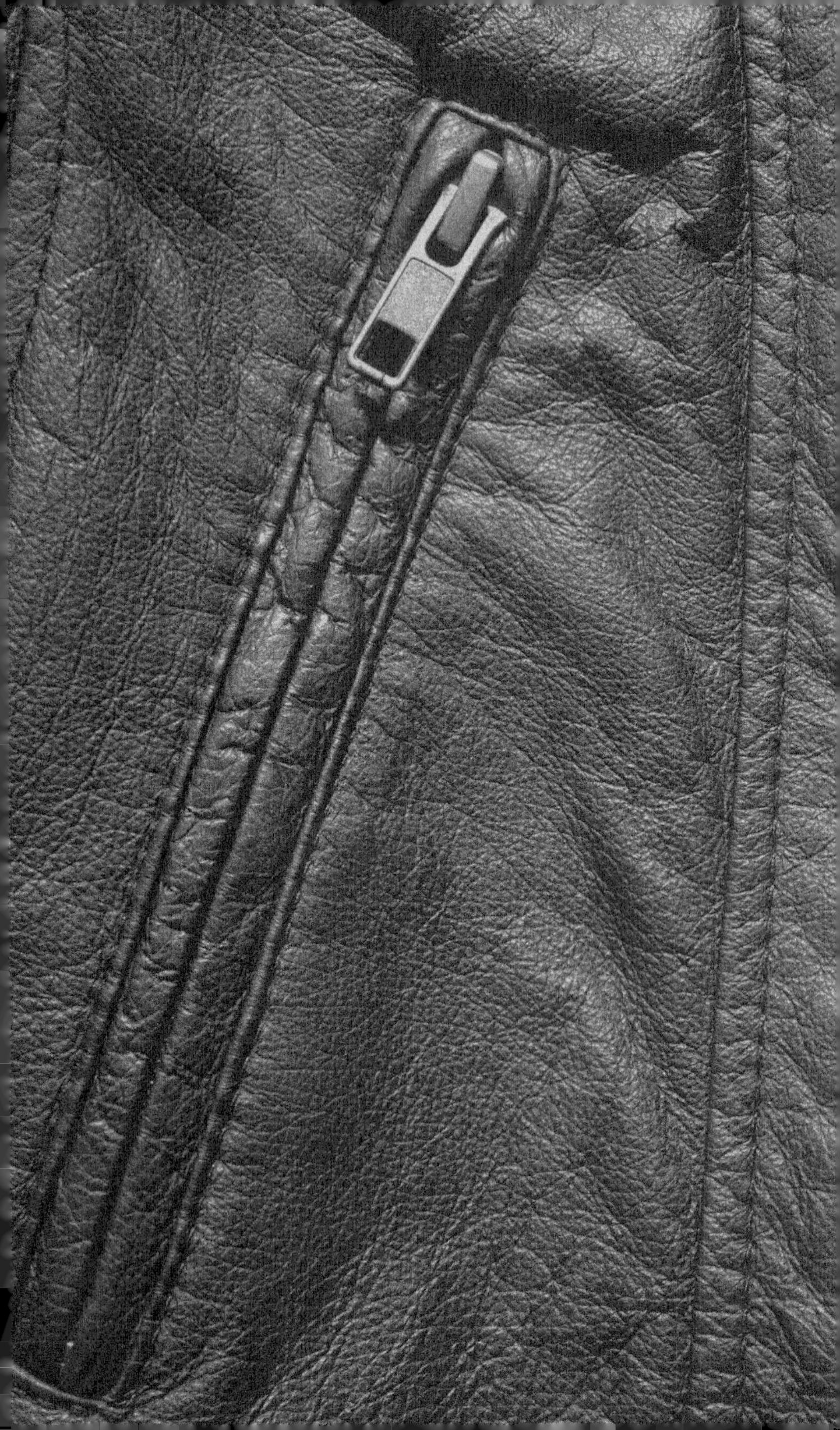

TWENTY

Aspen

I'm on Keene like white on rice the second he walks through the door early Sunday evening. And when I say *walks*, I mean hobbles. I'm watching my best friend *hobble* his way into our dorm. The sight alone has the same anger building inside me as when I saw that jackass from Washington nail him in the ribs during the game.

"Let me see it," I demand, grabbing the strap of his bag from his shoulder.

He frowns, letting the duffle slide into my grip. "Hello to you too, Pen."

I frown right back. "Hello? Really? You get beaned in the side and you wanna start with hello?"

His nostrils flare and instead of answering, he shoves past me toward his room. Not bothering to give me a second look.

What the fuck?

I follow him. Of course, I follow him, my fury only growing. Except now, it's also aimed toward him instead of the dickface who hit him.

He doesn't look or spare me a second glance, speaking straight ahead of him as he pushes open his door. "I was hit by a pitch. Big deal. It's happened plenty of times before."

Dropping the bag next to his door, I cross the room to him and grab his shoulder. "Don't you dare play this shit off, Kee," I snap as I spin him toward me. "Now take your shirt off and let me *see.*"

The minute I see his wince, I know I made the wrong move.

Shit.

His lip curls back in a sneer before he yanks his arm from my hold. "Yeah? Well, I'm not really in the fucking mood to be ambushed and then manhandled the second I walk through the door."

I bite my tongue and step back, putting some space between us when I don't want there to be any. It wasn't my intention to piss him off the second he walked through the door. It's just…

"I know this isn't the first time and it won't be the last," I say, calming myself by clenching and unclenching my hands at my sides. "I've seen it hundreds of times. But I've never seen one take you to the ground like that."

His scowl slowly fades as he fiddles with the hem of his shirt, glancing away from my imploring gaze. "I promise, I'm fine."

My tongue wets my lip and I grab the soft fabric, pulling him back into my space. The words are a whisper off my tongue. "Then show me. Prove it."

He gives me an exasperated look. "Pen—"

I raise a brow. "Don't make me dare you."

A slow smirk crosses his face and he shakes his head. "So stubborn."

"One of my most endearing qualities," I remind him, slowly lifting his shirt up.

He snorts. "If you say so." But then his arms raise, albeit slowly, allowing me to slip the fabric over his head with ease.

Brown eyes heat when they reconnect with mine as I drop the shirt to the floor between us. Neither of us dares break away from the other. I don't even think either of us are breathing when my hand connects with the skin covering his side. The contact is enough to have him glancing away from me.

Clearing my throat, I move my attention to where I'm touching him. I take in the massive bruise across his ribs, my breath hitching as the pads of my fingers trace over the black and blue and purple skin. It's welted and raised in places to the point where I can even see the stitching from the ball in one spot. But what has me wanting to cringe the most is the indentation, making it look like the ball is still lodged into his side entirely.

I've seen Keene's baseball injuries up close and personal before. None of them have ever looked like this.

"This is just from a ball?" I whisper. He winces when I brush over where the skin is raised, the area clearly more sensitive than the rest of the injury.

"Yeah, but I'm fine, Pen. Seriously," he says, trying to pull away from me, but my fingers wrap around his bicep to stop him. He glances down at my hand and sighs. "I've been hit by a pitch plenty of times. You've seen it in person, you've watched it on TV. It's part of the game."

Yeah, but your body wasn't mine *any other time this has happened.*

My attention flicks up to his face and I can tell how much pain he's in, though he's trying not to show it. Between the ball he took to the ribs and spending nine innings behind the plate, he's gotta be hurting. Sore muscles and aching bones.

"Did you take an ice bath for it?"

"Didn't have time there, so I took a quick one in the team's clubhouse before coming home."

He shifts away from me again, and this time, I let him go. He drops onto his bed with a thud, a low groan following as he buries his face in his pillow.

I clear my throat again before saying *stay here*, not bothering to wait for a response.

"Wasn't planning on moving until Monday morning," he calls, slightly muffled as I enter the bathroom.

I quickly fill the tub with steeping hot water, dumping in a few scoops of Epsom salts I know he keeps under the sink after long, rough days. His coach always harps on him about doing both ice baths *and* salt baths after spending the weekend behind the plate, since alternating between the hot and cold can help heal and soothe his aching muscles.

Yet somehow, he always manages to forget the *hot* portion of this cycle, because the container of salts is pretty much full.

A few minutes later, the tub is full with the salts tossed in, and I make my way back to Keene's room to usher him to the bathroom. He fights me at first, refusing to move from his place on the bed, but eventually I manage to get him to agree to get in the damn tub if I order his favorite Italian place for delivery tonight.

That gets his ass up *real* quick.

"Mmm, that looks like heaven," he says, staring at the tub as he starts stripping out of his shorts and underwear.

I busy myself with putting away containers when he undresses, then picking up his clothes to keep my eyes off him while he slides into the tub. A low hiss escapes him, and I'm not sure if it's out of pain or from the heat of the water, but I tamp down the urge to turn and check on him. The last thing I want or he needs is me ogling his body when he's in no shape to do anything about the stupid amount of lust he causes anytime I catch a glimpse of his bare skin.

So instead, I grab a clean towel from beneath the sink as I wait for the sound of water sloshing against the side of the tub to subside as an indication that it's safe to turn around. Even if it's completely idiotic and unnecessary, considering I've seen him naked hundreds of times now.

Something he's quick to point out, which isn't a surprise.

"You should know better than anyone, I'm not exactly shy," he teases. I turn to see that shit-eating grin of his aimed my way from his spot in the tub. "I mean, I answered a FaceTime call in the shower with you."

I feel heat rush to the tips of my ears at the mention of what happened when he was in Arizona, but I fight to keep the embarrassment from sending me to the safety of my room. "I just…was trying to be polite. Not ogle or anything."

"Because knowing you want me is such a bad thing, right, Pen?" His eyes roll. "I fingered my ass and basically made a live porn video for you. I don't give two shits about a little bit of eye-fucking."

He's got a point…

"Fine." I shake my head and take a seat on the edge of the tub, letting my eyes trail over the lines of lean muscle and smooth skin. "So wanna tell me about how things went today? Besides the welt the size of the moon on your side?"

He leans back, closing his eyes as he goes over how the game went before he took a fastball to the ribs. My eyes trace over his face as he talks, grateful for the few minutes to take him in without his knowledge.

He's got a couple bruises and cuts along his forearms, which isn't all that abnormal. His skin looks more tanned, though, and the freckles dotting his cheekbones and nose have darkened some since I saw him Friday.

"I can feel you staring at me," he says suddenly, opening his eyes. "Thought you weren't gonna ogle."

"Just making sure you're still in one piece."

He smirks. "Always the worrier. I swear, I'm fine. But if playing the injured card gets you to grant my every request, I've got one for you."

"And that would be?"

He licks his lips as he takes his time mapping my face with his stare. Unlike me, he doesn't care that I'm watching him, which somehow manages to make *me* more nervous.

It makes no fucking sense.

"Come in here," he finally replies.

"What?"

"You heard me," he replies, doing his best to slide up in the tub to make room for me. The issue is, we're both over six feet tall and nowhere near small. No damn way we both fit in there. *Comfortably.*

"Not happening." I laugh softly, but I stay seated on the edge of the tub beside him to keep him company while he relaxes. I think he gives up on the idea pretty quickly, when out of nowhere, his wet arm wraps around my waist, effectively soaking my shirt and shorts where his skin touches me.

"What the shit?" I ask, attempting to jump up. I don't make it far though, because Keene's arm tightens around me to hold me in place.

"Oh, no," he says in mock innocence. I can practically hear the smile in his voice as he presses his cheek against my back. "How'd that happen?"

I roll my eyes and remove his arm from me, albeit as gently as I can since it's the side of his body that took the hit. He still winces and I immediately regret not letting him keep it there.

"*I wonder,*" I say, my voice laced with sarcasm, but I still don't turn around.

Instead, I reach down and peel my now partially wet shirt over my head, tossing it across the bathroom. My shorts come next, joining my shirt, but my boxers are still dry so they remain on my body as my last layer of decency.

Decency. Right. Because Keene hasn't become very well acquainted with my cock by now.

His forehead presses into my back again when I move back into place. The heat of his skin directly against mine sends a shiver up my spine and goosebumps break out across my body like little zings of lust rippling through me.

"Are you gonna make me get your underwear wet too, or are you gonna take them off willingly and get in here with me?"

The words don't come out much louder than a whisper, a breath of air leaving his lips and sliding over my skin like a siren's call. It makes it almost impossible to deny him a fucking thing.

"We won't fit," I tell him softly.

"I can sit on your lap," he surmises and my dick likes that idea instantly, thickening behind the navy cotton of my underwear.

"You won't get much rest if you're sitting on my cock."

I feel his cheeks tilt up in a smile before he presses a kiss to my back. "Kinda the point there, Pen."

My heart hammers in my chest and my dick swells behind my boxers, loving the all-too-vivid picture he's painting for me.

Though I know I shouldn't, I rise just enough to shed the last layer of clothing on my body. Shifting, I slide into the foot of the tub, hissing as my skin comes into contact with the water that might as well be boiling.

"Jesus, how aren't you cooked right now? Did I make this too hot?"

He shakes his head and smirks. "It's perfect. The hotter, the better."

I shake my head. "Right, I forgot you like to boil yourself alive."

His smirk grows. "Not all of us like our baths to be as cold as our hearts, Pen."

Smartass motherfucker.

Like I assumed, the fit is tight, and that's being generous. Once my shoulders rest comfortably between the spout and the edge of the tub, I stretch out my legs best I can. The only issue is, there's nowhere for them to go unless it's directly into Keene's chest.

Looking up at him across from me, I give him an exasperated sigh. "This isn't gonna work."

"Yeah, it will."

"How—"

Keene does some quick maneuvering of my limbs before I can get another word out, and all of a sudden, we just fit. Perfectly.

He's between my legs, one of my knees bent toward the wall, while the other is outstretched and resting on the edge of the tub over his shoulder. He adjusts his body to match my position from his end. I try not to focus on the way he winces and grimaces whenever his bends or twists too far, biting my lip to keep from saying anything. Drawing even more attention to his injury will only make the entire situation that much worse.

"See?" he says in victory when we're comfortably relaxing in the miniscule tub, suds and salts floating all around us.

I chuckle lightly. "You live to prove me wrong, you know that? It gets you off or something."

His brown eyes heat with a quick flare and he raises a brow at me. "You'd know a lot about what gets me off, wouldn't you, Pen? But the last time I checked, it's usually got to do with your cock or mouth. Not your ability to be wrong."

My teeth sink further into my lip and I glance away quickly before said cock can start to get any stupid ideas. Like dragging him into my lap so we can grind our way to an orgasm, which sounds pretty fantastic right about now.

"What'd you do while I was gone, anyway?"

I wet my lips. "Nothing worth talking about."

His brow raises. "You played video games the entire time, didn't you?"

No, I missed you *the entire fucking time.* Not that I'd ever dare say the words out loud, because they feel like they'd be crossing into territory we really need to stay away from.

Because it's not the normal kind of missing him. Hell, it wasn't even missing the sex the few days he was gone, which is exactly the reaction I should be having if this is just sex between us.

There shouldn't be this…aching need inside me that's been growing for him.

But no matter how I try to deny it, it's there. It's shifted something between us, changed our dynamic already in ways that terrify me.

"You know me so well," I deadpan.

He smiles, big and bright and so fucking Keene. It has my heart stumbling in my chest at the very sight.

Then the shithead goes and ruins it the second he opens his mouth. "I know you better than anyone. Biblically, and otherwise."

The innuendo has my lips twitching, but my heart's still pounding.

When I don't respond, I feel his hand wrap around my foot before hot breaths float over my skin. It ignites my entire body more than the scalding bath water ever could.

He presses a kiss to my ankle bone, moving up on to my calf as far as he can reach without sitting up entirely. Then his hand begins trailing up my leg until it reaches the crook of my knee, fingers dancing along the way.

Just like the way he touched me when I was sitting on the edge of the tub, it sets off goosebumps.

"Does this turn you on? The soft touches?" he asks when my eyes finally move back to meet his gaze.

I swallow harshly when his fingers reach my inner thigh, inches away from my dick. It's been hard ever since I got in the damn tub, my naked skin pressing into Keene's. Now it's on full-out alert and all I can do is nod at him as the other hand starts taking the same path down my opposite leg.

His brow raises, and he smirks. "Really? I would've thought you'd prefer it when it's rougher. Harder. Needier."

Both his hands are millimeters away from my cock as it begs for his attention. He takes no mercy on me though, letting the tips of his fingers graze against the sensitive skin of my inner thighs.

Fuck.

I want him so much, it might kill me. I've *wanted* him for a while now. Craved the way he touches me. Kisses me. Fucks me with his mouth and hand. Like he was crafted by a higher being to know exactly what I need at any given moment.

And that's why I can't bring myself to stop this thing between us, even while knowing we're already in far too deep.

"Touch me," I plead when his thumb grazes the side of my dick. "Please, for the love of fucking God. Just touch me."

His smirk is filthy. "I already *am.*"

"You know what I mean," I mumble, shifting quickly to get his hand on me. But the moment I do, water sloshes over the side of the tub. Keene winces, as if my movement somehow caused him pain, and I freeze instantly.

Shit.

His eyes flash to mine and he must read my fear all over my face, because he smirks again and shakes his head.

"I'm *fine.*" His chuckle is deep and throaty, and the genuine sound of it instantly puts me at ease. Then he glances over the edge of the tub. My eyes follow suit, and I instantly realize why he winced, because the floor is completely soaked.

"Oh, fuck." I laugh.

"You put way too much water in here for both of us."

I shoot him a look. "It wasn't originally for *both of us,* asshat."

He grins, his fingers returning to my legs again. "Maybe, but it's a lot more fun this way."

My lip twitches, a smile forming because, yeah, he's right. I don't have the chance to tell him that though, because his hands grip the outside of my thighs and he drags me to him.

An awkward laugh slips out as he pulls me into his lap, more and more water sloshing over the edge of the tub. "What do you think you're doing?"

His smile is both devious and shy when he looks up at me through those stupidly thick eyelashes of his. "Well, seeing as you already decided the water belonged on the floor, I wanted to play along."

I snort out a real laugh this time, shaking my head. "Naturally."

"Of course," he murmurs. His expression softens slightly as his eyes roam my face. "And it's definitely not an excuse to touch you after being apart for three days."

My tongue darts out over my bottom lip, and I swear I can feel his cock thicken beneath me as he watches. "Not at all, hmm?"

Keene's eyes are half-mast and full of heat as they flick back up from my mouth. He shakes his head, the hand on his good side coming up to cup the back of my neck.

"Absolutely not," he whispers, pulling my mouth to his.

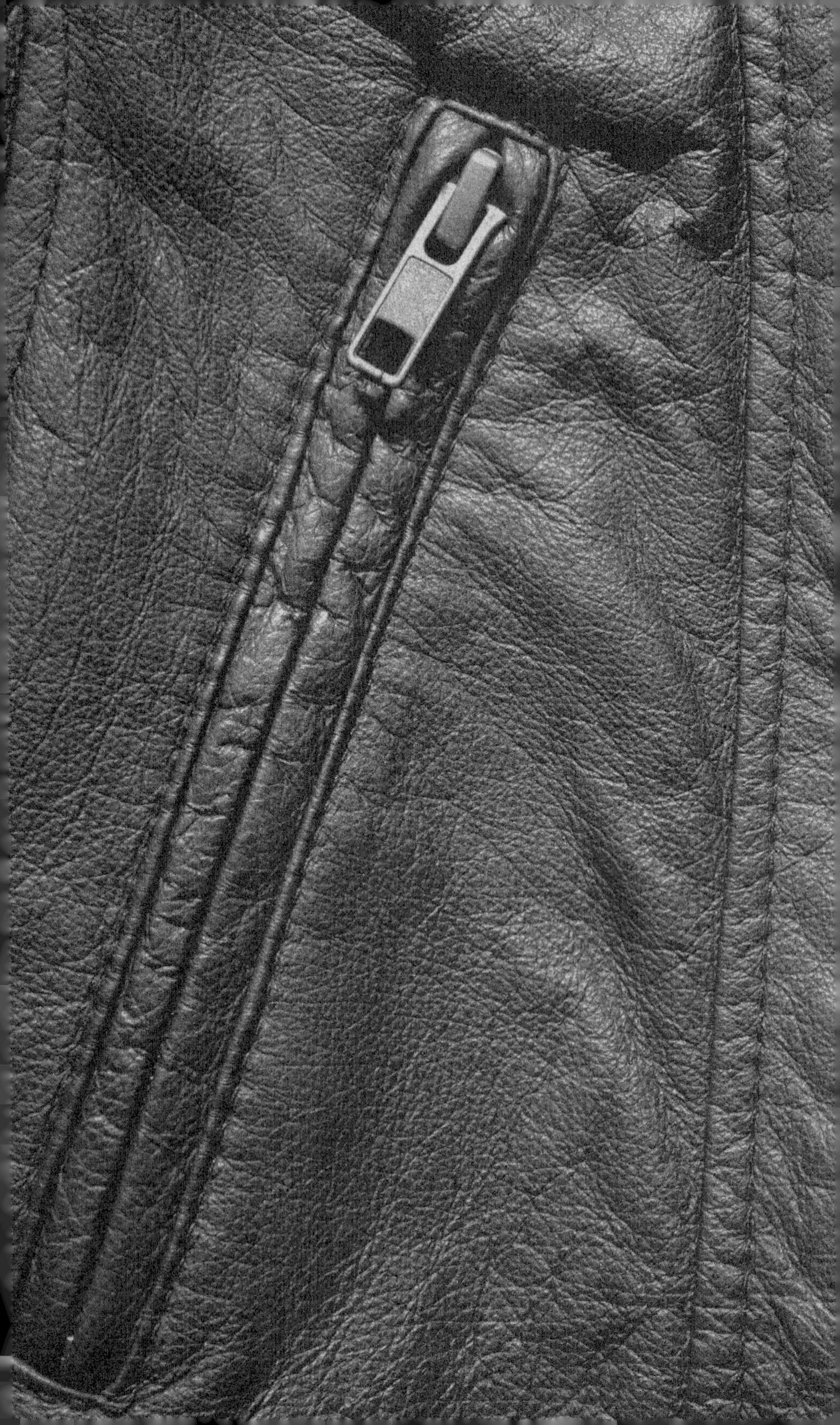

TWENTY-ONE

Aspen

A firm, muscled arm wraps around my stomach, stirring me from sleep. My eyes are blurry and stinging when I open them, and it takes me a minute to gain my bearings. I'm definitely in my bed, if the time glowing on the ceiling from my alarm clock is any indication. And it's telling me it's four in the morning, only a few hours since we fell asleep.

We.

Keene.

There hasn't been another person in my bed for months now, until tonight. His breath comes out hot against my shoulder as he inhales and exhales slowly. His soft, golden hair tickling my skin with each rise and fall of his chest.

I didn't realize he stayed in here to sleep, though I can't really say I blame him for knocking out before he could crawl back to his own bed after our bath.

And who am I kidding, anyway? I'm more than happy to have him here. A shocking turn of events, considering my distaste for snuggling or sharing a bed in general.

As gently as I can, I pull my arm and shoulder from beneath his head, letting it slide down onto one of the pillows. Though I try my best not to wake him, it doesn't matter. Long, thick lashes flutter against his cheekbones for a few seconds before two brown eyes blink up at me, full of hazy sleep.

And I feel a new kind of tugging at my heart. One that speaks more of longing than it does of friendship.

Jesus Christ, Kee. What are you doing to me?

"Hey," I whisper. Then I clear my throat, trying to get my words to sound less like a prepubescent teen. "I didn't mean to wake you."

He groans and rolls his head back and forth on the pillow a couple times, something he's done since we were kids. The first time I ever saw him do it, he said it was to shake the cobwebs out of his brain, and the gullible idiot I was at six years old, believed spiders crawled into heads every night and made their homes there.

Now, it just makes me irrationally happy if I see him do it.

His gaze collides with me and he gives me a sleepy smile. "You didn't."

I let out a soft laugh. "Really?"

"Mmm," he mumbles, leaning in to kiss me softly. Sensually. Achingly fucking slow. "Nope, not at all."

It takes everything in my power not to grab his face and spear my tongue between his lips or roll him onto his back and pin him to the mattress beneath me. Just the thought and his mouth on mine alone has my dick stirring beneath my briefs.

"See," he mutters when he pulls away. "Still sleeping."

Then the shithead rolls away from me to actually go back to sleep. I mean, yeah, it's four in the morning and we've barely slept, having stayed up way too late talking and playing games before getting in a little studying. I should probably take a page from his book and also get some more shut eye, if only for another hour.

The problem is...I'm not tired anymore. Definitely not by a long shot when Keene's hand reaches behind him, searching blindly for a moment before it comes in contact with my fingers. His own wrap around them and he tugs, pulling my body into his back, not letting go until he's got us spooning. Him being the little spoon.

I'd normally laugh at his ridiculousness, his incessant need for physical contact that's only grown since we've started hooking up. But right now, I'm just doing my best to not dry-hump the hell out of him while he falls back to sleep. Which is nearly impossible, with the way the warm, smooth skin on his back feels pressed against my chest.

Somehow, I managed to behave myself.

For a whole two minutes.

When his ass nestles back into my crotch, my dick right in his crease, all thoughts of keeping this to a PG-rated snuggle session quickly fly out the damn window.

Fuck it. In for a penny, in for a pound, right?

Instinct takes over before my brain can talk me out of this, and my mouth slowly moves across his skin. I kiss freckle after freckle peppered over his back and shoulders. I've become even more obsessed with them since we've started exploring each other's bodies, especially the ones dotting his collarbone and tops of his shoulders. Connecting them with kisses rather than ink from a marker like I wanted to do as a kid.

My tongue flicks out to steal a taste of his skin, and my cock is practically weeping as it rests snuggly between his cheeks.

The arm curled over his waist slowly slides back until my palm settles on his hip, careful to keep from brushing over the nasty bruise on his ribs. He's firm beneath my touch, his hard, well-earned muscles creating lines and paths beneath his skin that are visible even in the dim light from my alarm clock. Grabbing hold of him, I continue to work my mouth across his body as I press my hips forward.

The sensation it shoots straight to my balls is exquisite, so I do it again. And then again.

Keene must still be in that state between awake and asleep, because he grumbles before letting out my name on a sigh. "Pen?"

"Mmm," I mumble as I continue to trail my lips across his shoulders. The fourth time I rub against him, he presses back. It's barely noticeable, but I feel it all the same.

My lips brush a line from his shoulder to his neck, and I use the hand I have anchored on his hip to hold him tight against me, right where I want him. From the contented sigh that once again leaves him, he doesn't seem to mind.

Still doesn't keep him from murmuring out, "What're you doing?"

His voice is a gruff whisper, but it doesn't sound angry or even confused. It almost sounds like he wants confirmation of where this is leading. If I have anything to say about it, we're about to end up sweaty and covered in cum.

"Want you," I murmur those two simple words into his neck. Then I press my hips into him once more, as if he needed proof behind the statement. My mouth moves over his heated skin up toward his ear as I continue to roll my hips into him. It doesn't take long for him to get the picture, joining in to help our bodies move together. Grinding and chasing a release we're both desperate for. "Fuck. *Need* you, Kee."

"Then take me."

Hell yes. I love the way that sounds on his—

I stop all movement the second my brain is able to register what he just said, and the second it does, my body is leaning over his. As I search his eyes, wide and shining with unkempt desire, I lose my breath for a second.

Then he says it again, his voice hoarse, "Take me." His palm reaches up to cup the side of my face, and I see those two words spoken once more, this time with just his eyes.

Take me.

And up until this moment, I didn't realize how much I wanted to do just that.

Take him and make him mine.

My mouth crashes to his with brutal force as I roll us, layering my body over his. We grind some more, our covered cocks bumping and sliding against each other within the confines of our underwear. The friction is pure bliss, but it's not what either of us wants.

Quickly as I can, I remove both our boxers before my lips find his again. Then I do exactly as he said. I take him with my mouth, slipping my tongue between his lips to tangle with his. I take him with my body, caging him beneath me.

But it's not enough. Nothing with him ever is, and the thought alone is terrifying.

One knee slides between his legs and I grip his thigh, pulling it up toward my hip to get a better angle for our cocks to press together in the most delicious way I've ever felt. They slide against each other as we rut together, pre-cum leaking from the heads.

"Touch me," he murmurs, pulling back to break the kiss. His lips, swollen from our kiss, are parted slightly as he pants out a plea. "Christ, Pen. Please fucking touch me."

I smirk, biting his lip before I reach between us, gripping both our cocks in my fist the way he's done countless times before. Being the one to take the lead and set this in motion is new to me. Nine times out of ten, he's the one to make the first move, even if I was the one to urge him into it. And I've always been willing to follow him wherever he wants to take us—especially in this journey of self-discovery we're on—but right now, it's just different.

Of course, true to nature, Keene starts getting antsy and wants to take the reins back in his own hands. Literally. He bats my hand out of the way, taking over jacking us. And fuck, if it isn't even better when he does it. The perfect amount of pressure as he strokes us from root to tip. The mind-blowing feel of our heads pressing together when he rolls his palm over them.

My mouth lands on his jaw and I nip my way across it, loving the scratch of his stubble beneath my lips and teeth. Masculine and so fucking sexy in a way I've never realized before.

"We need lube," he says suddenly, his breath coming out in harsh pants.

I glance over, noting there's not a chance in hell I can grab it from here, and there's definitely no way I'll be ripping my body away from his for even a minute to get it.

"I can't reach."

His smirk is devious as he wraps an arm around my waist, flipping our positions instantly in one of the hottest maneuvers I've ever experienced. I mean, hell. No wonder some of the girls I've been with enjoyed being manhandled in bed. If I wasn't already hard as a steel rod for him as it is, I would've popped an instant boner the second he did that.

Keene leans away, coming back with a bottle of lube no more than a second later and popping open the cap. He nudges my legs together and then straddles me to rest on his knees, getting a front row seat as he coats my cock with lube.

"My test came back clear at the beginning of the season," he says, not meeting my eyes as he continues to jack me.

I understand what he's getting at immediately.

It's the condom talk. And fuck, if it doesn't make my chest inflate almost uncomfortably with the amount of trust he's putting in me. More than anything, I'm glad to have him on the same page as me.

I'm careful when it comes to sex, and I always—*always*—use a condom, so it should be fine for us to go without one. But the unknown worries me, and I don't want to put him at risk. I'd never want to do anything that'd end up hurting him.

But I've also never been able to deny him a damn thing. Not in this life, and I doubt in the next.

We both want this. Skin on skin. No secrets or walls. No barriers.

Not a damn thing between us, the way it's always been

It only makes sense that this wouldn't be any different.

"Whatever you want," I murmur. "I'll give you whatever you want, Kee."

He smiles softly, eyes flicking to meet mine as he rubs his thumb under the head of my dick. It feels too good, but it's not enough.

"Pen," he whispers, free hand dancing along my stomach, tracing over each indent of my abs, and his tongue licks his bottom lip.

"Kee," I mumble, though it comes out choked. Because the way he's looking at me right now, the amount of emotion in his gaze, I can't handle it. The fire in his eyes ignites every single cell in my body. My fucking soul.

"I want *this*," he tells me, voice hoarse. "I want *you*. Inside me. Fucking me."

Goddamn, I want that too. It doesn't matter that we haven't really talked about this. Real sex. Not apart from that one night weeks ago when

I watched him finger his ass in a hotel shower a thousand miles away, telling him I wanted him ready to take my dick by the time he made it back to me.

That was just dirty talk. Something to get him hot. Get him off.

It's nothing in comparison to actually sinking inside him. Feeling him clench around me as I drive into him. Taking every single inch of what I have to offer. Sharing something with him that…never in a million years did I think we'd share.

Which is half the reason I don't have it in me to question why this has happened, or more importantly, how it changes things between us if we cross *this* line.

Not now. Not anymore.

Not when I've never wanted anything more in my entire life.

"I want that too." I don't know if the words come out loud enough for him to hear. At this point, it might not matter. He has to know, if only from the look on my face alone. Still, he swallows, and I feel his body vibrate with nerves.

And God, I'm nervous too. More than he is, probably.

The next words sneak out from my lips without permission, the dual meaning in them crystal clear.

"I don't wanna hurt you."

He nods, eyes full of trust. "Then don't hurt me."

My chest aches at the need in his voice. The tremble in his tone. It's a vulnerability like I've never seen from him before. All I can do is nod, giving him permission to use me. And that's what this is, right? Him using me to figure out where his mind is and what he wants.

Right?

The thing is, I feel anything but used. Definitely not in the bad, dirty sense of the word, because I want this as much as he does. When it comes to the things Keene and I do together, the way we touch each other or how we are together, it just feels right. Like this is how it's supposed to be.

Grabbing the lube, I dribble some on my fingers and reach around him. I massage one ass cheek as I rub the liquid up and down his crease. He clenches when my fingers go to enter him, just like they did the first time, but soon enough, he's thrusting back against me.

"More," he pleads, and I add a second finger. I work him open agonizingly slowly, knowing he needs the prep time if we're doing this. But every thrust that stretches him more only makes my cock weep with envy.

Who would've thought one appendage could have jealousy over another?

By the time I get a third inside him, a thin sheen of sweat coats his forehead, and he's groaning with pleasure that has me ready to explode.

"I'm ready, Pen," he pants, eyes meeting mine. "Just get inside me."

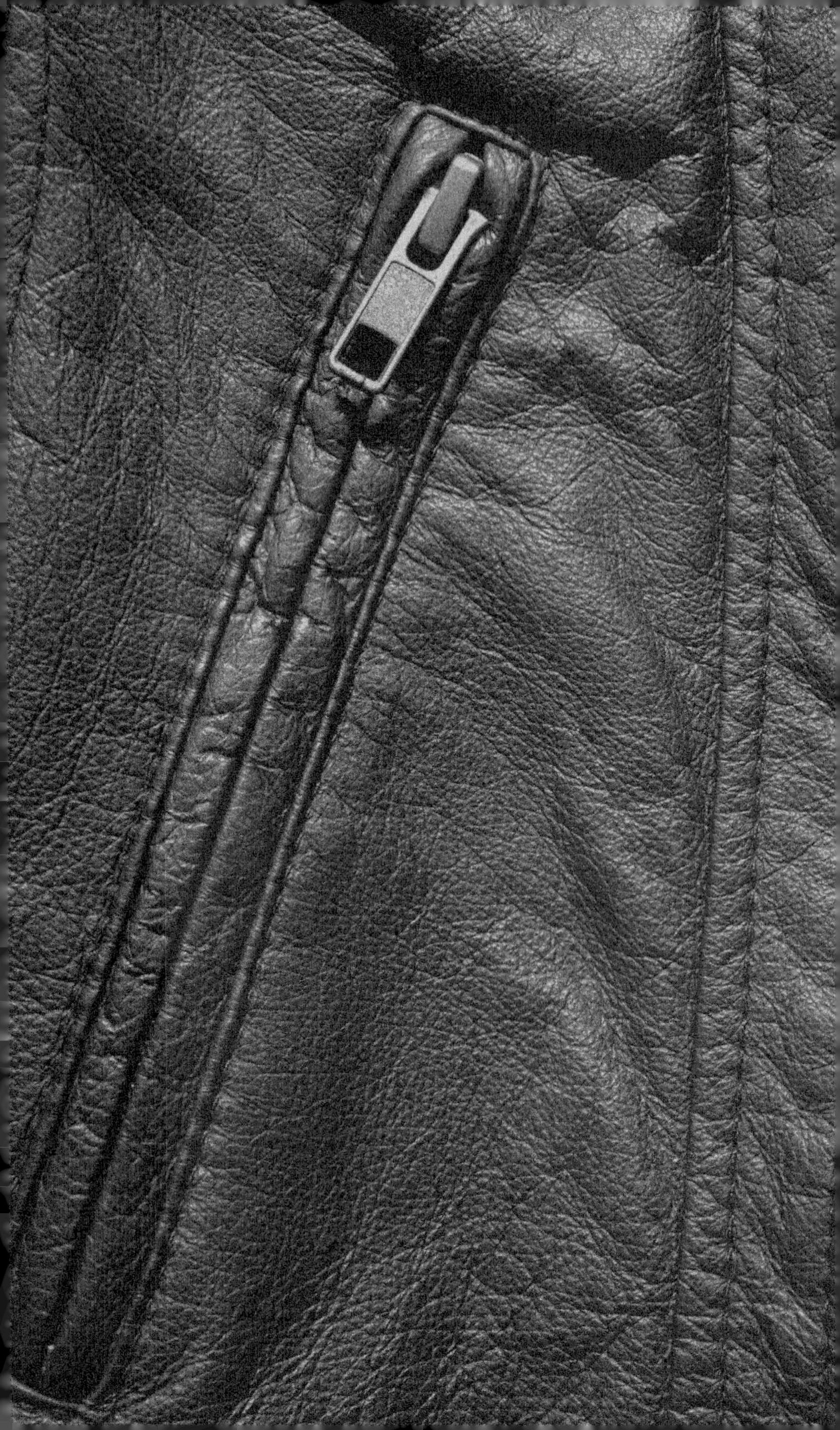

TWENTY-TWO

Aspen

Those four words every guy loves to hear take a minute to register in my brain. Way longer than normal, but maybe that's because of *who* said them, rather than the needy plea he spoke them with.

That's all it takes for the nerves to come rushing right back, freezing me in place.

Keene isn't fazed though; he makes a move to get off me, my fingers sliding out of him. That snaps me out of the slight panic, and I place a hand on his hip to keep him firmly in place.

I feel his eyes on me in the dim glowing light, questioning me.

"Stay on top," I utter, swallowing unsteadily. "I heard it's better for the...first time. So you'll control the pace."

He bites his lip, and the sight makes me fucking stupid. Add in the fact that his hand is wrapped around my cock, and I'm surprised I can even think at all.

I pull his torso toward me, lifting his ass off my body. He watches for a moment before a look of understanding passes over his face, and he moves to position us. The head of my cock presses against his hole, and my entire body becomes a ball of nerves all over again. Shaking with them.

I can feel his too. Radiating off him in palpable waves as they flow between us.

"You're sure?" I ask, my voice shattered glass.

Instead of answering, he lowers his mouth to mine in a searing kiss. One that tastes of passion and need and anxiety as he sinks down enough for the blunt head of my cock to slide past the tight ring of muscle. Keene gasps into my mouth, by far the sexiest sound I've ever heard from him. I swallow it whole, desperately greedy for his tongue, his lips.

I'm barely inside him—only just the tip—but the pressure is fucking insane. Tight and hot and so damn near perfect, I could die right now and it wouldn't matter.

But I'm acutely aware of Keene's quick breathing and every miniscule movement he makes.

His forehead presses against mine, breath hot against my lips. And then he does that thing he does where he reads my mind and takes the word right outta my mouth.

"Good?"

I nod as I snort out a slight laugh, doing my best to keep the rest of my body still. And also to not come before I'm all the way inside him. "I think that's my line."

He lets out a soft chuckle, brushing his lips over mine again. "I'll take that as a *yes,* then."

Is he insane right now? I'm fantastic. Like, I'm in literal heaven.

That thought only becomes more accurate as Keene impales himself another inch on my length with a tentative drop of his hips.

"Holy shit," I breathe, brushing my lips against his again in another searing kiss. "You're so tight, Kee. Can I permanently take up residence inside you?"

I hear him swallow, but he lets out a nervous laugh. "I don't know if that's a good idea. You're really fucking big."

Never in my life have I both loved *and* hated that statement.

His ass is squeezing my cock so tightly I might *die* if I don't either get balls deep inside him or pull out entirely. Or worse, become addicted to this feeling and thrust in without permission. From his pinched features and the way his neck is corded and strained, that's the last thing he needs right now.

My hand glides up and down his good side, the other anchoring in his hair. "Breathe, baby. Relax some more. We can stop if you need to."

Even if I combust into a million tiny pieces, I'll stop.

His gaze collides with mine, and it's then I realize the term of endearment that slipped from my lips by mistake. I've said it before in the heat of the moment, but it didn't feel like this any time before. It felt right, to the point where I didn't even notice until he just gave me that look.

And for once, I can't get a good enough read on him to know if he likes it or not.

His lips part as he lets out a shaky breath, sliding down further on my shaft. It's a tight fit, and I can tell he's uncomfortable with the way his forehead creases, partially in pain and in concentration.

"Kee?" I murmur.

Licking his lips, he nods to let me know he's good. It's not at all convincing, but the way his ass is squeezing my cock, I can't formulate a single thought besides wanting to thrust all the way in.

I don't, though, and instead, one hand moves to grip his ass cheek.

The other grasps his cock, and I start jacking him as he continues to ease himself further onto me. The pained expression leaves his face, giving way to pleasure as I finally bottom out inside him. I keep working him with my fists, letting him catch his breath and adjust around me.

I'm dying to start moving. As in, if one of us doesn't start riding or thrusting in the next two seconds, I might actually be sent to an early grave.

Death by sex. Not the way I thought I'd go.

When I look up at him to tell him we need to move, the realization that I'm *inside Keene* hits me, and I'm completely floored by what he's entrusted me with. Rendered speechless by this amazing, perfect human as I have a moment to take in his flushed cheeks and heaving chest for the first time. He's so fucking…beautiful. So brave and caring, and all I can think while our eyes lock is *mine.*

He's mine, from this day on.

Licking his lips, Keene gives another tentative drop of his hips, sending a bolt of pleasure zipping through my body like lightning.

"Oh, shit," he moans on a gasp, and I bite my lip to keep the line of expletives from spewing out of my mouth.

But when he does it a few more times, I can't hold it in.

"Holy mother of Jesus." My neck arches back against the pillow, every part of my body primed and ready to explode from the tight heat of his body sheathing me.

I don't think I'll last much longer than five minutes at this rate, and while I've embarrassed myself in front of Keene before when it comes to sex, I refuse to do it now.

But how the hell am I supposed to keep from blowing my load when he looks so sexy as he starts really riding my cock. Bouncing up and down on it, his lip tucked between his teeth as he takes both of us closer to the edge of ecstasy. All the squatting he does behind the plate built up the muscles in his legs and ass, and I watch in awe as they flex and move beneath my palms as he fucks himself on me.

I'm entranced by it. Captivated by him. The sight of him getting lost in the way my body makes him feel. The pleasure he's pulling from me with every thrust and grind of his hips.

Jesus.

Sex has never been like this with anyone else.

This, right here and now with Keene, completely transcends all other sexual experiences. It's all-consuming, and while I want to let myself follow him into bliss, I never want it to end either.

"You're the sexiest thing I've ever seen," I grind out. His gaze locks with mine, searing me with heat and want and lust.

"I could say the same," he pants.

He does that little drop thing with his hips again, his sac sliding against my cock when he pulls back out, adding a whole new sensation to fucking him.

Keene sets a pace for us that's somewhere between sensual and needy, easing up and down my length like he was born to take it, and as much as I want to let him ride me how he wants, I can't just sit back and watch. No matter how pretty the sight might be.

Natural instincts take over and I start guiding his body up and down, getting him at just the right speed to have my balls seizing and aching for release. The way his breathing starts becoming choppier and more ragged signals he's right there with me.

Leaning forward, a hand on either side of my head, he claims my mouth with a tantalizing kiss. It's all heat and sweat and tongue and Keene. As addictive as it is sexy. It makes me lose all sense of my carefully crafted control.

My grasp on his hips tightens, holding him still halfway impaled on my cock. Letting my body take over, I fuck up into him at a relentless pace. Harder, faster. Absolutely frenzied with the need to alleviate my throbbing dick.

"You were made to ride my cock, baby," I rasp into his ear. "We haven't even finished and I already can't wait to fuck you again."

"As soon as you make me come," he murmurs before capturing my lips with his again.

Not one to deny him, I wrap my palm around his length and start jacking him in time with my thrusts. He glides through my fist with ease while he bears down on my length. The way his teeth sink into his lip and eyes sink closed tells me he's so close.

"Oh, fuck. Right there, Pen."

I must peg his prostate just right, because he lets out a guttural moan against my mouth. I swallow it down as I let the overwhelming way he's enveloped all my senses send me over the edge.

Cum spurts from my cock, filling his ass as I ride out my orgasm. He meets each of my thrusts with one of his own, his pants and groans spurring me on to keep filling him with my release. His cock pulses in my palm as I continue to stroke him, hard and fast, until his teeth sink into my shoulder. Muffled cries of pleasure work their way from him as his release soaks through my fingers, coating my stomach.

Keene's arms give out, and he collapses on my chest in a mess of cum and sweat. But right now, I wouldn't have it any other way.

My free hand moves to his back, fingers coasting up and down his spine as we both take our time coming down from our post-sex high, reveling in holding him like this. Having this piece of him.

He's still doing his best to catch his breath when his head raises to meet my gaze.

"We're...so doing that again."

TWENTY-THREE

Keene

By the time we're showering to clean ourselves off—which takes far longer than necessary because I can't keep my damn hands to myself when Aspen is naked and within arms' reach—it's gotta be close to seven in the morning. He would've already been back from his run under normal circumstances, and I'd still be dead-ass asleep.

But this morning, and more importantly, last night? Nothing's normal about it.

My entire body is at war with itself, both regretting the lack of sleep and saying *I'll sleep when I'm dead* to ask for another round of sex.

I try not to let the latter get to my head, otherwise I know it's sure to explode at the memory of him fucking up into me and his cock stretching me so perfectly and—

Shit.

I wrap my towel around my waist to hide my erection from sight, not needing Pen to call me a nympho after riding his cock one time. Which he would, and I can't really say I'd blame him. But even as I calm my libido enough to start toweling off, I can already feel myself losing my second wind. Or maybe it's my third. At this point, I can't keep track.

All I know is I'm in desperate need of about ten hours of sleep to even have the most remote chance of being human today. And…I'll also need an entire bottle of Tylenol, seeing as I'm ridiculously sore, not just from the sex, but from the games.

My hand reaches up to brush my fingers through my damp hair, and I wince when the movement causes a sharp pain on my side. Turning, I find the bruise imprinted on my ribs looking worse this morning than it did yesterday, the shades of black, blue, and purple becoming more pronounced against my skin. They don't feel much better either, when I run my fingers over them softly.

Honestly, I feel like the team's trainer was right when he said there was a chance one or two of them might be cracked. The pain is…brutal. But hell if I'm gonna mention it and be put on the injured reserve list for getting hit by a pitch. Not in this lifetime.

Aspen cuts the water and steps from the shower, wrapping a towel around his waist. A frown mars his face when he catches my wince from dropping my arm back to my side, but at least he keeps his thoughts to himself.

Too bad they're screaming loud enough that it doesn't matter if he chooses not to verbalize them. I don't have to know him as well as I do to tell he's pissed. I'd be irritated to no end if he came home every weekend in the shape I do, covered in cuts and bruises, and I'm not nearly as protective as he is.

I meant it when I said it's part of the game, though, and it's the part he's just gonna have to accept. Especially if baseball becomes a permanent part of my life as a career.

I'd told Mom the same damn thing on the phone yesterday when she called me after the game, worried sick about the hit I took.

My eyes track him as he dries off, taking in the expanses of skin that've quickly become my personal kryptonite.

"Keep looking at me like that and you're gonna need another shower," he murmurs softly as he moves to stand in front of the vanity. His gaze lifts, meeting mine through the mirror, and my stomach flutters with those stupid fucking butterflies.

"I love when you threaten me with a good time."

The heat in his eyes is downright searing now, and what's sleep again? I don't know her anymore. I'm too busy being dick-drunk on Aspen Kohl.

"Don't even think about it," he mutters, as if reading my thoughts. "You need sleep, and I have class at eight."

He's right on both accounts. I also have class, though it's not until one. At least I don't have practice today, just a light day of weight training.

Pen slips by me out of the bathroom, but I grab his wrist.

"Skip with me instead," I murmur, dragging him toward my room this time. "I'm exhausted, and I know you probably are too. Let's catch some sleep, and then maybe get a late lunch."

He looks like he's debating it for a whole two seconds before a grin pops his dimple as his fingers lace with mine. My heart stutters in my chest.

"You are *such* a bad influence, Keene Waters."

My smile is instant, and he lets me drag him all the way to my bed where we both drop our towels to the floor. "That might be true but, Aspen Kohl, you're the biggest pushover I've ever met."

"I'll give it to you," he says with a laugh as he climbs beneath the covers, completely naked.

I join him, settling my good side into him, and he wraps an arm around me. It's protective and comforting all at once, and I burrow deeper against him. Legs tangle beneath the cool sheets, a juxtaposition with the intoxicating heat of his skin radiating against me.

It's so easy to get lost in him. Especially when we're like this. Just the two of us in our own little world where nothing else exists.

"You feel okay?" Pen asks, fingers dancing up and down my arm. Goosebumps break out over my skin at the soft caresses.

Nestling my cheek into his shoulder more, I murmur, "Yeah, I'm good."

He pulls back slightly, his *bullshit* look written all over his face. "Why don't I believe you?"

A small smile tugs at my lips, and I press them to his skin. "Hmm, maybe your mountainous pile of trust issues is to blame?"

His frown gets deeper. "Be real with me for five seconds, Kee. I didn't hurt you, did I?"

I shake my head. "Not at all. I promise, you didn't hurt me. I'm mostly tired. Yeah, I'm sore too, but it's mostly my legs. I might live half my life in a squatting position behind the plate, but it's a completely different feeling when an eight-inch dick is being shoved up there while doing it."

A crack forms in his grimace, and soon, a smile takes over instead. "God, you're such an idiot sometimes."

Your idiot, are the words that almost slip past my naughty lips, but I manage to keep them in. Barely.

He settles back in against the pillow beside me. Fingers continue to dance over my skin, tracing a sensual path up and down my arm, every once in a while skimming over to the edge of my back. Just having him touch me like this, soft and sweet, is enough to make me melt.

His nose burrows into my hair, and I hear him give the faintest inhale through his nose. If I thought I was a damn puddle for him before, it's got nothing on how I'm feeling right now.

After a few minutes of peaceful silence, he murmurs, "But you…liked it? The sex, I mean?"

Part of me wants to laugh, because how the hell would he think I *didn't?* But when he doesn't laugh or play it off, I realize—

"You're being serious?"

His silence speaks louder than words, and it doesn't sit right with me. I shift to lean up on my elbow, getting a better look at his face. I see the slightest amount of torment etched into a crease on his forehead, and he lets his eyes dart away by rolling his head to the side.

"Pen," I murmur, cupping the side of his face and dragging his gaze back to mine. When he still tries to resist me, I do the only logical thing I can think of.

I crawl on his damn body like it's my own personal jungle gym, straddling his hips the way I was only a few hours earlier. My muscles scream at me more than they did when I was riding his cock, and that delicious sore feeling radiating through my entire body tells me everything I need to know.

I loved every fucking second of him inside me. I just don't get why he'd be thinking any differently.

Of course, I realize my mistake of doing this the second his dick starts to thicken beneath me. During this conversation, I'd somehow forgotten that we're both naked.

"Get off me," he mutters, a frown on his face. But then his eyes soften, and his hands start rubbing up and down my thighs. The heat from his palms sears my skin in a way that's pure torture.

"Not until you quit being stubborn and actually hear what I have to say," I counter.

Arching a brow, I silently wait for him to disagree or put up some kind of fight. Yet, like I figured, he doesn't. Instead, two sapphire eyes roll, and a hand lifts off my thigh, sarcastically motioning for me to get on with it.

"I don't know why you think I didn't enjoy what we did last night, but I did. A helluva lot. Sure, I'm sore as shit from it, but, Pen…" I trail off, letting out something between a laugh and a scoff. "I can't wait to do it again. And again and again after that. I'd hop on your dick again right now if I thought you—"

"Not a chance," he warns, shoving me off him. "You need to rest, ya damn nympho."

Yep, there it is.

"I'm a slut for your cock. Sue me."

Something between a laugh and a snort escapes him, and he shakes his head. "A cock-slut? Really, Kee?"

I shrug. "If the shoe fits, I'll wear it without complaint."

This time he really does laugh, and the sweet cadence of it vibrates through my body and straight into the very marrow of my bones.

I'll never get tired of hearing that sound.

"So now that we've got that covered," I say, raising my brow, "where the hell did that come from?"

His tongue swipes out over his bottom lip, and damn if I'm not tempted to take it between my teeth right now. But this is more important. After all, he was the one who made the rule about us talking shit out if we were gonna hook-up. Being honest with each other about how we're feeling was *the* most important thing.

I settle back into his side with my arm tossed over his stomach, even managing to keep my hands to myself when I'm greeted with the sight of his erection thickening beneath the sheets. A true miracle for me.

But when he looks away again, it causes a niggling worry in the back of my mind.

What if he didn't like it, and that's why—

"I..." He cuts into my thoughts before trailing off again. His expression is unreadable when he brings his gaze back to mine and searches my face. "I just don't like the idea of doing something that will end up hurting you, Kee."

Why I didn't see this coming sooner, I'm not sure. I definitely should have, though, considering he's mentioned this very fear to me multiple times, last night included.

"You could've spent hours prepping me, but I don't think it would've mattered." It's the truth, and we both know it. It's just whether or not he'll accept it that's a toss up, so I go for a lighter approach. "Dicks are a lot bigger than fingers, you know? Which is a good thing, if you think about it."

Rolling his head a couple times against his pillow, he sighs. "You give me too much credit, sometimes."

"I think I give you just enough, actually. It's *you* who doesn't."

A yawn hits me out of nowhere, the exhaustion starting to take over.

Pen's fingers move up to my head and start running through my hair. The slow, continuous sensation coaxes me closer to slumber with every pass through the strands. "Maybe. But I'd never be able to forgive myself if I ended up fucking up somehow and making it bad for you. Especially when I know how important this is to you. Figuring out"—he motions toward my junk with his free hand—"what he likes."

My lips curve at the corners in a sleepy smile. "By now, we've come to a unanimous decision. We both like you. A fucking lot."

He snorts. "Glad to hear it."

"Good." I trace over his abs with my fingers, letting the tip slide in the valleys of each toned muscle. "And you know, pain and pleasure come hand in hand a lot of the time. Some people get off on the pain." I can feel him inhale to start making his rebuttal, so I quickly rush out the rest of my thoughts. "I'm not saying I'm one of those people who likes pain with sex. But that first moment, when it was mostly an uncomfortable burning sensation, didn't take away from what was going on. At all. Sure, it wasn't the best feeling ever, but once we started going at it, I was in heaven. I can't even describe it."

Some sort of groan rumbles in his chest, vibrating beneath my ear. "So what you're telling me is I *did* hurt you."

I laugh a little, because really? That's what he's getting from this?

"Everything you did felt good. Great, actually. I wouldn't want to do it again if it didn't."

I glance up to find he's gone back to silence. Fantastic.

Of course, not being one to just let things go, I give him a playful poke to his abs and smile up at him. "You don't need to treat me like I'm glass, Pen. You're not gonna break me. You should know that better than anyone."

A long, slow sigh leaves him, and I feel him nestle his nose against me before pressing his lips to the side of my head. It's a clear sign that this conversation is over, at least for now. Which is only proven when he murmurs softly into my hair.

"You're not doing a very good job at getting some rest, Kee."

Ah, yes. Deflection. His MO.

But I'm too damn tired to continue hashing this out now, so I do the only thing I can. I nuzzle my face against his skin some more and fall asleep to the sound of his heartbeat beneath my ear.

TWENTY-FOUR

Keene

After waking up from the world's best cat nap, my stomach is growling like a grizzly, and I'm in dire need of some sustenance before I get to the point of being hangry. Aspen offers to order us some take-out or grab something from the cafeteria, but I'm not feeling it.

Honestly, what's the point of skipping classes if we spend the whole day on campus or in our dorm? Kind of defeats the purpose, in my opinion, and that's exactly what I tell him as I bolt out of bed and start getting dressed. He follows, albeit reluctantly, until we're both by the front door.

"Let's get sushi. At the place downtown you love."

I shove my feet into my sneakers as I say this to find him yanking on his Vans.

"So we can brave the insane traffic and parking at this time of day?"

My eyes narrow on him, and I cock my head, watching as he slides on his leather jacket. "Have you always been this whiney, or have I just never noticed before?"

The observation earns me a glare, and he points his keys at me. "Keep that shit up and you can walk there yourself, smartass."

I raise my hands in mock defeat—even though I won this bout in our battle of wills—following him out to his car.

I'm still a bit sore, even after taking some meds, and squatting down to get into his Impala makes the achy feeling in my thighs and ass become more of a burning pain. Oddly enough, it also turns me on. Not in the way that has me pitching a tent in the parking lot. It's more of knowing *why* I feel like I took a Louisville Slugger up the ass last night.

Because...I basically did.

Okay, maybe a slight exaggeration on the size comparison, but Pen's dick is definitely nothing to bat an eye at.

I laugh softly at my unintentional pun, and Aspen glances over at me like I'm crazy. Of course, when I open my mouth and tell him *why* I'm laughing, his lips just quirk, and he shakes his head.

"I swear, Kee. You're so weird sometimes, it's hard to remember why I'm even friends with you."

"Oh, I know why." A smirk slides on my face.

His brow arches as he rests his forearm on top of the bench seat, backing out of the spot and starting toward downtown. "Please, don't keep me in suspense."

"It has to be my dashing good looks." I pause. "And the awesome seats I snag for you at my home games."

He snorts, shaking his head. "Yep, you caught me. Toss some front row seats to *college* baseball, and I'm a kept man."

"I always knew your love was bought," I say with a facetious sigh.

We both start laughing then, and I flick the radio to his favorite alternative rock station and lean back against the seat. I'm honestly about to pass out for another mini snooze until we pull up to the restaurant, but I feel Pen's eyes flicking to me every once in a while as he drives.

"What're you looking at?" I mutter, my eyes still closed.

"Your dashing good looks," he deadpans, and a small smirk curves my lips. Opening my eyes, I find his attention on the road, but a slight frown rests on his.

"What's up?"

He remains silent, then, "Are you sure you're okay?"

"Yeah, I'm fine. Why wouldn't—"

"The radio," is all he says.

The radi—Oh.

My stomach flips, and I fiddle with the sleeve of my hoodie like it's the most interesting thing in the world. I hadn't even realized I'd put his station on instead, and honestly, I sure as hell don't know why I'm feeling all warm and embarrassed about something as stupid as this.

"Yeah, I'm good," I mutter. "Just figured I hog the thing enough as it is."

All he does is nod, attention locked on the road ahead.

After that, an awkward air settles between us and doesn't get any better until we pull to a stop outside the restaurant. Once we're inside and seated at a booth near the back, he's still off, but at least he seems less…tense.

We haven't been here since the new semester started, and when I see one of the waiters walk by with a plate of shrimp tempura rolls, my mouth instantly salivates.

"And here I thought we were coming here because it's *my* favorite," Pen mutters before reaching over and snapping my mouth closed. "Careful, you're drooling."

Electricity sizzles where his skin touches mine, a crackled charge surging between us as I meet his gaze from across the table. It takes every ounce of willpower I have in my body to keep from mauling him on the spot, but somehow, I manage.

He licks his lips, and my greedy eyes track the movement. Of course, when I flick my attention back to where it belongs, I find I've been caught red-handed.

"Still drooling," he says, leaning back against the booth's backrest with a knowing grin on those perfect lips.

And just like that, all feels good and right again.

Except the half-chub in my jeans. That just feels fucking uncomfortable.

It's been years since I've eaten sushi for the first time, but after our food comes, I realize why I don't eat it often. It's because I still can't manage a set of chopsticks to save my life. All that hand-eye coordination I've spent years honing by playing baseball is completely useless against two tiny pieces of wood and a piece of sushi.

But with the way Aspen's lips curve into his sexy half-smirk each time I drop my California roll when it's inches from my mouth, popping that addictive dimple out, I care less and less. In fact, I'm more than happy to make a fool of myself if it means seeing that look on his face.

I've always liked making him smile before—it's not something he does often enough as it is—but lately, it's become a bit of a little game for me. A secret one, of course. But I try to catalog what it is I do that gets certain reactions.

How to get a genuine smile, where the dimple is deepest. What I do that makes just the corner of his lips twitch up in amusement.

All the little things I've started to pay more attention to, even if I shouldn't.

Even though it was my idea to go here, Pen ends up paying for lunch and my brain does that thing it never does. Overthink.

Actually, it does that a lot more lately, thanks to my hopeless attraction to Aspen, but it's still not a feeling I'm used to. I really fucking hate it, honestly. The uncertainty. Questioning every action he makes. Wondering what he's thinking whenever *I* do something, like swapping the radio to his favorite station when I never do that.

We're back to the car in a flash, heading back to campus, so I can get my butt to the gym on time.

As we walk down the paved paths across the quad in the direction of our dorm, I can't help but notice Aspen's still a little…different than he was last night. Not in a bad way, like how things were in the car before lunch. It's more that I keep catching him glancing at me out of his periphery. Watching me a little closer. Though I'm sure it's more out of concern than anything else—probably checking for signs of discomfort on my part—I wish it was for another reason entirely.

Which I need to shut down, right now, if only for my own good.

Wanting something like that is dangerous. Both to our friendship and to my heart. Because as much as I wish I didn't feel something more for Pen than just friendship, I do. I think I have for a while now.

I feel safe with him. Protected. Secure. Completely myself and more understood than I am with anyone else.

But this isn't just that.

It's that ache of longing in my chest that's setting off alarm bells.

"You good?" he asks, giving me a nudge with his shoulder as we walk side by side.

More than anything, I wanna reel him in for a kiss, right here in the middle of the quad. And maybe hold his hand while we make it the rest of the way back to the dorm. The kind of things that…couples do together when they're out in public.

But again, I hold out. Keep myself in check, proving that I have way more willpower than I thought.

"All good," I tell him. I hate that it's a lie, and even more, I hate how bitter it tastes on my tongue.

We said we'd be honest with each other when we started messing around in the bedroom. Aspen kept his end of the deal, opening up to me earlier when we got back into bed. But I can't bring myself to give him the same level of honesty about what's going through my mind right now, all under the guise that it's better for me to keep something like this to myself.

What I'm wanting isn't what we agreed to, and the last thing I want is to screw up what we have going by trying to change it. After all, we'd both said this would end if we felt like something would start messing with our friendship.

The urge to act all couple-y definitely falls into that category.

So, as hard as it is and as much as I don't want to, I fight the wants and desires my heart's begun aching for. I do my best to shove them to the back of my mind.

Out of sight, where they bel—

"Waters!" I hear my name shouted, though the recognizable voice has me wincing and looking for cover. It's no use, though. Avery's spotted me, and the only way I'm getting out of whatever conversation that's about to happen is by dropping dead on the spot.

When I start to slow, ready to turn and face my pain-in-the-ass teammate, Aspen grabs my sleeve and keeps us moving forward.

My brows furrow, glancing at him in question, but he shakes his head slightly. "Just act like you didn't hear him. C'mon, the dorm's right around the corner."

Sometimes I wish I could just take a page from Aspen's anti-social playbook and ignore people outright, but that's not me. Even if that person is one of my least favorite people on the planet.

"He knows I heard him," I hiss.

Sure as shit, Avery shouts out, "Hey, don't ignore me, asshole!"

"See?" My teeth clench and I come to a halt, ripping my sleeve free from Pen's hold. He stops a few feet ahead of me before turning around.

From the set of his jaw and the hard stare he pins me with, I can tell he's not happy. Probably because Avery's the definition of an asshole, and he has a habit of making my life—and Pen's, by association—a living hell whenever possible.

Which I'm sure he's about to do…right now.

"You're too—" Aspen starts, but I cut him off with a shake of my head.

"I know," I tell him.

He's always said I'm too nice for my own good. Too forgiving and understanding. It's not something I can really help, and most of the time, it's not a bad quality. I just like making people happy or helping out however I can.

And it's not like I make a habit of letting myself become a doormat. No matter how much some people—like the douche nozzle who just grabbed my shoulder to spin me around—wish I was.

While my expression is somewhere between bored and annoyed when I meet Avery's gaze, he looks…worried?

What the—

"You know, it's kind of rude to just keep walking away from someone trying to get your attention," he says, crossing his arms across his chest.

Well, there goes my theory of him being concerned about something. He's just a dick, same as always.

"Coming from a jackass like yourself, that's kinda rich, don't ya think?" Pen snaps from behind me. Venom and contempt lace his tone; not that I'm at all surprised. I think he's the one person who dislikes Avery just as much as I do, if not more.

Avery takes a step toward Aspen, attention fixated on him in a death glare over my shoulder, but I hold up my hand to stop him.

"Both of you, cut the shit. What do you want, Reynolds?"

His scowl moves from Pen to me before turning into a sneer. "Geez, aren't you just a ray of sunshine today. I didn't mean to interrupt your *date,* but—"

"Mmm, see that's where you're wrong," I cut in, cocking my head. "Because you *did* mean to interrupt. You made it perfectly clear that you didn't give two shits about what I was doing when you were shouting my name across the quad. What you wanted was more important."

Confusion is added to the disdain written on Avery's face. I can tell he's surprised by me snapping at him so quickly. Honestly, I'm a little surprised myself.

But fuck him for coming in here like a dick and—

"Wow," Avery says slowly, stepping away from me. "I guess I won't ask if I can snag you for some extra pitches tomorrow before practice." His gaze flicks to Aspen again. "Fuck him better next time, will ya? There's no reason anyone should be this pissy after getting laid."

I can feel the fury radiating off Pen from behind me, and I put my hand to the side to stop him without even looking.

Avery's just reaching. Being a douche because he can, not because he actually knows about what happened last night. There's no possible way for him to, unless he somehow snuck a camera into Pen's room without our knowledge.

The rational part of Pen's mind certainly knows this too, but it's not enough to stop him from popping off.

"Fuck you, Reynolds." Aspen seethes. His heart's pumping wildly beneath where my palm is pressed against his chest.

Avery just smirks and flips him the bird as he backs away.

"In your fucking dreams, faggot."

TWENTY-FIVE

Keene

The walk back to the dorm is silent and filled with more tension than there's been between us in weeks, only making me hate Avery more. Up until he decided to ambush the two of us in the quad, the day was perfect. Sure, it started out a bit strained, but after we both got out of our heads, it was amazing.

Then the douche had to go mess it all up by opening his ignorant fucking mouth.

It's bullshit.

I brushed his comments off easily enough the moment they left his lips, having to deal with the shit more often than I'd like to admit. From the way Aspen's still stewing, he wasn't able to do the same.

Waves of his anger hit me at full force, dragging me under in their toxicity with every step we make down the hall until we reach the door to our suite. He unlocks it without a word or glance in my direction, shrugging off his jacket and shoes silently.

It's killing me, not knowing what part of the run-in with Avery triggered this level of reaction. All I want is to erase it. Find some way to make things better. Rewind to this morning and never leave the comfort of his bed.

"You wanna game?" I ask as he crosses to the kitchenette and fills a glass of water. "Shoot some bastards in *CoD?*"

A shake of the head is all I get in response before he moves to his room…and shuts the door behind him.

The closing *snick* of it falling in place might as well be that of an impenetrable vault locking up every one of Aspen's thoughts. One he, and he alone, has the code to.

What's rolling through that head of yours, Pen?

I can tell he wants space. Needs some time in his own head before he shrugs this off, but it's hard to give him that. Not when I want to be able to take away whatever pain or discomfort he's feeling…especially seeing as I'm the cause of it.

In the end, it only takes five minutes of silence before I'm overly antsy and anxious enough to knock on his door.

"Yeah?" he calls, and I take that as permission to enter.

When I do, I find him lying across his bed, staring up at the ceiling blankly. Completely zoned out the way he gets when something's really plaguing his thoughts, which isn't a good sign.

Just being able to physically see him has taken some of the weight from my chest and tossed it to the side, but some of it still sits there, crushing down like an anvil, while so many thoughts remain unspoken.

"You good?" I ask softly from where I stand in the doorway. I'm not sure why I bother, since the answer's written clear as day with his body language alone.

That's the thing about knowing someone as long as I've known Pen. I can read him. Like an open book, pages splayed out before me. Knowing he doesn't give that power to just anyone—okay, pretty much *no one*—is what makes it all the harder to use it against him. Yet, no matter how much I don't like it, sometimes I have to take advantage of it. If only to get him to speak words instead of internalizing everything he's thinking or feeling.

"Actually..." I start, fiddling with the hem of my shirt. "Don't answer that. You don't need to. Just tell me what you're thinking instead."

I watch as he visibly swallows, and then blue eyes shift from the ceiling to my face. In them, I swear I see a million different emotions.

Pain. Fear. Regret. Longing. Hundreds more, I can't even begin to name them all.

"I don't know what I'm thinking, Kee. I don't know anything anymore."

The anxiety and panic in his voice wrap my heart in a vice, squeezing until breathing feels nearly impossible. I've never felt more helpless, not knowing what to do to make this better.

I'm dying to rush over to him and take him in my arms. Maybe run my fingers through his hair before kissing him breathlessly, to show him he has me. He always has me. Yet, I think the last thing he wants is for me to touch him right now. I mean...he can barely *look* at me.

So I settle for simply crossing the room to his bed and stand at the edge, closing as much of the distance between us as I dare, all while still feeling like it's hundreds of miles rather than a few feet.

"Can you try? Please?"

Taking a deep breath, I spill my own fears to him. Laying them out for him to see in hopes that he realizes he can do the same, and it wouldn't change a thing.

"I mean, is it me? Are you..." The words catch in my throat as I crack open before him. "Are you ashamed of me? Or about what happened last night?"

He sits up on the bed in a flash, eyes wide. "Absolutely not." Scooting to the edge of the bed, he throws his legs over and grasps the back of my knees. His imploring gaze shows the truth in his words. "Never in this lifetime would I feel that about you."

"Then…" I trail off, shaking my head.

His smile is sad, measured, as he looks up at me wordlessly. Then, as if sinking into my brain and finding exactly the right thing to do, he links his fingers with mine and tugs me down to the mattress with him. I follow without a fight, curling up to face him as soon as our heads hit the pillows. He raises our joined hands, his thumb tracing calming patterns across my skin before pressing his lips to each fingertip.

The gesture makes my chest tighten.

"I'm not ashamed of a single thing we've done together," he whispers while he continues to play with my fingers. "Yeah, we've hit some speed bumps before we got to this point, but you know me, Kee. Sex is sex. I like having it with you just as much—if not more—than I have with any other person I've been with."

I smirk, tracing his lips with my index finger after he kisses it again. "Good to know I'm keeping you satisfied, at least."

He lets out a soft scoff and lifts his gaze to meet mine. "Honestly, I should probably be more hung up on the fact that you're a guy, but I'm not. That shit hasn't even entered the equation for me since we started this."

That's where I thought he'd be hung up too. But if he means it when he says that's not the issue, then I truly have no idea what he's so hung up on either.

"Then help me understand, Pen. If it's not what Avery said…then what is it? Because nothing but the worst thoughts are going through my head by not knowing what's happening in yours."

His teeth scrape over his bottom lip, the action drawing out his dimple for the briefest moment. "I don't know how to explain it, really. There's so many different pieces to this weird puzzle in my brain, and the more I try to make sense of it, the more it doesn't make sense at all."

The corner of my mouth twitches. "Sounds about right to me. Overthinker."

Rolling his eyes, he settles in closer and slides one leg between mine.

"Well, smartass, I think to start…I've been struggling with knowing that this was never part of the plan."

I do my best not to comment on that, but he must see something written on my face, because his lips curl up and he gives me a playful shove.

"Look, don't knock my plans, okay? This is serious."

"Okay, okay." I laugh softly. "Plans are serious."

His eyes roll again. "We've always looked out for each other. Had each other's backs. Been the shield and armor when we've needed it. I just never imagined us having to protect ourselves from…this. From the judgment of Avery or any other asshole we meet that's like him. The prejudiced dicks who decide that the only right way to live is the hetero way. The *normal* way."

An unsettled feeling rolls through me, and though the last thing I want is to make things more and more about Avery being a complete dick, I'm still doing my best to not keep things from Pen. Which is the reason I open my mouth and tell him about what happened in the locker room after the game yesterday. All of it. Every shitty, arrogant, hateful word.

I'm not surprised by the way Pen's jaw ticks as I relive the sordid tale, but what does take me off guard is the way he pulls me in tighter against his chest. Removing as much space between us as humanly possible.

"That's exactly the shit I'm talking about," he whispers, his warm breath fanning over my cheek.

I can tell there's more inside his head he's not saying, if the tension in the way he holds me is an indication. But I've also known Aspen long enough to realize, if he really wants me to know something, he'll tell me.

So instead, I focus on what's clearly written on the lines rather than what might be hiding between them.

"You don't have to protect me, though. I can take care of myself just fine."

He loosens his hold, leaning back to look me in the eyes. "I know that. I swear, I do. But isn't that like…the number one job of a best friend? To make sure you're okay? That all the fuckwads in the world know not to mess with you, otherwise they have to mess with me too?"

My lips curl. "I see your point."

After all, I feel the exact same way about him.

"I hate feeling like I can't do that anymore, because I just don't know how. Not without asking you to stay in the closet for the rest of your life, which I could never do. And it's like…what if people can tell? What if everyone we walk by on campus can just tell we've had sex or sucked each other off, and it just starts people talking. That's something that could really impact you, especially with baseball in the future."

I get where he's coming from. While there's a few out players in hockey or football, there's not a single one in the MLB. But there's a slight flaw in his logic.

"You really think people can just *tell* we're screwing? Just by looking at us? Or more importantly, that any of them actually give two shits?"

He lifts the shoulder he's not laying on in something of a shrug. "At this point, it all might sound crazy. It does to me, and it's my own thoughts, ya know? And…maybe I'm worrying about nothing at all. I don't know."

"And here I thought you knew everything."

There's a slight curve to his lips, and his dimple appears. "I don't know a fucking thing except that I don't want to be the reason you get hurt."

His hand releases mine, then. Comes up and cups the side of my face, brushing his thumb across my lips as his eyes follow the path it takes. I press a quick kiss to the pad, my heart squeezing from the smile he gives me when I do.

There's so much trouble in his eyes when they lock with mine, filled to the brim like a dam about to break. "I meant it when I said that last night, Kee. Whether it be from someone finding out about us, or something else entirely, it wouldn't matter. There's no way I could live with myself for being the reason for your pain."

There's no doubt in my mind he means it. Though he doesn't let himself care for people often, when he does, he cares deeply. With his entire heart and soul—a type of loyalty that knows no bounds. Sometimes, even at the cost of his own feelings.

"And where do you fall into this?" I murmur. "Your pain? Your happiness? You seem so worried about me, but what about you?"

I don't know if the question takes him by surprise, and that's what takes him a minute to respond. Or if he really doesn't have an answer for me off the top of his head. Either way, I'm not expecting the answer I receive.

"At the risk of sounding completely fucking corny or like a total sap, I'm happiest when you're happy, Kee. It's always been that way, always will be."

I swear, my entire body trembles at his words as my mind tries to catalog this moment to memory. It's on the tip of my tongue to tell him the same thing, maybe even spill more of what I'm holding on to.

But I'm not willing to risk letting my heart do the talking instead of my brain.

"Well," I say, snuggling up into him, "my smile *is* infectious."

He chuckles, leaning in to press his lips to mine. "That, and it's completely addictive."

God, if I don't know that feeling all too well.

Rather than responding with something sure to ruin the moment, I kiss him harder, letting my tongue get the first taste of him in hours. Taking tiny pieces of him for myself with every brush of our lips and tongues.

Neither of us moves to take it further, even though simply kissing him gets me harder than a steel pipe every damn time. Instead, we just lay there, lips sliding against each other as hands map over skin with feather light caresses. Getting lost in the moment and in each other.

Just…being.

I'm the first to pull away, the tugging at my heart and war in my head forcing me to seek air.

There are so many things I wish I could tell him right now. Feelings that've been stirring inside me the more we explore each other like this. About feeling like we were always meant to end up here, even if we didn't realize it. Even if he still doesn't, from the sounds of it.

Maybe *this* was the plan all along.

But I keep these thoughts to myself, taking my turn to lock them up and throw away the key before they can burst from my mouth and effectively ruin everything.

"This feels right to me," I say, measuring my words to not give too much away. "So maybe we should just focus on that. Not about how this isn't the way we thought things would happen or the worries about the *what-ifs*."

He nods, a small smirk forming. "There's the Keene I know and love. Always going with the flow and talking me off the ledge."

That one four-letter word leaves his lips, causing my heart to stutter and stumble in my chest. Inflating painfully against my ribs until they might crack from too much pressure.

And they do splinter slightly when I force a smile back at him.

"That's what best friends are for."

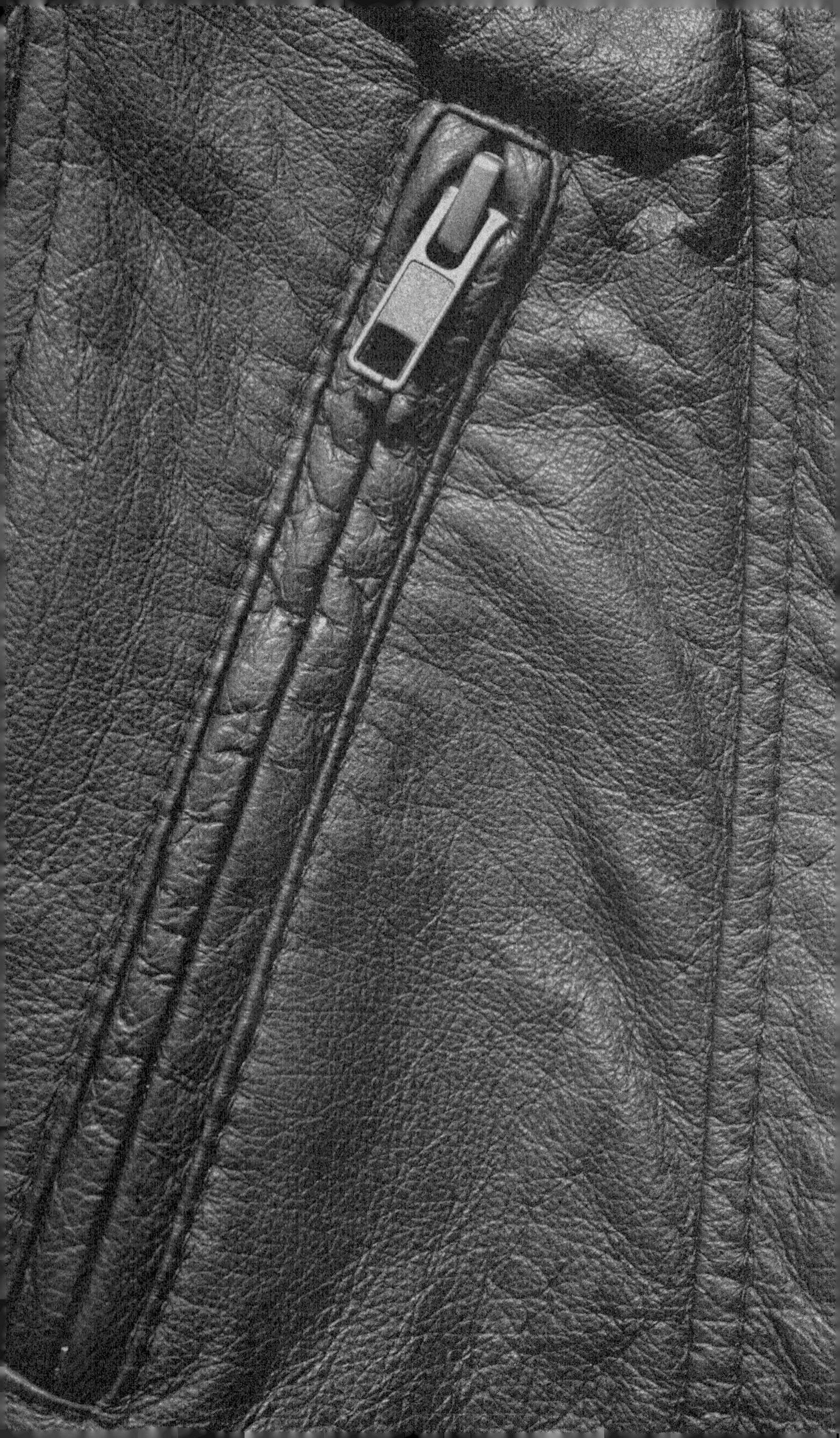

TWENTY-SIX

Aspen

A couple weeks have passed since the confrontation with Avery in the quad, and subsequently, the conversation Keene and I had in my bed. The one where I laid some of my biggest fears about this entire situation on the table for him to see.

I wasn't lying to Keene when I said my major concern was protecting him. He's my best friend, and I'd do anything for him. As if that wasn't obvious enough the day I convinced him that us sleeping together was a good way to figure out his bi-curiosity. A decision I still stand by a hundred and ten percent…even if it's messed a few things up in my own head.

But what I didn't say to him is I can't shake this feeling that *I'm* one of the people he needs protection from.

I wish I knew why my brain is latched on to this idea.

My head falls back against the brick of our dorm's roof—my favorite spot to come and think in peace—and I take a long drag from my cigarette. The normally calming effects of the nicotine never hit, and no matter how many drags I take, it doesn't seem to ease the swirling feeling in my stomach.

Maybe it's because I don't think I'm enough. Not what he deserves or what he needs in the long run.

Sure, I can fulfill the sexual aspect of this arrangement. Help him discover the pieces of who he is that've been missing. But when it comes to something more than that, I've got nothing to offer but a really shitty track record of letting my guard down with people I should trust, and a long string of emotionless hookups to show for it.

I scoff out a laugh, one of those people coming right to mind, and I wonder what she'd think of all this shit. After all, she's one of the few people to ever call me out on my shit.

Her words from the restaurant during our failed date echo through my head on playback, and I stare down at my phone resting on the concrete between my feet.

I think it's better for you to put the focus on yourself. But just know, I'm happy to help however I can.

Flicking ash to the ground, I internally debate on taking her offer to heart. Truly opening up to her, maybe getting some advice or insight that I can't go to Keene for in this instance.

Fuck it. What's one more bad idea?

Picking up the phone, I hit the call button and wait while the phone rings.

"Aspen?" a soft, feminine voice comes from the other line.

"Hey, Brist," I say, stubbing out my cigarette on the brick. "Catch you at a bad time?"

"Not at all, just on my way home from the gym. What's up?"

I pause, second thoughts starting to creep in. But then I shove them down and ask, "Any chance you can meet me?"

She's silent for a moment, and I think she's about to tell me no or to fuck off or some other variation of that. Then she surprises me.

"Give me thirty minutes to shower, and send me your location."

⋘⋘⋘⋘⋘⋘⋘⋘⋘⋘⋘⋘⋘⋘⋘⋘⋘⋘

True to her word, Bristol calls me from outside our dorm building just over thirty minutes later, and I run down to meet her before sneaking her up to the roof with me.

She looks around the rooftop, and I shove a loose brick in the door to prevent us from being locked out. As she's taking in the view of campus while the sun sets off on the horizon, I move back to the spot I was taking up residence in earlier and snag another cigarette from my pack. After a few moments, she joins me, her back hitting the brick with a soft thud.

Word vomit spews from my mouth before she has the chance to open hers.

"I'm sleeping with Keene."

There's a slight lift of her eyebrow, nearly imperceptible, and she lets out a low whistle. "Damn, Kohl. I was expecting you to ask about rekindling our friends-with-bennies arrangement; not finally out yourself to me."

"Why would you—"

Wait a fucking minute.

"Did you say *finally* out myself to you?"

She shrugs, a small smirk on her face. "Maybe."

I'm floored. Absolutely flabbergasted, staring at her with wide eyes and mouth agape. Something that clearly entertains her, because her smirk grows even more.

"Better be careful there, Kohl. You'll let the flies in."

I have no idea how she's joking at a time like this. She just flipped my entire damn world on axis with one fucking sentence.

After blinking a few more times, I'm able to form a coherent thought and string some words together to speak. "So, wait. You…called this?"

She snatches my pack of Marlboros from out of my hand and pulls one out. But instead of lighting it with mine, she starts peeling the paper off, letting the tobacco and other shit fall to the cement. "With you, absolutely. I always got a vibe. With Waters…I had an inkling, but I wasn't really sure."

"How?"

Her brow arches when she looks at me. "You've heard of this thing called *gaydar,* right?" When I nod, she smirks and continues, "Well, when you're queer, your gaydar tends to be stronger than that of a straight person's."

That definitely makes sense but—

Wait…

"You? You're queer?" She nods, and my jaw drops slightly, a slight worry hitting me that causes even more word vomit. "I didn't turn you into a lesbian because of that awful date, did I?"

She burst out laughing, shaking her head. "Oh, Kohl. I've been bi long before I met your cock, and I'll still be bi long after I've forgotten what it looks like."

I don't know if I'm supposed to be offended by that statement or not, so I just give a nonchalant shrug. "Okay, well…sorry. That was a little self-involved, I'll admit. You just took me by surprise."

"Understandable." She laughs. "But God, that reaction will live rent-free in my head for months. I wish I would've been recording it so I could make it into a GIF."

"You're a real comedian," I deadpan before taking another drag of my cig and mumbling to myself, "Wow. What are the fucking odds?"

The question was rhetorical and wasn't meant for her, though she had no issues hearing it since she's seated only a foot from me.

"The odds are pretty high, actually. Especially now that our generation is more apt to speak out—or come out."

I raise a brow. "No shit?"

She nods. "Straight isn't the default. No matter how many people want you to think it is."

Wow. I guess I've never really looked at it in that sense, but now that she's said it, I understand. Hell, I'd just assumed straight was my default for the past twenty years. Even when there might've been signs that I wasn't long before Keene and I kissed.

I'd see guys and I'd think they were hot. A specimen of male beauty or whatever. I just never had any physical urge to act, so I'd just assumed… it was admiration. Not an attraction. Looking back, I know now that I was probably wrong.

Especially with the way Keene and I are together, I know for certain I'm not straight. I might not know exactly *what* I am—and truthfully, I don't really care all that much to figure it out. I am who I am, I like what I like, and that's the end of it.

But, I think it's safe to say I like dick. Keene's for sure.

I was being honest when I told Keene I hadn't thought about him being a guy since that first momentary freak out, because it doesn't really matter to me. And even that bout of overthinking and analyzing things up the ass was more because he's *him,* not because he has a dick instead of a pussy.

"The more you fucking know," I mutter, exhaling a cloud of smoke.

"Is he the reason you needed to…how did you put it?"

"Figure myself out?" I say with a laugh. "Yeah, he was. He got in my head a little bit."

"It's bound to happen when you two are as close as you are."

Yeah, she hit the nail on the head with that one, especially if the night I took her on our disaster date is anything to go by.

"Is that when it started? If you don't mind me asking."

"Yeah, it was right about that time. We'd...sexted a bit. After he came out to me about his curiosity."

It's her turn to be shocked again. "Really?"

I nod. "Yeah. It was sort of on accident, kinda on purpose."

She lets out a soft laugh. "Oh, Kohl. So are you guys dating now or—"

"No," I say quickly, shaking my head. "It's...casual. Just while he figures himself out."

This time, she lets out a loud laugh. One that says my comment is the funniest thing she's heard in, well, this entire conversation.

"You're trying an emotionless, no-strings style hook-up with your best friend?"

I frown in confusion. "Yeah?"

If possible, she starts laughing even harder.

"What the hell is so funny? Is there something wrong with us keeping things casual?"

"I mean, I wouldn't say there's anything *wrong* with it. But baby, it's gonna backfire on your ass so hard, it's not even funny. Might as well light the fuse now."

Her comment sets me on edge. What she just said is exactly part of why I'm feeling so uneasy about this all of a sudden. It just took hearing someone else say it for me to finally figure it out.

If only I could figure out the *why*, now.

"Why do you say that, Brist?"

A perfectly manicured brow arches above her blue eyes—hers more icy than my cobalt. She must think I'm joking, because she blinks after a second.

"Oh. You're serious?"

Obviously.

"Honestly? He's always kind of looked at you like you hung the moon. For a while, I thought I was just seeing things; thought maybe it was part of this deep friend connection the two of you have. But now that you've told me this…" She shakes her head. "I mean, you two are about as casual as a white-tie gala. As in, not at all."

"It's just sex," I tell her again, but it sounds like a lie to even my own ears.

"You really believe that? Or are you just trying to convince yourself of it? 'Cause the way I see it, you two are either gonna become the greatest thing to ever happen to each other, or you're gonna toss his heart in a frying pan the moment he wants something you won't give him." Her eyes hold a dash of sympathy. "And Kohl, there's nothing casual about a seared heart."

My head sinks into my hands, and I thread my fingers through my hair.

On some level, I know she's right. I just let my possessiveness and protective nature when it comes to Keene overshadow the flaws in this idea.

I see them now, though. Clear as day.

I added sex, the one thing I've always tried to keep emotionless, to a relationship with someone who has the keys to unlock every single feeling I keep hidden. Of course it's gonna be impossible to keep it as casual as I would with anyone else.

I'm such a fucking idiot.

"You're thinking awfully loud over there," she muses. When I lift my head, I find her using the paper from the cigarette she shredded to make a pile of its guts.

"I think I fucked up."

She smiles, still focused on what she's doing. "Not yet, you haven't."

"How haven't I? I went and I took him to bed with the pretense of keeping this casual with no-strings, and you literally just told me it's going to implode on us in a spectacular blaze of glory."

The snort she lets out is anything but ladylike. "All right, cool it there, drama queen. You must've missed the part where I also said you two could be the greatest thing to ever happen to each other."

We already are! I want to scream. And I can't lose that, or him.

"Or end up cooking his heart like a fucking steak," I mutter. "Which sounds pretty terrible to me."

"You're right. But the thing is, you have the choice. The decision is in your hands about where the two of you end up."

"Just my hands?" Surely he has just as much of a say in this as I do.

She nods. "You're the one who doesn't let people in or allow them to get close. If you decide to pull that shit on him, there's no way it'll last." Finally, she looks over at me. "You told me Keene is like a golden retriever, and I can see it. He just loves and loves and loves. Never has met a person he didn't like. And he's also the kind of person who needs that kind of love in return."

Her usage of the word *love* causes my stomach to roll uneasily. No, actually, it feels like it's currently in the middle of the ocean during a goddamn typhoon. Rocking back and forth, no hope of escaping without taking some serious damage.

Swallowing roughly, I give life to the words I didn't even know were the truth until this very moment.

"I don't know how to give him that. Or how to be what he deserves."

Her brows raise. "And you want to be?"

I open my mouth, but words evade me completely. Just slip right from my grasp at a time when I need them most. But whatever it is I'm not saying, Bristol must get it, because she gives me a slow, solemn nod.

"Don't mess with his emotions, Aspen. Don't screw up what you two have." Her gaze is soft, yet I feel the firmness in her words. "Your friendship is something special. One I'd kill to have. So if you're gonna attempt this with him? Something real and true and more than just a few quick fucks while he explores his sexuality? You have to be all in."

My throat constricts tightly, but it's not nearly as painful as the vice currently wrapped around my heart.

"I don't know what I want…other than to keep him safe. From the world, and from me. I don't want to ruin him or hurt him or—"

Her hand lands on my forearm, giving it a gentle squeeze. "I know. You don't have to explain it to me."

Knowing I don't does ease some of the burden on my shoulders. I think part of the reason Bristol and I always worked in this friends-with-benefits style arrangement is because she and I are a lot alike. At least when it comes to something like being vulnerable with other people.

Which I think, funnily enough, is the reason I've been able to confide in her about this as easily as I have.

I stub my cigarette out on the ground beside me, hoping to tread lightly with my next question.

"How…do I even go about trying to give him more? If that's what route I wanted to take? Like, I've never even had a girlfriend…or a boyfriend, for that matter. Not a real one who knew me the way—"

"He does?" she finishes.

I take a deep breath and nod.

"You're overthinking this, Kohl. Just let him in. Show him you care. Don't start erecting walls where there's never been any before, and do your best to not freeze him out."

I blink at her, dumbfounded. She makes it all sound so fucking… simple. "Is that all?"

"It is, young grasshopper."

Great. So, basically, she's telling me to change my entire human nature if I decide to try to make things with Keene into something serious.

Defeated doesn't even begin to describe how I'm feeling.

"This'll be impossible." I give her a look of dismay. "How am I supposed to be able to keep any of that from happening with him? He might know me better than most people, but I also know me. There'll be a point where it's too much and I'll do something I'm not supposed to."

"Not if you try not to."

"Easier said than done, Brist. My heart might as well be stuck inside the fucking ice castle from *Frozen*."

She glances at me, a devious smirk on her face, and said heart sinks.

"What?" I ask cautiously.

Her grin only widens at my wariness. "Well, in the words of the great Olaf? Some people are worth melting for."

TWENTY-SEVEN

Keene

April

"Are you gonna tell me what the hell is going on yet?"

Aspen glances up at me as he tosses his bag in the trunk of the Impala, and I'm quick to follow suit with my own bag—the bag I didn't even pack—so he can shut it. He doesn't answer me as he hops into the driver's seat, so with a sigh of indignation, I open the passenger side.

All I know is that ten minutes ago, he told me to get dressed and get down to the car.

At first, I thought maybe we were just going out to dinner or something. After all, it was a rare spring Friday night where I'm free to do whatever the hell I want, since we have an off-weekend. But then he walked out of my room, carrying two overnight bags, and handed one to me.

In the time it took to get down to the car from our dorm, I've asked him the same question about fifteen times.

Where are we going?

Clearly, I've yet to get a real answer out of him. In fact, the only time he actually gave me an answer *at all* was the first time, when he just smirked and told me to get moving. Which still isn't a fucking answer.

"Earth to Aspen? Did you go deaf in the past fifteen minutes?"

When he doesn't respond, I pop my finger into my mouth before leaning over and shoving it in his ear, giving him a wet willy.

"What the hell, Keene?" He aims a glare at me after pushing me away from him, rubbing the sleeve of his hoodie in his ear. "Are you five?"

I cock my head. "I don't know, are you going to answer my question?"

"No, I'm not," he says, turning the keys in the ignition. "Isn't the point of a surprise to…I don't know…be surprised when you find out what it is?"

I bite my tongue and roll my eyes because…yeah, he has a point.

"You could've just said it was a surprise," I mutter indignantly.

"You could've just *gone with the flow*, Mr. I Don't Like Plans."

The glare I shoot at him is less about the dig and more about him being right, per usual. But to hell if I'm admitting it now.

"Fine." I sigh, leaning back in the passenger seat as he backs out of the parking space. "But I get control of the radio the whole way there."

⫷⫷⫷⫷⫷⫷⫷⫷⫷⫷⫷⫷⫷⫷⫷⫷⫷⫷⫷⫷⫷⫷⫷⫷⫷⫷⫷⫷⫷⫷⫷⫷

Aspen pulls the car into the driveway of a tiny little cottage in the coastal town of Cannon Beach before killing the engine and looking over at me.

"We're here."

My brows furrow. "Where is here, exactly?"

"Your surprise."

My eyes flick from him to the house. It's cute, I guess. Quaint, and far enough from town that there isn't much traffic. Just from peering around it as we pulled in, I can tell it's seated right on the beach.

"Unless you bought me that house, I don't think I understand," I say slowly.

His brows raise and eyes widen, looking at me like I've truly lost my mind. When he realizes I'm serious, he sighs and shoves the car door open, letting it fall closed behind him as he makes his way back to the trunk. I follow, meeting him at the back of the car to grab my bag.

"Did you take one too many balls to the helmet this season to think I could afford to buy you a coastal property at twenty years old?" he asks as he walks up the front path to the door. There's a lockbox next to the door, and Pen enters a code before pulling out the keys and slipping them into the door. "It's a rental. *Our* rental, for the next two nights."

He pushes the door open, letting me walk into the foyer first. My immediate thought as I take in the open concept house that has a view straight out to the ocean is…damn. It's beachy, but with plenty of modern touches and upgrades. Homey and welcoming, but still clean.

"Wow," I murmur, dropping my bag beside the front door and heading to the back door. There's a deck off the living room with some outdoor seating and—

"Are we allowed to use the hot tub?"

Pen materializes behind me, his arms wrapping around my waist and chin settling on my shoulder. "Would you kill me if I said no?"

"Possibly."

He chuckles, his warm breath coasting over my skin. "Well, I guess it's a good thing we can."

I settle back into his hold, my entire body vibrating with joy and excitement. I try to tamp it down, careful not to read too much into the plans he made to surprise me with this. But my stupid heart gets the better of me every damn time when it comes to him.

"Why'd you do this?" I murmur, turning in his hold.

His hand slips beneath the fabric of my shirt, fingertips skating softly over the skin of my lower back. It makes me shiver, especially when paired with the intensity of his stare.

"So we could have a little getaway before life gets crazy with finals and baseball and shit. I..." He clears his throat softly. "I didn't think we'd see much of each other past this weekend, so..."

The thought hangs in the miniscule amount of space between us. Heavy and overwhelming.

His focus shifts to the ocean that damn near matches his eyes, and then back to me, and my heart stumbles in my chest at the vulnerability he's showing while he waits for me to say something.

But I can't. I can't even fucking speak.

So I do the only thing I can.

My fingers slip around the back of his neck, and I haul him into a toe-curling kiss.

His tongue wastes no time entering my mouth, and he walks me a few steps until my back presses against the sliding glass door of the porch. He takes and takes and takes some more, pillaging my mouth like it's his to own before snagging my bottom lip between his teeth.

We're both hard behind the confines of our clothes, grinding and groping at each other with a frenzied need. My hands slip their way under his shirt. His fingers work the button on my pants.

I have half a mind to have him turn me around and fuck me right here against the goddamn door; that's how needy I am for him as he continues to suck on my tongue like it's his favorite candy.

"I'm going to assume that you like it?" he murmurs, a lilt of amusement in his tone between kisses.

"I love it," I whisper into his lips, yanking my shirt over my head when I break away. "Thank you for doing this."

"Always." He brushes his nose against mine, and a little piece of me dies inside at the gesture.

Something's changing with him. With us. And I have no idea why.

It's like all these unwritten rules we've had for the past few months flew right out the window of his Impala on the way here. Now, I'm left standing here, desperately grasping for them, if only to keep my heart safe.

But they're already long gone, and as much as I should be ecstatic, I'm terrified.

I've always felt safe with Aspen, but this might be the first time I've felt like I need to guard myself from him too.

He steps away from me slowly, leaving me breathless against the glass as he slips outside and uncovers the hot tub with a swift move. Steam billows out of it, floating through the air and adding to the lust floating between us.

Lust that only gets worse when, right in the open and where anyone else could see, he drops his pants and underwear.

He's left completely naked before me, his erection bobbing out in front of him in a way that has my mouth watering. My eyes lock on it, on the blue veins and pale skin as he stands before me like some kind of god waiting for me to get on my knees and worship him.

As if I don't already have every waking thought devoted to him already.

Without removing his gaze from me, he hops over the edge of the hot tub and slides his sinful body down until the smooth, hard expanses of his torso are submerged.

Once his dick is out of sight, I manage to snap out of my reverie and focus back on his face.

"You coming or not?"

His sapphire eyes practically glow in the lights from the jacuzzi as he waits patiently for me to join him like I normally would, under any other circumstance.

But the line we're toeing right now is anything but normal.

We're playing with fire, and if I'm not careful, I'll end up being the one who gets burned.

Maybe that's why every part of my body is screaming at me to turn and go back inside to the safety of the cottage. Walk away from him before it's too late. Salvage what's left of this friendship, knowing it was better to have him like this for a short time rather than not at all.

All these thoughts blast inside my head like alarm bells and sirens.

But I ignore the warnings.

Shed the rest of my clothes.

And jump straight into the flames.

The next morning, Aspen wakes me up at what might be the butt crack of dawn with a swat to my ass and kisses over my shoulders. At first, I think it's for sex—which would be fucking insane, considering we went at each other for three rounds last night before my dick finally called it quits. Then I hear him murmur something about starting the day, so I try grumbling, rolling away, and going back to sleep.

But this is Pen. He's not one to take no for an answer, especially when it comes to *plans*. One of which he says he has for us at freaking six-thirty in the morning.

A freaking sociopath, my best friend.

As it turns out, he drives us a little bit north of Cannon Beach to a hiking trail famous for a bunch of different movie filming locations. And while *Twilight* might be the main draw, it's when I see another movie listed on the trailhead map that gets my stomach swirling with anticipation.

Probably because *The Goonies* was one of my all-time favorite movies growing up. I think the two of us have seen it close to fifty times over the course of our lives. And I have to admit, a sunrise hike beside the ocean is breathtaking, and I'm sure Aspen ended up with plenty of amazing shots of the scenery.

Afterward, we return to the rental to rinse off the sweat and grime together…which turns into trading blowjobs under the rainfall-style shower head. The little delay of events makes it so the two of us are starving by the time we head back into town, stopping at a small cafe for breakfast. And honestly, while I love *The Goonies* something fierce, I think the highlight of the trip so far is the omelet I scarf down in maybe three minutes flat.

No lie, I think there might be crack in it or something, because after one bite, addiction sets in, and I'm ready to be *that person* who asks the cook for a recipe.

"Don't you dare think about it, Keene," Aspen mutters, shooting me a glare over his glass of orange juice. *With pulp.*

Like I said, a sociopath.

"I'm just saying, it might be the greatest thing I've ever put in my mouth."

A dark brow lifts, a filthy smirk forming on his lips. "And why weren't you saying that an hour ago while I fed you my cock?"

One sentence. One fucking sentence from him is all it takes for me to pop an instant boner, even in public. Which is kind of a problem, no matter how much I love his dirty mouth.

I lean forward, closing the space between us from across the table. "Maybe because I was a little too occupied to speak."

"Mmm," he hums, lifting his glass to his lips. My attention latches on to his Adam's apple while it bobs from him taking pulls of the drink.

If I wasn't hard before, sure as hell would've been now.

The day's only just begun by the time we leave the cafe, and we spend the rest of it exploring the areas around town, vegging out in the hot tub at the rental for the second time in a twenty-four-hour period, and just… enjoying each other's company.

I'm honestly shocked when Pen does something as simple as holding my hand as we walk down the main street of town. When he's not too busy taking pictures, that is. Not to mention the way he reels me into a kiss before we walk through the doors of a tavern a couple towns away where we have dinner.

By the time we're back in Cannon Beach, the sun is a couple hours from dipping down past the expansive horizon created by sand and sea. It's honestly one of the most stunning things I've seen, the sunset over the ocean. We watched it from the deck of the rental house last night, wrapped in nothing but towels and each other.

I'm just glad we've made it back in time to watch it again. Or, at least, that's my thought until Aspen pulls into a parking spot near the boardwalk leading down to the beach.

"More activities?" I ask, a smirk on my lips. "You're starting to spoil me, Kohl. Better knock it off before I start getting used to it."

Or maybe the real issue is that, in less than twenty-four hours, I already am. And I have no fucking idea how we're supposed to just go back to what's been normal for the past few months.

"Don't sit there and act like you haven't loved every single thing we've done today."

He doesn't even wait for me to answer, climbing from the driver's seat and waiting for me to join him at the front of the car.

"We're not going swimming, are we?" I ask as we hit the edge of the beach. It might be April, but we're in the Pacific Northwest. Only insane people go swimming when the water's that cold. I can see one now, a lone black dot on the horizon sitting on an orange surfboard.

Pen shakes his head, a chuckle slipping from him as he toes off his shoes and socks before he sets them off to the side of the boardwalk. I follow suit, though I'm still fairly skeptical.

The only reason I know, for a fact, he won't randomly try to drag me into the surf or dunk me is because he's got his camera bag slung over his shoulder.

"What happened to going with the flow?"

I can go with the flow just fine. My last name is *Waters,* for fuck's sake. I just have no interest in getting hypothermia and dying. Or getting so cold that my dick decides to flip inside out and permanently retreat back into my body.

"Trust me, Kee. Now, c'mon," he says, grabbing my hand and linking my fingers with his. My stomach flips at the smile he gives me before saying, "I have another surprise for you."

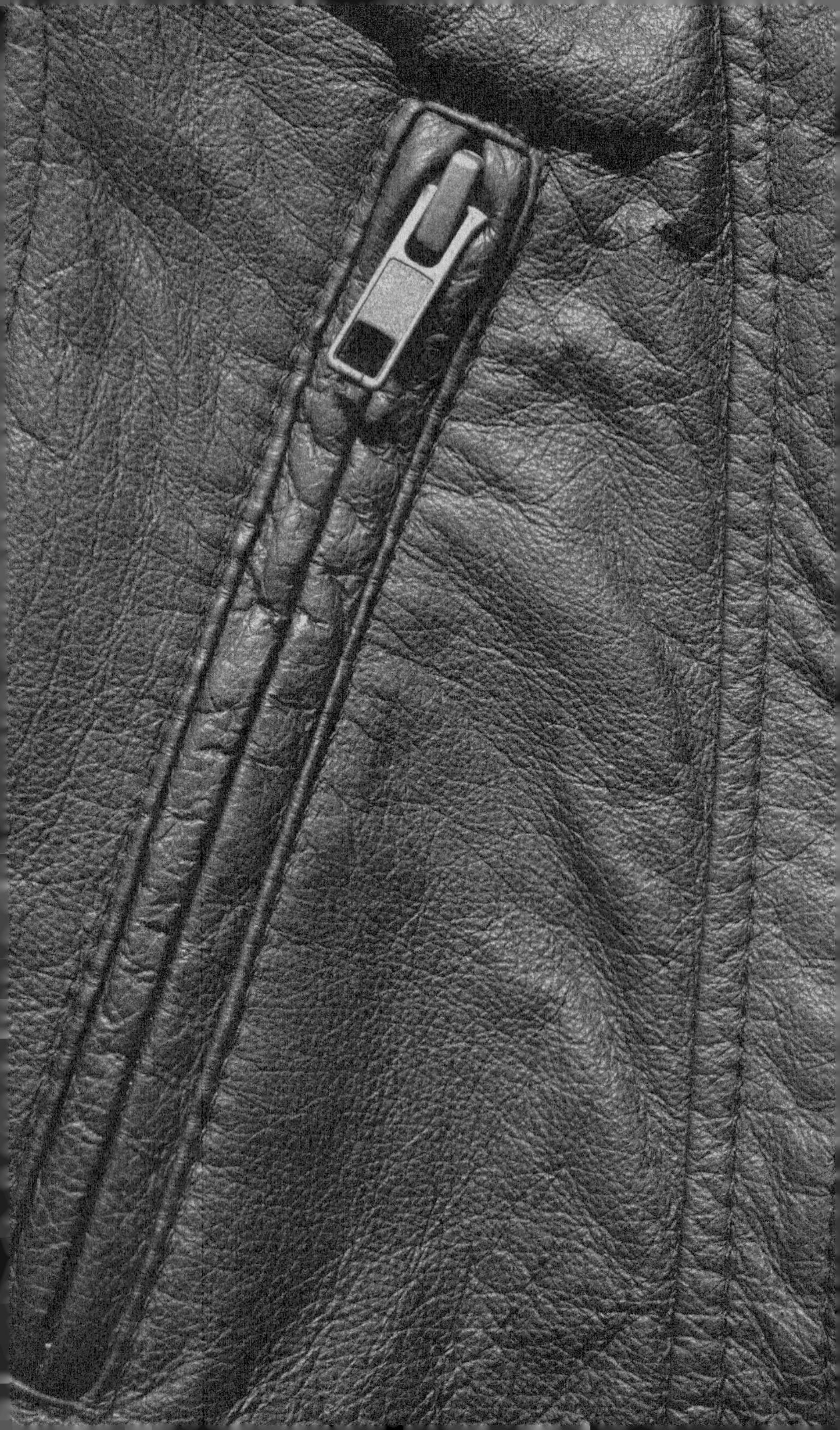

TWENTY-EIGHT

Aspen

"What do you mean, another surprise?" Keene asks as I drag him off the boardwalk and into the sand. It squeaks between our toes as we head toward Haystack Rock, just off the coast.

"You act like they aren't your favorite thing in the world. You almost shit yourself when we planned that surprise party for you after you won the State Championship junior year."

"Yeah," he says with a nod. "Literally almost shit myself, because I wasn't expecting it."

"But you still liked it," I counter, making my original point. "And this doesn't really involve anyone jumping out from behind furniture."

He lets out a laugh, his fingers squeezing mine before finally relenting. "Fine. I guess the first surprise was okay, so—"

"Just okay?" My brow hitches up when I look over at him. I know for a fact he's had the time of his life today; I made damn sure of it.

His grin grows. "Oh my God, do you need me to stroke your ego now or something? You know what I meant."

Rolling my teeth over my bottom lip, I hit him with a heated gaze. "It's definitely not my ego that I want you to stroke, Kee."

A tiny hint of pink hits his cheeks while he continues smiling. "I think that can be arranged. Later."

Oh, I'm counting on it.

I have every intention of laying him down and worshiping every inch of his gorgeous, carved body all damn night. Just like I did multiple times last night.

But, for now, it can wait.

Once we get close enough for a good angle of the town's famous icon, I pull Keene to a stop beside me. He looks confused as I drop my bag to the ground.

"Just give me a second. Stand right there with your back to the rock."

Of course, the second I pull my camera free, slinging it over one shoulder and across my chest, Keene makes a noise I can only describe as irritation.

My gaze rises to meet his. "Problem, Waters?"

"More pictures of me? Seriously?"

I have to laugh at the indignation laced in his tone. "Just cool it, okay? It's not what you're thinking."

It's not. I have something a little different planned than taking an obscene amount of pictures of Keene. He must not believe me, though, from the look on his face as I unpack my tripod. I wouldn't be surprised if he was trying to figure out a way to toss me into the freezing cold ocean.

It takes only a few minutes for me to get the tripod set up before snapping a few photos of Keene to adjust my settings. He glares, of course, and flips me the bird.

"It's not what I'm thinking, my ass," he mutters. "I swear to God, I'm gonna steal that thing from you one day and fill your SD card with pictures of you sleeping."

There's no doubt in my mind he'd do something like that in retaliation, and it just makes me laugh as I set the camera on the tripod before adjusting the rest of my settings and putting the autofocus on Keene.

"Calm down, pretty boy. And whatever you do, don't move from that spot."

"Fine. If it gets me back to the hot tub faster, I'll do whatever you say."

I snort and shake my head. Leave it to Keene to try and ruin another part of his surprise with an attitude the size of Everest.

"Hey, Kee?"

"Yeah?"

I glance up at him from over the camera, clicking the final setting for the timer. "How good are you at catching?"

He blinks at me as if I'm stupid and frowns. "I'm literally a *catcher*, Pen. What kind of question is that?"

"Just making sure," I murmur to myself.

With everything ready to go, there's nothing left to do but click the shutter and quickly bolt around the tripod toward him. Which I do, only confusing him more.

"Better think fast," I say as I jump into his arms. My legs wrap around his waist and I cling to him like a damn monkey climbing a tree before planting my lips on his.

He catches me, even with being taken by surprise for the first half-second. But then his hands grip my thighs, just below my ass, and he tugs me to him as his mouth molds to mine. One of my palms cups the side of his face, and I dive in for more, kissing him like he's the air I breathe.

Our tongues roll and mate together in a slow, seductive dance that I never want to end, and even though I know the camera's long since stopped snapping images, I keep kissing him.

Because I can.

Because he's mine.

Minutes pass before Keene pulls away. His lips are red and swollen, his voice breathless when he whispers, "Was that the surprise?"

I nod. "You'd said you wanted me to get out from behind the camera for a change," I murmur before pressing another kiss to his lips. "I just figured it would be a lot more fun to do that with you."

Instead of responding, he kisses me again. This time, more fiercely. Hungrily. Like he wants to devour me whole in this very spot. I'd let him. Fuck, I'd let him have whatever he wants if it meant I never had to give this moment up.

"You're getting me hard in public," I murmur into his lips as he continues to nip and suck at mine.

"Now you know how I felt at breakfast, having to listen to your filthy mouth."

A chuckle rumbles up from my chest. He has a point, though doing that wasn't at all intentional. However, what he's doing right now is one hundred percent planned, and if he wants to play dirty, I've got no qualms about doing the same.

My feet kick at the backs of his knees, taking both of us down to the ground in a tumble of limbs. I land on top of him, and he bursts out laughing the second his back hits. We're both covered in grains of sand that we'll probably be washing out of our hair for a week.

"A jackass, like always."

If wanting him on the ground beneath me so I can roll my hard cock against his makes me a jackass, I'm more than happy to claim that title.

Giving him a slow rock of my hips, he moans, and I swallow it down with another searing kiss.

I'd take him right here and now on the beach if I knew we wouldn't get arrested. Sure, the beach has been mostly abandoned as it is, with only a few other tourists and a lone surfer out in the ocean, but that's enough to keep me from putting my idea into action. I'm putting a pin in it for later tonight, though, when we have the cover of darkness and our own stretch of private beach.

My lips curl up into a grin when he pulls back enough to meet my gaze, then fixating his attention on my mouth. At first I think he's gonna cuss me out some more—which is the reason for my smile. I never expected him to say what he does next.

"Your smile makes me stupid," he mutters, reaching up to run his thumb over my bottom lip. It tracks over to the left side, dipping down to where my dimple is making an appearance. "This makes me pretty stupid too."

His declaration makes me smile more, his finger sinking deeper into the divot when I do. My heart stumbles and stutters in my chest as he continues to touch me in a way that's both foreign and familiar all at once.

In reverence. With…love.

Maybe that's part of the reason I get this aching feeling when I have my hands anchored in his hair as he works my cock with his mouth, or why I can't get enough of the taste of his tongue as it spears between my lips. Because it might be new and crazy and terrifying, but it's also everything I could ask for.

And all I know is…I want more.

More of Keene, and in ways I've never wanted anyone else.

In ways I've never wanted *him* before now.

You have to be all in.

I glance up when emotions start clogging my throat, only to find a surfer with an orange board standing near the edge of the waves just… watching us. From the looks of it, he has been for a while now. And instead of feeling weird about it or wanting to push Keene away, I find myself wanting to do the exact opposite.

I wanna put on a show. Pull him closer. Kiss him again.

Claim him right here and now.

So I do.

Even if the surfer dude is the only one around to see, it doesn't make Keene any less mine.

The thing about the Pacific Northwest is that the weather can change on a dime, and today is a perfect example. After another thirty minutes of taking stupid, goofy pictures both together and of each other, I notice storm clouds starting to roll in off the coast. I barely have time to get my camera equipment together in my bag and shove it under my shirt before the downpour starts.

I guess it's not a terrible thing, since it washes any remaining sand from us by the time we make it back to the Impala completely soaked. But the smile on Keene's face as he shakes out his dripping hair is so worth it.

Turning the ignition over, I pull out of the parking lot and head down the road back to the cottage. On the way, I feel the heat of Keene's stare on me, devouring every wet inch of my body with his eyes alone.

It makes me hot all over, but not as much as his tongue catching a drop of water cascading over his lip.

I groan. "Keep staring at me while doing that, and we aren't gonna make it back to the house."

Of course, he takes that as a challenge, sliding across the bench seat until he's directly next to me. "Doing what, exactly?"

I don't answer him, trying to concentrate on the road ahead and not crashing my car, but he makes it really difficult when he palms my cock over the wet denim of my jeans, rubbing and squeezing my thickening length until we pull into the driveway.

"Get inside," I mutter through clenched teeth before bolting for the house. He's right behind me as I unlock the door and shove it open with purpose, finally out of the rain. I'm in the foyer a second later, and he slams the door closed behind us before pulling me against him and diving in.

Lips devour lips, tongues battle with each other, fighting about which one belongs in whose mouth while we grind and roll together in a wet, panting mess. It's frenzied and needy, while still being seductive. Sweet nips and gentle caresses paired with complete desperation for the other.

It's deliciously addictive. Pure, passionate sin rolled into one mind-boggling kiss.

But I've come to realize, it's not just his kiss that I'm hooked on. It's everything about him.

Keene.

My best friend.

The *only person* who has the power to completely ruin me.

And I might just let him.

The thought has me grinding to a halt, because this is exactly what I've tried to protect myself from, especially when it comes to this thing between us. This beautiful, epic, and potentially tragic thing that absolutely terrifies me.

Can anyone blame me, though? I can't destroy everything we've built together for our entire lives if this goes wrong. Because I could lose everything in my life, every damn person or thing I hold dear, and I'd be okay.

Just not him.

God, never him.

My heart thumps wildly in my chest when I pull away, chest heaving with effort. And then I do the scariest thing I've done yet; I let myself crack open a little more for him.

"I want you. So much, I can't think. Can't breathe. I can't do anything but want you."

And I do. In every sense of the word, I want him.

Need him. Crave him.

Every piece of who he is, I want to claim as mine.

He swallows, his face more serious than I've probably ever seen. Almost like he's in pain. "You already have me."

Four words, and my heart explodes.

I reel him back to me, my mouth hungry and greedy for him. His tongue slips past my lips again, and I take pull after pull of it while I push him back against the door. My hands work their way beneath his shirt, determined to feel his soft, smooth skin against mine as soon as possible.

He rolls his hips forward, the length of his cock creating the perfect amount of friction against mine beneath our wet clothes. But I want nothing between us. I want to be surrounded by him. Enveloped in him.

Taken captive by every single thing about him that I've fallen in love with.

The second he rips his mouth from mine, I'm desperate to reel him back in for more. But God, there's something to be said for how beautifully wrecked he is right now, pressed up against me. Hair drenched from the rain, mouth red and swollen from my kiss. I don't think there's ever been a sexier sight in my life, and it only solidifies my thinking from on the beach.

I want more, however I can get it.

Giving this up would be like living without oxygen.

Impossible.

We continue to stare, drinking one another in as we catch our breath. I can see a tiny spark in his eyes where something mischievous is forming.

"What is it?"

His tongue darts out, catching a drop of water trailing over his lip like he did in the car. And when his look turns downright devious, I have a feeling I know exactly where he's going with this before he even asks the question.

"Don't you dare?"

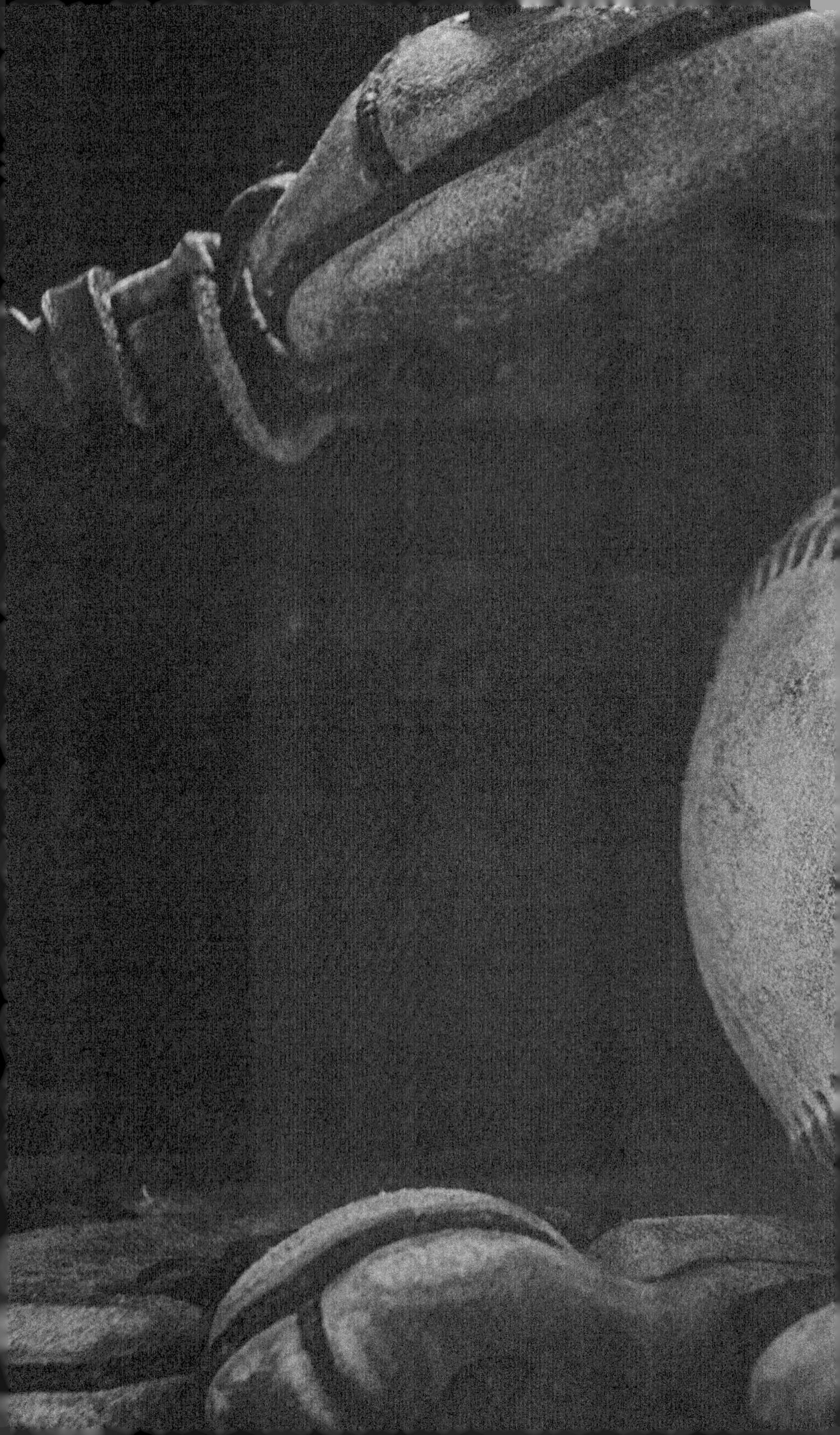

TWENTY-NINE

Keene

The moment my words register, a wicked grin to match my own appears on his face. Then he pops that little dimple below his mouth in the most addicting way. "Do you even have to ask?"

I smirk, trailing my hand down his chest. My fingers dip under his shirt, pulling the damp fabric over his head and tossing it across the room. It lands with a loud *thwap*, leaving his skin completely exposed.

"I dare you..." I whisper, letting my fingers glide the length of his spine, before circling around to the front of his jeans, my knuckles dancing over his skin there. The button pops open with ease and I smirk when his breath hitches slightly with anticipation as I push them to the floor.

I love knowing what I do to him. The way his body responds to mine when I touch him.

We might be in this weird space between friends and more than that right now, and I might be going insane while trying to dissect it, but I know *this*. The way my body melts under his touch, sings for him alone.

"You dare me…" he repeats, his eyes igniting my skin. It doesn't stop when he glances down to where I'm undressing him, painfully slow.

I've had this idea in my head for a while, how to separate my emotions from the sex we've been having. And with all the emotions swirling around in my brain and chest while we've been here on the coast, I think it's time I try to lock them up and enjoy this for what it is.

Just sex.

It's the only way to detach. Guard myself, before it's too late.

Leaning in, I brush my lips lightly against his. Not in a kiss, but a featherlight caress meant to taunt him.

"I dare you to fuck me," I murmur against his mouth. "And when I say fuck me, I don't want the way we've been having sex, all sensual and shit. I want you to *fuck me*."

To prove my point, I rub the heel of my hand against his erection, stiff and ready for me. It makes my cock twitch against his hip, getting impossibly harder. I want to take my time with him, drive him as wild as he does me on a daily basis with something as simple as a look in my direction and one of those sexy, dimple-popping smirks he reserves just for me.

But God, I'm torturing myself as much as I am him, so I forego the idea of a slow seduction, moving from zero to a hundred in the blink of an eye.

Tugging my own soaked shirt over my head, I let it join his on the floor before swapping our positions and pressing him back against the door. He's cold against me, slick with the remnants of rain water, and when I go to flick his nipple, goosebumps break out across every inch of his pale skin.

He licks his bottom lip, that grin of his turning downright sinful. "Am I not fucking you good enough for your liking?"

His hands slip into my pants, kneading my ass in his hands and driving me even crazier for him.

"Mmm, that's not what I said." I wrap my hand around his cock, giving it a couple slow tugs. "I want whatever you'll give me...however you'll give it to me."

There's an arch to his brow. "But you want me to be rougher? Dirtier?"

Licking my lips, I nod. "I want the filthiest parts of you, Pen. I want it all." Deep blue eyes flare with heat, an unchecked amount of lust and desire swirling in their depths. Then he leans in, whispering against my lips and making my toes curl.

"Then get on your knees, baby. I'm about to fuck your face until you can't breathe."

Holy shit.

I've never dropped to my knees faster in my life, stripping him of his underwear until he's standing before me in all his sexy, naked glory.

The expanse of pale skin before me is mouthwatering perfection, and I can't help but want to touch and lick and worship every inch of it.

I used to tease him about how white he is, always telling him he makes Casper look tan on his best days. Even when we spend weeks on the road where we hike and spend a lot of time outside, he never gets much darker than he is now.

But as I run my hands down his taut stomach and lick at the blue veins popping out near his hip, I don't think I'd want it any other way. There's nothing I'd change. I'm obsessed with everything about him.

My tongue runs the length of his cock, working up from root to tip before lavishing attention on the crown, already shiny with a bead of pre-cum. I swirl it around the head and flicking at the nerve beneath, and though I wasn't going for torture, it must be from the way Pen's chest rumbles out a low groan.

"Don't play games with me, Kee," he mutters, fingers sinking into the hair at the back of my head and tugging me closer. "Open. And swallow."

With a small smile on my lips, I obey his command and let him slide his cock along my tongue. The moment the head hits the back of my throat, I inhale through my nose and take him further. My nose brushes against his skin, the musky scent of him overwhelming me as he starts to move.

It's slow at first, controlled as he always is while he lets me get a feel for it. But soon enough, he's moving faster, hips snapping forward and fingers anchoring painfully in my hair. More pre-cum catches on my tongue, the burst of masculine flavor making me crave more of it.

I'm so desperate for him, it's insane.

And that makes me so screwed.

My grip on him tightens, holding on for dear life as he starts to fuck my mouth with absolutely zero finesse. The length of him glides across my tongue, slipping down my throat on each thrust, and the look on his face is nothing but sweet, blissful ecstasy as I take everything he has to give me. I swallow around the length the way that drives him wild, and he lets out another sexy moan that goes straight to my own aching cock.

"Shit, don't do that if you want me to fuck you, Kee," he rasps, pulling himself free from my lips and yanking me up to stand. He plants a blistering kiss on my lips that makes my stupid, love-sick heart sing before breaking away far too soon.

Fingers weave with mine and he drags me down the hall toward the room where we're staying, the remainder of my clothes left behind in our wake.

Pen releases me, immediately moving for my bag and grabbing the bottle of lube I keep stored in there. When he turns, his thick length coming back into view again, a shiver runs down my spine.

Anticipation builds more as he crosses the room to me, dropping the lube on the comforter and taking my face in his hands and kissing me.

This kiss is different from the last, more slow and sensual, like it was at the beach when I held him in my arms. Full of emotion and memories and friendship, tasting of the future.

A future you don't have.

This time, I'm the one to break away because my heart can't take the way it makes me feel. It's too much, making my entire body tremble with want and need and love and lust, torn between what this is and what I know it could be. It only escalates when he searches my face, giving me the softest smile imaginable.

"Bend over the end of the bed for me, baby."

Turning away from him helps ease the ache in my chest, but only just.

I follow his command, and the second I do, I feel slick fingers teasing my hole before the first sinks inside me. There's a split second where my body tenses, ready to reject the intrusion, but I relax and let him sink the digit in me further.

I've become addicted to the stretch my body gives him, the way we fit together perfectly at every turn. I'll never get tired of feeling it.

He kneels behind me, adjusting his angle before another finger slides into me. He really starts stretching me then, preparing my body for him as he peppers kisses at the base of my spine and across each cheek.

My prostate is easy enough for him to find now, and he plays with the little pleasure button inside me, taking turns tormenting the nerves and scissoring his fingers as he sinks them in and out of me.

It doesn't take long for him to have me panting and needy as I grip the comforter in my fists. He hasn't even touched my cock, let alone put his dick inside me, and I already feel primed and ready to explode at any second.

Pen's not helping matters when every time I think I'm gonna come, he eases off my prostate and goes back to stretching me. It's the most delicious kind of torture, but damn. I rue the damn day I decided to mess around with edging him.

Payback's a bitch, and it's gonna be the death of me.

When my balls seize for what might be the eighth time without being granted release, I let out a frustrated sigh.

"I want you inside me, Pen. I want to feel your dick stretching me. Owning me. Not your goddamn fingers. I fucking need it, so stop playing games and drawing it out. Just give me what I want."

He lets out a low chuckle, pulling free from my body and trailing his fingers up my back as he stands. My ass clenches around nothing but air, missing him filling me, but becoming more desperate for what's coming next.

"Someone's impatient." He grabs the bottle of lube from beside me, and I glance over to watch him coat his cock with the liquid.

God, it's a sight to behold.

"You would be too if you were just being edged for the past twenty minutes," I snap.

His lips twitch for the briefest moment. "I have no idea what you're talking about."

I'm about to call him out for being a damn liar, but knowing Pen, he'd only go on to torture me more for his own enjoyment. And thankfully, I'm rewarded for my silence when he kicks my legs further apart and positions himself right behind me.

Lips brush over my spine in a feather-light caress, and another piece of my heart shreds.

I can't handle the soft touches, knowing they lead to nothing. To nowhere. Because to him, this is just sex.

It's time I get on the same page.

"I'll never hurt you," he murmurs, teeth scraping against my shoulder. "I'd rather die."

The vulnerability in his words slices me open, leaving me raw and bare like never before. And I don't have it in me to tell him that he's *already* hurting me.

He fucking hurts me with every touch, look, or kiss, painting an impossible picture in my brain.

That this is real.

That he might love me.

But I know he doesn't.

Not the way I love him.

"You're not gonna break me," I tell him for what might be the thousandth time, but the words taste bitter on my tongue, like the lie they are.

He takes them at face value, though, pressing yet another kiss to my skin.

Warm breath floats across the back of my neck, and when his cock nudges my rim with the slightest amount of pressure, the combination of sensations makes me shiver.

"Good. Because I'm about to fuck you like I hate you."

Then he thrusts his hips forward, impaling me completely with one single move. I gasp, my entire body lit on fire in the best way, and it only grows. Building in the best way as Aspen pulls out almost all the way before slamming back home.

It's hard and fast and brutal, but it's everything I've wanted. As he pounds into me, claiming me as his, I feel whole. Completely owned by him.

The slap of his hips against my ass and the sound of heavy breathing fill the room, creating a soundtrack we get lost in as our bodies take us close to the edge of release. I've been halfway there for a while, and I know it'll only take one or two strokes of my dick before I come completely undone.

"You wanna be owned, huh, Kee?" he pants, grabbing my hips and dragging me back onto his cock. "Is this what you want?"

"Yes," I whisper, caught between the truth and a lie. Because I don't want him to own my body alone. I want him to take my heart and soul too. Everything I have to give, I want him to own. Make his and protect it. Cherish it.

But what I want is something I know I'll never have…and I'd do well to remember that.

"Then get there," he mutters. "I'm close."

My palm wraps around my cock, and his palm lands on the small of my back a moment later, pressing down so my ass lifts higher. The new angle has him swiping over my prostate with every punishing thrust, sending me closer and closer and closer.

And I shatter.

I come on a cry, fists clenching the comforter. A full-body orgasm racks every inch of me as hot cum coats my fingers and drips onto the floor between my feet. Aspen's not far behind me, his movements becoming more sporadic and far less controlled as he finally slips over the edge with me. He rides out his orgasm, the grip on my waist tightening enough to bruise until he slows to a stop.

A deep, sated breath leaves him, his forehead landing on my back as we both take a minute to come down from the high of our release.

His fingers skate back and forth over my hip, a loving but owning caress, and it creates a knot in my throat so large, it's almost impossible to breathe around.

I'm desperate for some air, some space to get myself under control before I do something insanely stupid. Like crying right in front of him. Or telling him I want more.

Or do the worst thing possible. Because those three words are right there, on the tip of my naughty tongue. Somehow, I manage to swallow them down, nearly choking on the acidic taste of deceit.

But I know it's for the best.

It's always for the best, keeping emotions separate from sex. That's what he said, right?

I'm the first to move, pulling away enough for his cock to slip free from my ass. He doesn't let me get far, though, his hold on my hips tightening. The warm dripping sensation of his cum sliding out of my hole greets me after a few seconds, beginning to trail down my leg.

"That what you meant by owning you?" he whispers, and I glance over my shoulder in time to watch him swipe up the cum seeping out of me before shoving it right back inside. "Claiming you?"

My heart might as well be in a vice as I nod, telling him yet another lie. Tears begin blurring my vision, and I turn away quickly. Hell if I'll let him see me losing my shit after sex.

"Gonna go shower," I mutter, freeing myself from his grasp and rushing to the safety of the adjoining bathroom.

Tears track down my face, and I swallow down the sob trying to work its way from my chest as I yank the shower on full blast to drown out the mangled sound that manages to slip free.

I've gone and fucking done it now. Proven that, no matter how hard I try, I can't turn off my feelings for him.

There's only one way to survive being so stupidly in love with him.

We have to stop.

Otherwise, I'll destroy everything.

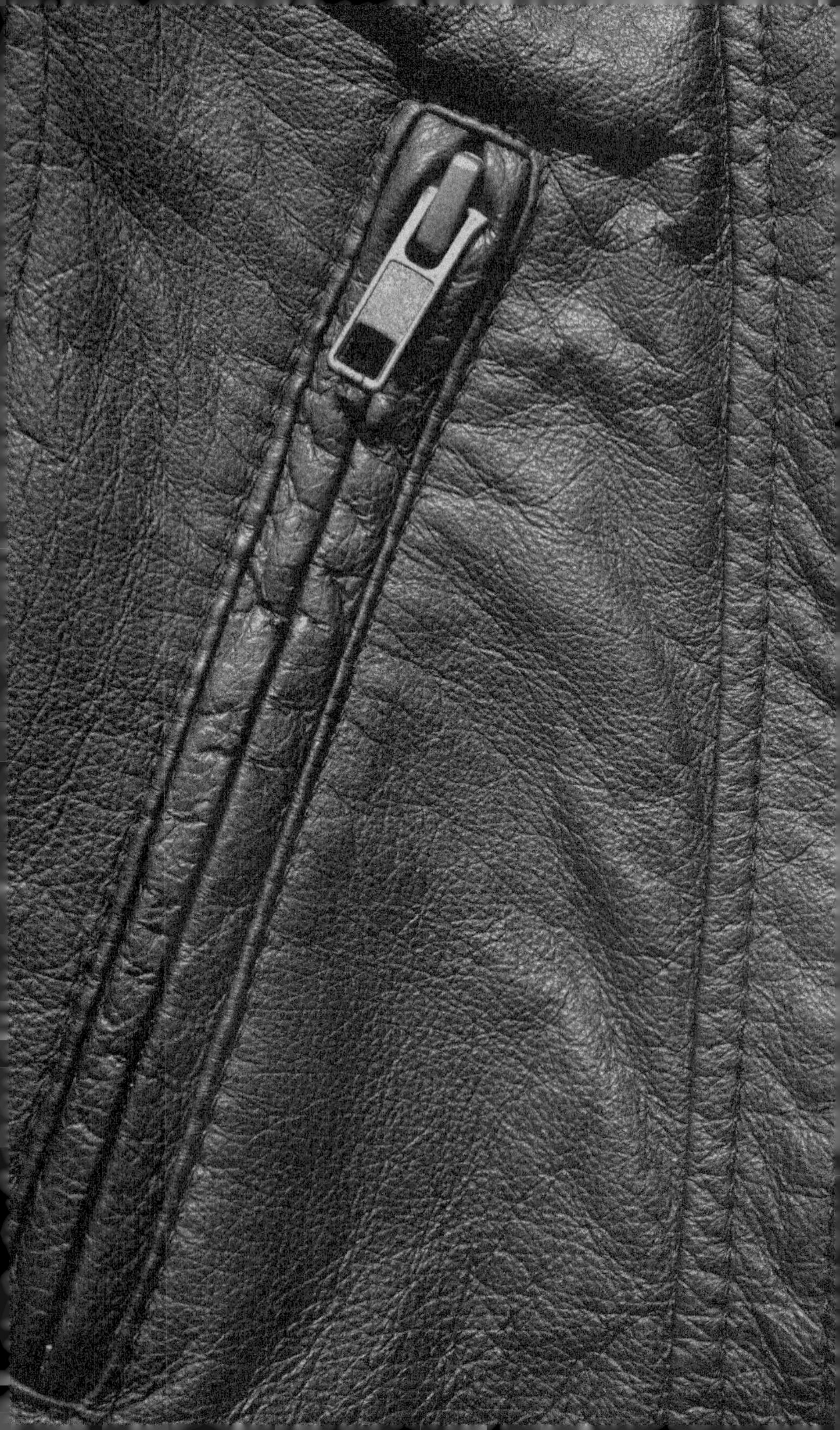

THIRTY

Aspen

Me: Something's wrong with Keene.

Bristol: What did you do?

Me: Why are you assuming it's something I did?

Bristol: *gif of the unamused kid in Spongebob pajamas*

Bristol: Please. You're the emotionally stunted one here. It has to be you.

Me: I appreciate the vote of confidence, as always.

Bristol: Absolutely. Now spill. When you texted from Cannon Beach, it sounded like things were good. What changed?

Me: That's just it. I have no idea.

Me: We were at the beach, and everything was great. I did everything you said. Let him in, showed him I care. And for a second, I was seeing it. Us. Me and him.

Bristol: So it comes back to…what did you do?

Me: Nothing!

Bristol: When did he start acting weird?

Me: ...after we had sex.

Bristol: So you did do something.

Me: I fucked him the way he asked me to. Hard and rough and claiming. And, no offense to you, but it was some of the best sex of my life.

Bristol: None taken, I guess.

Me: He seemed fine after it. Went to the bathroom to shower. Came back out, and he seemed a little out of it. Thought it was just post-sex haze. We watched the storm on the balcony after. Snuggled in bed the way he likes. It was everything.

Me: But the next morning, he woke up like a completely different person. Almost...detached? The complete opposite of himself. He barely spoke the entire ride home.

Bristol: Did you try talking to him?

Me: Don't type to me in that tone. Of course, I tried. He gave me a one-off comment about being tired, but it's been weeks, and it's not better.

Bristol: THIS HAS BEEN GOING ON FOR WEEKS AND YOU'RE JUST TELLING ME NOW?

Me: I was trying to fix it on my own. Obviously, I can't.

Me: I don't know what to do. I wish I knew what was wrong so I could fix it before it's too late.

Bristol: Just don't give up. He's never given up on you.

THIRTY-ONE

Aspen

May

Tonight's Family Night for the Wildcats, a yearly tradition they have at the last home game of the regular season. Each of the players have special seats in the rows behind the home dugout, reserved for the loved ones who helped teach them about dedication, commitment, hard work, yada yada yada.

Honestly, I think it's just a bunch of pomp and circumstance, but I have to admit, I love knowing there's a seat reserved for me with Keene's mother and sister. Not that I didn't have one last year. It's just…this one seems different somehow. Maybe because *we're* different now.

We're not just us, as in Keene and Aspen, best friends.

We're *an us*, as in…shit. Well, I don't know what we are anymore.

Not boyfriends. Not just friends.

Lovers, maybe? As cringey as it sounds, that might be the correct term. We're certainly not fuck buddies or friends with benefits, because even if neither of us has said much about it, there's something more here.

More equaling feelings. Emotions, no matter how much I haven't wanted to admit it. They're raw and real and scary ones, because they're true, and they run deep.

Twenty years deep.

The anxiety that causes only gets worse with Keene being a little off ever since we came back from the coast. Still is, though I think it might be getting better. I don't really know how to describe it, I just feel it, even though nothing's really changed.

We haven't had sex since that day at the cottage, but that's mostly on me. I've been busy with my studio final, pulling all-nighters most of this week to make sure it's done in time. And man, do I feel guilty for it. Or maybe I'm just overthinking everything I do or say, now that I'm starting to really sink into the idea of an *us*. Because the last thing I want is to go on and screw it up.

"This is us," Loraine—Keene's mom—says, motioning toward the seats all decked out with maroon t-shirts donning the number twenty-eight on them. "Wow. The school really went all out this year."

I chuckle and shake my head, knowing damn well that it was all Keene, not the school. He wanted to do something special for tonight, the sap he is when it comes to his loved ones. Though it might be one of my favorite qualities when it comes to him.

Loraine and Lexi, his sister, both settle into their seats, me smack dab between them. My guess is the choice of seats was also Keene's decision, which are right behind the edge of the dugout closest to home plate. Gives a great view of the game for his mother and sister, and as for me, I can also catch glimpses of my man's ass as he does his thing behind the plate.

Win-win.

For some reason, my mind snags on the words that just ran through my brain. Two in particular.

My man.

I mean, I've called Keene that before plenty of times over the years, just never in the context of…well…mine. My best friend or my number one, sure. But never just *mine*. I have to admit, the possessive side of me loves the way it feels and sounds, even just in my head.

As if summoned by my thoughts alone, Keene appears in front of me, finger gripping the net that hangs over the dugout as protection from stray bats and balls.

"Hey, guys." He smiles up at us, and for the first time in a few weeks, it truly meets his eyes.

"Hi, honey!" Loraine says, jumping up at the sound of his voice. She gives him a quick peck on the cheek as best she can through the net, holding up the shirt he'd left on her seat. "Look at what the team did for us! Isn't that so cool? Did you know?"

Keene shrugs and gives me a look. "No, I had no idea, Mom."

"Yet it's funny how no one else had a shirt waiting on their chair," Lexi mutters under her breath. Not very well, because Keene and I both heard her loud and clear, though Loraine seems to be oblivious to her daughter's point. Or maybe she's just gotten really good at ignoring Lexi's snide comments over the years.

I give Lex a nudge with my foot, a signal to shut up, as Keene glares daggers at her for a moment.

"The team had the option to put them on the reserved seats or have them picked up at will call," he says through gritted teeth. "I chose to do this."

Lexi rolls her eyes and lifts her phone in front of her face, texting up a storm. Probably bitching about being at a family event for Keene when she'd much rather be doing…whatever teenagers do these days.

Probably making videos for TikTok.

"Aw, c'mon, Lex," I say, nudging her again with my foot. "Can't you just be supportive and act like you love your brother for one day?"

She ignores me entirely, just keeps tapping away at the screen.

"Alexis," her mother scolds, using her full name before grabbing the phone from her daughter's grip. "I've had enough of your attitude for the day, and we just got here. Now wish your brother good luck before he gets on his way."

If looks could kill, Keene and Loraine would be six feet under right about now.

"Good luck or whatever," she mumbles, crossing her arms over her chest. Then, as if realizing *I'm* the cause of all her problems—or at least her phone being taken away—she glares up at me. "And don't think I don't realize you're just defending him because you've been butt buddies since before you could walk."

I do my best not to wince or give a reaction to her comment; I really fucking do. After all, this is Lexi, and she lives to push both of our buttons. But I feel the way my body tenses at her words, and more importantly, the newly found accuracy to them.

"Alexis Ann!" Loraine exclaims, a frown taking over her face. "That's enough."

"It's fine, Mom," Keene says, shrugging. His typical move when something's eating at him. "I've gotta run anyway."

He turns to head toward the stairs that lead down into the dugout when I call out his name, nearly forgetting the surprise I brought for him.

"Kee!" I call just as his head is about to disappear under the roof of the dugout. He pops it up, just enough for me to see his nose and eyes, raising a brow.

"Got you something," I say, lifting a bottle of lemon-lime Gatorade. His favorite.

"You're my favorite human ever," he says, smiling. "I knew I forgot something at the dorm."

He'd probably forget his damn head on game days, that's how in the zone he can get. Especially on days that are important to him. Like when his mom and sister are coming to watch, not knowing about the slideshow each member of the team put together for their families.

"I know," I shrug, playing off the way his words make my pulse thrum.

"Like I said," Lexi grumbles. "Butt buddies."

This time, Keene's the one to roll his eyes. "Come to the other end of the dugout so I can grab it?"

I could just as easily shimmy it under the net where we are right now, but the look in Keene's eye as he makes his request lets me know he wants a second of my time away from the prying eyes and ears of his family.

Thankfully, we're here pretty early. Loraine's doing, of course, being the overly supportive and extremely enthusiastic mother she is. Yet because of this, the stands are still pretty empty and we have a bit more privacy down on the other end of the dugout. Only just a bit, though.

I hand him the drink, letting my fingers brush against his during the hand-off.

"Thanks." He grins, opening it and taking a few slow pulls of the liquid. My eyes latch on to the way his Adam's apple bobs as he swallows. The urge to lick it soars through me, making my dick twitch in my pants.

Not that I wasn't already admiring how good he looks right now. Eyeblack smear beneath his eyes, his catcher's helmet sitting backward on his head. And hell if he doesn't fill out his uniform to damn near perfection.

"Stop looking at me like that," he snaps softly, capping the bottle and setting it on the roof of the dugout.

I play innocent. "Like what?"

He just arches his brow, his non-answer more than enough to tell me he knows I'm full of shit. No surprise here, because I am.

"Lex is really on one today," he muses, changing the subject entirely. Not exactly where I thought his mind would go after the very public mental undressing I just gave him, but okay.

"That's just Lex. She's fine."

Alexis and Keene haven't always had the best relationship, and it became more and more strained as she got older and he took on more of a father-like role for her, rather than just a big brother. Add in that he's a golden boy—her words, not mine—and I guess there's a bit of resentment beneath the surface.

He lets out a snort. "Imagine how pissed she'd be if she knew how true her *butt buddies* comment was. She's had a damn crush on you since what? When we were eight?"

I smirk, vividly remembering little four-year-old Lexi chasing us around, begging for a kiss because one of her friends was kissed by a boy in their Pre-K class. Being the gentleman I was, even at that age, I refused and told her that her first kiss needs to be with a boy she really liked.

Clearly I was absolutely clueless and didn't yet know girls only seem to want what they can't have. That was the day Lexi Waters' obsession with me was born.

"Sounds about right."

He licks his lips, glancing down at mine. "Sucks to be her, I guess. Though I can't say I'm all that mad about it."

Yeah, me neither.

And I'm more than happy to see that playful, flirty side of him come back out. I've been so busy and didn't realize until now how much I've really fucking missed it.

"Now who needs to stop looking at who like that?" I point out, cocking my head before changing the topic to a much safer option. "Kick some ass today, okay? Or there'll be hell to pay."

He sees right through my attempt to tame the conversation though, using a hand on the dugout to lean toward me. God, his growing smirk is something straight outta an X-rated movie. Full of heat and desire and capable of melting me from the inside out.

"And do I get a reward if I listen to that request? Or was that a really poor attempt at threatening me?"

Doing my best to keep us from being overheard—because more and more people have started filing down to their seats—I mirror his stance and lean in even more toward him until my mouth is only inches from his ear.

"I'll fuck you through the weekend starting the second you walk through our door if you do," I tell him, letting the tips of my fingers brush against his. "And that's a promise."

If I thought the look he was giving was filthy before I made that comment, it's nothing compared to the way lust has completely taken over his face when I pull back. Those brown eyes are dilated, and his tongue swipes over his bottom lip subtly as he stares at my mouth some more.

I wish I could kiss him right now. Lay one on him right here, in front of the world. But it's not only fear holding me back. It's timing.

We haven't so much as had the chance to talk about *us* or what the future holds once we move back home this weekend, let alone how he wants to handle coming out to people, if at all.

My concerns about how it will impact his career is a huge one, and if I have to give up kissing him in public to make his dreams come true, I will.

"Keep looking at me like that, and I won't be able to walk back to my seat without giving the entire stadium an eyeful of what I'm working with below the belt," I warn him, raising a brow.

He blinks a couple times, as if coming out of a trance. "Shit, you're probably right."

As if on cue, one of his teammates calls his last name, causing him to peek under his arm into the dugout. His fingers rub against mine while he chats with…I think it's Reyes? I can't be sure.

One, because I don't really pay much attention to the rest of the team. And two, because even if I did, I wouldn't be able to right now with the way the pads of his fingers trace over my knuckles. It has my entire body lit up like a Christmas tree, and I doubt he even realizes he's doing it.

Touching each other is just subconscious to us now.

"We're gonna infield quick," he tells me when he looks back up. It's then I notice a bunch of his teammates filing out of the dugout to take the field. "Then we gotta get this show on the road."

I nod, not really sure what to say at this point. Normally, I'd kiss him and squeeze his ass if we were in our room before he left for the field. I did that before he left today too. Yet my body is craving to do it again. Right now. Where everyone can see.

It's not the right time.

Keene's free hand moves up to the maroon helmet sitting backward on his head, fiddling with it the way he does his hats when he's nervous. My eyes narrow in on the action.

"Why are you fidgeting? You do this all the time."

He shrugs. "Not with my mom and sister here."

Of course. I should've figured he would be anxious about their presence. He has nothing to prove to them in regards to his ability on the field. Both of them know how hard working and dedicated he is to playing ball. So that only leaves…

"Your family is gonna love what you put together," I tell him in reassurance, looking down into his eyes.

And as if that's all he needed to hear, he beams at me. But it's in the weirdest way. Like he knows something I don't. "I hope so."

"They will because they love you. And they're really proud of you." I don't say that I include myself in the *they* I just spoke of because…shit. Because I need to figure my own crap out before I dare say that to him.

The love part, that is.

You have to be all in.

"Good. I wanna make them proud. Because I love them too." His eyes soften and he gives me that look again. This time, I really can't place it, so I just nod.

Two of my fingertips give one of his a subtle squeeze before I pull away, turning to head back to where Lexi and Loraine are sitting, sodas and peanuts in hand. Lex tosses a bag of them at me, and I bat them out of the way, hitting her smack in the face.

She calls me an asshole, but I just smirk. "Karma's a bitch, Lex."

And then Loraine scolds me for cursing at Lexi…even though she just called me an asshole. Yeah, tell me how that one makes any sense.

I'm sliding back down into my seat between the two of them when I hear, "Hey, Kohl!" being called in Keene's deep timber. Glancing up, I find him leaning against the rail of the dugout, still where he and I were just talking.

I raise my brow in response, figuring he'd make some comment to back his sister up. Instead, the fucker opens his damn mouth and shocks the ever-loving hell outta me.

"I dare you to put your money where your mouth is after the game," he taunts, that cocky smile returning. "Regardless of the outcome."

Oh, baby, you think I'd have it any other way?

I nod, doing my best to keep my grin from taking over my entire face. "You're on."

"What was that about?" Lexi asks a moment later. When I'm able to peel my eyes away from Keene as he saunters out to his position behind the plate for infield practice, I look down at her big, hazel eyes.

"Nothing, really," I say with a shrug. "I just told Keene I'd kick his ass if he didn't do well today."

Yeah. *Kick* his ass.

Right...

THIRTY-TWO

Aspen

The team goes through two players at a time between each half inning, showing the slideshow of images each player gave to have displayed on the scoreboard for the crowds to see. It's the top of the seventh now, and I'm even starting to get jitters, so I can only imagine how Keene is feeling from having to wait.

He's slow out of the dugout to get into position behind the plate since he was left stranded on base in the bottom of the previous inning, though it never fails to amaze me how quickly he can throw all that gear on. When he climbs up the steps of the dugout and appears, he glances over his shoulder to look at the three of us.

His smile lights my soul on fire and I can't help but grin back and do my best not to notice, once again, the way his pants hug his ass or how fuckhot he looks immersed in his element. The last thing I need is to sport a chub from staring at him whilst sitting between the two members of his family who mean the most to him.

Thank God, halfway through the warm up, the moment finally arrives.

"And now introducing the family and loved ones of number twenty-eight, starting catcher for the Wildcats, Keene Waters!" The announcer's voice booms over the stadium as clapping and cheers fill the space.

Keene glances up at his mom, sister, and me again, lifting his mask as he does. He's got the biggest, dopiest grin on his face when he sees the tears in his mom's eyes as the first image of their family is brought on the screen. When I look over to my other side, I notice even Lexi is smiling at her big brother before looking up at the scoreboard.

Laughter ripples from my stomach as I watch the images flick across the screen in the slideshow. I helped Keene pick out the images he wanted to use for this a couple weeks back, especially the one of him and his sister covered in whipped cream when they decided to have a war, using the spray cans as guns when they were ten and six. I remember the day like it was yesterday, and from the giggles bursting from both Loraine and Lexi, they do too.

My attention moves from the screen down to the field again, where my heart might as well stop. Because instead of looking at the scoreboard, where images of his loved ones are flashing, he's staring at me.

Not his mom or sister.

Me.

The smile on his face just about kills me. There's so much emotion in it besides joy and happiness, though anyone who doesn't know him as well as I do wouldn't just see those two things. And they'd also think he was looking at his family members, not his best friend turned…lover.

The oohs, aahs, and laughter that reverberate over the crowd each time new photos come on linger in the background as he and I smile at each other, and goddamnit, I don't think I've ever been more at peace in my—

A ring of gasps echo through the stadium, pulling Keene and I from the little bubble we were just living in, ignoring the rest of the world.

And *fuck*.

The second I look up to see why everyone seemed to collectively go into shock, I wish I didn't look. I wish I could rewind three, five, ten seconds ago to that little bubble Keene and I were just in, oblivious to anyone or anything around us. To when shit was simple and we could smile and grin at each other without a care in the world. Without worry or fear or, most importantly, judgment. Like we have a secret no one else knows, because we do.

Correction: we *did*.

Because fast forward to this moment we're in, one that seems more like a nightmare than a dream, and the secret? Our secret?

It's not a fucking secret anymore.

My heart catches in my throat—or maybe it's vomit trying to work itself free from my stomach—as I stare up at the screen of the scoreboard. At an image I know I didn't have any input in adding to Keene's slide show. Because if I did? I sure as fuck would've said *hell no*.

Seeing as it's one of the two of us kissing on the beach—me in his arms, legs wrapped around his waist—I'd think that's pretty understandable.

"Aspen?" Loraine whispers, though how I hear it over the murmurings floating through the crowd, I'm not sure. Words like *gay* and *couple* float over my skin with heat from people behind and beside us. And though we live in a very progressive place, I swear I catch the word *faggots* murmured too.

More than once.

Loraine says my name again, grabbing my arm this time to get my attention. When I look down at her, I'm not surprised to find the questions written on her face. But what I'm not prepared for…is the pity in her deep brown eyes.

I swallow harshly, shaking my head without realizing I'm doing it. As if my body and mind is rejecting this as reality. But from the way her hand moves down to squeeze mine in reassurance, I know it has to be.

Time grinds to a halt as my eyes lift to find Keene.

He looks like a deer caught in headlights, eyes wide and alert as he stares at me. The shock and disbelief on his face are more than enough to tell me this wasn't his doing. Not intentionally, at least.

Not that it fucking matters now. The damage is done already. Thousands of people are gaping up at a giant photo of the two of us kissing, me in his arms.

His mask slides off his head and falls to the ground, and it's like the action alone is enough to silence the thousands of people reeling by this extremely public coming out we were just forced into. Not that it matters, because I can't hear a goddamn thing over the blood roaring in my ears. The only reason I even know Keene is trying to get my attention is because my eyes are fixated on his face and I recognize my name on his lips.

I've watched him moan it enough times that it's permanently ingrained in my head.

My feet move on their own accord and I take a step backward. Away from him. Each time he moves to get closer to me, I feel my body moving and tripping back up the stairs toward the concourse behind the lower level.

When he reaches the netting, he drops his mitt to the ground and grips the material in his fists. "Pen."

Somehow, I hear it this time. I hear the aching plea in his voice, and it breaks me more than the hurt and sorrow in his eyes. It shatters the heart pounding in my chest more than this moment ever could, and more than anything, I wanna go to him. Let him assure me we'll get through this together, because we're Pen and Kee and we can get through any-fucking-thing as long as we have each other.

There's never been a day on this planet where I haven't chosen him. But my body and my mind are at war with my heart, and the pieces of me in charge right now, they're not screaming to go to the person I love. They're chanting words of fear and self-preservation. Even when they shouldn't. Even though it makes no sense for me to want to bolt.

Which is why my head…it just keeps fucking shaking. Silently saying *no*. Denying this is really happening, and in turn, denying him.

I'm halfway up the stands without even realizing it, but when I almost fall on my ass, a hand lands on my back. I look behind me to see a woman, her eyes full of the same pity Loraine had in hers, and it's enough to snap me out of the fog.

I gotta get outta here.

My feet propel me farther from him—my best friend—and I do my best to avoid making eye contact with a single person in the stadium as I make my way up the remaining rows of seats.

And I hate myself for it.

For not being able to protect him from this. For not being more careful. For dragging us and our friendship into such a beautiful yet tragic descent into Hell.

That's what it feels like, having our business aired like this in front of thousands of people. Business we had no intention of sharing with the world anytime soon.

Bristol's words come smashing back into my consciousness, her omen now a prophecy.

You two are either gonna become the greatest thing to ever happen to each other, or you're gonna toss his heart in a frying pan the moment he wants something you won't give him.

You have to be all in.

Tears prick at my eyes, and I realize I've been fooling myself all along.

I can't be this guy—the one I've seen forming in Keene's mind when he looks at me through his rose-colored glasses. The guy who can do hearts and flowers and shit. Taking something that is meant to be purely physical and mixing in emotional intimacy and romance.

I've never been that guy; I've never wanted to be him either. I just don't know *how* when all I've truly wanted was to get through life with as little emotional damage as possible.

And this? Right here and now?

It's damage on a catastrophic level.

"Aspen!" Keene shouts my name as I run up the steps. Once. Twice. His voice is full of anxiety and fear, something I certainly understand at this moment.

Not enough to turn around, though. Or dare look back.

Because if I look back, I'll see all their faces. The mixture of disgust and sympathy swirling through the crowd is palpable, and I don't have it in me to be subjected to their judgment about something they don't understand.

Something *I* don't fully understand.

Maybe if I did, I'd be making a different choice right now.

"Pen!" Keene calls for what might be the millionth time. It rips from his throat in a cry so feral, it shakes me to my core. Causes earthquakes of fear and tidal waves of emotion to wreak havoc inside my body.

The tiniest part of me still hopes and prays I'll turn around.

It doesn't matter, though.

Because I'm already gone.

THIRTY-THREE

Keene

I'm still in disbelief as I look back up at the picture of Aspen and me from a few weeks ago, when we took the trip to the coast.

The one from that rare weekend away from school, practice, games. Just the two of us, enjoying the ocean and each other.

When we were free to just be *us*.

My heart aches more because the image on the screen…fuck, it's my favorite one we've *ever* taken, and over the years, we've taken thousands.

Aspen's in my arms, my hands cupping his ass as he wraps his legs around me. He basically looks like a monkey climbing a damn tree, but it's the smile on his face as he kisses me that sends my heart into overdrive.

Anyone with eyes and half a brain can tell that I'm head over fucking heels for him. They don't need this picture for proof, they only need to catch the way I look at him.

But in this picture…I swear, I can see that same emotion written on his face.

Love.

It's not the kind of love two best friends have for each other, either. It's the deeper kind. The complete infatuation. The get-married-and-grow-old-together kind of love.

Two-halves-of-a-whole love.

And...my other half just bolted from the stadium like his life depends on it.

Which is more than enough to send me after him.

I tear off the field and into the dugout, whipping my helmet off and slamming it against the concrete wall.

"Waters!" Coach shouts from his spot out by the third base line, but I shake my head at him and storm through the door leading to the locker room, practically ripping the thing off its hinges.

Not bothering to undress or even remove my cleats, I grab my bag and rush toward the exit.

A million thoughts race through my head, most of them surrounding where Aspen would've gone. Back to the dorm? Back home? I honestly don't know, and all that does is send fear zinging through my body.

If I need to run there—wherever there might be—to get to him, I will.

I don't even have it in me to be pissed at Avery for that stunt he pulled. I might not have proof it was him who somehow got that picture on the scoreboard, but I know it was that fucker. It has to be. He's the only one on the damn team who's ever made any sort of comment about my sexuality to begin with, and he's the only person to sink to this low of a level.

But, right now, Avery doesn't matter.

The look on Aspen's face as he stared up at the screen in the outfield? That most definitely does. The panic as his eyes met mine from his seat... it made me sick. More sick than realizing it was *that* picture blasted for everyone to see, or the connotation behind it.

And while the game wasn't being televised, this is the twenty-first century. I'm willing to bet my future in baseball that this little *outing* will end up getting posted online. Maybe even going viral, because people these days have a disgusting ability to find entertainment in watching someone else's pain and embarrassment.

It takes no time at all to get out of the stadium since the game is still going on, and while my panic is rising by the second, it comes to a grinding halt when I find Aspen waiting at the Impala in the player's lot.

Pissed off and pacing, but at least he's still here.

Probably because he knew I'd come running after him. Just like I've proven time and time again, I'd chase him just about anywhere.

My heart hammers against my rib cage as I come to a halt a few feet away from him. He doesn't bother to stop his movements though, barely casting a glance as he continues to wear down the rubber of his shoes on the concrete.

Sweat streaks down the side of my face, surely smearing the eyeblack across my cheekbones, but I don't care. I don't care that I'm trampling over concrete on steel cleats either, nor that I just walked off the field in the middle of a major game—the latter being something I'll probably take some serious heat for tomorrow.

I just care about him. Making sure he's okay. Because as much as I was prepared to come out to my family in due time, I have no idea where Pen was with it. Which makes this shit all the worse.

Blazing eyes flash to me with a quick glance, and he continues to pace. *God, he's furious.*

"Pen," I whisper, inching toward him some more. "Talk to me. Are you okay?"

When he doesn't answer, I do the dumbest thing I can do at the moment. I push for more, grabbing his arm to halt his movements. It works, but when he yanks his arm from my grasp, a small piece of me dies inside. I don't even have to look into his eyes to know they'll only kill me more, because I can't stand to see his anger or his pain. Not now, not ever.

"Are you okay?" I ask again, my voice impossibly softer.

"What do you fucking think, Kee?" he snaps, combing his fingers through his hair a few times.

I do my best not to wince at the venom in his tone, but it's hard not to. Part of me worries he thinks *I* was the one who publicly outed us. Still, I have to say it. Just in case.

"I didn't—"

"I know." A sharp breath slides past his lips in a huff. "If what you've told me about how things have been going this season is any indication, I have a pretty good idea who had this brilliant idea."

I simply nod in response, thankful we're on the same page about something with this whole mess.

But the sheer amount of panic on his face when he turned and bolted from the stadium—away from *me*—spoke volumes. As mortifying as it was to look up and see my personal business put on display for thousands of strangers to see, without my consent no less, at least he was there. At least I had him with me. We'd go through it *together*, because every emotion he was feeling in that moment, I was feeling too.

The only difference is he's too blinded by fear and rage to see that this doesn't have to be the end of the world.

That I have his back, just like I know he has mine. No matter what's thrown at us.

Only, that's the way it used to be. And when two words leave his lips—

the last ones I was expecting to hear—I realize that was *then*.

Before.

"I'm sorry."

I open my mouth to ask…something. Anything. *Why?* or *How come?* being a couple that come to my mind first. But what's the point?

He doesn't have to say another word aloud for me to know everything he's thinking. It's written all over his face, his body language. It was crystal fucking clear the moment he bolted from the stands, even when I called his name.

This thing between us…is over.

I just didn't want to believe it.

You should have, though, a tiny piece inside me taunts. *You should have known this would happen if you got too attached. Just like you should have stopped it; ended things and ran when you still had the chance to get out of this with your heart intact.*

My jaw ticks, and I glance away from him to regain my bearing over my emotions. An effort that feels futile the second I make it. "So that's just it, then?"

His fingers continue raking through his onyx hair from my peripheral. "What do you want me to say, Kee? Things weren't supposed to end up here."

"Just because people know doesn't mean…" I search for the words. "We were going to both come out eventually, right? I mean, it might not have been the way—"

"Don't do that," he warns, his tone low and serious, and when I look back to him, I find more contempt in his eyes.

"What?"

"Pretend like this is just gonna be okay."

I blink at him, at a complete loss. "But…it is. Look, Pen, if you're worried about your—"

"God, how don't you get it? I don't give two shits about me. What matters is how this might affect you for the rest of *your* life." He bites out a curse, now pacing again. Meanwhile, I'm left in shock at his declaration. "This could follow you *everywhere,* Keene. For the rest of your life. It might not be as bad as a sex tape, but it's still fucking bad. It could be the reason scouts don't come to recruit you or—"

"Then I'll deal!" I shout before I can think better of it, tossing my hands out to the side. "This isn't the end of the world, Pen. If it means I can't go pro, then—"

"I'm not gonna be the reason your entire future falls apart!"

I open my mouth, ready to disagree. But then I close it, internalizing the best way to respond to that.

Because…really? Does he really think I'm stupid? Or that I don't remember the day he cracked his chest open a little wider for me to see all his fears about us? About my future? About not being able to protect me?

I remember every damn word that came out of his mouth that day, just like I memorized the shape of his lips as he said them.

But it's all a bunch of bullshit. Layers and layers of it, heaped up in a mountain that he's hoping might be high enough I won't want to attempt climbing it. The problem is, I know him too well. I can see that there's something else going on here. There has to be.

"By doing this," I whisper, "you're making sure it does. You're taking everything we have the chance to be and throwing it away without even trying."

He shakes his head, halting before me. "We don't have the chance to *be* anything, Keene. We never have."

The words are a punch to the gut, and I'm left slightly breathless. "How can you say that?"

"Because it's the truth."

A scoff leaves me. "Right."

He glowers. "Don't fuck with me about this."

"Why not? We both know it's bullshit."

"It's not!" he snaps right back. "It's not, because I can't be what you need me to be, Keene!"

It's on the tip of my tongue to scream at him, shout from the top of my lungs that he already is everything I need. Every want and desire and craving and wish I have all leads straight back to him.

If only he wasn't too fucking blind to see it.

"I'm not asking you to be my protector or my savior or anything of the sort. I'm just asking you to be my best friend, the way you always have been." My throat constricts, the vice on my heart tightening. "I'm just asking you to lo—"

"I can't," he growls, cutting me off before I can utter the word again, just four letters long.

I swallow the shards of glass lodged in my throat. "Can't or won't?"

His eyes are hard as they lock on mine, the tick in his jaw firmly set. But I see cracks slowly fissuring along the surface of his facade, growing deeper with each passing second. "Can't. I *can't* give you what you want."

My head and my heart battle for control, creating an all-out war within me. Swords clash against armor, slicing off piece after piece until bloodshed is inevitable, leaving me bleeding internally without a hope of surviving.

It should be easy, choosing myself. To save myself the heartache.

But I've never been able to choose anyone over him.

I step toward him slowly, like approaching a trapped animal. "You already have, Pen."

He shakes his head, and I watch him swallow harshly before he steps away from me. The distance between us might as well be the Grand Canyon, only growing deeper and wider.

His voice is raw as he whispers, "I can't do this."

That one stupid word infuriates me when it leaves his lips for what might be the millionth time since I found him. *Can't*. It sends wave after chilling wave of rage rolling over me, crashing and breaking and dragging me under their icy depths.

And I drown in it until I snap.

"So you can fuck me, but you can't date me? Is that what it means when you say you *can't*?" I snarl, poison coursing through my veins. "You're willing to take everything I have to offer you, but heaven forbid you give me a damn thing in return, right?"

His gaze softens, but only fractionally. Probably because fighting back like this isn't really my thing. And when it happens, it's never toward him. "I have nothing to give you."

My nostrils flare at yet another cop-out, bullshit response, and I shove the last word he spoke to the back of my mind. "You have *everything* to give me. You're my best friend, for fuck's sake! God, Pen, you're supposed to know me better than anyone, yet somehow you're too blind to see I'm—"

"Stop," he cuts me off, his head shaking again. "Please, stop."

In love with you, I finish internally.

It physically pains me to keep this from him. I want to shout it from the rooftops, let the whole world know how crazy I am for him. That he's the only person I fucking see.

Because I *am* in love with him. Maybe even before this all started with that dare of a first kiss back in high school.

It's always been Aspen.

"Give me one good reason," I grit, stepping into his space again, and this time, I don't stop. My hands come to rest on either side of his shoulders, pinning him against the driver's side door. His attention flicks between my eyes, his fingers gripping the pack of smokes in his pocket. As soon as they're pulled free, I yank them from his grasp. They're crushed in my fist moments later, completely worthless to him.

Just like my fucking heart.

"Because," he hisses, cobalt eyes colder than I've ever seen them, "you're about to cross a line we'll never be able to come back from."

I can't help it. I bark out a laugh, removing my hands from near his body in fear I might strangle him for his completely idiotic statement. "You're kidding, right? Crossing lines? Don't you think it's a little too late for that?"

"Kee—"

"No, Pen. Shut up and listen to how *stupid* you sound. Lines haven't just been crossed. They've been blurred for a while now, and I think you know it." I pause for a brief moment, shaking my head. "And let's not forget the way they were fucking obliterated the moment your dick slid inside me the very first time. Because best friends don't *screw each other*."

He doesn't say anything. Doesn't rebuttal or make excuses, let alone own up to the truth in my statement. And his lack of response telling me everything I needed to hear. So much so, I can't help the rage boiling inside me. The pure, unfiltered fury taking control of my body as I stare at him.

My best friend.

My other half, if only he'd just *try*.

"You're such a fucking coward, Aspen." I scoff to ease the ache in my chest. "Apparently, that's never gonna change."

It only gets worse when he nods, agreeing with me rather than pushing back the way he wants. I can handle some conflict. At least if he'd fight me, I'd know all hope isn't lost for good. That he hasn't completely given up.

The last thing I want is his indifference.

"You've always been the brave one. Always willing to jump without fear. But that's not me, Kee. I can't give you that because I'm not capable of it. Of anything you're asking for."

Every word slices through me with an aim for my heart. It cuts and cuts and cuts some more until there's nothing but a shredded, bloody hunk of meat left in my chest.

The worst part is, I don't even hate him for it. I hate myself for letting it happen.

Tears prick at my eyes, and I blink them away before they dare to spill over. "You might think that, but you're wrong. You've shown me. When we were on the coast, with every single thing you planned out for us. Or when you skipped class with me. Or every time you drive me to practice or watch one of my games or take a bath with me after a rough day or let me pick the music in the car. Each one of those acts is *proof* that you're more than capable of giving me every fucking thing I could want or need."

Another shake of his head is all I get for a long time while I watch him weigh and measure his words. His jaw is set and tense, but it's still just a front. The slight waver in his eyes gives him away. The anxiety and fear tearing him apart from the inside, slowly creeping toward the surface.

And more cracks form.

"If anything, just add it to the list of things I regret when it comes to what happened between us. For making you think this could be more. Not following the rule *I* set out to begin with. All it's done is hurt you. I *keep* hurting you, Kee. At every fucking turn. I see it when you look at me, and half the time, I don't even know what I do wrong. But no matter how much hurting you hurts *me too,* I can't just stand here and lie to you by saying I wouldn't take it all back if I could."

And there it is.

The one obstacle I doubt we can get over.

It hits me like a punch to the chest, right where my heart is, before the fist wraps around it and squeezes. Crushes the organ in its grip. The weight of his words land hard enough that I'm forced to take a step away from him, but I know the second I do, my heart will be torn out in the process.

But I keep moving back, trying to distance myself from the object of my affection…and inevitable destruction.

Blood pours from the wound he's created, and I can't help the strangled noise that comes from my throat as I try to keep myself together. Patch the hole before I bleed out at his feet.

"And here I thought you said you'd rather die than hurt me," I rasp at little more than a whisper. "But here you are, doing just that by not even giving this a chance."

His teeth roll over his bottom lip, and I watch as each of those tiny little cracks in his armor spiderweb out like a broken mirror. He clears his throat a couple times and blinks back the slightest hint of emotion but does nothing to erase the gravel in his voice when he murmurs another rough, "I'm sorry."

He doesn't even look at me as he yanks the door to the Impala open, ready to run away again. But the masochist in me won't let him. Not yet. Not until he realizes what this will do to us. The permanent repercussions of him shutting down and freezing me out.

His arm is in my vice-like grip before he can slide into the driver's seat. Squeezing hard enough to hurt, yet knowing it's nothing compared to the woodchipper he just threw my heart into without a fucking care.

There's still a palpable amount of sorrow in his eyes when he meets my gaze. It's almost enough to pull him into my arms, take his pain as my own the way I have my whole life.

The way we've always done for each other…until now.

Let. Him. Go, the voice inside me demands. *Save yourself while you still can.*

It feels wrong, though. To draw this line in the sand between us, already knowing we'll be on different sides. He's so much as told me that's the only outcome for us.

But I do it anyway, though it might kill me more than it could ever save me.

"You talk about crossing lines like those are the things that matter here. But if you walk away from me right now…" I start, my teeth grinding together as I force the words out, "…there's no turning this around. *That's the one line we've yet to cross, Pen. So do it. Go, if that's what you want.*" I shake my head, my voice cut and shredded by shards of glass. "Just don't bother coming back."

Though it rips me apart to do it, I release my hold and step away from him. Giving him the space to decide.

To pick me…or his pride and fears and every other bullshit reason for us to not be together. To get through this as a team.

His Adam's apple bobs, and I still see the emotion he's choking back. The shimmering of tears, unshed and pooling in his eyes. But he still doesn't let them go.

Or let *me* in.

Even when that's all I want anymore. To see and know and love every damn piece of him. Including every fear and flaw and fucking insecurity.

But I never stood a chance against them. I see that now.

My tongue runs over my bottom lip, and I let out a grated laugh.

"I know you well enough to realize you're going to rip this conversation apart in your mind one day soon. Overthink it, analyze it to shreds. But just remember, when that moment happens? You're the one who chose to end this…and *I* was the one who wanted to fight."

His eyes sink closed, head hanging momentarily as I watch him take a long, steady breath. The single tear that slides down his cheek is enough to fracture what remains of my heart, because all I want is to brush it away.

I think he's about to say something when his lips part slightly, a small amount of hope surging forward.

Stupid fucking hope, because instead, he swallows again.

Schools his features. Gets in the car.

And then he drives away.

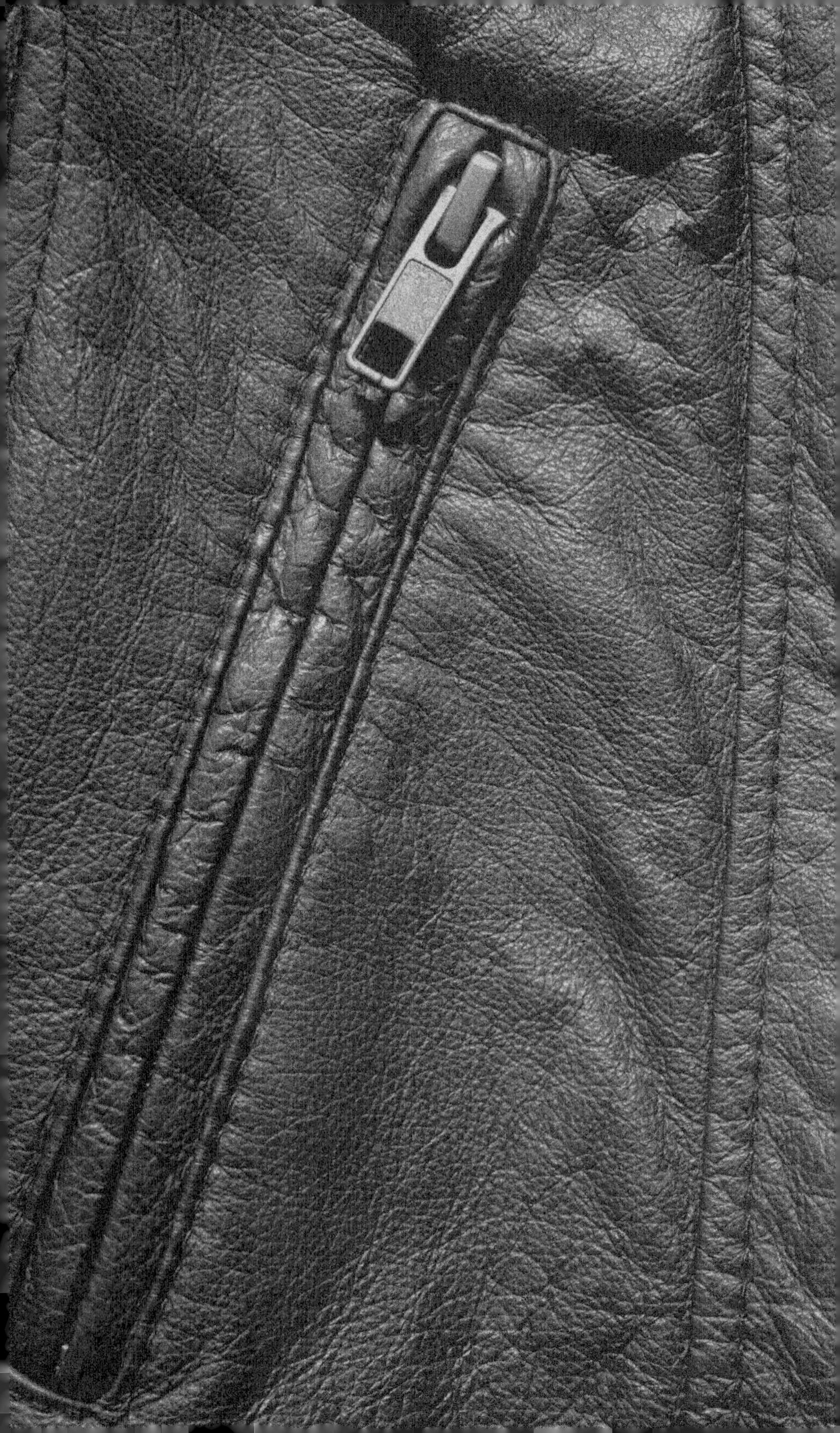

THIRTY-FOUR

Aspen

I f staring at my ceiling in complete and utter misery was an Olympic sport, I'd be a fucking gold medalist by now.

It's been only a week since the debacle at the baseball game, but it feels like a million years have passed. The moment I left the stadium, speeding away in my Impala, I moved my happy ass out of the dorm suite. I knew Keene wouldn't be back in time to stop me since he was dealing with the repercussions of our very public *outing*, and like the coward I am, I slipped away like a thief in the night.

Of course, by the time I got home that evening, Mom had already been called by Loraine and heard about what happened at the game. She was waiting for me on the couch, and the second I opened the front door, the saddened look on her face told me she knew.

She knew *everything*.

That was all it took for me to break on the spot. I dropped my bag at the front door and bolted to her. Ran to the safety of her arms, and clung to her like a lifeline.

That night was a week ago, and while she's given me the space I've needed since, I know it's about to change when I hear a soft knock on my door not long after she gets home from work.

I roll to my side and sigh, still wanting a little more time to lick my self-inflicted wounds in private. So while I'm doing my best to ignore her, the rap of her knuckles comes again against the wood, making it impossible.

"Can I come in?" her soft voice comes from the other side of the door.

No.

The answer is always no. When she asks at dinner if I want a second helping. If I want to talk about what happened. If I've heard from Keene at all recently, or made an effort to reach out.

If I'm okay.

Always no, though I never verbally admit to the last one. What right do I have to complain about how shitty I'm feeling when I was the one who *chose* this? I actively made the decision to walk away from Keene.

Now, I have to live with it.

"No," I say, loud enough I know she'll hear me.

Instead of going back downstairs or to her room like she normally would, I hear the telltale sound of a handle turning and my door creaking open anyway. My eyes sink closed and I pray to any god who might listen for her to go away. Leave me alone to stew in my misery.

She doesn't say anything as she crosses the room to me, nor when she slides onto my bed with her back against the headboard. I keep my back to her, feeling too many emotions already clogging my throat and well in my eyes.

"You need to talk about it, sweetie," she says, settling her palm on my back.

It's the gentle tone of her voice, combined with the pressure of her hand on me, that sets me off.

My body shakes as silent sobs rip from my body. No sound or even tears escape me. I just tremble in her grip as the day I destroyed my friendship with Keene flashes through my mind. It already lives there, a vicious tape on repeat. A devastating reminder of my biggest regret, filling me with enough self-loathing to drive the sanest person completely mad.

Mom's hand soothes me, rubbing my back as I break before her, letting out every ounce of pain I've been holding on to for days now.

Pain for me. For Keene.

For the *us* we could've been, if only I wasn't so fucking terrified to let him have me the way he wanted.

I don't even know when the tears start, only that Mom gently brushes one after another off my cheek as they fall. Some slip past her too quickly, coating my lips in the salty flavor that reminds me of the breeze off the ocean in Cannon Beach.

And I sob harder.

It could be minutes or hours that pass before I calm myself enough to turn to her.

Her warm eyes are teary too when she looks down at me, and I can tell the sight of me losing it has brought her close to the edge. Still, she remains strong for me. The way she always has, ever since Dad died.

"I fucked up, Mom," I whisper, folding my arm and nestling my head into the crook of my elbow. "I really fucked up this time."

"Yeah, you did," she says, her hand on my back moving in slow, soothing circles. "But the good news is, you and Keene always manage to work it out in the end."

My head shakes rapidly as I try to calm my breathing. "Not this time. There's no way."

"What makes you think that?"

He told me as much.

"I just know. And even if I got him to forgive me—which might be impossible with the way I hurt him—we won't ever be the same."

Her fingers sift through my hair now. "You don't know that for sure, Aspen."

I do, though. I know my best friend, who has too big of a heart and is far too forgiving. But even he has his limits. And even if—and this is a big *if*—he can find it in himself to forgive me, I still don't think I can forgive myself for this. For hurting and betraying him on such a deep-seated level.

When I don't answer her, she continues sliding her fingers through my hair, humming softly while she does it. It puts me at ease, the gentle scraping of her nails against my skull. Calms me and grounds me in a way that nicotine can't even touch.

The only thing with this same power is…Keene.

"Can I ask you something that might sound kind of silly?" she asks after a few minutes.

My shrug of a response is enough to give her permission to continue.

"Do you think being in a platonic relationship with Keene is any different than being in an intimate one? Besides the sexual aspect, of course."

I cringe and look up at her. "Christ, Mom. Are we really doing this?"

She gives me a small shrug for an answer.

I can practically hear her words from when I was younger—during that infamous birds and bees talk—saying *if you can't talk about it, you shouldn't be having it.*

The thing is, I have no issues talking about sex. But talking about it with my *mom?* That's a whole other ballpark I wasn't prepared to be batting in today. Especially if it's in reference to batting for the, uh…*same team.*

Clearing my throat, I sit up and lean back against the headboard beside her.

"Yeah, I do think that our friendship changed when Keene and I started the…physical stuff and…" I trail off, shaking my head. "It was just different. Of course, it was. Why *wouldn't* it be?"

"But I'm asking apart from the physical stuff, sweetie. Did you care about him any more or less than you have before? Was it harder or easier to be honest with him about how you're feeling when you added the physical stuff to your relationship?"

I roll my teeth thinking about it.

"No," I finally decide. "I guess it didn't change any of that. Not really."

"And why is that?"

Wracking my brain for a few moments does no good, and I come up empty-handed. "I don't know."

"Because you've never had to worry about keeping your guard up with Keene. In fact, you've always been each other's biggest warrior and fiercest protector." She adjusts her position from beside me slightly, and I lift my attention to her eyes. "Over the past twenty years of your life, you and Keene have been inseparable. A dynamic duo. Partners in crime. Whatever you wanna call it, that's what the two of you were. And during that time, he did all the grunt work you've kept everyone else from completing. He found a way into your heart the way no one else ever has."

"Yeah, but…he's my best friend. If I can't trust him, who can I trust?"

"Exactly. You trust him more than anyone else. Sure, it started as friendship, but that was just laying the foundation."

I must look lost or confused, because she gives me yet another patient smile. My mother, the saint.

"You might not see it this way, but you've always loved him, Aspen. It was obvious how much you meant to each other since you were old enough to walk. Anyone who was around the two of you for more than ten minutes could see it. So after all this time, and the friendship and love you've shared? I'm not surprised falling in love with him was the next step."

The empty hole in my chest grows, throbbing and aching for the missing piece Keene holds in his hands.

"Loving someone because you care about them is different than being in love with them. The hearts-and-flowers kind of love."

Her brow raises skeptically. "Are you saying this isn't that kind of love?"

I hate how simple she's making this sound. Like the answers have been right here, staring me in the face the whole fucking time, but I've just been too blind or stupid or both to realize it.

My voice is hoarse when I whisper, "I love him with every inch of me. And that's the last thing I wanted to happen."

She frowns, her hand coming to rest on my shoulder. I see the unspoken question in her eyes and hear them in my own thoughts too.

If only the reason for them made sense to everyone else as much as they do to me.

"I didn't want to fall for someone. Anyone. Ever. It's never been in the cards for me. When I pictured my life ten years from now, I never saw someone…sharing a bed with me or kissing me good night. It wasn't something I planned on, and it's not something I wanted."

"Are you sure about that?"

"What else would it be?"

"Something you were too afraid to allow yourself to want, perhaps?" I don't miss the way she fiddles with her wedding ring. The one she still wears every single day, despite not being married for over a decade now.

The vice around my heart constricts painfully. "Does it matter which it is?"

She nods. "One of those is nothing but a fear. And those can be overcome, if you try."

Clearing my throat, I give her an agonized look. "Maybe you're right.

But this isn't the way it was supposed to go with us." I shake my head, grief consuming me further. "He's my best friend, not my…"

"Partner?"

I nod. "I can't let myself want him like that. Because…what if it doesn't work?"

"And what if it does?" she counters. "And isn't that worth taking the chance that what you two have could be something extraordinary?"

My head sinks into my hands. "I don't know. I just know I don't want to lose him. That's not supposed to happen with us. None of this was supposed to happen."

The elephant in the room sits between us, because my actions thus far have only ensured that I've already done just that. I lost him.

A glance up reveals her lips rolling inward, forming a thin line while she thinks. The action pops out a dimple similar to my own.

"So…you're on the verge of losing your best friend—and possibly the love of your life—just because things aren't playing out the way you thought they should?"

I open to my mouth to deny it, but when she puts it like that, I feel like a fucking idiot. Thankfully, she spares me the humiliation of having to admit it aloud, continuing with her point.

"I hate to break it to you, sweetie, but life never goes according to plan. Not for a single person I've ever met. Which is why you have to learn to adjust, take things as they come."

Every ounce of my body knows she's right.

Because, despite what I told Keene outside the stadium that day, I don't regret him or the time we had together. I don't regret helping him or loving him or anything that transpired between us.

I just hate that I couldn't protect him the way I always have in the past.

More so, I hate being the catalyst for the moment that photo ended up on the screen.

I might not have done it—aired our business to everyone there that night—but I planned the trip where the photo was taken. I sent the photo to him before his game the week prior to Family Night, hoping it would cheer him up a little bit from whatever funk he was in.

I'm almost positive that's how Avery got his hands on it, though working out those details feels completely pointless now. The damage has been done, and there's no chance of undoing it.

Mom reaches over, takes one hand in hers, and gives it a reassuring squeeze. "You have the chance to make this right. Because the way I see things between you and Keene? You're the unexpected inevitable."

Her words hit me in the chest, damn near knocking the wind out of me.

You're the unexpected inevitable.

But God, if that's true, why do I feel like I don't stand a chance of getting him to even listen if I tried to plead my case?

"I don't know how to make it right." I give her a small, helpless shrug, tears pricking at my eyes again. "I don't know where to start."

"*I'm sorry* is usually a good place," she says, knocking her shoulder into mine. "Especially when you've hurt someone. And I'm sure you realize you've probably got quite a bit of groveling to do after how you've pushed him away."

My free hand reaches up, fingers threading through my hair. "I know. And that's the worst part of it all, because as much as I want to make it better, how can I when I'm the reason for it in the first place?"

Her smile is delicate, and her palm squeezes mine again. "You're doing that thing you do."

I frown. "What thing?"

"Overthinking yourself into circles."

My laughter is caught somewhere between genuine and forced, especially when I recall Keene's parting words.

You're the one who chose to end this...and I was the one who wanted to fight.

"As always, right?"

"You don't have to, sweetie. The way I see it, you fell for your best friend. Someone who you've known and trusted for most of your life. And while I think that's something worth fighting for, you're the one who has to do some soul searching and decide for yourself."

My eyes sink closed, and I let my head fall back against the headboard. I wish she'd tell me exactly what I need to do, how to make this right. Give me the roadmap or instruction manual, and I'll follow it to a T.

Life doesn't work that way, though. So I need to find my way through this on my own. Which means I have a shit ton of soul searching to do, just like she said.

Mom must realize I'm maxed out on emotional talk, because she lets out a soft sigh, patting my leg a couple times before standing. I glance up, tracking her movement to the door where she pauses and turns around.

"You didn't ask for my two cents, but as a parting gift, I'm giving it to you anyway." Her eyes and tone are as soft as ever, but her words leave little room for debate.

"Okay," I whisper, a sudden knot forming in my throat.

"There are far worse things in the world than falling in love, Aspen. No matter who it's with."

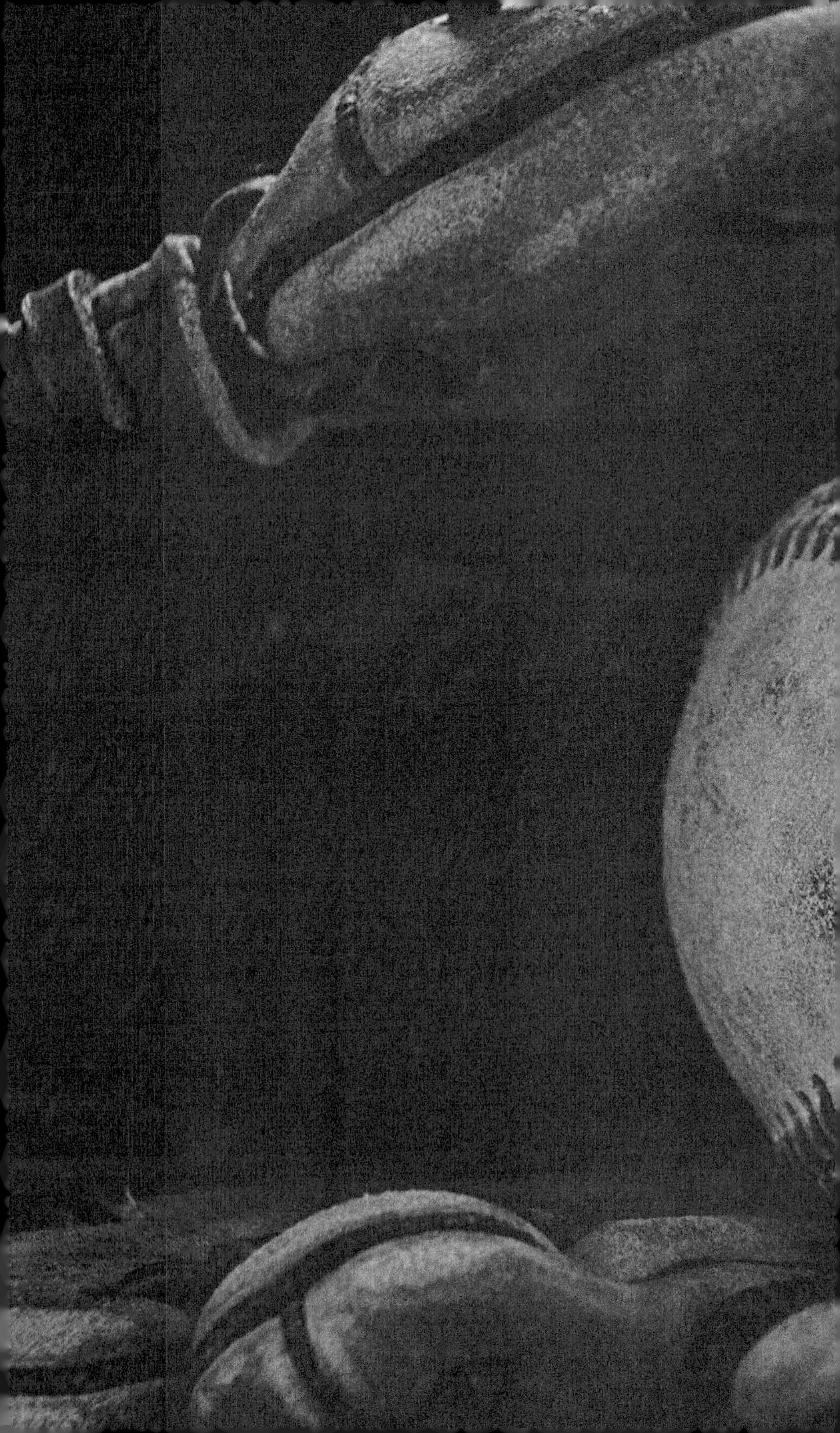

THIRTY-FIVE

Keene

July

A tap on my shoulder scares the shit out of me while I'm in the middle of playing yet another round of *Escape From Tarkov* on my PC. I probably jump a foot out of my desk chair before shoving one half of the headset off my ear and spinning in place.

As expected, I find my sister standing there, looking over my shoulder at the computer uneasily. Sometimes, I swear she thinks I'm gonna be watching porn whenever I'm on the thing. Which is sort of awkward, considering I've barely left this spot all summer.

"What is it, Lex? I'm in the middle of a raid."

Her hazel eyes, the same shade Dad's used to be, dart back to my face and she shrugs. "Mom said that dinner was ready. She told me to come get you."

Rolling my eyes, I spin and turn back to my game. "Not hungry," I mutter, shifting my headset back into place. "Don't forget to close the door on the way out."

I start playing again, but after a couple minutes—and right when I'm about to get to my extraction point—someone pops out from behind a building and lights me up. I'm dead in under two seconds, and I let out a sharp curse before yanking the headset off entirely, letting it clatter to my desk.

"That was anticlimactic," a voice mutters behind me.

My sigh must make my irritation hard to miss, along with the glare on my face, because when I turn to find Lexi sitting cross-legged on my bed while she stares at me, her eyes pop a little wider.

"I told you to leave."

"No, you actually told me to close the door on my way out. But I never left." As if knowing my next statement, she adds, "Mom told me not to take no for an answer since you haven't left your room all day."

I grumble a little at that. The whole point of not leaving my room is so I didn't have to talk to anyone and I can mourn the death of my friendship with Aspen in peace. Mope around and be pissed and sad and completely destroyed without having anyone watch.

Mom is the one I'm trying my best to avoid, though. It isn't fair to her because I know she cares, but the last thing I want to talk about is him or how I'm feeling right now. Which is exactly what she'd try to make me do, just like she has every single time we've been in the same room since we talked after the dramatic events of Family Night.

I just need a break from her constant bombardment of questions.

Have you talked to him?

Do you know where he is yet?

Why don't you try reaching out first?

Or one of the hundreds of others she has ready in her arsenal.

Plus, if I don't leave my room, there's no chance for me to look outside at the Kohl's driveway across the street, only to feel another rush of disappointment when I don't find the Impala sitting in its usual spot.

Of course, why would it be, when Mom let it slip a few weeks ago that Pen just up and left. No call or text to tell anyone. He'd only told his mom that he'd check in periodically—again, according to *my mom*—and ever since I found that out, all other information's been strictly withheld from me.

But seeing as I'm a masochist, I check for updates on his social media platforms to get a clue of where he is or who he's with.

It's pathetic, but not as pathetic as the ache in my chest when I come up empty every single time.

"Do you wanna talk about it?" Lexi suddenly asks.

My attention shifts back to her, brow raised in question. "Are you being serious right now?"

Another shrug. Jesus, is that all this girl does anymore?

"Well, not talking about it is clearly doing you a whole lot of good. And I'm currently out of tea to keep me occupied since the news about Derek cheating on Laney has already fizzled out. So your drama will just have to do."

I scoff. "Thanks, Lex. I feel the love."

"No problem. Now spill."

Shaking my head, I make a buzzing sound with my lips. "Not fucking talking to you about this shit. It's weird. Not to mention you were in love with Aspen since you could walk."

She rolls her eyes. "Yeah, but he's yours, Kee Kee. Always has been."

I open my mouth to disagree, to tell her it sure doesn't look that way right now, but she starts picking at her cuticles, seemingly uninterested in what I have to say. Which irritates me, because she just came in here and told me to spill my guts to her, only to act like she could give two shits?

Yeah, that's not gonna fly.

So I give her some of the juicy bits while still keeping it PG-13 enough for my little sister. And boy do I have her attention from the second I mention the first kiss at the end of high school.

That leads to the incident at the party earlier this semester. The weird tension between Pen and me until we finally talked about what the issues were. And then his stupid idea to *explore things together*. I unload all of what happened with us in a beautiful display of word vomit.

And then I tell her about how it all came crashing down, thanks to Avery fucking Reynolds and his brilliant idea to go through my phone while I was in the shower one day after practice, only to find that photo and send it to the team's PR coordinator from my email account, asking them to add the image to my family slideshow at the last minute.

The only reason any of this was found out is because Kaleb watched it with his own two eyes. Having been smart enough to realize I wasn't the one to hand that photo over willingly, he came forward to tell Coach and the school's athletic director about what he knew the day after Family Night.

Avery was tossed out of Foltyn, and the rest, as they say, is history.

I also clue Lexi in on *why* Avery decided to detonate my entire life the way he did.

As it turns out, he's none other than my Toppr pal, balls4lyfe.

Needless to say, I didn't see that one coming.

Sure, I knew balls4lyfe was one of my teammates, but I thought maybe it was one of the younger guys I didn't know that well. Hell, I even thought it might've been Kaleb, since I never see him with girls. Overall, Avery was the last person I suspected, thanks to all the homophobic, asshole remarks he'd made over the two years I'd known him.

So why did he light the fuse on this ticking time bomb?

I guess it messed with him hard when I broke things off that day when we were unknowingly on the bus together. Or, at least, *I* didn't know it was him when it happened.

He knew he was talking to me the whole time though, thanks to those *damn freckles* on my stomach. It's such a unique pattern that he's seen quite often in the locker room, and pairing it with my admission about unresolved feelings about my sexuality and that we pinged within such a close location on the bus and at the Chi O party…I'm honestly not surprised he put two and two together.

Add in that I admitted to seeing someone—and the only logical person for it to be was Pen, since I'm never seen with anyone else—and jealousy took over. And a bit of fear, thinking I knew who he was too, and that was the real reason why I cut ties.

And here we are.

Me, with my life in fucking shambles…and Avery, kicked out of school for being a douchebag.

The only reason I found all this out was because of the long-ass text message he sent me, apologizing and explaining everything from his side. Probably looking for some sort of absolution, if I had to guess.

I didn't respond and blocked his number just to be safe.

It's by the end of that ridiculous saga that Lexi is staring at me, wide eyed and in complete shock.

"Holy…shit," she mutters, shaking her head. "Your life's a mess, Kee Kee."

I snort. "Thanks for the reassurance, Lex."

"But, apart from this Avery guy being a complete dick, this doesn't seem very complicated to me."

Leave it to a sixteen-year-old girl to think of falling in love with my best friend, who doesn't do anything more than emotionless hookups—only for us to be outed publicly in front of thousands of people—as *uncomplicated.*

If that's really the case, high school must be a joy these days.

I give her a dubious look. "Really? That's what you have to say about everything I just told you?"

She shrugs. "Okay, look. I'm gonna give it to you straight—which is a funny thing to say considering you're not."

I chuckle at that, my lips quirking at the corners. Damn kid. "Okay, Lex. Give it to me straight."

"Aspen's your best friend. He always has been, right? So is it really worth losing that friendship just because he doesn't want to be your boyfriend?"

The way she deduces it so dramatically is something of an artform. Truly. Because it seems like she was barely listening to a damn thing I said the entire time I was talking.

"How can I be friends with someone I love, especially when he doesn't feel the same? That sounds like a miserable existence to me."

She frowns. "I mean, why couldn't you be? You've always loved him, so there's not much change there."

I roll my eyes. "I mean, *in love* with him."

This time, she nods. "I know. And I stand by what I said. You've always felt that way about him."

Has she lost her damn mind?

My head cocks to the side, and I stare at her, a mixture of bewilderment and awe etched into my frown. "I didn't even know I was bi until this year."

Her brow raises, as if to say *so what?*

I scoff, reading her attitude easier than a picture book. "How would I have been in love with him for our whole lives if I never knew until recently that I like guys? It makes no fucking sense."

And now she's looking at me like I'm the stupid one. "Love has nothing to do with how you define your sexuality. It's all about the heart."

I blink at her, not sure I heard her right. And then I blink again, because I'm convinced she was just taken over by some Greek philosopher or self-help guru. But nope, it's still my shithead little sister sitting in front of me.

Well, fuck. I guess it's true, what they say about girls maturing emotionally way faster than guys, if she just pulled that shit out of thin air.

But as her words sink in through the surface, an agonizing ache forms in my chest. One that doesn't go away, even when I rub at the space where my shredded heart still beats behind my ribs.

Clearing my throat, I meet her gaze and sigh, the words on the tip of my tongue tasting like the ash from Aspen's cigarettes. "His heart doesn't want mine, Lex."

She snorts, shifting on my bed to make herself more comfortable. "That's a load of crap if I've ever heard it. He's been in love with you just as long as you've been in love with him. Maybe even longer."

I shake my head, both in denial and disbelief. There's no way she's *not* pulling a bunch of bullshit out of her ass now. "You've officially lost me."

A roll of the eyes is what I get, then, "Try to keep up, Neanderthal. Why do you think none of the relationships he's ever had lasted?"

"He didn't have any relationships."

"My point exactly," she says, clapping her hands together. "And why do you think that is?"

I guess I've never really thought about it. But when I take a moment to really analyze it, I don't come up with a whole lot.

"Because he never liked them enough to do more than fuck them?"

Her face curls up in disgust, and she cringes. "Ugh, no. Stop. I get that you two are soulmates or whatever, and I'm fine with that…but for the love of God, don't talk about my first crush that way. You'll ruin what's left of the fantasy."

It's my turn to grimace at the image of my sister fantasizing about— *Okay, nope. Not touching that with a bucket of bleach and a ten-foot pole.*

"Then why? Why wouldn't they last? It's not like he hasn't had fuc—" I catch myself and reroute, "I mean, *friends* that he kept around for a while. He and Bristol were seeing each other pretty regularly for almost a year."

The arch of her brow tells me I must truly be an idiot if I'm not seeing the answer.

Well, someone get me a damn dunce cap, because I still can't figure it out.

"Okay, I'm just gonna spell it out for you, because you're kind of a lost cause." She pauses, ever the drama queen. "It's because he couldn't trust them, dingbat. You know, the foundation of any relationship, but especially when it comes to dating? And if he couldn't trust them, then I'd bet a whole year's worth of allowance that he also couldn't be himself around them."

The kid's definitely got a point there. I mean, it's like Pen always told me. He keeps the emotions out of sex, even though we both know it can be so much better when you care about the person too. We're living proof of that.

Lexi takes my silence as permission to keep going. "I mean, let's be real here. Did any of them even know about how much he loves photography? What he's going to school for? Or even something more superficial, like his favorite video game or color?"

I shake my head. "I don't think anyone knows that stuff about him, Lex."

"Ah, see. But *you* know those things." She crosses her arms, clearly pleased with herself. "You're the only person he trusts to see the real him, Kee Kee. You're special to him. You always have been. What else would you call that besides love?"

The pieces all make sense on paper; I have to give it to her. They're still not quite believable enough to make me do anything about it, especially with how he left things. Namely, by straight up just running away from the problem.

And honestly, I'm far from ready to reopen a wound that's barely begun to heal.

Sighing, I lean back in my chair. "How the fuck did you get so smart?"

She shrugs, her face the picture of impassiveness. "Two X chromosomes."

My lips quirk, and just like that, her composure cracks and we're both busting a gut like no other.

Once we finally manage to calm ourselves enough to speak, I rise from my chair and hold out my hand for her and drag her from my bed. "C'mon. It's time for dinner."

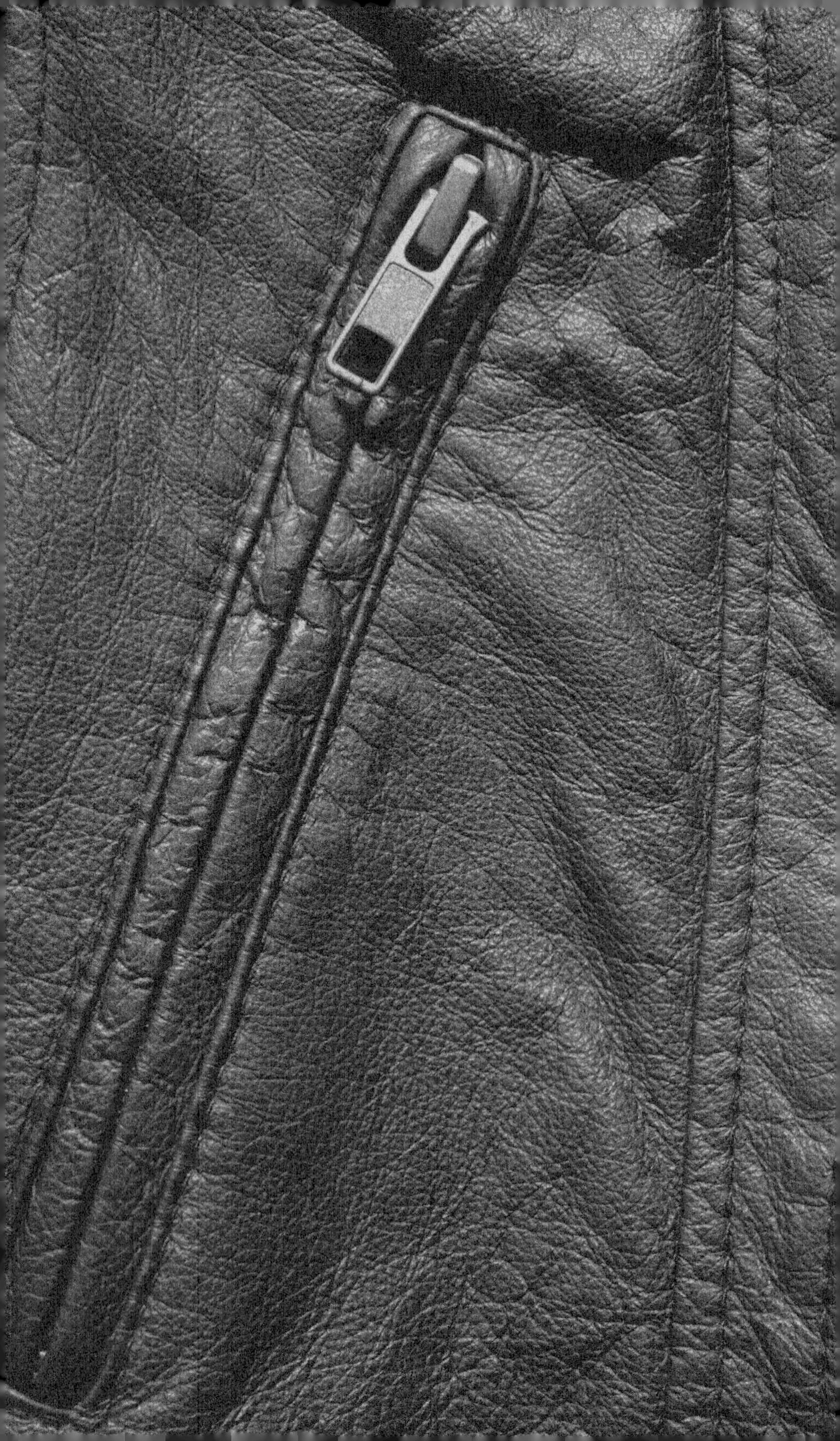

THIRTY-SIX

Aspen

Late August

I don't realize I'm heading to the dorms until I'm already there. Already throwing my car in park in the closest spot and walking up the path to the building, desperation clawing at my throat. It's like my body went on autopilot on the drive back, and all I could think about once I hit the Oregon state line was getting to him.

Then again, I shouldn't be surprised. My heart has always been connected to Keene. Called to him in a way it never has for anyone else. If only I wasn't stupid enough to take that for granted, choosing to cherish his more than my pride.

I guess eight weeks on the road, doing a lifetime's worth of soul searching, will clarify some shit. Put it in perspective until the things that matter take their place, front and center.

And God, did it ever work.

Seeing him is the only thing that matters right now. I didn't bother getting gas or stopping at home to drop off my bags. All signs pointed to him and only him.

To get him back, tell him I love him…and most importantly, that I'm sorry.

I just hope I'm not too late. Because months apart can do a lot. Change a lot.

Just look at the amount of growth I've made in that time.

Who's to say Keene hasn't found someone else? Someone actually worthy of his love and time and affection. Who won't run away like I did.

That fear alone would've sent me running back here. Straight to him.

Or, as straight to him as possible, considering I have no way of getting into his dorm with my ID card this year. Which I didn't really think about until I'm standing locked outside the dorm building.

"Shit," I mutter, pacing in front of the door.

Even if I snuck in as someone else came out, the RA at the front desk is sure to send me straight out here again. Even if it's the same blonde girl from last year who was known to have a little leniency. Damn sticklers for the rules.

Then again, I used to be one of them, keeping to a rigid structure to live by. That is, until Keene went and flipped my whole world upside down.

Trying another option, I pull his contact up on my phone and hit the call button, but it goes straight to voicemail.

Damnit.

My options have dwindled down to one thing now. Sitting and waiting, hoping I catch him coming or going and can convince him to hear me out. It's warm and breezy for late August, and the clouds swirling overhead look like thunderheads.

But I'm not gonna leave. Come rain or storm or Hell or high water, I'm seeing him.

I'll wait here all fucking night if I have to.

Guess all that paying attention I did in science class paid off, because those clouds were definitely thunderheads. Sure as shit, it started pouring down about half an hour ago, and even though I'm under the overhang of the dorm entrance, the wind's making it close to impossible to stay dry.

My brain's telling me to give up and come back in the morning, but the stubbornness in my heart won't let me. And it's a good thing too, because about an hour later, I finally spot him rushing up the walk to the dorm. His duffle's held up over his head as he sprints toward cover from the storm. He's so occupied with trying to keep himself dry, he almost runs straight into me when he reaches the top step.

Thankfully, he glances up when he hits the landing, halting in place when his brain registers my presence.

And the look on his face…well, let's just say he doesn't look thrilled to see me.

Soaked to the bone, jaw set tight, and eyes cold, he asks, "What're you doing here?"

I wet my lips and swallow. "I came to see you."

He snorts. "Why? To let me know you're back? Or were you planning to let my mom clue me in on that little fact weeks later too?"

Fuck.

Not my finest moment, letting Loraine break the news that I left on a journey of self-discovery by myself. He wasn't supposed to know *at all,* because I didn't want to hurt him even more than I already have. Yet another mistake I've made when it comes to us, since the look on his face tells me it did.

But I knew I couldn't tell him. If I saw him or spoke to him, I wouldn't have gone. And if I hadn't gone, I wouldn't have figured myself out and I wouldn't be here right now, ready to beg on my hands and knees for his forgiveness.

"It wasn't like that," I whisper, shoving my hands in my pockets. "I just couldn't—"

His lips thin into a line and he scoffs. It's enough to cause me to stop mid-sentence, needing to know what he has to say, no matter how much it hurts. Except he starts laughing. At first, it sounds ironic, but then it turns into something a little more manic and empty. Neither of which sound right on him.

"Two months, Pen," is all he says.

And the amount of guilt I feel crashes down on me all at once as I nod, still holding his gaze.

He scoffs again, a newly lit wave of fury in his eyes.

"Months have gone by, and save for a single goddamn text on my birthday, I haven't heard from you. You left the goddamn state, not bothering to say goodbye or even clue me in on your plan to get as far away from me as you could. Shit, you could've been dead on the side of the road or joined the cabbage patch and I wouldn't have fucking known."

His anger flows into me, igniting my own anger inside me. Not at him, but at myself, though it wouldn't appear that way from the outside.

"It wasn't about *you*, Keene," I hiss. "It was about me. About figuring myself out so I didn't bring you down with me."

"That's just it, though! You made this about you, when we could've figured it out together!" he snaps, his cheeks beginning to tint with anger. "Just like everything else before that day, we could've walked that path *together*. Leaned on each other the way we have since we were kids. *You're* the one who took that away from us. *You* chose to run away when shit got tough instead of trusting me to be there to catch you when you fell!"

His words cause me to wince as guilt rushes through me. The truth in them is blatantly obvious, and it causes the self-loathing in me to escalate dramatically.

"I'm sorry," I whisper, doing my best to calm myself. "I wasn't thinking—"

"You were thinking, Aspen," he says, shaking his head, droplets of water flinging off the ends of his hair when he does. "The problem is, while I was thinking about you and me and *us* in that moment on the field, you were busy just thinking about yourself."

The words cut deep, as the truth often does.

All I can do is nod.

He's right. The only thing on my mind was saving myself. From pain or judgment or embarrassment; at this point, it doesn't matter.

I screwed up, and now it's time to own it.

But before I can, he asks a question I wasn't really prepared for.

"Where'd you go?" His jaw ticks as he stares at me, clearly making an effort to stay calm. Something Keene's never had issues with until now.

"Utah," I murmur, not meeting his eyes. My voice is practically non-existent and so rough, it sounds like someone shoved gravel down my throat and forced me to swallow it. "And Colorado too."

The flash of anger on his face is quickly replaced by hurt, and it rips me apart from the inside out.

"You did the trip—*our trip*—without me?"

Nodding again, I whisper, "I did."

And somehow, saying those two words out loud feels like more of a betrayal than leaving him standing there alone on the field or in the parking lot. Because I didn't just betray him. I said fuck our friendship and our tradition and everything we built, putting my own needs before us.

Another wave of guilt hits me, threatening to pull me under the dark, murky surface.

God, I wouldn't blame him if he hates me or never wants to speak to me again.

I get the feeling we're pretty damn close to one, if not both, of those options too. Especially when he shakes his head and moves to brush past me to get to the door.

"Kee."

His nickname is enough to have him pause, turning just enough to catch my gaze. And no matter how hard he's trying, he can't hide the hurt in his eyes. Being the one to put it there fills me with self-loathing, and I know what I have to say might only make it worse.

But I have to try.

"All I'm asking for is five minutes. Please." My tongue darts out over my lips and I swallow down the shards of glass lodged in my throat. "I dare you to give me a chance to fix this. To make this right between us."

Using the game is cheap. A cop out. But it's my only hope.

"*Pen.*" He sighs, probably because of the dare, but I shake my head and grab his hand. It might be a mistake, touching him without his consent. Yet I do it anyway, because without his skin against mine, it feels like he's already gone.

Like I've already lost the one person on this planet that I was made for.

"Hear me out. Please. I know I fucked up—"

"Fucked up? That's what you wanna call it?" His scoff turns into a laugh of disbelief as he rips his hand from my hold. "You didn't fuck up. You fucking *destroyed* everything we had. Years of friendship, out the window. And for what? Because you were embarrassed? Because you were afraid?"

"Of course I was afraid, Keene! If the world knew, that made it real.

And if it was real..." I trail off, words evading me once again at the most inopportune time.

Keene doesn't seem to have that issue though, laying into me with fire in his eyes.

"It was real whether the world knew it or not. You felt it as much as I did, the shift between us. And in the end, *you're* still the one who chose to walk away. You're the one who couldn't handle it. Who was too afraid."

"I know—"

"No, I don't think you *do*, Pen," he snaps, anguish written all over his features. "Because if you knew anything, you wouldn't have walked away when I needed you most. When we needed *each other*."

There it is again, the ripple of guilt when I hear him say those words.

I needed you.

Regret courses through me as I think about that day three months ago. Walking away from him was the hardest thing I've ever done. Even as I did it, I knew it was the wrong move. I knew it would end up being the greatest betrayal he's ever felt, and from the person he thought it'd never come from. One that cut deepest, because out of the few things we always knew we could count on in life, each other was always number one.

No matter when or where, we had each other, and that was all we'd ever need.

But when it was time to prove it? To put up or shut up? To stand together as a team, us against the world?

I blew it.

Tossed it in the air like a hand grenade with a lit fuse and bolted from the line of fire. Knowing that is punishment enough to last a lifetime, especially if it causes damage to us that's too deep to repair.

There's only one way to find out.

"Don't you dare?" I whisper the three words that started this entire mess over two years ago. A knot the size of a baseball lodges itself in my throat as I look at him, at the face I've known for my entire life, only recently realizing it's the face of my future, no matter how unplanned it might've been.

Brown eyes sink closed, a pained expression creasing his forehead. "Pen…"

Fuck.

I can tell he's about to say no. Maybe make some kind of excuse not to answer at all. But even though I have no right to ask for a definitive answer, I need one. I need to know if we can ever go back to where we used to be. Or become something even better.

"Kee, you heard me. Yes or no?" I ask, imploring him to give it to me straight, yet terrified the answer might actually be *no*.

His throat works to swallow and he shakes his head, sorrow etched into his features. My stomach sinks at the sight before he even had the chance to get the words out.

"No, Pen. I can't anymore." He worries his bottom lip between his teeth the way he always does when he's trying to keep his words to himself. I don't have it in me to ask for them. They don't belong to me anymore.

I must be a goddamn masochist though, because I can't let it go. I can't let *him go*. Not without giving it everything I can. Because at least if this is truly done and over, I can say I did everything in my power to make this right between us. At least I'd have the chance to speak the truth I've been too afraid to admit to not just Keene, but to myself.

You're the unexpected inevitable.

The truth in those words is why I dig the knife in deeper, finding myself begging for him to kill me with yet another rejection. "Please, Kee.

I'll do anything."

His jaw ticks and he shakes his head again. Another no. And with it, another piece of my composure cracks. It feels like my heart is fracturing within my chest. Fingers find themselves wrapped around his forearm this time, the contact spreading warmth through my entire body where his skin ignites beneath my palm.

Soft and warm and home and Keene.

"Please, baby." My voice is barely a whisper over the pouring rain. "I have no right to ask for this from you. But please. Just one more time."

"You don't deserve it."

"I know I don't."

"You're lucky I'm even entertaining this right now."

I nod sadly. "I know."

He scoffs out a laugh. "You keep saying that, but I don't think you do, Pen. Sometimes I swear you don't remember that you weren't the only one outed in front of thousands of people that day. I was too." A grimace mars his face as he shakes his head, eyes full of so many emotions, I can't possibly place them all. "And you wanna know what was worse than having that image flash up on the scoreboard without my knowledge? Watching you walk away from me like I meant nothing to you."

Another crack forms within me. "I'm sorry. I'm so fucking sorry."

Keene nods, his lips rolling into a thin line as he looks me over. His gaze moves over me like he's seeing me for the first time. Like he has no clue who I am anymore, and the thought alone is enough to make my heart feel like it's being torn from my chest.

"I forgive you," he finally says, after the world's most unbearable silence. "There's no use in harboring anger or resentment toward you for something we can't change."

I swallow. "Why do I hear a *but* at the end of that sentence?"

"Because…" He lets out a sigh and rubs his forehead. "Because I can forgive you, but I can't just forget it happened. You hurt me, Pen. And I didn't just lose the guy I was sleeping with that day in the parking lot when you walked away from me. I also lost my best friend."

"That wasn't my intention. That's why I'm here, asking this of you. Begging you. *Daring* you to show me what an idiot I was for ever walking away. Nothing is more important than you, fucking *nothing*."

He smiles sadly. "Your pride. Your fears. Those were more important."

"Not anymore."

"I wish I could believe you."

My eyes sink closed, a cool wind whipping over my exposed skin and making me shiver.

"I dare you to let me show you we can go back to how it was before."

A look of surprise crosses his face before flickering into something like irritation. "Before we had sex? Before everyone found out? Before—"

"Before I was stupid enough to give up the only person who's ever meant anything to me. I'm done running from this or fighting it. There's no use anyway." My heart catches in my throat. "It was always gonna be you and me in the end."

When I expect his gaze to soften, it only hardens.

"There was a time I thought that too."

No, no, no. I'm losing him.

"Then I dare you to do what I couldn't. What you wanted all along." I step closer, slide my hand down to weave my fingers through his. "Stay. Fight for this. For us. For what we had and what we both know we can be."

He looks down at our entwined fingers, his jaw pulsing as he works to keep his emotions in check. Ones floating right under the surface when he meets my gaze again.

"There are just some things people can't come back from. Wounds that'll never fully heal. You *broke me,* Aspen. Ripped my fucking heart out of my chest where I stood. So I can't just wait here forever, holding on to the hope you'll figure it out and change. That's literally insane."

"Kee." My free hand moves to cup the side of his face as I whisper his name. The anxiety and anger rippling through him is palpable, and it kills me, knowing I'm the reason behind it. The last thing I ever wanted to do was hurt him. The one thing I swore I'd never do.

He leans into my touch for the briefest second, eyes sinking closed.

"Let me go, Pen. Please, just let me go."

I can't.

No matter how much he wants me to, no matter how many times he begs for it. I know I can't let him go. Not now, when I know what it's like to live without the other half of me.

But I just might have to learn how. Indefinitely.

Goddamnit.

This isn't the way I wanted to do this, but I'm out of options.

And if I know anything at all—if I've learned anything in the past few months without him—it's that I'll regret not putting everything I have on the line right now, while I still have the chance.

Which includes my heart.

Letting my hand slide around to the back of his neck, I tamp down the emotions threatening to break free. I push the fear away and put everything I have—heart and soul—on the line the way I would never dare with anyone before him.

For anyone *but* him.

"I dare you to let me love you the way you deserve to be loved. Wholly.

Completely. And out in the open, where the world can see." My throat constricts around the words, but I continue to push them out anyway. "I love you. I'm so stupidly in love with you. And I dare you to love me too."

While he's done his best to keep it together thus far, it's three little words, eight letters too late, that cause a tear to slip free. It hits my palm, and I wipe it away with my thumb like that's all it takes to make it so it never existed.

"I already did, Pen," he whispers, voice mangled and raw. "But it wasn't enough to make you stay."

My forehead settles against his, both hands cupping his face now as regret fills the sliver of space between us.

"It was enough to bring me back to you. I'll always come back to you, baby. Because you and me? This is it. The real deal. Just let me show you."

I crowd into him closer, erasing any and all distance between us as I back him into the wall. Our wet clothes plaster us to each other, and the heat of his body radiating through them is the only thing keeping me warm anymore.

"You've seen me push people away, time and time again. Never letting them see me for who I really am because I was too afraid of giving them that kind of power. To know what makes me tick or how to hurt me, so I put on the armor." My thumb brushes his lips, my attention locked on them as I speak. "But you've always known where the cracks were. Just like you've always known how to protect them. Fill them with pieces of yourself. And when you did? You made it impossible to live without you."

The ache in my chest eases with every word pouring from my mouth, so I let them go. Give him every vulnerable part of myself that's always been his to begin with.

"You're the thing I can't live without, and I'll wait for, fight for, and chase you to the ends of the fucking Earth to prove it to you. So please, just tell me you'll give me another chance. Please tell me I haven't fucked up enough to lose the one person on this planet that was made for me, and me alone, to love."

His fingers dig into my drenched shirt, grasping onto the fabric for dear life as the most agonized expression crosses his face. Never before have I seen someone this torn; completely shredded between their head and heart.

I know which finally wins when his grip loosens, and he pushes me away. His head shakes as he steps toward the door, but the image quickly blurs out of focus from the tears pooling in my eyes.

"I can't," he says, his voice grated as he glances away from me. "At least, not right now."

My jaw ticks, and I clear my throat.

Fuck. Is this what it felt like for him three months ago? When I said no? When I walked away?

If it was even a fraction of the pain coursing through my entire being, I don't blame him for saying he can't or won't let me back in. Because this pain? It's fucking unbearable. It feels like an anvil was dropped on my chest, and I'm struggling to breathe. Yet breathing is the only thing I can do to survive.

"Okay," I manage, clearing my throat again. "If that's what you want. I understand."

"It's not a no, Pen. I just need time," he whispers. "Please, just give me some time. Some space."

Those are the last two things I want to give him right now, when we're no closer to fixing this than we were the day I left. They feel like the most deadly combination in the world, extending the chasm of space already between us.

But if this is what he wants—what he *needs*—I'll give it to him.

I'll do whatever it takes.

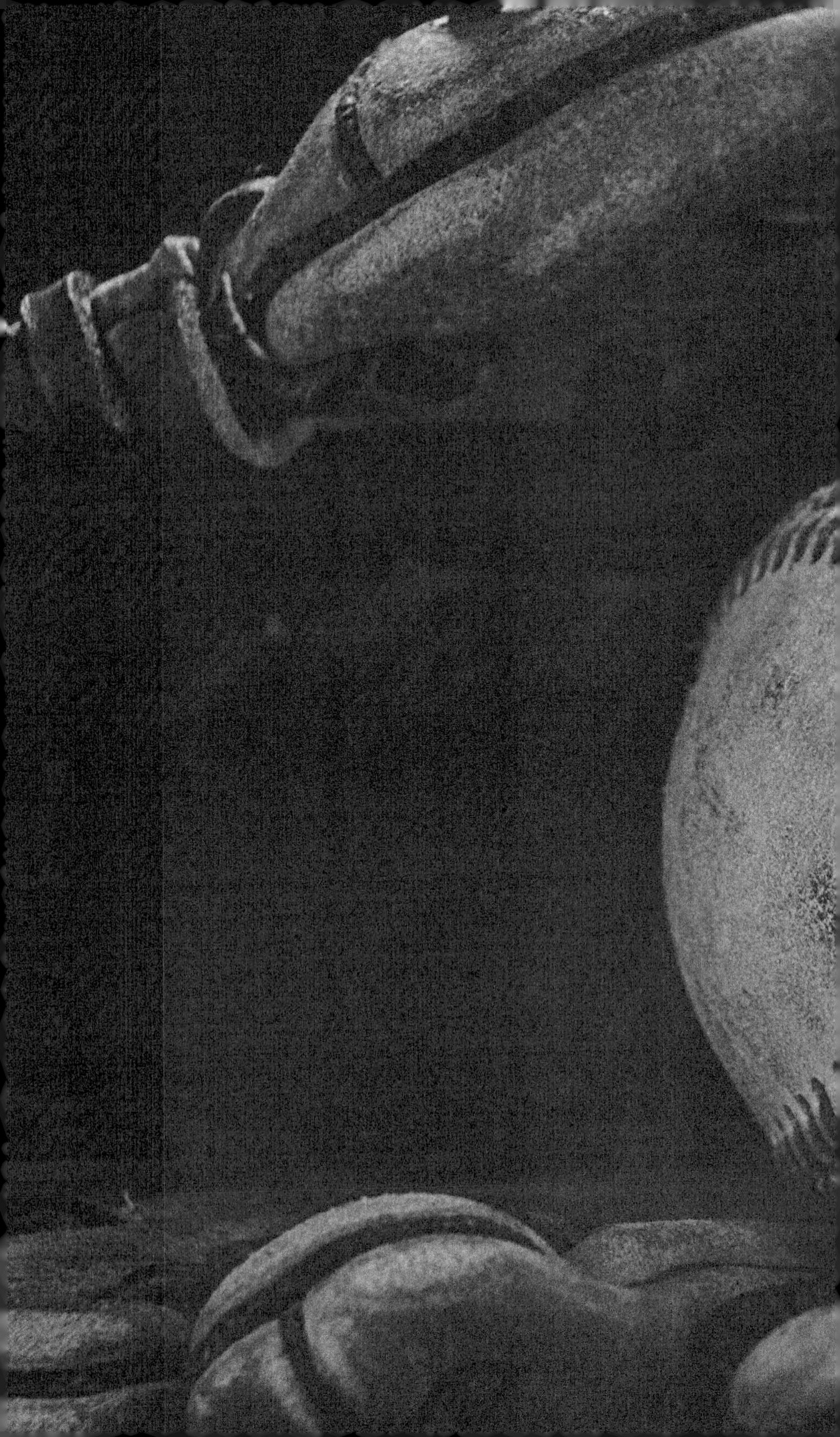

THIRTY-SEVEN

Keene

September

Three weeks have flown by since my conversation with Aspen outside my dorm. Twenty-one days since he sought me out and put everything on the line, not unlike how he dared me to use him as a sexual guinea pig. To explore what I now realize is my bisexuality. The only difference between those conversations are the responses.

No, that's a lie. So much more has changed since we first decided to see what this attraction between us really is.

He and I are both two completely different people than we were a few months ago, when this all started. We've grown closer. Together. Made discoveries about who we are and what we want and what it truly means to love someone with your entire being.

Well, at least I thought we had. Until he left me standing like an idiot on the diamond. Then again in the parking lot.

And then ran away like a fucking coward for two entire months.

I realize I can't stay mad at him forever. Especially knowing, while we might not live together this term, there's a good chance I'll run into him at some point on campus. Even if Foltyn College is a massive school, and I know the spots he frequents to create a mental *no-go* zone, it's still not big enough to avoid coincidental run-ins.

So to prepare for that, I shut down any feelings I still had for him. Put them in a box in the back of my mind and threw that damn key away. And I was ready for the moment I had to see him again. Or so I thought.

Then I ran up to that goddamn building to find him standing there, looking sexy as ever and soaking wet. Skin slightly tanned the way he only gets in the summer, and those damn blue eyes looking at me the way I was only able to dream of for months.

And that was all it took. Seeing him again instantly reawakened every emotion I tried to lock down, and it took everything in my power not to run straight to him the second our eyes locked. In that moment, I realized no corner of my mind would ever be far enough away to completely erase the love I have for him.

Yet, somehow, I managed to keep my distance.

My brain was smart enough not to trust the battered heart still struggling to beat in my chest. Even if being near him made it feel a little more whole again.

So I asked for space. For time, despite hearing everything I've ever wanted come barreling out of that smartass mouth. Including those three words. The ones I've felt for no one else but him.

Three weeks might not seem like much time. But it was enough.

Which brings me to where I am right now, on this beautiful mid-September morning. Standing outside the apartment Aspen rented for the year.

My fist raps on the door in time with the pounding of my pulse. It hammers beneath my skin, sending adrenaline rushing through my veins.

But it's not fear I'm feeling, but anticipation. To finally make this right between us. To claim him as mine, and tell him every goddamn thing I feel for him. Every stupid, reckless emotion that lives inside me are ones only he's capable of making me feel, and I'm ready to embrace them.

If only he'd open the damn door.

I knock again, louder this time. But as seconds tick into minutes, the adrenaline I was feeling quickly turns into disappointment.

Of course he's not home. That's my fucking luck, isn't it?

Just when I go to turn around and make my walk back to campus, the door is pulled inward and Aspen appears in the doorway.

Shirtless, with only a towel wrapped around his waist.

A slight nagging feeling ripples through my gut as I take him in. It quickly turns into fear, thinking someone else is in there, and that's what took him so long to answer the door. And though the thought should be quickly dismissed by the water dripping from his wet hair or still coating part of his chest—clearly from a shower—it doesn't. It only makes it worse.

But damnit, if my stupid fucking heart doesn't also soar at the sight of him.

I'm a lovestruck fool when it comes to Aspen Kohl.

"Hi." He breathes the word out on an exhale, blinking a couple times as he looks at me. Hell, he probably thinks he's imagining me standing here. Can't really blame him, what with the radio silence he's been receiving each time he's sent me a text over the past few weeks.

Usually they said good morning. Sometimes a check in or *thinking about you* in the middle of the day or a photo of whatever he's working on in class.

But every single night? He sends me a single text with three words in it.

I love you.

Every. Fucking. Night.

As if I needed the reminder of how he felt about me. Pretty sure his declaration that night outside my dorm has been playing on a permanent loop since I left him on the stoop to brave the rain alone.

Part of me still doesn't believe it actually happened. Like I just dreamed it up somehow.

Maybe that's why he sends the text every night. To make sure I know it's real. After all, there's no mistaking the words when they're typed out, plain as day.

A smile takes over his face as he stares at me, the dimple below his mouth popping as he does. But the unease in my gut from his state of undress has me in knots, no matter the look on his face. Or the way he said *hi,* sounding just as disgustingly in love with me as I am with him.

But that's just it.

He loves me. He *told me* he did. He wouldn't tell me he loves me, only to turn around and fuck someone else. There's no way in hell.

Right?

I clear my throat, fiddling with the hat resting backward on my head as I glance away from him. "If you're busy, I can come back later."

Aspen's face falls for a moment, confusion painting his features. "Why would I be busy?"

I motion to him and his current state of practically naked, and his eyes dart down. His head shakes, and a smirk is on his face once again, eyes dancing in delight as they come back up to meet my gaze.

"I just got back from a run. Was in the shower when I heard you knock on the door."

Oh.

It should've been the logical assumption from the towel and water still beaded on his skin, but my mind ran away with the worst possibilities all the same.

I roll my teeth over my lip and nod, ignoring the slight flush of embarrassment heating my cheeks and ears. At least Aspen doesn't call me out on it when he notices. And I have no doubt he does from the way those damn blue eyes dance, but I'm still grateful.

"Then can I come in?"

"Yeah. Of course." He steps out of the way, letting me slip past him into the apartment.

It looks just as I remember it. We picked it out *together* last spring, just before we went to the coast, and when I turn back to look at him as he runs his fingers through his hair, my chest aches a little.

At what could've been.

At what still *can be*.

God. My mind is all over the place right now. Torn in two different directions. Because on one hand, we need to talk. Really figure shit out. But all I want is to strip that towel from his body and make that shower he took completely pointless.

The real trick is knowing where to start.

"Place looks nice," I say awkwardly, and what the fuck? Why am I acting like a nervous imbecile right now? What is it about this guy—my goddamn best friend—that's got me losing every viable brain cell.

His tongue darts out over his bottom lip, and he gives me his dimpled smile again, but this time, it's almost sheepish. "It'd be a lot nicer if you were living here too, like we'd planned."

A weird sound comes from the back of my throat. Something between a squeak and a cough.

"Uh, yeah," I respond. Again, just as awkwardly.

Oh, Jesus Christ. Someone take me out back and put me outta my misery.

Like always, Pen reads my damn mind and takes pity on me. "I take it you're not here to just shoot the shit?" He moves deeper into the apartment to the kitchen, adjusting the towel on his hips. His tone is light, but the way he moves is rigid. Tense.

Hell.

I'm here to tell you I don't need time anymore, but I'm screwing it up before I can even get more than two sentences out.

I let out a deep breath and shake my head. The tension in the room damn near triples when I do, Pen's back and shoulders going stiff.

"Well." He sighs, turning to lean back against the island. His arms flex as he crosses them across his bare chest. "I guess there's no use beating around the bush."

There's a tinge of defeat in his tone as he speaks, and I watch as he begins shutting down and figuratively curling into himself before my eyes. It's written in his body language, completely obvious in his face.

That's when I realize…

He thinks I'm here to end this. For good. That I'm here to tell him no, I won't give him another chance. I can't love him or trust him after what happened.

He thinks he's lost me.

The look of sheer desolation on his face is enough to bring me to my knees. And if I thought for one goddamn second he didn't love me, his expression alone would've been more than enough to change my mind.

"I wanted to let you know I, uh…have some ground rules." My teeth roll over my bottom lip while I think. I honestly didn't put much thought into what I really wanted from him other than just…him. But I'm smart enough to know I can't dive right back into this without some things changing between us beforehand. "Because if you want this? And I mean really, truly want this? Then I need some reassurance."

His arms fall to his sides, eyes widening a fraction. Just as quickly, he wipes the surprise from his features and nods. "Okay. Name them. I'm all ears." There's a short pause before he adds, "I'll give you whatever you want, Kee. Anything."

God. Where do I even start?

My moment of hesitation has him moving toward me again, but before he can reach me, I hold my palm up. It has the desired effect, causing him to stop a couple feet from me with a frown creasing his forehead.

"I can barely think right now as it is," I tell him. "The last thing I need is you touching me."

A small, frustrated huff leaves him. When I meet his gaze, those blue eyes are blazing with a mix of emotions. Lust. Anticipation. Excitement. But the one missing?

Fear.

It's enough to have my mouth dropping open, letting a glorious display of word vomit seep out without much thought.

"No more hiding. The whole *coming out* process happened, even if we didn't want it to, and since it has, I have no plans to keep this a secret. I wanna hold your hand on campus. Kiss you whenever I feel like it, in front of whoever the hell is around. And I wanna do those things without worrying you'll cringe or pull away from me."

He licks his lips and nods. "Easy. I want the whole fucking world to know you're mine, Kee. The same way I'm yours."

My heart strains inside my chest, doing its best to reach across the room to find its other half. But my head still needs more from him.

"You don't get to make decisions about us on your own. We talk about shit and work through things together. If we do this, I'm your partner.

Your equal, in every way that counts."

"Done."

My stomach rolls as the next one comes to mind.

"I can't handle more rejection from you, Pen. I can't handle loving you and losing you all over again. So if there's even the slightest chance you're gonna back out of this down the road, I need you to say something now. Let me go, and let me be. Because I'm giving you the power to hurt me all over again, and I wanna know my heart is safe with you."

I watch as he works to swallow before clearing his throat. His jaw ticks tightly and he nods. For whatever reason, I'm surprised again with how quickly he's agreeing to my terms and conditions.

"I'm in this. For the long haul." Emotion rattles in his voice, making it shake uneasily. "Until we're both old and gray and can't get our dicks up, let alone ride one." A short laugh breaks past my lips, and he smiles at me, flashing that dimple. "Living without you isn't an option anymore, Keene. It never really was."

Elation takes over me, but confusion takes over when he asks, "So what else?"

"What?"

"For your list of demands. What else is there?"

"Uh…" I chuckle ruefully. "I think that's all of them? Were you hoping for more?"

He shakes his head, his grin turning sly. "No, not at all. I just thought for sure *no smoking* would make the list somewhere."

I wanna laugh, because at this point, that's one of the lowest priorities. My *only* priority is making sure he doesn't completely destroy my heart all over again. So instead, I just shrug. "I can't ask you to be perfect."

"Good thing you don't have to ask, because I already quit."

My brows raise in suspicion. "Since when?"

"Since the day you crushed my pack in your hands and told me if I walked away, there's no coming back." One hand reaches up to run through his hair nervously, and if saved by the damn bell, his phone buzzes on the counter. He makes a move to silence it, but just before the screen goes black, I swear I see—

"Was that…"

Aspen's brows furrow as I cross over to him, grabbing his phone from the counter. He doesn't try to make a grab for it, probably under the assumption I wanted to see who was calling him. In reality, I couldn't give a shit about *who* it was.

What I care about is—

Fuck.

His lock screen. It's the picture of the two of us from our trip to the beach. The same one that outed us at my game. Him in my arms, kissing each other like it's the only way we can breathe.

But why…

"You're probably confused, right?" he says with a soft laugh, and when I glance up to his face again, I find him watching me intently.

"A bit," I admit, entering his passcode.

And sure enough, the picture is his background too.

"It's one of my favorite pictures I've ever taken," he starts, grabbing the phone from my hand to look at it. A smile, small enough that his dimple stays hidden, crosses his face. "But for a while, I couldn't look at it. It only reminded me of the day a massive choice was taken from us by it being put up on that screen without our consent. A memory of when I wasn't strong enough to stand beside you." He swallows harshly and clears his throat, but it's still lined with gravel when he goes to speak more. "Yet the moment it captured was the same moment I fell in love with you. Or, at least where I realized the love I've always felt for you shifted into something more. Something I never knew I wanted. Something I was stupid to give up in the first place."

I bite down on my tongue to keep from saying anything, and instead try to focus on not blurting out that I love him too. Even when I feel the heat of his skin against my palm when he reaches down to squeeze my hand tightly.

The world starts to disappear around me, blurring at the edges as my emotions well in my eyes. I can't help it. I feel like I'm being ripped apart. Torn between wanting to take things slow—if only for the sake of my heart—and mauling him right here in the kitchen, consequences be damned.

"I want you to know I'm done keeping secrets or hiding what I'm feeling from you. About you. For you. It was a fool's effort to try to begin with, because you've always known my heart better than anyone else." His voice thickens. "You and me, Kee. It's always been you and me."

He repeats those words he told me weeks ago outside the dorm. The ones that prove this—*us*—was inevitable. I realize now, he's right. We were always gonna end up here, because there's no one in the world Aspen trusts with his heart. Except me.

Before, it was just to see it and know what lies within it.

Now, I get to own every inch of it.

He's made damn sure of it too. Because every demand I've listed… fuck, he didn't flinch. No second guessing. Just a simple yes to every one of them. Knowing him as well as I do tells me he probably knew them all before they were even spoken out loud. And he made sure he could handle it before he even came to find me weeks ago.

"You sure there's nothing else?"

My attention moves back to his face, and the way he's looking at me has my stomach doing barrel rolls and cartwheels galore.

Emotion. Love. Lust. It's all written there, in plain sight.

God, when did the roles between us change?

I've always been the one to wear my heart on my sleeve. To let people see right inside me, even when I shouldn't. Except, right now, that's exactly what *he's* doing, and I'm the one holding back. Staying guarded.

But if this is gonna work? I have to meet him half-way. And I have to give him everything he's willing to give me, no matter how fucking terrifying it might be.

"Actually, there is."

A brief flash of worry flickers over his features before he schools them. "Okay," he says slowly.

My thumb moves absently over his skin where our hands are connected, the action calming me enough to make the jump.

"I love you too."

Aspen blinks at me for a second before his brain catches up. The second it does, he beams and grips the back of my neck with one hand, my waist with the other, and hauls me flush against him. "Never in my life have I been happier to hear four words come outta your mouth."

Then he crashes his lips to mine in a kiss so passionate and powerful, I feel it all the way in my toes. I've never felt more alive or at home than I do at this moment, and it's all because of him.

"You and me," I whisper against his lips before capturing them again, more hurriedly this time. Aspen takes the lead though, spinning us so my ass is pushed against the counter and he's caging me in. Daring me to try to break free.

As if I'm not exactly where I want to be.

Our mouths fuse together down to the molecular level, allowing our tongues to tangle and mate. He brands his words, his promises, into my heart and soul with every brush of his hands through my hair and press of his hips into mine. And I tell him how much I've missed him, how much I love him, with every swipe of my tongue against his or soft caress of my fingers across his heated skin.

If I have a say in what happens next, I'm about to use every inch of my body to show him both of those things too.

THIRTY-EIGHT

Aspen

The path to my bedroom is fairly simple. Straight down the hall, and it's the only door on the right. But with Keene's mouth glued to mine and my hands mapping every inch of him while I strip him down, it's a lot more difficult to make it there without tripping, stumbling, or running into walls and doors. Clearly, because we do all those things before we finally manage to fall onto my mattress together, both of us naked save for his underwear. I hadn't even realized I lost my towel until my naked cock brushes achingly slow against the fabric of his boxer briefs.

"I love you so much," I utter against his lips before grabbing the bottom one with my teeth in a light nip, rolling my hips into his. The feel of him is still so unreal to me. Hard and smooth and perfect.

And now? All fucking mine.

"I *am* pretty lovable, so I don't blame you."

A chuckle slips past my lips at his usual cockiness. "Good. Because we aren't leaving this apartment until I've shown you at least a dozen times how much I mean those words."

He licks his lips, his tongue swiping over my mouth before he smiles. "A dozen? Pretty sure we'll have to stop and get some form of sustenance."

"That's what delivery is for," I tell him as I move to nibble at his jaw. My teeth scrape over the light stubble there, reveling in how it feels against my lips and teeth. I don't know how I ever thought I could live without this.

Not only his body. But just everything about him.

His laughter when he makes a stupid joke, or the secret smiles he casts my way from behind the plate during a game. The smell of his hair when my nose is buried in it. The security he gives me at every turn.

If I could craft the perfect person for me out of thin air, it'd be him. There's no doubt in my mind about that anymore. Just like I know that choosing this—him—is what I should've done all along.

I find his lips again, and soon enough, we're going at each other like two animals in heat. Downright needy and desperate for more. My tongue rolls against his and I suck it into my mouth as his hips rock up into mine. Our hard dicks bump and rub together in the most tortuous friction imaginable, and I know the only way either of us will be anything close to sated is once we've wrung each other dry of cum and sweat.

A rumble works its way from his throat when I flick his nipple with my thumb, and he breaks our kiss. The way he looks up at me, an infinite amount of love and trust in his eyes, causes my heart rate to skyrocket.

"I've missed you so much," he whispers, palm cupping my cheek.

I turn my face, kissing his hand. "Me too. I was going insane without you."

The words come out with a lot more emotion than I thought they would, and I clear my throat, not wanting to get so caught up in my feelings that I can't enjoy this. Because living without him the past few months has been close to impossible. I never want to go back to that, and from this moment forward, I don't plan to relive what those weeks were like.

They're over now.

This is all that matters.

As if reading my mind, he smiles and murmurs, "Never again."

I nod in agreement before capturing his lips, this time in a kiss of promise. A promise of a lifetime of friendship *and* love. Of being everything each other needs.

"It's always been us," I whisper against his mouth. "Walking away from you was the worst thing I've ever done. I'll regret that time apart and the way I hurt you for the rest of my life. And while I know I can't change it now, I'll make damn sure to prove it'll never happen again."

His lips curve into a sexy smile, and instead of responding, he just kisses me again. Claims me, faults and all, still choosing to love me.

Kissing quickly becomes not enough for us, and while Keene works to rid himself of his boxers, I quickly dig through my nightstand for the bottle of lube I keep stashed there. Flicking it open as I look down at him beneath me, I'm overwhelmed with so many emotions.

Love. Gratitude. Security. Everything I never knew I wanted or needed.

Maybe that's why, instead of coating my own cock with the liquid, I reach for Keene's.

His eyes slam closed as I begin stroking him slowly, twisting at the head the way he loves. "Fuck, Pen."

I smile, loving the way he loses himself in this. In us. "That's the plan, baby. To fuck Pen."

Just as quickly as his eyes sank closed, they snap right back open. Wide and alert and full of both lust and want. "What did you just say?"

"You heard me," I whisper. "Or are you gonna make me beg for it?"

I lean my body over his, taking his mouth with mine as I bring my cock to join his. They slip and slide together, each bump of the heads sending bolts of lightning down my spine at an unprecedented rate. Pre-cum leaks from both of our heads as our lengths glide against each other, mixing with the lube until we're both panting and needy for even more.

I don't think I'll ever get used to how amazing it feels to be like this with him. How I ever lived without this from him before is just…mind-boggling.

"Would you?" he murmurs, forehead resting against mine. "Beg for it?"

Yes. No doubt in my mind, if that's what it'll take. If I can do anything right now, it's to show him how much I want him. How much I mean it when I say *I'm in this.*

He's what my forever looks like, and all I want is to prove that to him.

"I would. I wanna feel you," I murmur against his lips, not bothering to wait for him to respond. "I want you to own and have and love every single inch of me. My partner and equal in every way humanly possible."

He swallows audibly, looking up at me with more love than I thought humanly possible. "You really mean that, don't you?"

I nod. "I really do."

The tips of his fingers scrape against my skull as he rakes them through my hair. "I think I just fell more in love with you. If that's even possible."

His words make my heart soar, pounding in my chest harder and faster than it ever has before. "I dare you to prove it," I say, grinding into him. "Take me how you want me, baby. Because I'm only ever gonna be yours."

He bites his lip, fighting to keep his smile to himself. It doesn't work, because a moment later, a filthy smirk takes over that sexy-as-sin mouth of his. The sight of it is intoxicating, full of so much love and hope, I can't help grinning right back.

"On your back, Kohl," he rasps, batting my hands away so he can wrap his fist around his cock. "I want you beneath me. Feeling every inch of my body against yours as I sink inside you."

Holy fucking shit.

Excitement rushes through me as I roll off him and onto the mattress, and when he settles between my thighs, my entire body vibrates with anticipation.

Every single time before this, Keene's always let me have the upper hand. Take control, set the pace and the tone, and lead us both to pure ecstasy. He put all his trust in me, every ounce of faith he could possibly give another person.

And he chose to give it to *me*.

It's only fair I do the same for him.

Though as much as I wish I could say this is all for him, I have to admit, it's for me too. I need to know how it feels to have him inside me. Owning me, mind, body, and soul. To fall apart because of him, only to feel more whole and complete than ever before once it's over.

Teeth scrape against my thigh as he lubes up his fingers and starts to loosen me, pressing in and out of my ass at a relentless pace. We've done this a few times before with one finger, maybe two, so the stinging burn isn't all that unfamiliar. But when I say a few times, I mean count on one hand the number of times when my curiosity got the best of me while he was sucking on my dick like he'd never get a taste of it again.

But when that third one slips inside and the burning only gets worse, my chest tightens a little bit. Fear starts seeping in, taking away from the pleasure he's giving me.

Keene wraps his fist around my dick and jacks me slowly, timing his strokes with each thrust his fingers make. "God. You're fucking perfect, Pen. I can't wait to make you lose your damn mind."

My eyes slam closed as I try to lose myself in the pressure building inside me. It's uncomfortable as hell, though, and I'm smart enough to realize three fingers are still a lot smaller than his cock. And I'm not sure it's gonna fit.

Of course, I know it will, seeing as he was where I am right now several months ago and he's able to take my dick without so much as a wince. But I remember the first time, and how worried I was of hurting him.

That same fear builds inside me right now, clawing its way into my brain to form doubt. I'm not afraid of the pain. I know I can take it, I just might be sore tomorrow. It doesn't take away from being terrified he's going to love it, only for me to hate every second of it. I'll feel like absolute garbage if that's the case.

I've done the work to push this fear of not being enough for Keene out of my mind. Spent weeks alone with nature to learn to conquer it, but it still doesn't make it easier to push down when it hits, even if I'm actively choosing not to let it influence me.

After all, it doesn't belong in my life. Not anymore. But my face must give away my every thought, if Keene's words are anything to go by.

"I can hear you thinking," he says, curling his fingers up inside me. He brushes over my prostate again and again, and it momentarily pulls me from the hole I'm digging inside my brain. "Look at me."

I listen, opening my eyes to find him looking down at me. Heat and desire sear into me from his stare as he continues to fuck me with his hands.

"Get outta your head, Pen. Just feel and let go."

Blowing out a breath, I do as he says. Move my focus to feeling every brush of his lips or skin. Soon enough, I'm able to lose myself in him again, just like he said. In the pleasure of being loved by this man.

His fingers leave my body not much later, being quickly replaced by the head of his cock. I clench on instinct as it nudges against my hole, but thankfully, he's not put off by my body's natural reaction. Instead, he starts kneading my ass cheeks in his palms in an effort to loosen me up.

"Just relax for me, babe. Trust me," he whispers, pressing his hips forward slightly. The crown of his cock slides in past the tight ring of muscles, and I already feel so full of him, I don't have any clue how I'll possibly take the rest of him.

Still, I force myself to relax. Focus on the way his palm shuttles over my cock and his mouth trails a heated path over my skin.

"That's it, Pen. Just like that." He peppers kisses along my jaw, moving to my lips before taking them between his teeth. "You're so fucking perfect."

I almost laugh at that, because if the past few months are any indication, I'm the furthest thing from perfect. But goddamnit, if he doesn't make me wanna at least be the perfect person for him. Become everything he could ever want and need.

Rather than arguing with him, I reach up and bring his lips to mine in a searing kiss. His tongue fucks my mouth, sliding and flicking against mine as he tunnels deeper. The second he bottoms out inside me, his hips flush against my ass, I break away from his mouth and let out a soft gasp.

"Are you okay?" he asks, instantly pausing his movements. "Am I hurting you?"

It hurts all right. Not in the way I expected, it just burns like a motherfucker and I feel like his cock is a second away from ripping me in half. But no way in hell am I about to bitch out. This beautiful, amazing, strong man does this for me. Takes me inside him, trusts me with his body and his heart. Two things I'd go to the ends of the Earth to claim as mine forever.

So I want this. I want him. All of him.

And he deserves all of me too.

Letting out a deep breath, I grit my teeth and shake my head about a thousand times. "You have to start moving. Please."

My voice is strained, and I can tell from the look in his eyes, he's completely against the idea, but he listens, pulling out and gives a slow thrust of his hips.

His lips caress mine, the softest, sweetest touch that has me melting beneath him. "You feel amazing, Pen. Are you doing okay? Can I keep going?"

I nod a few times, breathing through my nose. Every nerve ending in my body has been lit on fire by him. His body, his presence, his love. All I can do is lie here. Lost. Reveling in the heat.

I moan when his thrusts become harder, more measured. The pain finally starts merging, mixing with pleasure, and my hands grip the pillow behind my head for some sort of hold on my sanity. "Keep going. Harder. Take what you want from me."

My legs wrap around his thighs, hooking my feet around his ass to pull him into me again to accentuate my point. We both groan in unison at the sensation of him pressed so deep inside me.

"Just want you, Pen. Every piece of you."

His hips start to move in long, slow rolls, taking his time while he drives me insane with need. It doesn't take long for him to start picking up more speed, my body becoming more pliable beneath him. Melting into a puddle of love-sick, lust-drunk goo.

The stretch my body gives him as he starts pistoning his hips relentlessly is unreal, snapping them into me like a man hell-bent on breaking me in two. I love it, though. I love every forceful thrust and tortured groan he gives me, and soon enough, I'm lost in pleasure. Lost in him.

And that's before he pegs my prostate with the head of his cock. When he hits that little button, all bets are off, and I'm about to tell him we're swapping the roles of top and bottom in this relationship.

"Fuck, baby," I say on a rough breath. "Don't ever stop."

He chuckles slightly, straightening before grabbing my hips and yanking me to him. The new angle I'm taking his length at sends a shiver rushing through me, and I moan again. I can barely think or breathe, only capable of allowing the pleasure he's giving me to take over my entire being.

I feel him everywhere. From my fingertips to my goddamn toes.

"You've never looked sexier in your fucking life," he murmurs. "So wrecked for me."

I'm not just wrecked for him; I'm completely destroyed. Decimated. So far past gone, it's laughable.

That used to scare me, giving someone so much of me. Handing over the capability to completely ruin me. But the thing about Keene is...I trust him enough not to use that power. Instead, I know with my entire heart that he'll safeguard it. Protect and cherish it, because it's something I've never given to anyone other than him.

Because he's always loved me, flaws and all. Long before we ever could've imagined this turning into anything more than friendship.

Keene's hand trails over my abs before wrapping his palm around my dick. He strokes in time with the rock of his hips, the dual sensation of his hand and cock the perfect, most blissful form of torment.

And I'm right there. So fucking close.

"Come on, Pen," he growls, fist tightening around my shaft. "I want you there with me. I want you milking my dick with this tight ass."

His thumb rubs the spot beneath the head of my cock as his dick swipes over my prostate, sending me over the edge in a wave of ecstasy I've never experienced before. I explode, stars forming behind my eyes as he continues to jack my length until he's milked every last drop of cum from my body. A full-body orgasm of epic proportions.

My release coats my stomach, and his fingers are slick with it when he releases my cock to grip both of my hips. His tempo increases, becoming more and more sporadic as he loses himself right behind me. The feeling of his cum filling me, marking and claiming me as his once and for all, is the greatest in the world. Unmatched by anything else.

Nothing compares to being loved by Keene Waters.

He slows his movements before coming to a stop, dropping over me with his forearms on either side of my head to stare into my eyes. There's a hint of worry in his, the unspoken questions in them, obvious and loud. And more importantly, completely unnecessary for him to bother asking.

I don't say a word, wrapping my palm around the back of his neck and bringing his lips to mine. My tongue slides into his mouth in search of his, and they move together in a sweet, lazy dance, like we have an infinite amount of time together to spend just like this.

If I have it my way, it'll be the rest of my damn life.

"I love you," he whispers against my mouth, like it's a secret just for me.

But I don't want it to be a secret anymore. I want the entire world to know I'm his the same way he's mine. That he's *always* been mine, even when I was too stupid or stubborn or blind to see it.

It's always been us. Ever since the beginning.

"I love you," I tell him, reeling him in for another kiss. "So much more than you'll ever know."

THIRTY-NINE

Aspen

November

My nose burrows into Keene's hair as we lay in a mess of tangled sheets, sweaty limbs, and a mixture of our cum after one of the filthiest rounds of flip-fucking we've had yet. And over the past two months since he's come back into my life, we've been doing *a lot* of it.

It's been hours since he's arrived after his last class of the week, daylight having long since faded into a cool autumn night. The breeze floats in from my open bedroom window, cooling the sweat lingering on my skin.

At this moment, I don't think I've ever been happier or more content with the unexpected wrench life decided to toss at my plans. In fact, I've never been more grateful, especially when I have Keene tucked into my side, right where he belongs.

A lot more has happened since that day too. We've fallen into a new, comfortable routine with each other after all that time apart. One I wouldn't trade for the world, seeing as it includes more sex than anyone could ever ask for and Keene spending pretty much every night at my apartment.

All the joys coupledom has to offer are completely at my disposal now, and though we've only just made this thing between us official, it's hard to remember a time before what we have right now. A time when I wasn't able to whisper three little words to him whenever I felt like it or hold his hand in the quad or kiss him when he brings me lunch at my architecture studio.

No one's given us a second glance whenever we're out in public together and sharing any form of PDA. Either they don't notice, don't care, or I'm out of ear-shot to hear if they have any sort of judgment to pass on us for being true to who we are and the person we love.

At this point, I'm more than happy to let Keene claim me as his in front of whoever he wants. Especially now that Avery's gone from our lives for good. Don't get me wrong, I would be fine with it if he was still around, but his ass getting booted from the baseball program and the school, thanks to the little stunt he pulled, is just the cherry on top.

I'd found this out during the forty-eight-hour period Keene and I spent doing nothing but fucking each other senseless and catching up on the few months we missed. And he told me the whole damn saga about Avery and Toppr and how that damn picture of us ended up on the scoreboard during the game.

In the end, I guess I should thank Avery for handing me the worst moment of my life on a silver platter and making me grow from it. Without that day happening, who knows where Keene and I would be right now.

And honestly, it's a breath of fresh air, having everyone know about us. I'm so far past the point of caring about the persona I put out for the world to see the past few years we've been at Foltyn, detached and emotionally unavailable to anyone being the most prominent. Now, I'm just focusing on being the best version of me. Both for myself and for Keene.

It feels…exactly how it was meant to be.

Maybe that's why I'm anxious for more. For him to be here all the time, not just sleeping over when he's too tired to go home after sex. Which is an almost nightly occurrence as it is.

Considering where I was a few months ago, I think wanting more—wanting *everything*—with Keene can only be a good sign.

I shift beside him, my arm that's slung over his waist moving up and down his side in a gentle caress as I press a kiss to his temple.

"Don't you dare?" I murmur into the blond wisps.

While we usually take a more direct approach with what we want from each other now, we still toss in dares every once in a while. Keep the friendship alive along with the romance. Enjoy the banter and the innocent fun of getting under each other's skin.

I especially love the sex dares, and God, if I don't have quite a few planned for him when he's gone for away series this coming season.

The smile in his voice is evident. "For you? Absolutely."

Though I've phrased it as a dare, I don't end up asking it as one. Mostly because…I want him to say yes to this because *he* wants it. The thought that he might say no sends a rush of anxiety through me that I quickly tamp down.

"Move in with me."

Those four words I've been holding onto since the day he came back to me, offering forgiveness and a second chance, come tumbling from my lips before I can take them back. After all, I've been hesitant to push this, knowing that he's wanted to take things slower this time around. I can respect his desire to go that route this time, rather than just diving in off the deep end like before. That's how things got messy and complicated.

So, like the good boyfriend I am—or at least, I'm trying to be—I agreed to those terms. But the new semester is just around the corner and...I don't know if I can go another six months of not living with him all the time. I'm already miserable as hell whenever he shows up with a fucking duffle bag every week instead of just taking half of my walk-in closet.

He rolls his body so he's half on top of me, those brown eyes wide as he searches my face. "What'd you just say?"

"You heard me."

His tongue darts out over his bottom lip, a little nervous and a helluva lot sexy. "No, I'm not sure I did. You might need to repeat yourself a few more times."

"Move in with me, Kee." My hand comes up to cup his jaw. "You're here all the time anyway. You spend every goddamn night here except maybe once a week," I point out.

It's not necessarily apprehension I see when his gaze roams over my face, but what concerns me is there's no excitement anywhere to be seen. And that makes me worry. That maybe it's too soon to be bringing this up after all, though it feels only natural at this point.

"Say something, baby," I murmur. I sneak my fingers into the hair at the back of his head. "Please."

He wets his lips again, searching my face. "You're sure about this?"

"We'll make sure to do it right this time." I hook my finger under his chin and reel him in, pressing a kiss to his perfect lips. "You'll be closer to the stadium and work-out facility too, which is great when the season starts."

A convenience we'd known about when we picked the place together, knowing it was directly across from where Keene spends the majority of his spring semester. Of course, it's on the clear opposite side of campus from most of his classes, but I choose to leave that part out.

"This is true," he murmurs, a small smirk on his lips.

I nod. "And it's not like we haven't lived together for two years already. The added sex and snuggles are just a bonus."

"Hmm. Yeah, but I already get that now. Without paying rent."

By now, I can tell he's just fucking with me, and that's more than enough to know my worries about his answer were completely unnecessary. He's just waiting for me to convince him some other way. I'm not really sure how to play along with this game of his…until an idea hits me. One I've thought about a few times over the past couple months, yet have been too chicken to do anything about.

"Well," I say slowly, tracing the bow of his lips with my index finger. He snags it between his teeth, giving a light nip before releasing. "I could always sweeten the deal. Just for you."

Heat flares in his eyes, and I see a hint of curiosity in them too.

Consider his interest piqued. "I'm listening."

The corner of my mouth curves up and I wet my bottom lip. A movement he tracks without fail. "Do you remember that one conversation we had last spring? About…nude photo shoots?"

His eyebrows might as well shoot through the damn ceiling. "I remember."

"I'm not saying this is a bribe, but…" I look around the bedroom we're in from my spot in the queen bed. "You've seen that the lighting in here is really great in the morning."

He nods slowly. "You're right, I have noticed that."

"Yeah, see? It would be the perfect time and place to get in some shots." I lean forward, stealing a slow kiss from him. "And maybe a little pre-class cardio afterward."

"You make a compelling argument, Kohl."

"Mmm," I murmur, kissing him again. "So what do you think? Convinced?"

He chuckles, his smile against my lips sending me to the damn moon.

"Well, with an offer like that, how's a guy supposed to say no?"

"That doesn't sound like much of a *yes*, either, Waters."

Laughter, the most decadent sound, spills from his lips and he gives me a devastating smile. "Of course I'll move in with you. Weirdo. But I'm cashing in on that offer to shoot you naked the second all my shit is in this apartment."

No part of me cares about giving up my safety from behind the camera. Not for Keene. So I just grin at him, feeling on top of the fucking world. "I knew you couldn't resist me."

His eyes roll. "Never in a million years."

We both laugh then, and I pepper his face and lips with more kisses, a ridiculous amount of happiness radiating through me. How can I not be happy when I'm fortunate enough to call my best friend *and* roommate the love of my life?

Eventually he shoves me back, trying to get some air from the way I'm smothering the hell out of him, still smiling and laughing.

"When would I move in? I'm sure you already planned an exact date before I even—"

I chuck him in the shoulder playfully for making a dig at my plans before rolling him to his back. He knows as well as I do, my incessant need for planning has benefitted us more often than not.

And...also caused a lot of issues, but that's besides the point.

"I was thinking in the spring, asshat. Gives us a little more time to make sure we're in a good place. Still takes things at a slower pace."

He nods in agreement, smiling up at me. "Yeah, and it gives our moms a little more time to adjust to the news."

I smirk right back, and he reaches up, index finger poking at my dimple. "They could definitely use a little more time to get used to us being together."

We kept the secret of us reconciling our friendship as well as starting dating from the two of them until just this past weekend. Truthfully, the only reason we decided it was time to let them in on what was going on with us was because Thanksgiving is right around the corner. We weren't about to break the tradition of the Kohl and Waters' families spending it together just because we wanted to keep our relationship to ourselves for a little longer.

Mom was thrilled when I told her. Of course, she was. I had no concerns when it came to her being accepting of me and Keene in a romantic sense. After all, she was the one who really put things in perspective for me.

It was when Keene and I walked into his house across the street later that afternoon that I thought I might lose my lunch. I knew Loraine was still upset about how I'd reacted at Family Night. Even more by how I treated Keene all summer. But the minute my hand slipped into his and I told her he's my everything...I could tell she was just as happy for us as my mom was. And it was a huge weight off my shoulders the second her arms wrapped around me and said I'd better take care of him. Or else.

That's all I'm trying to do now. Make good on that promise to her.

"I'm actually surprised you haven't pushed for this sooner," he admits.

I frown down at him. "Would you have done it if I'd asked sooner?"

He shrugs, a small smile playing on his lips as his fingers skate over my abs. And that little smirk is all the answer I need.

"When would you have said yes?" I ask, the tiniest bite in my tone.

Another shrug. "I mean, I probably would've said yes if you asked me that first day I came over."

My eyes widen, and I gape down at him in disbelief. Like true, utter shock. "You're shitting me right now."

He blinks at me innocently. "Not at all. After topping you for the first time? I'd have agreed to anything. You could've committed murder and I would've said *cool babe, where we hiding the body?*"

My frown deepens. "You're my best friend. You're supposed to say that anyway."

His mouth parts slightly, ready to come back at me with some smartass comment...only for him to nod in concession. "Touché, Kohl. Tou-fucking-ché."

"Also, can we just recall the fact that *you're* the one who asked to take things slow? And now you're telling me I could've had you here every waking hour of the day that you weren't in class two *months* ago?" When he just shrugs yet again, I let out a huff of indignation. "I literally hate you sometimes."

"Should've asked, dude. Not my fault. I didn't realize you'd become all clingy and shit after taking your little journey of self-discovery."

"It was *soul searching*," I retort. "And it's not my fault either."

His brows raise slightly, as if to say *really?*

I give him a sheepish grin. "I mean, can you blame me?"

"Well, no. Like you, I'm also pretty damn irresistible."

"Exactly. So sue me for wanting you here with me. All the time." I lean down, my tongue licking at the seam of his lips. "In my bed. In the kitchen. On the couch."

"Basically what I'm hearing is that you just want a live-in booty call."

"Oh, absolutely." My hips roll down into his as if to prove a point, and I'm elated to find him hard again. "You should be so lucky I chose you for the job."

His eyes slam closed as he arches up, grinding against me in return. "Then you should be so lucky I accept."

I take his mouth with mine to keep from disagreeing with him. If anyone should be feeling like the luckiest person alive right now, it's me.

Because he's giving me another chance to love him, whether or not I actually deserve it.

I'm gonna make sure I earn it, though. I have to.

He's my other half.

My unexpected inevitable.

My fucking everything.

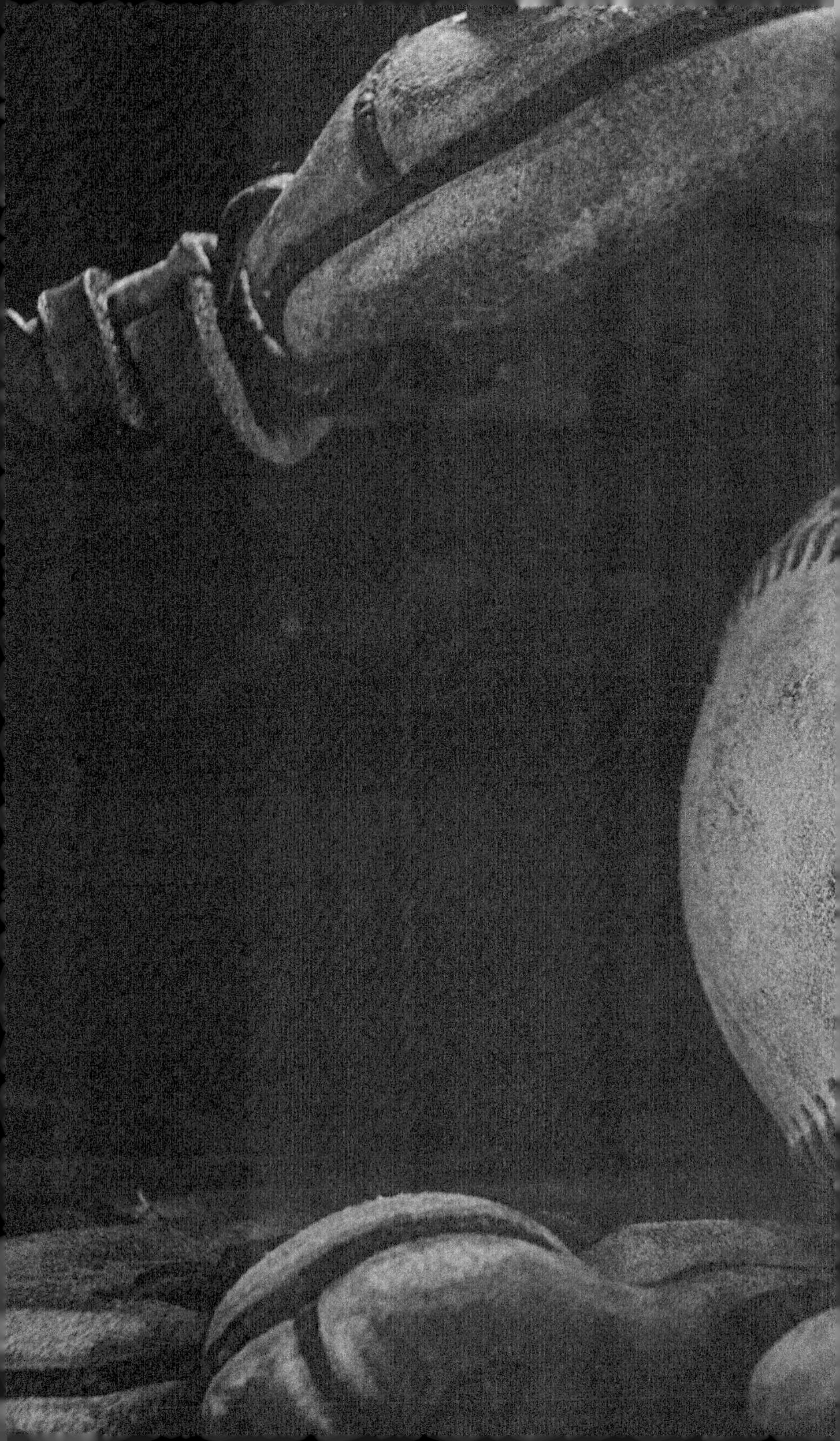

EPILOGUE

Keene

Four Years Later - April

Opening Day for the MLB every spring has always been one of my absolute favorite days of the year, and this season, the anticipation whirling through my body is nearly doubled. Actually, it might be somewhere near quadrupled, because today is entirely different from any other Opening Day I've ever attended.

Because…it's finally my turn to be the one on the field.

The anticipation mixes with anxiety, and even a little fear, as the announcer starts calling off the names of the starting line-up for the Sacramento Storm.

"Starting on the mound for the Storm is number twenty-three, right-hander, Beckett Hurst. And behind the plate, number twenty-eight and rookie, Keene Waters."

My stomach churns to hear the crowd's wave of applause echo throughout the stadium, filling me to the brim with even more anxious energy. As if that's even possible.

It's surreal, hearing my name announced in a major league stadium, let alone one I've sat in as a kid with wide eyes and big dreams. To make them all come true...nothing compares.

Just like nothing compares to having my best friend by my side through it all.

My attention flicks to the stands momentarily, finding Aspen right behind the home team dugout. Exactly where I want him. Exactly where he's been for a majority of the games here in Sacramento this season, now that I've officially been called up from the minors to take the starting catching position.

He's been offered a spot with the wives and girlfriends of my teammates plenty of times before, but I think he prefers his solidarity from the WAGs on game days.

Probably because he doesn't classify himself as a wife or girlfriend—which, to be fair, he isn't. Then again, even years after we've become an official couple, Aspen's distaste for labels still stands. About...pretty much everything.

He still hasn't put one on his sexuality, but I don't see the need for it if he doesn't.

I know who he is, just like he knows who I am. As long as we're both happy and comfortable in our own skin, I can't ask for more than that.

Though, I'm eternally grateful that he doesn't cringe at the term *boyfriend* or *partner* now. Truthfully, that's the one label he wears with pride, no matter where we are or who is watching.

To me, that's all that really matters.

I smile at him—the love of my life—while he's texting on his phone. Probably emailing someone from the office, the damn workaholic he is ever since he started his job with a local architecture firm here a few months ago.

I use his distraction as an opportunity to take him in without his knowledge. It's only fair, seeing as he gets to stare at my ass for the next however many hours while *I'm* trying to focus on doing my own job—while simultaneously trying to battle vomit-inducing nerves. Knowing he's here helps the latter, though. And damn if he doesn't look sexy as hell with a backwards cap covering his hair and in a gray and teal jersey, embossed with my number and name on the back. Something I can't wait to strip him out of after the game. Or maybe I'll fuck him wearing that, and only that.

After all, I'm in the big leagues now. Who says I can't have my boyfriend be my own personal cleat chaser?

He must feel my attention on him, because only a few seconds after I look at him, his gaze lifts to meet mine. Those cobalt blue eyes ensnare me, just like they do each time I catch him looking my way.

They never fail to speed up my pulse like a love-struck teenager all over again.

A small grin forms on his lips, and he mouths three words to me.

Kick some ass.

Not exactly the three I was thinking he'd say, but hell, I'll take it. I'll take any and all support he throws my way, which is never in short supply. Honestly, it's all because of him that I even survived the past three years in the minors.

I know paying my dues is part of being a pro athlete. I've been preparing for it ever since I was a kid. But hell, no amount of mental preparation was enough to get me through weeks on end without being able to physically touch Pen.

It made my time in the minors my own personal hell.

No one was at fault for the situation either. He was still up at Foltyn working on his graduate degree, meanwhile, once I was drafted to the Storm after senior year, I was sent to their double A team over in Kansas.

Fucking *Kansas*. Literally the worst flyover state imaginable, not to mention two time zones away from where Pen was in Oregon.

But we made it work. For two miserable years, we did the long-distance thing.

Thankfully, after he graduated, he decided to take a bit of time away from searching for a big kid architecture job—his idea, surprisingly—so he could do a bit of traveling with me during the second half of our season. He still worked some, bringing his camera with him to whatever city our series was in and shooting urban scenes and even some games.

He even captured a photo of me behind the plate that ended up in an issue of a nationwide sports magazine called *The Field*, which paid for his travel for the rest of that season.

Though I'd have loved him to follow his passion for photography—especially if it meant freeing up his schedule to travel with me as much as possible—he's still the Aspen I fell in love with all that time ago. Ever the realist, always a planner. And if his job at this new firm allots him the sense of security that comes with following that plan, I'd never dare to ask him to give it up. Just like he'd never dream of asking me to leave the game I've dedicated my life to.

It just means we have to get a bit…creative when it comes to long stretches of away games.

Needless to say, I rarely ever shower without him there with me on FaceTime.

Even all that time apart doesn't take away from the spark between us. We're as insatiable for each other as ever, not only when it comes to sex, but also just in the general sense of the word. Maybe it's the unhealthy level of codependency our moms love to tease us about, but regardless, I don't care.

There's not a single thing about him or us or our life together that I'd change. Not when it allows me to fall more in love with him every single day.

"You ready for this shit?" Beckett, my pitcher, asks when I reach him on the mound. He's one of the only other LGBT players in the league, and I'm fortunate as hell to have him to hang out with. Someone who not only understands the lifestyle of living half our lives from hotel rooms all over the country, but also gets what it means to be a queer professional athlete.

It helps that he's just a year older than me too, though he was pulled up from the farm team in Kansas after only one season rather than my three. He's just that fucking good.

He's also become the closest thing I have to a best friend...though the true owner of that spot will never be anyone other than Pen.

Blowing out a deep breath, I give Beck the most honest nod I can muster. Which must not be a whole damn lot, considering he laughs and smacks me on the arm with his glove.

"Aw, c'mon now. You've got bigger shit to deal with today than playing a measly 'ole game of baseball."

He's right, I do. Then again, him mentioning that only really serves to make my anxiety worse instead of better.

But then his eyes flick over to the dugout, and my attention follows on instinct.

I'm prepared to find Pen sitting there in his seat, looking as intoxicating as he did a few minutes ago when he caught me checking him out. But I have to do a triple take, not quite believing my eyes because the four seats next to Aspen are occupied by our mothers and my sister.

My heart catches in my throat when the three most important women in my life start waving and cheering like their lives depend on it.

All three of them had told me a few weeks ago that they wouldn't be able to make it today for my first game. Both my and Aspen's moms said they had to work, even though they tried their best to get out of it to fly down from Portland. And Lexi...well, shit. She's been off living her best life at Leighton University in Chicago, so I thought there'd be no way she would be able to get here in the middle of the semester.

Yet, somehow, all three of them are right there next to Pen.

"What the..." I glance back to Beckett and narrow my gaze on him. "Did you know about this?"

He just grins and gives me a shrug. "Seems like you're not the only one with tricks up your sleeve, Waters. That boyfriend of yours is a sneaky one."

"He sure is," I murmur, more to myself than anyone else. Then I turn back to my pitcher. "Payback is a bitch if I find out you had anything to do with this, Hurst."

Beck knocks me on the shoulder again. "Totally worth it to see the look on your face. Now, let's get this show on the road, man. We've got a game to win before you can get the hard part of your day over."

I nod and he gives me a wink, knocking my catcher's mitt into his glove before I jog back to my place behind the plate.

On the way, I watch as the four people I love most in the world all clap and cheer just for me jogging.

Jesus, they're crazy.

But I'm also crazy lucky to have them. Because, just like that? All my nerves have completely dissipated. Having my family here on what might be the most important day of my life...it grounds me. Not to mention, it means the damn world to me.

And he made it all possible without me even knowing.

"*I love you,*" I mouth to him, a stupid grin plastered on my face. He mouths the words back to me, just in time for the umpire to call up the first batter.

Pulling my mask down, I slip into the headspace where nothing outside the diamond exists. It's just me, my pitcher, and the batter in the box.

The good thing about playing at this level, though? My pitchers make my life a fuckton easier than I had it in college, or even the minors. And I can tell Beck is planning to bring the heat today, striking out two of the three outs in the first inning alone.

"Damn, you're on fire," I muse as we make our way back to the dugout to take our turn at the plate.

He smirks at me, all devious and calculating. "You think you're the only one with someone to impress in the stands, Waters? Think again."

A grin tugs at my lips, and like it's the most natural thing in the world, my gaze finds Aspen again. He's already staring at me, a smirk just big enough for his dimple to appear sitting on his lips.

"God," Beck mutters from beside me, his attention flicking between me and my boyfriend. "You two are like…disgustingly sweet."

I can't help the laugh that slips out. "That tends to happen when you *fall in love,* Hurst."

"Yeah, well, keep that shit to yourself, will ya? Some of us wanna play the game without going into diabetic shock."

I shake my head. This guy. He talks up some mad shit, but I know he's just fucking around with us. After all, he's one of my only teammates I've trusted with the whole saga about me and Pen. Not just the part that went viral on YouTube during that godforsaken Family Night game at Foltyn College.

I'm talking all the way back to high school. To that game of Don't You Dare, where I ended up kissing my best friend.

It's hard not to laugh, looking back at how this all started between us.

It was never meant to be more than a dare. A kiss between two best friends, and nothing more. Yet that stupid little dare ended up giving me the kind of love I could only dream about, and a life together that we never imagined.

And what Pen and I have now? I've realized it's only just the beginning.

I slide out of my catcher's gear in trade of my helmet, ready to head out to the on-deck circle.

My eyes meet Pen's again the second I step out of the dugout, and from his expression alone, I know what he's thinking. He wants to know if I'll make good on the dare he gave me during our car ride to the stadium earlier. And while I can't really guarantee my success with doubling on my first major league at-bat, I sure as hell plan to try.

But he's not the only one who'll be tossing out dares today.

Little does he know, I have the biggest dare of all to ask *him* later tonight.

To let me love him, for the rest of our lives.

Good thing, when it comes to dares, he always—*always*—says yes.

THE END

ACKNOWLEDGEMENTS

Damn, this book.

When I came up with the idea for Aspen and Keene, I had no idea they would be the most difficult relationship for me to write to date. For over a year, I plotted, outlined, wrote, deleted, reoutlined, and screamed at my computer when it came to these two. And now that they're finally here, it feels a bit surreal.

To my husband for dealing with me getting cranky for how hard these two made their story. For always giving me words of encouragement, and for always being my biggest supporter. You're my rock and my number one. I love you.

To my alphas/betas; Abby, Michelle, Sam, Amy, and Sarah. Thank you for pouring over this manuscript for me, giving me the best feedback possible so these two can shine at their absolute brightest.

To Sarah Sentz, for this cover. It was the perfect Keene, and I'm so glad I was able to snag it from you for their story!

To my editor, Z. You're the best dude. Honestly. I can't even put into words how much your help and support means to me, especially when I cancel date after editing date with you!

To my proofer, Amanda. Thank you for making sure these boys are in tip-top shape to meet the rest of the world, and for being so thorough!

To my street team. My Enclave. Y'all are the best, and I couldn't ask for a better group to be by my side. Thank you for being part of my team, and for the never-ending support.

And to all my readers. Thank you, once again, for giving my words a chance, especially when I do something so far off from my normal "brand" of story. For the edits, the reviews, the overwhelming love you give every set of characters I throw your way. This journey is hard, and often, really lonely. It's scary as hell too, but you guys make it worth it.

Thank you, from the bottom of my heart.

— CE Ricci

ABOUT THE AUTHOR

CE Ricci is an international best-selling author who enjoys plenty of things in her free time, but writing about herself in the third person isn't one of them. She believes home isn't a place, but a feeling, and it's one she gets when she's chilling lakeside or on hiking trails with her dogs, camera in hand. She's addicted to all things photography, plants, peaks, puppies, and paperbacks, though not necessarily in that order. Music is her love language, and traveling the country (and world) is the way she chooses to find most of her inspiration for whatever epic love story she will tell next!

CE Ricci is represented by Two Daisy Media.
For all subsidiary rights, please contact:
Savannah Greenwell — info@twodaisy.com

Printed in Great Britain
by Amazon